WOLF WIND

JANE WADE SCARLET…

… was born in Essex, but moved to Wessex at the age of twenty-two – the same year that saw the publication of her first novel, *RIDE THE WIND TILL DAWN.*

Jane now lives in Dorset, in a house filled with mermaids and the colour red.

To my children, Katie and Rory

And to my sister, Sally,
whose courage and determination
inspired me to keep on writing

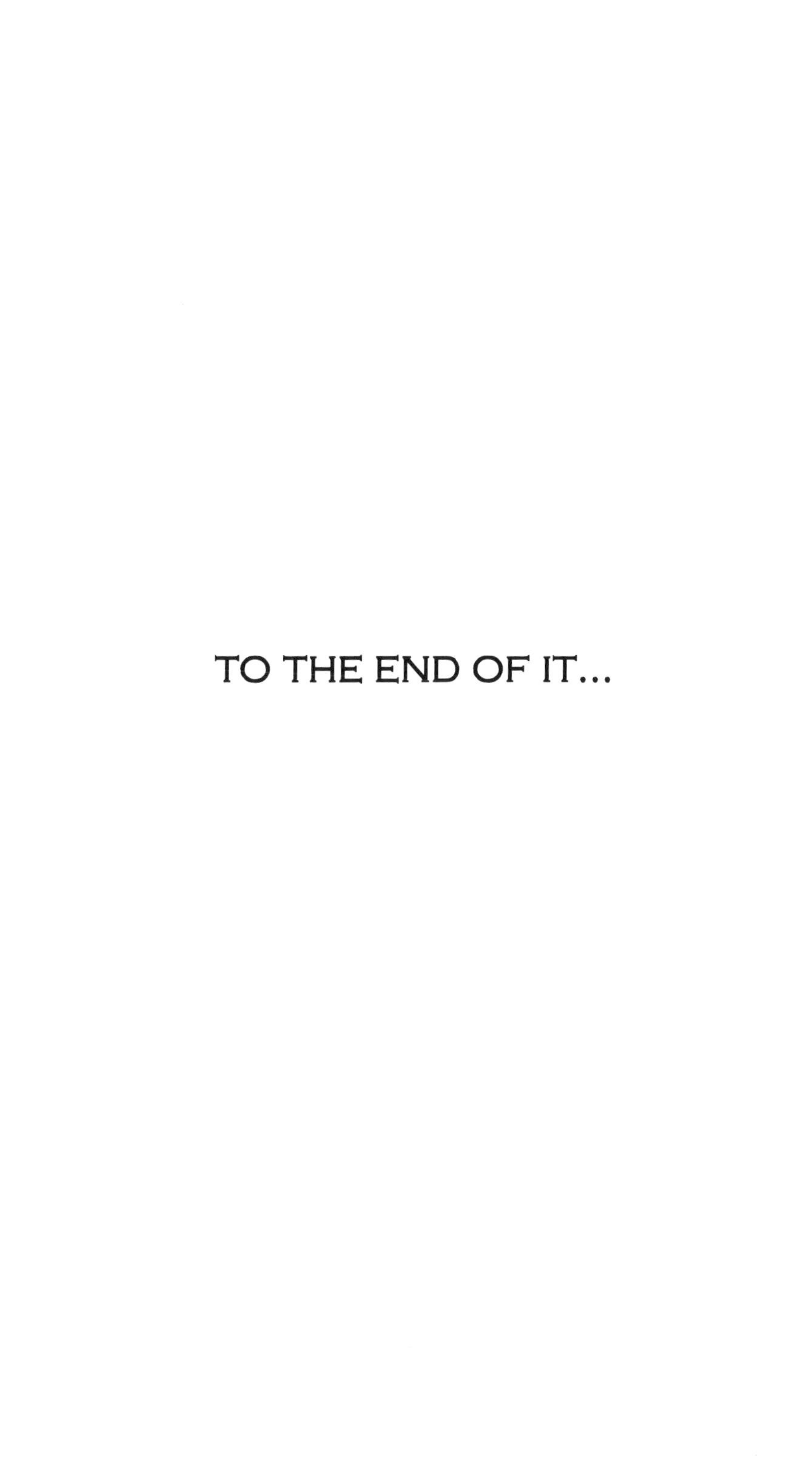

TO THE END OF IT...

ONE

THE LAND was undulating like the back of a worn-out mare. Martha opened her hands to the house wall as though to seek its protection, for it seemed that the distant hills were coming towards her under the swirl of cloud shadow and a jump of dust eddies, playing invisible tag and tumbling away into vast mysteries. But it was not possible for hills to move, and so she drew her hands back until only her fingers were touching the side of the house. A house that felt familiar but no longer friendly; bitten and sawn by unjust winters and the serration of dust. It felt of weary wood, but for her it was an anchor that stilled the heaving land until it was safe to step away, crossing the hollow yard where the handful of chickens jabbed their beaks with hope but little conviction, winding dry fingers through her apron and angling them like birds' wings at her forehead to help her to see. Although there was nothing to see, for the girl was in the field and the man was meeting with the bottle in town. And the boy was nowhere.

Martha's voice was dry and insubstantial, lost to the air, and she coughed as though her throat was unused to speech. 'Where is that damnable boy,' she said, leaning her head back and opening her mouth large; pushing the words past the end of the house wall and along the rise, to where the dirt track dropped towards a shingle road that followed the valley into town. It was here that her words clawed the horizon, and the dust scattered before them as if in fear, tormenting the eyes of the piebald mare that was pacing the rough road, bow-backed by the supply sacks that sucked at her flanks like a growth.

Old and hard-worked, the piebald was troubled by stiffness, and her shuffle of legs barely shifted the grit powdering the surface of the track. The boy was walking beside her, one hand grasping the rawhide rope halter and the other raised to discourage flies. Lean and ragged, he was burned by sun and toughened by wind, his hair falling like a web of fine sand across his face. As the woman's words entered his thoughts he turned away from the vision of her, standing by the end of the wooden house in the trouble that lay ahead, and his eyes narrowed to amber slivers in the late sun.

The boy swallowed the old bitterness as he brought the mare to the final rise before descending into the valley's throat, towards the farmstead that was patched with worn ground and surrounded by basic fields and a gasp of crops and livestock. The air above the house roof and the simple barn across the yard lay as heavy as menace and it fought every step the boy took, until the way behind him had dwindled and retreated, and he was wading between chickens' beaks into the sting of the woman's scorn. He brought the sagging mare to a halt and began to undo the knots he had tied outside Tobias Kendall's store, in the town where no one knew him and no one cared.

'You are late.' Martha scowled over the aimless hens while he loosened the mare's load. 'You are always late.'

The boy felt the bite of her eyes as he tugged the ropes free. 'The mare is weary,' he said. His voice was muted, as though he had pulled the words from deep inside, and he only registered the swing of her arm a second after the blow had jolted him backwards. He stood still then, and a stretch of rope fell across his dust-grey feet like something that had died in his hand.

She shouted in his face. 'The mare is not weary. You

loiter and you slacken. You squander time and you always blame the mare.' She was close to him now, her spit hot on his skin. He looked up, his eyes growing hard, like a puma coiled for the pounce. Take care, they warned. Take care.

'The mare is old and the sacks are heavy.' He had spoken so quietly that the words dissolved and she would not heed the warning, and she did not take care. All she knew was the exasperation in her head and the heat of the day and her isolation beneath the enormous sky.

'Liar.' She grabbed his shoulders and began to shake as though she held the boot-blackened rug from the house floor between her hands. 'Loathsome liar.' Measuring the words between each shake, then shaking nothing because the boy had twisted from her grip. He was watching her through dangerous eyes, and she stood small and vulnerable before him. He lifted his arms; it was a bid for leniency, but all she saw was menace. She stepped back in the dust and screamed through a mask of fingers, and the piercing of it stabbed him and drew the blood from his body. The chill of it crept up through his feet, until he shook with cold.

'How dare you?' Martha's hands dropped from her mouth. 'After all we've given you.' Her steps stuttered as she went towards him, and the boy could not move. 'We took you in from nothing. You were nothing, and you are nothing. How dare you threaten me?'

The whites around her eyes were shot with red veins and cruel lines carved her face, etching the story of her life. Hens squealed, he could see them pecking and the feathers floating, he could see the mare with her head hanging. He saw it all over the top of the woman's hair, because she was shorter now. Once she had compelled him with her height, at the beginning when the rough boards of the farmhouse might have become a better place for him. Now he was the compeller, and he smelled

Martha's fear as she raised her arms.

He felt his balance go beneath the onslaught. He saw the ground rushing up and struck it brutally. Wrath had made her stronger; she grabbed his elbow and wrenched him to his feet, and he swayed against her, fist-dented. He could only follow as she dragged him to the grey-board barn where the chickens had flocked, nipping spots of blood from his legs as he was forced through the doorway and into the haze. His head hit the wall as he tumbled. He made no effort to rise when she swung the heavy door back and crossed it with the wooden board, and when the evening gloom fell from the rafters he made no move to scatter it.

The boy came awake to darkness. It absorbed the barn walls and the hayloft platform above, and engulfed him in silence. He was lying on prickles of straw, and a mist of patterns swirled above his body as he gathered himself together once again, afloat on a raft of oblivion that was destroyed by the door crashing back on its hinges. The darkness cringed away, and he followed the swing of light and saw the man straddling the threshold like something skeletal left behind from a nightmare. The ground shivered as the man came closer, his face ravaged by grotesque shadows from the lantern in his hand. The boy's feet scuffed for balance when the man grabbed his throat and squeezed as if he did not want to let go.

'Dirt scum. Dog scum.'

He was hauled upwards and thrown towards the lesser darkness of the open door. From the small corral behind him the piebald mare kicked the fence and squealed in fear as he fell through the night and hit the ground. It was the scent of freedom in the space under the hidden moon that lifted him to his feet, and he stood ready to run. But it was a brief time. In a gasp, the moon peered out from its hiding place and he saw them: the two others standing in the yard. The briefest of times and he hesitated and then it was past, but they stood there still, watching him under the pale light. The lantern sparked the faces of the straight-backed woman and behind her, way behind almost to the house, the girl who was hiding in shadows under a cloak of heavy hair as if she, too, was standing ready to run.

'Do not move, dog scum.' The words fouled the air. 'You move before I've finished, and I shall kill you.'

The insect scritch was stilled, shocked into silence by the man's voice that fell heavy on the back of the boy who stood in the yard. Nothing stirred but the breeze flap of the girl's long gown, and the singing sound as the lash sliced the air towards him.

TWO

THE MOON was weighing her down for it hung low in the sky that night. It wore a solemn face as though it was judging her, and the sad light it offered coated everything with a glaze like a snail's glistening left on a wall; the moon-silver trail of something secret that had passed in the dark.

Sage strained for quiet, but the yard was abuzz with insects; it was almost like she did not need to watch her noise or hush down the throb in her chest, for her pa would have remained unaware. He was snoring hard on the other side of the house; so completely asleep that he would not see his daughter climbing through the window into the sombre light, followed by her shadow as it played over wood grain mountains in the barn wall and made a shimmering of the boy lying on the ground.

Her skirt beat around her legs as she hastened forward, because why was the boy so silent? Oh Lord, was he dead? She had not seen him disobey the order not to move; not once, not even after her pa had finished what he was doing. If it had been her standing before the whip she knew she would have moved; did not matter about the fear of it – she would have moved. Was he killed? No, he was lying curled on the ground as if in a sweet sleep, and when she kneeled beside him she could hear the breath in his throat. His shirt was so torn she could see the lick of moonlight over his skin, and in the cool night he was hot under her hand. She called his name and his eyes tried to open as though her voice was a key in a lock; he looked afeared as he turned, expecting to find some horror behind him, and she put her hand on his mouth to stop the shout. He saw her then; he bit his lip to quell the sound, and it seemed to her that he did it also to quell the hurt.

Sage swept up dust when she rose, but if it gritted his eyes he did not show it, and she had no time to hesitate. She opened the barn door as quiet as was possible and loosed the chestnut gelding from where her pa had haltered it to the wall. The fear flared in her again when the door grated the ground with a rough-wood drag and she froze, testing the air, but in the distant hollows of the house she could hear it still: the snore of the man who was lying there next to her ma and dreaming of the power of his one-sided battle. The thought was like a prod of courage, for she did not give nearly so much heed to the noise the chestnut's hooves made when she led it out into the yard; out towards the place where the land opened into another world.

The boy was on his feet now; he followed her into cooler air that was hung with the sound of scratching, as if the insects were keeping busy as they hovered above the ground. He stopped when she stopped, and Sage could feel him watching her with eyes that were as clear as glass, brown and sparked with gold. She pulled herself up on the chestnut's back, gripping a handful of mane as she leaned down one arm to help the boy up behind her; and it was smoothly done, although she knew from the shake in his breath and the fierceness of his arms around her waist, that it had afforded him some pain.

'Just hold on to me the best you can,' the girl said, so quietly for the fear of being overheard that she wondered if he had taken in her words, but she felt the bounce as he nodded. His arms tightened as though he was sending his thanks, and she grew warm and rich from that pressure around her waist.

The chestnut was drooping, like it was seeking its entitlement of sleep, but Sage kicked it straight to a canter. The boy's muscles stiffened as the shock sliced through his back, but she had no more time to waste for the horse was already disturbing the hush of night as it clattered up the rough road; she could almost see the slither of sound snaking into the house through the window she had left open to welcome her return. Although the snoring would not be disturbed by any siren, because after her pa had been drinking he lay in deep hollows of nonsense, his head clogged with whisky and his ears closed to all.

And then the girl thought of her ma, lying there next to him as near as anyone should want to be, awake and staring up at shadows. Her ma would hear the sudden clatter of hooves on the shingle road, like the rattle of wind through the poles she stood in her garden to keep birds from marauding her vegetables, and perhaps she might believe that it was a late lonely traveller, lost in the waves of land that crashed against their homestead. But she was too familiar with the response from her man's fists should she collapse his sleep, and so she would hide her knowledge from the skeleton beside her and lie waiting for the cockerel to doodle away the stars and bring the day to life.

A thread of moon-silver was playing with the horse's mane. Sage's hair flapped like curtains caught in the breeze, and the curtains wrapped around the boy who was a shadow clinging to her back. They rose together with the gelding's canter; the hoofbeats flowed behind them and left silence on the road that led to Oasis, so that all she could hear was the echo of hooves stumbling from the ungainly slopes that rode alongside until they had reached the edge of the town. She pulled on the halter then and brought the animal to a walk, guiding it to the square in the centre where the stores were closed and shuttered. The gelding strained its head towards the horse trough outside the drinking saloon, for even in darkness the smell of water was tempting. It might well strain, but Sage could waste no time in allowing it to drink. She kicked it towards thc farthest end of the town, where the hard-packed earth turned wild and stony, and distant hills reached up to catch the falling moon. She drew the animal to the side of the road in the place where young trees grew bravely with silver in the flap of their leaves, and the boy slid to the ground because he knew they had arrived. Her back was cold as soon as he left the horse, and she shivered for the loss of him as she dismounted.

He stood taller than Sage, for she had never grown much; he was strong, his muscles hardened by work, but still he needed her support to walk through the small gate in the picket fence and up to the shadowed house. He fell against her as she reached for the bell pull beside the door and she laboured under his weight. Nothing stirred to answer the obedient chime that seemed to echo inside the house, but when she tried a second time a window slid up above their heads.

The girl stepped back with the boy in her grasp and her eyes met the woman who stared down at them, leaning from the window with her head black against the moon sky; asking them what they wanted in a voice that was strained low so as not to break the sleep of others.

'Please, ma'am, we need the doctor.' The girl's voice was quick, rasping as though her throat was raw, but it was only because of the boy and the burden of him. And the woman could see him too, but still she took a moment to call back.

'He'll be right down; stay where you are,' she said, as if there was anywhere else they were likely to go in the dark of the night, with the moon acting coy behind its veils of cloud and the boy growing weaker in the girl's arms.

It didn't take long for the door to open, freeing a gush

of brightness that surrounded them as though it wanted to play for a while, and the woman was there as well, the edges of her long white gown burning with lamplight. She stood as ramrod straight as the plait of honeyed hair that was hanging over her left shoulder, and when she reached out the boy leaned towards her slightness as she brought them into the house. The woman closed the door on the emptiness outside, and they crossed the passageway and entered a room lined with wooden panels and rows of books. A room that smelled of dark wood and leather, and of a sharpness that made the girl think of the ointment that her pa would rub on the chestnut's legs after hard riding. There was a desk with drawers at its sides and a long couch, and that was where the woman put the boy so that he sat on the edge of it, huddled over himself as though he had fallen asleep. She took a taper to a lamp waiting on a low table, and the wick had been trimmed well for the light flared proudly, and in its revelation Sage could see how much her pa had ripped the boy's shirt in his exertions; she could see the red streaks shining and looking so much the worse for that merciless light.

'What's going on down here?' The man's voice was low and brown; he stood tall in the doorway like a furled leaf in his green robe. Sage's hair swept her face as she looked up at the sound of him, and his eyes told her that she had brought the boy to the right place.

'His back is…' But she could only start to say it, because the doctor had already crossed the floor and rested his hands on the boy's shoulders. And it was like the boy knew also that he was in the right place, for it seemed he put himself willingly into the care of those hands.

The man turned him slightly and frowned at what he was seeing. It was not a frown like the girl received from her pa, with anger clawing black lines between his eyes; no indeed, it was a frown that said that this man would try his best to rest even the balance of the thing that was twisted. He said, 'Lucy, would you please fetch some hot water?' and Sage was surprised to find the woman still standing there, for the dark-haired man had taken all her mind.

He had taken the woman's mind also, for she jerked when he spoke as if she had been sleeping, and left the room in such a hurry that her gown fluttered and folded around her legs like a pet cat. Sage watched her leave, and then she felt the buzz of the man's eyes resting on her, ripe with questions. 'I believe I may have noticed you in the town,' he said, 'but Lucy and I are newcomers to Oasis. My apologies; we have not yet grown accustomed to our new neighbours.'

'I am Sage Madison, sir, from the valley road. The boy works on our farm.' And she wanted to say that when he arrived on that day, all those years ago, she had been advised to call him brother, but the conversation was growing into a social thing and there was no time for it.

The doctor was shaking his head; she could see from the narrowing of his eyes that he was trying to remember. 'And on occasion he collects provisions from Kendall's store. Yes, I've seen him there.' He returned his attention to the patient and again his eyes narrowed, but this time because the strong lamplight was helping him to see what had happened to his back. 'This boy is in a bad way, Miss Madison. Would you tell me how this has come about?'

And now the time to answer had arrived, and with it came the shame and the anger; but it was easy for the girl to keep them out of her voice, as she had learned over the years so to do, when she said, 'My pa beat him.'

Her pa had beaten him again. But this was one time too many.

She watched the woman, Lucy, returning to the room, moving aside the space she had left when she went out. She held the bowl of hot water with careful hands and its steam stroked her youthful skin and flirted with the dark man's face. He looked up at her and smiled, and the smile carved older lines around the mouth that was asking his young wife if she was all right. But she ignored him as she set the bowl on the table beside the couch, and turned instead to Sage.

'May I offer you a hot drink?' she said, as if this was a friendly call. 'It is early morning and somewhat chill.' But the girl shook her head, for the shame and the anger together would be hot enough to keep away the cold when she rode the chestnut back along that bitty stony road; hot enough to keep away the fear when she climbed through the farmhouse window. And perhaps the heat might keep her strong when the dawn arrived and the boy was gone and her pa had unbuckled his fury.

Strength was one thing, discovery was quite another; the fear of it took her quickly to the door. The man turned away from the lamp to watch her, his eyes darker behind the shadows that were crossing his face.

'His name is Cub,' Sage said. 'And I want you to help him get away.'

Dr Ryker stood by the couch as his wife hurried down the passageway after the girl; he heard the muffle of their voices and the click that was the door closing. He heard his wife returning to the room as the boy fell against him, and the snatch of a sigh that was as distant as the question in her voice. 'Help him get away? Why would she say such a thing?'

But her husband stumbled under his patient's weight and she turned quickly to support him. And that was when she caught sight of the boy's skin under the stalwart lamplight, and stepped away with her hand pressed to the comfort of her face. 'Have you seen his back, Daniel?'

He nodded. He said, 'Lucy, I need your help to remove

his shirt,' and she stared at him for a second or two before taking her place beside him at the couch.

THREE

IT WAS after a stretch of hours that Cub came back to himself, when the day's heat had already been absorbed by the walls of the room. The leather of the couch where he was lying sang like a soaped saddle in the rich light, and meant nothing to him until the fog of recollection cleared, leaving an outline of stark images with sharp-toothed edges. Movement shifted at the corner of his eye, and he looked out of the window to the wind-writhe of tree shadows. All was peace, but his back was on fire and he knew there was someone standing behind him at the open doorway, stirring a float of dust with his breathing.

Bandages pulled at Cub's damaged skin as memory dragged him to the farmyard, where Madison belched whisky in his face and the two women watched from the shelter of the house walls. There was no part in the nightmare for the dark-haired man who came up to the couch, but the boy had his feet on the floor and was ready to run.

'Take it easy, son.' The man backed off with his palms raised. 'My name is Daniel Ryker and I intend you no harm.' He grabbed the chair parked in the kneehole of the desk. It grumbled across the floorboards on its metal wheels and rocked slightly as he sat facing the boy, elbows on knees. 'Do you recall what happened last night?'

Cub edged away from his eyes as if he did not want him to learn too much. He remembered that Sage had carried him to the doctor's house on the back of the gelding. She had broken the bonds and left him floating.

Ryker straightened up, rubbing his beard as though seeking its help to think. 'Miss Madison is a courageous and admirable young woman.' He paused. 'She told us her father had caused those wounds to your back but she did not say what you had done to deserve them.'

A frown crossed the boy's face like a cloud, and the doctor was struck by his youth. He could not have been much more than sixteen, this boy known as Cub, and the wounds on his back had been fiercely made. What reason could there possibly be for such violence?

'I have always displeased him.'

'You mean this has happened before?'

'It has happened before.'

'It makes no sense that a farmhand should be treated in such a way when he is free to seek work elsewhere.'

The room was sun-hot but the boy's skin crept with ice. 'Not free.'

'Then you are no ordinary farmhand.' The dark man had seen the shudder and he feared a fever. He reached out to check the pulse in Cub's wrist and the boy flinched. It was not so sudden but still he flinched, and the doctor hid unease with his eyes on his watch face. The patient's pulse was normal, but there was tension in his whole body. The man returned the watch to its pocket and sat back, and the extra space between them was a relief.

'I am no farmhand,' the boy said. Sunlight struck gold from the centre of his dark eyes when he stared through the window. 'I am the farmer's son.'

Ryker straightened. 'His son?'

'That is what he calls me.'

'Then what I cannot understand,' the man gestured at the bandages around the boy's chest, 'is how a father can treat a son in this way.'

'He drinks. Maybe he forgets.'

There was silence in the room, and such stillness that

the soft creaking of wooden boards in sunshine sounded like heavy boots crossing the floor. He drinks. He forgets. The invisible farmer took on a form in Ryker's mind that was barely human.

'Miss Madison. Your…sister? She urged us to help you to get away.'

Sage had wished it and Cub was impatient. He stood ready beside the couch, shoulders hunched against the pain in his back, but the dark man frowned. 'Not yet. You should wait.'

'He is hunting me.'

The boy's eyes were feverish; burning too brightly in the sun-gold room. He might leave the house now, but with his back still in tatters he would last maybe half a day. That was not the way it should be done. The doctor did not know quite how it should be done. 'Stay here a while,' he said. 'Wait until dark.' Let me decide what to do then, he thought.

'No.' It was quiet in the unreal limbo of the doctor's house at the end of the dusty town, but there would be no peace over the slope of the land where the hard-life valley lay forgotten. 'I need to leave now.'

'But you're not strong enough.'

'I will become strong.'

'I cannot allow you…'

'You will not stop me!'

They were both on their feet, facing up to each other like mismatched pugilists at a travelling fair: the tall, neat man and the hungry boy. The thin boy, toughened by years of manual labour, the light shining from the back of his dark eyes like points of flame.

Dr Ryker shook his head. 'Do you intend to fight me if I stand in your way?'

'If I have to.' The boy stared up at him, but as if he was seeing beyond the man, beyond the comfortable house to the valley and the farm. 'He is hunting me,' he said.

The movement of life was intermittent outside the window, and he stepped away from it, seeking the safety of shadows. The doctor saw this, and pulled the drapes across the glass with the sound of something coming to an end.

'He is a father, searching for his son,' he said, missing the drag of pain on Cub's face. 'And it would be better for you,' he challenged the boy across a thin spill of light on the floorboards, 'to return to him of your own accord.'

The room shrank like a trap. Cub took a step towards the door as though it was the gateway to freedom. 'You don't know that.'

He wanted to run; it was obvious in the way he was standing, the underfed boy with eyes like a caged animal and the husk of white bandages around his chest. The doctor held out a hand as if to slow him down.

'I have to leave now.'

'And go where?' Ryker frowned and drew back until his face was sharp in lines of shadow. 'Just where will you go?'

'I will go to the hills.'

'And if you were to reach them, which is unlikely, what will you do then?'

'I will find a horse to carry me.'

The man shook his head. 'You will find a horse? Just how might you manage that?'

'It will be,' Cub said. 'There is nothing more to say.'

His determination was a punch in the face. Ryker was knocked back by its power, but only for a moment, for a wayward fury had begun to build up from his feet.

'You are a stupid young fool!' He was shouting now; he didn't know why. 'You'll be killed out there on your own.'

'Dr Ryker.' The boy was trying to smile, but it was an unpractised movement. 'I will be killed if I stay.'

'For pity's sake, Daniel!'

They had not realised that the door had opened. They felt the sudden breath of air from the passageway before they were aware of Lucy Ryker standing on the threshold, her long skirt still shaking with agitation. 'The windows are open. Do you wish everyone to hear you?'

The doctor closed the door behind his wife and stilled her consternation with a hand on her shoulder. 'You have no other choice, Cub.'

'You are right,' the boy said. 'I have no other choice.'

He had started to shake. Lucy stepped further into the room as if to protect him, but the contempt in her eyes was for her husband alone. He saw darkness and danger as if there was an illness inside his head, but he could find nothing else to say. His silence was making his wife smile, as though he had finally done something to please her; but it felt wrong. He turned his head to the window where the sun was hanging heavy through the gap in the drapes, leading his eye towards Cub's destination. The swell of hills seemed ludicrously gentle from a distance, but they stretched beyond reach when the house door rattled under two short knocks.

Daniel followed the sound into the passageway. His wife came further into the room and slipped an arm around Cub's shoulders as if it was the natural thing to do. She smelled of lemon and lavender, and a wisp of hair swept away from her coiled braid and kissed his face. The voices at the door were quiet; almost inconsequential.

'Sheriff Russett?'

'Apologies for the bother, Dr Ryker, but I require your assistance.'

'How may I help?'

'Looking for a runaway. Son of Haine Madison from the farm in the valley dip.'

Daniel spoke as if feeling his way. 'Haine Madison? I don't recollect ever meeting this gentleman.'

The sheriff gave a laugh but there was no amusement in it. 'It appears that the boy made an unprovoked assault on Mrs Madison yesterday, and absconded sometime during the night.'

Cub sucked a breath as if in pain, and Lucy Ryker drew him closer until her scent was filling his head.

'I didn't know that,' the doctor said, whiplashing the words. 'Perhaps I'm needed there. How badly hurt is she?'

'She was more shocked than injured, by all accounts. Keeps querying why their son should have done what he did.'

Sheriff Russett paused, and his voice was muffled when he spoke again. 'Adopted son, more than likely; that's the way I see it, anyhow. I need to ask if you or Mrs Ryker might have sighted this renegade in town.'

'Not us. We haven't left the house today.'

'Well, I reckoned it was a long shot.' Russett's voice grew stronger as he prepared to leave. 'But my thanks for your time, Doctor. The boy could be dangerous, at least by Madison's account. Seems there might be Indian blood in the background. It's my guess that he'll try for the hills like any fool, in which case he won't be difficult to track.'

His voice withdrew from the door threshold and grew paler the further away he walked. 'He answers to the name of Cub,' he said, and then he chuckled. 'You might say that we are partaking in a cub-hunt.'

Daniel Ryker returned to the room where the boy and the woman stood together. He saw determination in his wife's face, and held up his hands as though surrendering to her strength of will. But he turned angrily to the boy.

'An unprovoked assault!'

Cub shook his head. 'I did not attack her.'

Small but fierce, the doctor's wife stepped forward. 'You just need to look at this boy's back to know who was assaulted, Daniel. And then tell me why he should be made to return to such a life.'

Ryker lowered his hands. He seemed slighter in the light squeezing between the drapes, and Lucy moved towards his uncertainty. 'Now I shall go and find some clothes for Cub, and you will harness the bay mare. We must both help him to escape further ill treatment.' She touched her husband's cheek with her palm, like a painless slap, and he held her hand to his face as if he agreed with every word she said. His eyes were on his wife's, but his nod was for the boy alone.

Lavender and lemon followed Lucy like a soft wave when she and the doctor left the room. Cub heard the muffled sound of a clock ticking away the minutes that lured Haine Madison ever closer. His scalp prickled as if the man was standing behind him, and then Lucy was back again. She had brought him a shirt, an old jacket, a scuffed leather pouch filled with food; she had brought him a battered tinderbox still frothed with cobwebs, and a sheathed hunting-knife on a worn leather belt. 'Daniel's knife, from when he was a boy,' she said. 'He has no need of it now.'

She helped Cub to dress. The jacket hung from his shoulders, but the knife-belt gripped his waist as though it had always belonged. He thanked her, and she closed her eyes when he spoke her name. Her husband's footsteps were too sudden outside the door before he pushed it open, and he did not see the rush of colour that had risen in his wife's face because he was beckoning to the boy.

Lucy did not follow them as they moved around the side of the house, swathed by the syrupy light of the day's end and the trees that edged the roadway. She stayed behind in the room with the leather couch, holding her breath until she could hear the sway of the buggy as the horse stepped out. She pulled back the drapes to see the vehicle taking shape through the window, and then as suddenly as the buggy had appeared it was swallowed up by the dust and the echo of its wheels.

The woman let the drapes drop, and turned in the premature gloom to face the memories that were still warm in the room.

FOUR

NIGHT HAD taken hold by the time the doctor's buggy reached the foothills, and a bitten moon was climbing the sky. Cub stood on the rising slope and gazed high to the stumble of rocks and hidden places. The grass rustled with the movement of wind and everywhere there were secrets, concealed by the dark.

Driven hard, the bay mare's breath scorched the air, and Cub lifted a hand to her neck before turning to the silhouette of the man sitting beneath the stars. 'Dr Ryker, thank you,' he said. His voice sounded awkward in the stillness, but it was more comfortable than the silence.

'I think you should…' Ryker hesitated. He turned his head as if he had heard a sudden noise, and stared back the way they had travelled like a man who thought he had left something behind. He reached into a pocket inside his long jacket. 'No. You'll find this more welcome than my advice.'

Cub opened his hand for the fistful of bank notes that were still warm from the man's body, and after a while the silence crept back again, until it felt uneasy to be standing there, on the cusp between the known and the soon to be discovered.

'It's growing late; I should get back.' The doctor stared through the darkness to where his wife was waiting for him to return alone, but his voice was carried by the night wind towards the start of the high land where the boy stood. And when the man stretched his hand over the side of the buggy Cub gripped until it hurt, storing away the memory of human warmth for when he was alone in a place where hills were his only company.

'I trust,' the doctor said, jerking the reins, 'that we may never have to meet again.'

The little mare stamped and rolled her eyes, white in the darkness. She curved the buggy around and broke into a canter, and the wheels spat loose stones in the air. Cub listened to the sound of her hooves until the vehicle was swallowed by the silence of distance. The money Ryker had given him was crumpled in his hand and slick with sweat, and he reached down to pull off his boot, laying the paper flat under its loose lining. Every step he took would feel like walking on riches.

Lucy Ryker's leather pouch pulled tightly at his neck, wafting the scent of lemons as though the doctor's wife was standing before him. He adjusted her memory along with the strap, and bent his body to the rising land.

Three days later the pouch was empty and Cub was as famished as a winter wolf; but the hills were behind him. In the dew-cool morning he turned his back on them, sharp with rocks and tumbled with hidden gullies, and looked out on rolling countryside, a vastness of struggling trees and desperate vegetation.

He had walked through the days and the nights to leave Madison behind and outdistance the sheriff's cub-hunt, and now his legs could hardly lift him from the damp grass into another day. He did not see the new sun raising steam from the earth as though the ground was boiling; he did not feel the blow as sleep crept behind him with its hammer, and the last things he sensed were a turquoise sky and the music of the dawn.

When he woke, the sun had risen to its zenith and thirst was leaf-dry in his throat. The itch of his healing back felt like a thousand insect bites; his legs ached but still he walked. Mirage-pools taunted from a distance and soaked into the air when he came closer, and Cub slipped one hopeless foot in front of the other and tried not to see the visions in his path. After a while he caught the scent of water, that would have brought saliva to his mouth if he had not been eating dust, and he followed the promise of a clear stream sparkling with rainbows as rich as any jewels. But what he found was as depleted as an echo, almost a memory in the thirsty ground had it not been for the sunlight glinting from splinters of water in the murk.

Cub fell to his knees by the edge of the swamp, muddying it further with dried earth that filled the air and the cracks in his lips. He scooped up what he could of the water and drank deeply and unwisely, swallowing small stones and lumps of mud with the sluice of liquid, and when he had finished his stomach cramped like a vice. He rolled in a ball, his legs to his chest, and retched until his throat was corroded, but what water he had managed to swallow stayed inside him, and after a while the pain receded enough for him to drag his dismantled carcass towards a nearby tumble of rocks. They gave pitiful shelter from the sun, but he was too far away from reality for that to matter. Crushed by paralysis, he was no longer aware of anything much.

Cub dreamed that it was early evening, that the sun was shining low in the west, and the man standing behind him had a canteen full of water in his hands. When he woke the man was still there. The boy's breath chattered through his teeth as he tried to roll to his knees, but the man dropped to the ground and forced him back down with a hand on his shoulder. Cub's heart beat high in his throat, but there had been kindness in that hand and the boy made no other move to rise.

'You're not dead yet then,' the man said. Leaves in the scrub clattered like bird scarers and a play of wind jumped through the grass on the other side of the exhausted stream, but Cub lay still and could not breathe. And when the water was offered he drank until there was nothing left. The man lifted his hat and dragged a sleeve across the sweat line under his hair, shaking the last drips from the canteen and shrugging as if that was a good thing. He pushed in the stopper and straightened up, rocking on his heels, for he was as rounded and solid as a tree trunk. 'You've been right out of it. Long time. Ten hours since we found you, boy.'

How fast could Madison travel in ten hours? How close was the farm now, and the whip sleeping in its coils in the farmer's belt?

'We thought the sun had got you. It would have been common courtesy to bury your corpse, say a few words, but then the ranch foreman found you was still breathing. Guess you're just lucky.'

'Lucky.'

'Is what I said. Lucky. We could have headed out and left you to the coyotes.' The man scratched his head and fitted the hat back in its place. He yawned and stared up at the leaves dancing in the tough little trees. 'But now you're okay.'

He was hunted, he was alone, he was frightened; but he was okay.

'You hungry as well as thirsty, boy?' the round-faced man said.

His name was Abraham, and he was a cowboy cooking critter stew in a dented pot over a reluctant fire. 'It would be best not to enquire into what kind of critter,' he advised. 'After a week under the sun you need to eat with a blindfold or you may not eat at all.'

But Cub's empty stomach cared little for that, and he made short work of the hot meat that was handed to him on a flat tin plate. The squat man crouched down and stirred the succulent something in the pot, feeding the crackle of flames with green twigs, and as the fire sizzled in the smoke he spoke to the boy of the horses the ranch men had been tracking.

'Found spoor this morning, so fresh it was steaming, and then we came across your corpse in the grass; still breathing, like I said, so someone had to make sure you kept breathing for a while longer. Well, my horse took a walk on a sharp stone last night, so it happened to be me. You owe your life to my unsure-footed steed.'

Abraham glanced at the black pony standing by the tethering rope with its nose in the grass and its tail shaking out flies, and as though it sensed his attention the animal stopped chewing and threw up its head.

The man dropped the raddled spoon into the cooking pot and climbed to his feet, and from where he was sitting Cub could feel the ground stirring. 'They're heading back,' the cowboy said. 'And by the strength of that thunder, with more horses than they started out with.'

Abraham went over to where the land rose like a breaking wave and fell away to the open plain, and Cub got to his feet and followed. He could see dust churning the air in the distance, like a storm gathering above the consternation that was coming their way. It was still afar, but after a while the dust boiled higher and fell flaring like a horse's mane, and Cub could hear men shouting as they came closer on their wild-eyed mounts, leading a huddle of mares on the end of taut ropes.

The air all around was filled with furious screams and the bite of grit, of a dismount of dusty riders and after a while of terrified mares trapped in leg hobbles. The three ghost-grey cowboys unsaddled their mounts and led them away to the tether, where Abraham's pony whickered greetings. Two of the men cleaned wind-whipped faces with grimy neckerchiefs and beat wings of dust from their hats as they headed for the cooking pot, lighting small cigars that flickered like fireflies in the evening. But the third stood talking with Abraham by the tethering posts. The mares were quiet now under the darkening sky, snuffling messages to each other and stretching down for the meagre grass, and they took little notice of the talkers: one as rounded as a tree stump; the other so thin that when the wind scurried across his body he was lost for a moment inside the flap of his shirt.

Concealed by tree shadow, Cub considered the line of animals. He would have to take one of the cowboys' ponies, for the mares they had chased were no more than fillies ready for mating. It had been four days since he had told Daniel Ryker that he would find a horse, but he could wait a few hours more. Late that night he would pass by the sleeping men on silent feet, and then he would be gone – on a well-ridden mount over open plains where the hiding would not be easy. But what other choice did he have?

'Found them snuck in by a rogue stallion. That's why it took us so long to get back with them.' The thin man's voice seemed too strong for his emaciated body; it crashed into the boy's thoughts and troubled the mares at the tethering rope. 'Bad brute, wild as a wolf and just as mean. Took a piece from the foreman's arm and left him with the memory.'

Abraham raised an eyebrow. 'Is that so?'

'It is. And here's the foolhardy thing, for Mr St John and The Saddler chose to knuckle down and rope the beast. Took them quite a time to bring all its four feet to the ground.' The thin man glared at his own feet, mousey hair breezing away from his face. 'And now they have two chances, as I see it: either they'll manage to drag the golden boy back here or die in the attempt.'

He looked up then, for something in the distance had caught his sight, and as he stared out to the bounce of plain below him his cheeks caved in, then rounded out when he smiled. 'Have yourself a look out there,' he said. 'See them coming?'

A small group had taken shape on the plain, beneath the singe of sunset. Cub stepped out from the shadows and sharpened his sight, his hands like a hat brim above his forehead. Out in the cloud of dust were three horses, but only two with riders. The third was unrideable, rearing like a dancer, a soaring fury silhouette-black against the evening sky. The riders advanced slowly, as though in pain, hampered by the stallion battling the ropes that had captured him, and as they neared the edge of the camp the horse's screams reached the men watching, and the falling sun burned away all evening shadow until what was left shone like gold.

'Palomino,' breathed Abraham. 'Would you look at that?'

The two men fell silent, muzzled by the stallion's rage, and Cub stood quietly behind them as the horses crossed the outskirts of the camp. The small dark hooves of the palomino slashed the air and he felt it like a sharp pulse in his throat. He knew the weariness that ran like sweat from the horse's flanks, and its fear of the men who were gathered around the fire where steam was still rising from the cooking pot.

Brought to a standstill the stallion shivered as though in fever, shaking his head against the ropes that sang with strain as they stretched from the riders' saddles. The men from the camp saw this and thought him broken-winded. They approached recklessly with loops of rope, to join the couple that were so tight now around the animal's neck the muscles bulged back from their cinch, amber-dark with sweat. But still the horse was not beaten. He reared so high above the stumble of fools at his feet that it seemed he must fall backwards on to the hoof-paddled ground, and he screamed one last time before the ropes throttled the sound from his throat.

And in his mind Cub screamed too, one last throttled time, as if he and the horse had been bound together.

FIVE

WITH MUSCLES straining the cowboys dragged the ropes to two trees along the bank of the empty stream, twisting a mesh of knots as the stallion fought the air. They left him trapped between creaking branches that danced the dance of the struggling horse, and headed for the other life that had returned with the sounds of evening and the smell of stew bubbling over the fire. The men collected together, hunching down by the glinting flames, but Cub stood away from the light and watched the stallion shaking his head against the tightening ropes. The heat of battle steamed from the palomino's back and vanished into the dusk, and Cub felt alone with the song of the insects; alone with the golden horse.

'Some crazy animal, huh?'

The voice cracked the gentle air and Cub's skin crawled. A tall man was standing a buggy's distance away from him, with spread legs and the darkness pushing at his back. The man raised his hands, palms forward, and stepped closer, and as the campfire flared over tinder the harsh lines around his mouth softened, lifting when he smiled. 'Didn't mean to cause you fright, son,' he said. 'Name's Ryde St John. I'm the foreman of this small band, and you are a stranger who travels the land on foot. Some might see that as curious.'

The insects had fallen silent; Cub could hear the wind flute playing through the grass as St John stared at him, his face licked by a leap of flame as one of his men fed the fire with twigs. 'A curious stranger who has gone without sleep.' He chuckled, and slapped the boy's back. The lash wounds burned, but the man didn't see Cub wince for he had already turned away to watch the stallion melting into the night.

'Some crazy animal,' he repeated, pulling the blood-spattered rag tighter around his left arm. 'A killer.'

'Not a killer. A wild horse that fights for his freedom.'

'You think?' In the sputtering firelight Cub could see St John watching him with eyes that were asking too much. 'You could be right,' the man said, a smile playing with the lines around his mouth.

He gripped the boy's shoulder. 'Let's go and get warm,' he said, steering him away from the darkness where the palomino stood, towards the frolic of the campfire and a seat on the hard ground. One of the cowboys threw a handful of wood into the hungry flames and the new light that shone on the sprawl of men was comforting, but Cub wanted to be back at the stream bank where the angry horse was carving a paler shape out of the blackness. Although when loaves were broken and passed around he stayed put to eat his fill of the dry, stale bread.

The foreman leaned back, pointing scuffed boots to the flames. 'You've gone without food as well as sleep, it seems to me,' he said. His stare was hidden behind the patchwork of light and shade on the edge of the fire's halo, but it was still sharp between the boy's shoulders.

'It might be he's just a growing boy,' Abraham said, brushing crumbs from the folds of his jacket and yawning mightily behind a fist.

St John snapped a blade of grass; shadows wove deep lines around his smile as he chewed. He lay down, shifting for a while to get comfortable, and slipped his hat over his face. One of the men started to tell a joke, and Cub drew back into himself, so that when the foreman spoke again he was the only one to hear under the laughter.

'D'you think you will ever get to where you're headed?' St John lay as if asleep, but his eyes were narrow beneath the hat brim, examining the boy who sat cross-legged and motionless at the edge of the firelight. 'D'you believe you will even last that long on foot?'

The centre of the exhausted fire shifted and sighed, and Cub gazed into its shimmering heart as it fell. 'I have to try,' he said, and when he turned towards the darkening figure on the ground he saw the man's eyes, and again they were asking too much.

One of the men called out. 'What are you planning for that mean stallion, Mr St John?' And Cub remembered hearing that trumpet voice as the two cowboys had ridden in, throttling the palomino with their ropes. A hush drifted over the camp, broken by the chuffs of tethered horses and the scream of a small animal in the talons of the bird that flew over their heads like a dark spirit, and the foreman seemed to pull away from the night as he sat up, dragging back his hat so that shadows frowned across his forehead.

'That mean stallion, Saddler, is a mint of money on legs, so I guess we should try breaking him.'

Abraham slapped his knee, and it was an angry sound in the quietness. 'Without the Lord's blessing, we'd only finish up breaking ourselves. That is one devil of a brute.'

The foreman aimed a finger in the air above the man's head. 'When I look at him all I can see is that his sire must have been some rich man's prize stallion. His colouring is too fine…come on now, his carcass is too fine, to be a full blood mustang. That beast's sire was a prince among horses, and it mated with a wild mare.'

'Maybe you're right; or maybe the beast itself is a runaway gone savage,' called the man with the trumpet voice, and a head of hair so dark that he seemed to merge with the night. 'And by now how many of our mares are already carrying wild stallion seed?'

'As to that, Saddler, we can only wait and see. But one thing is for sure, if we set him free he'll soon have those mares in some enthral again, and just how many more foolhardy weeks can we spare chasing the crazy creatures?'

The faces of men around the dying fire were practically unrecognisable now. Their disembodied voices racketed through the darkness like stones thrown at a casement, and one was louder than the rest. 'He chewed your arm and now he has a taste for human meat. He has to be destroyed.'

'No!'

Cub was on his feet, and when the cowboys stared up at him he saw the guns at their waists. He reached for the hunting knife, remembering the man in the buggy under the foothills, and the woman who waited for her husband to return. He touched the handle that had been worn smooth by Ryker's hand, and stepped away from the circle to where the night could hide him. 'The stallion is afraid, but he will fight to live.'

'Whatever I decide,' St John got to his feet and stretched arms above his head until his hat fell and small bones clicked. 'Now is not the time.' He leaned down to pick up the hat, and turned towards Cub. 'And there's no need for the knife, boy. We are all strangers' friends here.'

Cub lay awake under the blanket of night, listening to the language of the wind until it was an echo in his brain. The others lying on the hard ground were deeply and sonorously oblivious, but he waited for a further time's length before stepping past the dead mound of the fire and the shapes of sleeping men. He slipped away into darkness towards the brink of the stream and the place where the air was alive with the chatter of insects. The two tree trunks stood firm like legs stockinged in knotted rope and the golden stallion rested between them, his head bowed so low that the pale mane grew down into the earth. Without a sound the boy moved nearer, and then he stopped before the silver crest and spoke.

He spoke gentle sounds that echoed the whisper of water and the breath of wind; he spoke with words that swooped and tumbled like kites over fields of magic. And the horse's ears flickered, searching for the words he spoke. The stallion raised his muzzle and snuffled for the scent, and cocked his head to one side and listened like a dog. He saw Cub standing before him; he saw the boy take a step forward and bring a hand up to be smelled, and when the horse felt the velvet touch on his nose he sighed and waited and listened and watched, his breath warm on the boy's arm as he spoke, and the time passed and still he spoke.

Cub sank to his knees on the ground beside the slender legs, two with white socks and two without, and pulled strength inside him from the peace of the night as the horse ripped at the stunted grass. And after a while he wove back through slumbering men like a dark wraith, and fell asleep on his earth bed. And the only movement was the flicker of wind in the bird-scarer bushes, until the man raised his head from his saddle pillow to stare first at the stallion by the stream, and then the boy lying as still as death on the ground.

Dawn was spreading silver light over an early mist and already the fire had been rekindled with fresh wood like new life in an old nest. Oily black coffee was poured and a mess of cornmeal began to bubble in the pot. Ryde St John held up a tin dish for his share of it and called out to Cub over the circle of cowboys.

'It's in my mind that once we settle over the palomino we shall gather up the mares and head back home. Are you going on your way, son, or do you want to come along with us?'

The question was clear, but Cub could not read the man's eyes, for they lay in shadow like sockets in a skull. 'I shall go on my way,' he said.

'Well, that is your choice, but here you are in the middle of nowhere at all and a long way to somewhere in particular.' The foreman lifted his head and his eyes were cold, watching the boy's face. 'And you have no horse.'

Cub met his stare and felt off balance. And then he remembered how black the night had been when he had left the stallion grazing, and that the last two things he had known before sleep swallowed him was the rip of grass beside the sturdy trees, and the beginning of the unease that had coloured his dreams.

'I have come this far. I shall go on.'

'But I have made my decision,' the foreman said, laying down the dish and the bent spoon, its bowl heaped with his next mouthful of mush. He rose from his place and crouched down in front of the boy, and the men watching him fell silent. 'This is what I have decided,' whilst lying too awake to settle in the armpit of night, as the palomino pulled grass from the stream bank and wild animals killed in the distant hills. 'You tame that stallion to bear a rider and I'll let you take him for your horse.'

Time jerked, like the half second pause before pain registers, and then a rollick of sceptical laughter scattered the lingering mist like wind through smoke. But Ryde St John ignored it as he watched Cub, the lines on his face deep, his pale eyes flickering from one to the other of the boy's. The laughter drove the mist around the foreman's dry grey hair until it seemed that his head had reached the clouds. 'My men think it's a joke,' he said. 'But I am deadly serious.'

There was disquiet here, crisp enough to snap the air and sharp enough to stun. Cub peered at the golden horse by the stream, creamy now in the swirls of vapour, and then he turned back to the steady grey eyes that were asking too much. And he nodded.

All the laughter had whisked away. Somebody snorted. Abraham banged his fist on his knee and got to his feet. 'You cannot allow the boy near that horse. The devil beast will break his fool neck.'

'I don't believe that's going to happen,' St John replied coolly, his eyes still flickering into Cub's. 'What do you say, son?'

'But the kid is just a kid. Let one of us saddle the brute, for we will know better when we have got ourselves killed…'

'No,' Cub called out, his voice shaking a little for the pulse was fierce in his throat. 'I will do it. I will tame the stallion to bear a rider.'

The foreman sank back on his heels and picked up his dish of congealed paste, and the harsh lines around his mouth lifted in a smile. 'After we've broken our fast with this sorry substitute for a decent feed,' he said. 'That is when the boy will do it.'

SIX

COBWEBS OF mist burned away in the sun, and a little breeze brewed up from the scurrying clouds to play spirals with dipping trees. It tangled Cub's hair into a crest as he stood before the stallion by the stream bank, and knocked at the hats of the cowboys who had gathered there after the fast had been broken; brought together to watch the dubious taming of Abraham's devil beast, or maybe just to dissuade the boy from breaking his fool neck. Either way, disbelief and ridicule were in the air, and at first, the men heard nothing of the strange soft language that was hanging like whispers in the wind, but over time, and as Cub's voice grew, it felt as if there was another there, an echo after the chant; and the double beat hypnotised the listeners so that they, like the stallion, found themselves falling into the magic.

More time passed, and Cub lifted a hand to sweep the horse's flanks, breaking crusts of dried sweat into dust that shimmered in the light before he began to unknot the choke of ropes that had already left white wounds in the small trees. And still he spoke, trapping the pale stallion in webs of gossamer language, just as he trapped the hobble of mares and the men who stood there listening. The words sang from his throat as he pulled one of the lashes from the horse's neck and twisted the other into a rough halter; and the stallion moved its tail to scatter an insect that had landed on its rump.

And when he was ready Cub gripped the mane with his

left hand and pressed down on the haunches with his right. The animal snorted and shook flies from its head as the boy swung his leg across the golden back. It was lightly and swiftly done and there was a hush by the stream, as if even the breeze had ceased playing to watch the stallion faltering on stiffened legs, and the slight figure leaning over its neck with the end of the halter rope between his fingers. Cub pressed with his knees and the palomino moved, with a fierce shake of his head. And as they stepped away from the trees with the damaged bark, the boy looked up to meet Ryde St John's eyes.

The cowboys sent stones clattering as they stumbled back to life. The noise woke the stallion and he reared up to attack the air and the men beyond the air with sharp black hooves, and Cub wheeled him around to leap the pitiful stream. Seconds later the wounded trees had been left behind, and the men receded to a memory and then to dust as the horse bolted across the empty plain. Birds were frightened into the sky, their wings skimming the boy's head as he lay forward over the white mane.

Abraham was weary; he sat on the stony ground and listened to the stallion galloping into the empty land, and he was curious at the way the sound seemed to echo inside his chest. 'Mr St John,' he said, as though trying out the foreman's name for the first time. 'I want the boy to be okay.'

His eyes sharpened to black points by the sun, the foreman followed the streak of gold and the wake of dust under the visor of his hand, and spoke without turning. 'Abe, the boy will be okay.' And he was sure of it, because he had seen the sun rising in Cub's face when the stallion had reared beneath him and leaped the stream.

It was midday, and that same sun was thrusting high when Cub and the stallion returned, falling from the heat haze on to a low cloud of dust. The men in the camp stopped what they were doing to watch them coming; slowly, for the horse was near to exhaustion, hooves barely raised as he crossed over the rough stones. When they were close enough the stallion dropped his head to search for the water hiding in the depleted stream, and Cub slid to the ground and whispered words to the flick of the ear; words that allowed him to leave the horse by the crumbling bank and walk to where the cowboys were saddling their ponies.

Ryde St John smiled, and tipped up the brim of his hat with a forefinger; but the shadows clung to his face as Cub came to a stop before him. 'It was a good ride?' he said.

The boy raised his head. 'It was a good ride.'

'You tamed the stallion to bear a rider, so I must give him to you.'

Cub heard the hunger in the man's voice; he saw it in his stare. 'The stallion was never yours to give.'

'Never mine to give.' The foreman shook his head and the smile grew, deepening the lines around his mouth. It disappeared when he turned away. 'The stallion will always belong to the wild,' he said. 'But now he also belongs to you.'

They gave him food again, and afterwards the thin cowboy choked the fire with a spray of soil and Cub retrieved Lucy Ryker's pouch from the bank, where the tethering trees were still bleeding from their rope-welt scars. The leather felt like a memory, and in his mind the doctor's little bay mare rolled her eyes again, white in the darkness where the hills rose in their tucks and creases, and Oasis was a town he had once known. But that was another life now, and beyond time.

Ryde St John came up to the dip of the dying stream where Cub was standing with the pouch in his hands, and the man knew that he would have given his soul to learn what magic had been woven to chase the devil from the stallion that was waiting on the other side of the water. And he knew that it was still in his power to rip the secret from the boy. The boy who was ready to mount the horse and take the wisdom with him.

'Just tell me one thing,' St John called out.

Just tell me how you did it, he thought. Teach me the language that sang in my head when you whispered those words, and the stallion listened and loved you for it. But know that I would have killed you for the knowledge.

Cub looked round. Dry mud powdered his boots as he waited to know the one thing he had to tell the man who had offered escape from Haine Madison's whip.

St John hesitated. 'Just tell me the name you've chosen for this stallion.'

'His name is Wolf Wind.'

For he is wild like a wolf and he runs with the wind.

'That's the name a runaway might choose for himself,' said the foreman. And then he folded his arms across his chest and became formidable, and the boy saw him as if for the first time.

'I am known as Cub.' He looked down at the water glinting through fissures in the mud. 'And if you meet those who seek me, and they should ask you…'

'If they should ask me to describe a boy who walks across the vast plain to somewhere in particular? Well, I shall say that I know of no such young fool. But if they should ask me to describe one that can tame a wild horse to a rider just by whispering into its hot brain, then that would be another matter.'

'And that would be another boy,' Cub said, and he turned away from the man's voice and the threat in it to where the stallion stood, trailing the halter rope from the end of his muzzle.

*

They rode towards the endless ache of the plain and the corrugation of hills, and the land thrummed from the big stallion's hooves. They travelled through the day and took rest at night, one standing in the moon's shadow and the other seeking sleep on the hard earth. Cub fell to hunting small animals that he killed with Ryker's knife and cooked over the scarlet and amber of a tinderbox fire. And one night after he had eaten he fed the doctor's bandages to the flames, freeing his mind from the memory of the beating as he unwound the tattered strips from his body.

But some memories were too stubborn to fade, like the bitterness that had gleamed from foreman St John's eyes as he watched the boy mounting the stallion to ride from the cowboys' camp. Darkness had been a pall above the man's head, and that memory lingered like a warning, so that when the nights were lonely and the way before him seemed hopeless, Cub would know that there was a limit to everything. Even freedom.

It was a new day, and already half consumed; the time when morning gives way to afternoon and the sun can climb no higher. Cub stood beside the place where the soil had been battered dry inside a ring of angry scrub. There was a spring here, a small surge of water that rose from the ground and dived down again into a secret pool. Springs were becoming fewer, and the boy would have missed this one but for the patch of succulent grass that had caught his eye, its colour too vibrant for an ochre landscape. He kneeled on the green earth and drank deeply, and Wolf Wind lowered his fine head and drank in his turn. And the appreciation of a full belly lifted the boy's attention from the slithering in the wicked scrub, so that when Wolf Wind shied he had no time to react before the snake struck.

A sharp pain pierced his ankle, and Cub spun round to see the many-coloured thing curving on the ground. Before he could move again he heard Wolf Wind scream, and he knew a turmoil of gold as the stallion reared and trampled and the snake died writhing. And then he had to move. He pulled the hunting knife from its sheath and slashed the puncture holes on his ankle, once then twice, his eyes jerking from the quickening threads of blood to the pulp that was once the snake, to the restless stallion that paced beside him with thunder in his throat.

The boy stretched his hand for Wolf Wind's mane, but the scent of blood was in the stallion's nostrils and he shied from its terror, kicking out at the scrub as though a legion of snakes writhed in the thorny snag. Cub limped after him with the language soft in his mouth and the pain sharp at his ankle, but shock had weakened him. He pulled himself up to the horse's back like an old man who had forgotten how to ride, and wrapped his fingers in the pale mane to stop himself falling as Wolf Wind carried him away from the bushes that coiled like a witch's circle around the juicy grass.

The sun was curving towards the west, struggling against the pull of evening as the shake of hills dipped and danced a low valley slide towards a haphazard town, so new it was still rasping from the saw and echoing from the hammer. Cub shielded his eyes from the fire in his head and saw the apology of ill-placed buildings bordering a main street of packed mud, already worn to a bare rock gleam by rain and heavy wagons. It should be innocuous, but he felt sick with foreboding. The palomino caught the menace and smelled the stink of men; it fought the ground for every step and Cub gripped with the last strength in his legs to force it forward. And when that began to fail he lay across the white mane with the magic in his mouth; but the horse was crazed by fear and the words fell away.

Unbalanced by fever and hoof echoes knocking from the new sidewalk, Cub shifted on the stallion's back. The white boards, freshly cut from the heart of the tree, were dazzling the devil in the boy's skull, and each window they passed reflected the sun in flash after flash until his brain was numb. He could not see the people who had been brought to their doors by bustling curiosity, or the middle-aged man dressed in cotton and calf-hide, leaning against a slatted wall further down the street; standing so close to an open window that its swirling drapes were playing with his russet hair. The man's eyes were half closed in the sun, but as the horse paced level they widened to a pale blue, as sharp as ice. He pushed away from the wall and started striding the sidewalk parallel with the stallion, watching the boy, noting the sheen of fever over his skin. The spur at his heel clipped the wood and rang like a bell as he stepped down into the pool of sunshine, and the palomino heard it like the reproach of men with ropes in their hands.

Cub's sight was blocked by shades of brown a second before the stallion beneath him screamed, rearing so high that the man stumbled backwards, hands raised to protect his head. The boy lost his grip on the horse's back and the ground filled with his shadow as he fell. The pain in his skull was sickening, and then there was darkness.

SEVEN

SOMETHING WAS spinning a web inside his head, a buzzing silver spiral; desperate colours bleeding between the threads like a groan of bruises. It hung tethered to trees beside a stream where plains smouldered under the sun and everything was as brown and dusky as the woman who smelled of lemons. Her hair was waving like hills. She held him tightly in a place where flames writhed and she was too hot, too deep, too dark…

But a crack of light was opening and he dived up to the shine, scattering mist until he could see beyond to ghosts in the flicker, and behind them to where there was peace. He called for the spirits to take him, but they faded and there was pain instead. Sudden darkness sucked the light away and he fell, and fell, until there was nothing left.

'He opened his eyes, Clem. Did you see?'

'There was nothing to see. You probably imagined it.'

'I did not imagine it. He looked straight at me.'

'You mean, the way he's looking straight at you now?'

'Yes. Well, no, of course not. His eyes are closed now. But I know that he's reviving, for he called out to us. Even you must have heard that.'

'Reyna, he's been calling out words aplenty ever since Father brought him into the house, and none of them has made any sense.'

'Oh, why must you infuriate so? He opened his eyes and he spoke to us. And I shall tell Uncle Thackeray.' The girl tucked a floating hair into place, dislodging red-brown frizz from its fastenings. 'Clement Dart, why are you so hopeless?'

Her skirt flared, conjuring a breeze as she left the room. Her crisp white apron barely skimmed the floor; from behind she could have been a child playing in her mother's clothes. 'I am as hopeless as everyone probably expects,' the young man snarled at the empty threshold, his shoulders sagging like the old armchair in the corner, its plush rubbed to a thin skin by the pressure of many backs.

The chair, now draped with Daniel Ryker's shirt and wool-weave jacket, comprised just about the only items of furniture in the small, tight room, apart from a narrow chest, and the bed where Cub was lying. But even in his fever-drugged state the boy knew he did not want to be there. He hit the papered wall with his hand when he turned, and tried to clasp the pattern of flowers that climbed it to the ceiling. Tried to catch a painted stem so that he could climb also, away from the sickbed where wild things were burning and too many people had crowded in to watch. Where Lucy Ryker was holding out the leather pouch, holding out the hunting knife with its wicked blade; holding out her arms to embrace him.

He hit the wall again when he reached for her and Clement pushed his hand down to the pale cover. He pushed hard, with his back to the door, so that the girl would not see as he twisted one of the boy's fingers, and could not read what was written on his face when she came into the room, bringing with her the man in the calf-hide jacket who had stepped in front of the stallion.

'Has he fallen?' the girl said. 'I heard something fall.' She brushed past the young man and saw the boy lying helpless in the bed, but she did not see the bruise that was starting to grow around his finger joint like blood leaking under the skin.

Clement stepped back, knocking the chest with his

heel. It legs juddered and water slopped over the rim of the glass bowl on its surface, but the older man soothed the wood with his hand, and raised his head when the girl beckoned him.

'I saw him open his eyes, Uncle Thackeray, but Clem does not believe me.'

'Because there was nothing to see, Father.'

'Which does not entirely mean that Reyna was wrong, does it?' the man said, removing his hat and smoothing fox-red hair over his collar. He straightened his shoulders, and the jacket gave off a scent of woodfire and rainfall.

His son scowled at the window, where the forget-me-not blue drapes swayed cheerfully in the breeze. 'I guess I could have been completely mistaken,' he said quietly. 'Please forgive my erroneousness.'

Cub ground his head into the pillow and flinched as if the words had stung. The calf-hide man felt the boy's forehead, and his eyes narrowed to silver slits. 'Try not to mutter, Clement. If you don't wish us to hear what you say, then there is little point in saying it.'

'No, sir. Sorry, sir.' The young man leaned against the chest and twisted the bowl between his hands until the water stormed, but the father had already turned away and did not see the flash of angry lights in the son's glare.

'I don't think our young stranger will be coming back to us for a while yet, Nugget,' he said, resting a hand on his niece's shoulder. 'If, as you say, he did open his eyes I doubt that he would have seen you through them.'

'But he called out to us, Uncle!'

'It may have sounded like that, honey, but has he not been delirious ever since I brought him here?'

There was a moment's hush in the room as they all stood looking down at the boy in the bed, and then a dog barked from the street, a harsh sound squeezed through a tight collar. The man raised his head to the window and the drapes shuddered. 'While Dr Fortune is out of town,' he said, 'you are the only person capable of nursing this luckless boy, Nugget.'

The girl's earnest face pinked, and her eyes grew even wider under her unruly curls. 'In that case I will stay with him, Uncle Thackeray. And if I consider there has been an improvement of any sort, then I shall be sure to advise you.' She settled herself on the side of the bed, like a little russet-feathered hen in a white apron, and squeezed out a rag that had been soaking in the bowl where water still scuttled. 'And Father too, of course. When he returns home,' she said, pressing the cloth to Cub's forehead. It fell to the pillow when he twisted sideways; she made a moue with her mouth, picked it up and pressed again.

Clement and his father walked away, down the narrow stairs and into the kitchen at the back, where the dog from the street could still be heard complaining through the open casement. And when he reached the far wall Thackeray turned so abruptly his son rebounded off the hide jacket that was filling the room with the smell of outdoors.

'Just tell me what this is all about?' The man's voice was constrained. Too quiet to have penetrated to the front of the house or lifted through the ceiling to the rooms above.

His son stepped away and bumped up against the table. It felt like a buttress; its legs scraped the floor under his weight and the sharp sound winced in the churchlike hush. 'I'm sorry. I don't understand.'

'It isn't that difficult. I want to know the reason for your behaviour.'

Clement stared. 'My behaviour, sir?'

'You have taken on the character of a child who has been sent to bed without supper. I want to know what has brought it about.' Thackeray frowned. 'And keep your voice down. Show some discretion.'

The young man leaned back on the table and smiled.

His wide mouth lifted, but his pale blue eyes were chilly. 'I want to know what he's doing here, Father. I want to know why you chose to put him in my bed.'

'Where do you think I should have put him? In your cousin's bed?'

'What? No.'

'Should we have drawn lots? Perhaps you would have preferred your virtuous uncle to have given up his pallet instead?'

Thackeray Dart moved abruptly, as if he could no longer stand still, crossing to the far wall and back again, rubbing the hairs of his moustache between thumb and finger. Disarmed of their spurs, his boots made very little noise on the bland floor covering, but the table leg cringed as he passed.

'You know how troublesome it is having to live like this: keeping our balance when we're sliding on pebbles; trying not to spark attention. Having to be grateful to my brother-in-law because he has given us a home out of the depths of his goodness.'

'It was for Mother's memory. That is the reason we are living here.' Clement hunched into his round shoulders; he stared at the floor, and then at Thackeray's boots when they came to a halt in front of him. The room was too still. When the young man peered up at his father's eyes they were as cold as dead fish.

'Idiot boy,' the man said. 'It was for his wife's memory. She persuaded Norgate to give us a roof for her sister's sake. But it has been an entire year since Rosie passed, and even the saintly Ralf's patience stretches thin and brittle. Why else would he take himself away from his home and his daughter so frequently, when his business is right here in this town; in the front room of this house?'

Thackeray closed his eyes and shook his head. 'Oh, no; we don't need to agitate any still waters at this stage, Clement. I am not yet ready to move.'

‘But the waters are already agitating, Father. Can you not see? That boy, he is the one doing the agitating, but we will be the ones that are swamped.’ Clement stood straight and faced the older man in the shadowy pool lying across the floor. ‘Things changed when you brought him here.’

‘I brought him here so that things would change. I brought him here so that Reyna would change.’

They stood in a moment of silence, and then sounds knocked suddenly from the floor above as if something had fallen, and after that the silence returned. The young man and his father looked up to the dark of the kitchen ceiling and back at each other.

‘She needed someone to care for,’ Thackeray said. ‘She is a caring girl.’

‘I know that. I want her to care for me.’ Clement hung his head, and his father bristled.

‘Stand straight, boy. No husband-hunting woman is going to look twice at an apology on legs. If Reyna is to notice you then you need to stop acting like a cousin.’

‘But how can I when I am her cousin…?’

‘For sure, but when she comes to care for you it must be as a prospective spouse. And this is where that boy upstairs is going to help. He is awakening her femininity and her compassion. The rest will be up to you.’

Thackeray walked quietly towards the doorway. The corridor narrowed before him and trickled to a halt by the street door, light shafting through its top window like false rays of the sun. ‘Do not let me down, Clement,’ he said, and his voice slid through the dust hanging in the air and shivered the hairs on the young man’s neck.

EIGHT

NIGHT PASSED, along with the next day, and Cub lay trapped in the small tight bedroom in the wooden house on the main street of the new town. The brisk young girl with red sparks in her hair sat beside him, rearranging the sheets over his body and tucking the sides in with maternal precision. She forced water through his fever-clenched teeth and cooled his forehead with dripping twists of cloth from the glass bowl. And while he lay sleeping she just sat there, staring at nothing through the window and crooning a sweet something that sounded like a lullaby.

Then at the end of the third day a man dismounted his tired gelding at the front of the house, and when the young girl heard the rattle of the sidewalk under his feet she ran down the stairs to meet him at the door. Clement heard the sounds from where he was sitting, cleaning boots at the kitchen table, and his father straightened up by the window that opened out over the yard and said, 'Ralf Norgate has returned.' His eyes met his son's, and the look that passed between them was like frost.

'Father, welcome home.' Her face alight, Reyna closed the door on the raucous evening and hugged the man with trail dust in his hair. His moustache lifted with his smile as he feasted on the sight of her, for the few moments before she grabbed his hand and pulled him towards the stairs. 'There is something I need to show you, Father,' she said, oblivious of the dust and the fatigue. And in her enthusiasm, he was oblivious also.

'What is it, Nugget?' he said, the emblem on his vest glinting in the light that was stretching through the door window. 'Have you found another worthy cause requiring your attention?'

She pinked and lowered her eyes, clutching her hands together at her waist. She was the image of her mother, and the man felt his heart dipping with loss. 'Nothing worthier,' she said, and when she took his arm again he floated on the memory of his late wife as he followed their daughter up the stairs.

Two of the three doors sharing the short passageway on the next floor were closed. The one that was open led into the small room at the front of the house, where Clement Dart had been sleeping for the past year. For a moment Norgate was lifted with expectation that the space would be empty and all evidence of his nephew removed; and that all evidence of the boy's father would have disappeared also from his makeshift lodgings in the parlour. He had not expected Reyna to bring him to an inhabited room, nor the stranger who was lying in the bed.

'You must know what I am about to ask, Nugget.'

'He fell from his horse, Father, and I have been caring for him. He fell in the street and Uncle Thackeray brought him here. Dr Fortune is nowhere around and I want to be a nurse, Father, I so want to be a nurse.'

'Hey.' He gripped her shoulders and gave her a little shake. Her tears flicked up and caught the untidy strands of hair around her face, and he realised with shame that he had been away from her for far too long. 'Hush now, Reyna. Be calm, and then tell me the whole story.'

'He came into town three days ago on an unruly horse. An ungrateful horse. It reared beneath him in the street and he fell, and my uncle brought the boy to the house so that I may look after him, Father. Uncle Thackeray has honoured me with such trust.' Her face was a beam of light through the riffles of red gold hair; it filled the man with gut-twists of emotion.

'Dear girl, I can see that the honour is deserved.' He touched her cheek, and it was fiery hot. 'But you must take care of yourself before anyone and anything else, Reyna. When did you last eat, child?'

She seemed perplexed. 'Last night. I think. Perhaps last night – or before that. It does not much matter, Father.'

The man shook his head and the metal star at his chest clattered with light; it flashed into the half-closed eyes of the boy in the bed and a message made its way to his brain. A sharp message that cleared the fuddle and the mist and slid like a blade into his consciousness.

'It matters greatly, Nugget. For if you are hungry, how can you care completely for your patient? Go now, find something to eat, and then we'll try to discover what we can about this young man.'

He stood listening to his daughter's feet heading down the stairs, reluctant at first, and then speeding to the bottom. He heard her voice from the distance, followed by the voice of his brother-in-law; his wife's sister's husband. No relation to himself; surely no responsibility. Irritation pricked him like a familiar cloak of tiny nails. Oh yes, he was certainly home again.

Thackeray Dart climbed the stairs and let himself into the bedroom where his son had slept, and where his son's usurper now lay in the lap of strange dreams and visions. Ralf Norgate heard the footsteps along the corridor but he did not turn until he knew that Thackeray was standing behind him, his bulk shrinking the space in the small room until the atmosphere was hard and brittle. Ralf stood looking at the boy in the bed, sweat-streaked and blithering; he looked at the drapes hanging limply before the window. Then he turned around.

'Thackeray.'

'Ralf. Welcome home again. I trust your business was a success?'

'Yes, it was – comparatively so.'

'Ah, well.'

'Tell me, Thackeray.' He considered the man's eyes, and they shifted under his gaze. He felt the customary pull of annoyance in his gut, but that was always a symptom of being home now, and it meant hardly anything. 'Just how long has this young man been in fever?'

'Well, I don't truly know, Ralf, but he's certainly been suffering since I brought him into the house.'

'What do you think could have caused it?'

'Hazarding a guess, I suspect that he has been bitten by a snake, for I found a recent knife slash across his ankle that I suggest was cut to let out the poison.'

'I guess so.' Reyna's father moved towards the bed and placed a hand on Cub's forehead. The boy shuddered at the touch. 'He is burning up,' Norgate said to himself, as though he had forgotten the man behind him. But the room had moulded itself around the scent of leather and saddle wax and the man refused to be forgotten.

'Indeed. The bite has weakened him. He may be tough, but there's nothing to tell us how long he has been this way. I fear the continued absence of Dr Fortune, Ralf, for despite young Nugget's admirable attention, the boy needs professional help.'

The sheriff nodded, squaring his shoulders. He turned around to face his brother-in-law, as well as the door that would allow him to descend to the kitchen and the more welcome company of his daughter. But a burst of words came from the bed, dry-throat delirium that caught the sheriff's attention. 'Is the patient known around here?'

'No. I have asked, but no one has ever set eyes on him. There are some interested people in this town, who find the unusual mighty enthralling.'

Ralf looked up at him. 'This is a new town and a small

one, Thackeray. I expect that you and your son were equally as enthralling when you moved in last year.'

The silence in the room crackled with animosity, but it eased when Thackeray stepped away. 'Well, although not itself enthralling, this might well hold your own interest,' he said by the doorway where the day's light fell short and his face was a mask of shadows. 'Wolf Wind.'

Ralf frowned, shook his head to clear it. 'What is that?'

'Unfortunately, brother-in-law, it is beyond even my knowledge.' Thackeray's voice was crystal clear, but his mouth barely moved. 'Just two words that the boy was overheard to mention. Two words and no more.'

'But the only clue we have as to our strange young guest's identity.'

'You are wrong there, Ralf,' and how pleased he was that this was so, 'for there is also the horse he was riding.'

'Ah, yes.' The unruly horse. The ungrateful horse.

'A stallion. Palomino. Big. Too skittered to control, but the boy was riding bareback. The animal galloped away when he fell. Disappeared. Odd, don't you think?'

'Indeed. Odd.'

'And there is one other thing.' Thackeray stepped out through the door into full shadow, and when he turned again Ralf found it difficult to see the man's eyes. 'The boy has been whipped. Recently, for the wounds are not yet fully healed.'

NINE

THE NEW town sounds of hammer and saw became as familiar as the cock's crow and the dog's howl, and Cub's fever worsened. He grew weaker, sinking into the hollow of the mattress. For two more days, as the sun stretched across the sidewalk and shadows puddled the ruts in the road, Reyna sat in her weary place beside the bed and the bowl, watching the sweat drying in streaks across his face.

The next day a wind brewed, rustling clouds over a disheartened sky. The girl woke from jagged dreams to the clatter of a gate in the street; still in her night gown, sleep-laden, she stumbled along the passageway. The air inside Clement's bedroom seemed unusually dismal: gloomy, swirling with movement, as groggy as soup. She pushed it aside to reach the window, pulling back the drapes and opening the casement to the playful wind, but when she turned around the room hung still and silent.

The boy was lying half out of the covers, one hand raised to the pillow, the other dragging him to the floor.

'Oh no.' She moved towards the bed as if to capture something there. 'No. You cannot be dead.' She batted away the shadows that hovered above his head, and when she grabbed his shoulder it felt too cold. 'Not after I have tried so hard.'

She pushed him back on the bed; she shook him until his teeth clattered. And when she realised what she was doing she just stood there with her fingers to her mouth, and her sight so blurred that she did not see his eyes opening, or the way he was looking up at her furious grief. But then a bird flew past the window, so close that its call seemed to come from somewhere inside the room. They both turned to the sound, and when she saw him move Reyna let out a cry that broke in half behind her hands. She cleared her sight with a wipe of her sleeve, just to make sure that the boy was alive, that he was staring at her.

Staring at the doorway with his eyes widening as a furore leaped the stairs, and the man from the street stood there, half-dressed, gripping the door as if it was a shield. Cub remembered sliding from Wolf Wind's back, and his fall to the ground when everything had come to rest like the start of a deep sleep. He searched his mind for an explanation of what had happened since then, but he couldn't find anything that made sense.

Calf-hide man came further into the room; he spoke short, sharp words. 'What's wrong? I heard you call out.'

The girl started at the hair on his chest and the undershirt, the bare feet showing beneath the legs of his pants. 'Uncle Thackeray. I apologise; I must have woken you.'

'For sure, Reyna, it might be that you've woken the whole house,' he said, and half turned at the stumble of boots that brought her father to the bedroom door. He, too, held the edge of it like a shield, as if he was protecting himself from something that was inside the room.

'Is anything the matter, Nugget?' Ralf Norgate's face was open as he stared at her, but closed swiftly, like the shell of a prey, when he saw his brother-in-law. 'What are you doing here, Thackeray?'

'Following up the distress in my niece's cry.' The men faced each other from opposite sides of the small room, and the air shimmered. 'I have always understood it to be my duty to protect her. You know that.'

Reyna heard the sincerity but not the attack, and she

smiled. Her father heard only the criticism and saw the smile; and he felt excluded.

'I am grateful for your concern, Uncle, but I do not need protecting,' the girl said. 'For as you can see, my patient has recovered.' She beamed down at the boy in the bed and her face was angelic with pleasure. She did not notice him flinch as she reached out to feel for heat in his forehead; it was Thackeray Dart who noticed, with his quicker eyes and his sharper mind, and he thought of the welts that crossed the boy's back and began to figure.

'How are you feeling?' Reyna leaned down and spoke slowly and loudly as though Cub was far away. She stroked the back of his hand, and her palm was hot and dry and her eyes sparked. He struggled to answer.

'Don't try to speak, son; there will be time enough later for words.' The man stood beside the girl with his paw on her shoulder; an old fox with grey in his hair, glancing flint-eyed at the one who was still hesitating by the door. 'You see, Ralf,' he said, 'this good thing might never have happened had it not been for the diligence of your daughter's nursing.'

'Thank you, Uncle Thackeray.' Reyna giggled, making herself a coy bunch beneath the touch of his hand. 'To heal the sick is all I have ever wished.'

'Oh, I know that, Nugget. And I'm sure your father is also aware of your ambition. Are you not, Ralf?'

But the sheriff was just standing there, frowning down at the bed, and the boy who could not meet his eye. Frowning when his daughter noticed that the boy was shaking. Thinking he was cold, thinking he was ill again, she drew the sheet up to his chest and felt his forehead once more for fever. He was cool now for the fire had burned away, but still he was shaking. She turned her head and saw her father's frown, and she did not understand.

'It is remarkable.' Ralf felt the crumple of faith in her look. He collected himself. 'Just remarkable, what you have achieved, Nugget.'

She had her mother's face, as round as a plump peach, and she smiled at him with steadfast trust just as her mother had done. The trust that he had betrayed when he brought his beautiful wife to live in the wilderness where the killing disease was lying in wait. He turned away with the memory behind his eyes, and before him stood Rosie's sister's husband, with that knowing grin curling one side of his mouth.

'Thackeray.'

He spoke quietly, and the man cocked his head. 'What is it, Ralf?' he said, and even his voice had cunning, as though every word was woven into a trap.

'Come with me, Thackeray; there is something we need to discuss.'

The fox sighed and held up a placating hand. 'Sure, Ralf. I shall be down in just a minute or two.'

'Now, Thackeray. Come with me now.'

'I gather this is such a thing that cannot wait?'

'I believe it to be – something that cannot wait.'

Thackeray Dart studied the set face, the stolid features and the dutiful air, and he sighed again as if to make a point. The sound was almost loud in the quiet room despite the clatter of early morning life outside the window. 'Well, if you insist,' he said, and turned back to his niece. 'Your father and I shall be but a short while, Nugget. Why not prepare a bite of breakfast for our young guest? And you could venture into the parlour as well and wake your good-for-nothing cousin. No doubt he is still asleep, even at this busy time.'

The girl nodded, for she was happy now, talking to the boy in the bed about what had been and what was to be, unaware that Cub was pressing against the head rails like a creature in a trap.

Reyna's father led Thackeray Dart down the echo of stairs to the plain wooden door at the front. He unlocked it with a well-used key, and Thackeray walked before him into a room buttered with early sun, where deep shelves stretched half-empty across the walls and a rough board desk stood prominent, facing square-paned casements on either side of the street door.

Ralf opened a drawer in the desk and leaned in, shuffling the contents with both hands, and his brother-in-law waited behind him in the middle of the room. Thackeray favoured one leg after the other; yawned and scratched his chest; folded his arms – and Ralf froze as the man's shadow reached out and blackened his sight. He stepped away blindly, smacking the desk with his hip and bringing the chair to manic life. Thackeray restrained it as it jounced across the floor, his hands stroking the polished arms until the rub of skin on wood raised the short hairs at the base of Ralf's skull.

'Is everything well with you?' Thackeray smiled. 'You appear to be somewhat disconnected.'

Ralf kneaded the back of his neck. 'There's something in here that I consider of importance.' He turned to the desk and opened the second drawer, hiding his sight, stilling his irritation. His brother-in-law slung one leg over the corner of the desk and watched the investigation with a little smile.

'And what exactly is this important thing?'

'I thought I'd left it here and yet I do not…Ah, well.' Ralf Norgate took out a handwritten sheet of paper and pushed the drawer shut. 'Here it is now.'

He drew the chair back and sat down. The other man had not moved from his perch, and the sheriff waited in silence for him to do so. When Thackeray's shadow lifted away the new light that spread through the office was as sharp as relief.

'I have been making enquiries about the boy that you fetched into my house.'

'Making enquiries?'

'Sending out messages, Thackeray. Trying to find out who he is, where he comes from, who there is to contact.'

'I see.'

'A stranger in my house. One lucky enough to have survived snakebite fever.'

'Is it luck, or Reyna's ministrations?'

Ralf looked up at the man, half-dressed and ridiculous. He thought of his late wife and of her compassion; of how she had always expected him to display the same sensitivity. 'She is a child, Thackeray, not a nurse.'

'Reyna is a kind, caring and dedicated child, Ralf.'

The sheriff banged the desk with the heel of his hand, and the sound shuddered off the far wall. 'Damn it, man. Do you not think I know my own daughter?'

'Difficult to tell,' Thackeray Dart spoke softly over the shocked echoes. 'Owing to the length of time you seem to spend in absence from her.'

Ralf stood then, urging the chair away. 'And what is that supposed to mean?'

'Let me explain.' Thackeray smiled, turning towards the window where a horse could be seen trotting through a cloud of road dust, its rider's spurs chiming with each bounce of the animal's hooves. 'Let me explain on Reyna's behalf.'

'No, Thackeray. I wish you to explain on your own behalf.' It was the over-confidence of the man; he wanted to shake him to fragments; he wanted to grab his throat. His fingers cramped, and the sheet of paper collapsed inside his fist.

'There are times when the house is so quiet, Ralf, that I can hear Reyna crying.'

'What?'

'Crying. In her room. In the year that my son and I have lived here, not a full week has passed but you have been missing for some of it. Not one full week.'

'I do not think…I have not…Well, that is nothing but

a damn lie!'

Thackeray leaned forwards and rested his weight on the desk, scattering notebooks and papers, sending a horseshoe ink blotter rocking over the edge.

'Do you know who looks after your daughter when you are away on yet another one of your so important investigations? Making your so essential enquiries. Who do you think it might be, Ralf? It is myself, and my son, Clement. And have you not yet understood why it was, twelve months ago, that your Rosie – God rest her soul – why she insisted that you should take us into her house for the sake of her sister? Of Hannah, my wife.'

Sheriff Norgate stared at the year's fury burning in the man's eyes. Lashed by flecks of spit, he stood with his fists ready, the piece of paper unrecognisable now. And he wanted to kill.

'Perhaps you should tell me why it was, as it seems you are quite prepared to do?'

'She knew you so well, brother-in-law. She was leaving a young, desperate girl in the care of a careless man, and that is why she asked me to take over your responsibility. Your wife invited me to become a guardian for Reyna, Ralf, because she could not trust you to do the job.'

'That is not true. You are…' Something had caught in his throat, strangling what he wanted to say. Trying to strangle what he had not wanted to hear. 'Rosie never liked you. If she allowed you to live here it was purely for Hannah's sake, not for any other.'

'Sure, it was for Hannah's sake. But about the other you are mistaken. Rosie was very fond of me, Ralf. And she liked Clement very well indeed; well enough for her to desire that he and Reyna should become betrothed.'

'Betrothed? What in hell are you saying?'

'Your wife wanted her daughter and my son to love one another. To marry.'

'You're quite insane.'

'Be careful what you call me, brother-in-law, for you might be labelling the sister of my Hannah with your names.'

'How am I to believe you?'

'By knowing that I'm telling you the truth. It was her dearest wish.'

'Rosie said nothing of this to me…'

'She could never talk to you about it, Ralf. Because even your own wife was frightened of you.'

Norgate lashed out with his fist, catching the man's jaw. Thackeray rocked away; his bare feet making dry scuffles on the floorboards. He stood for a moment with his back to the sheriff, then very slowly, he turned around.

'She was afraid of you, brother Ralf,' he said. 'Had you indeed never been aware of her fear?' He raised a finger and pushed it slowly into the man's chest. 'And if you ever hit me again I shall make sure that you learn the same fear of me.'

Ralf Norgate watched him leave, and the place on his chest where the finger had pressed itched with anger. The door closed and he was alone in the room, but his neck prickled with the daily onslaught that reached out for him from the windows; the parade of life across the stamped street and the spring of the wooden sidewalks. He needed to think of the people of the town, who trusted him enough to put their lives in his hands, before he followed his brother-in-law into the heart of the house and tore him apart in front of his daughter and his nephew. And the boy. The boy whose life he was holding in his hand.

The sheet was warm, and as crushed as a piece of linen. He pulled up the wayward chair and sat at his desk, opening the paper like a flower. The words had been penned with good ink – for the ink used by the telegraph office, proud and new at the end of the street, was always good. Even the damage inflicted by rage had failed to diminish the reply that had resulted from his enquiries.

It had come from the sheriff of a small town lying over the pointed hills. A short report from Sheriff Clay Russett of Oasis. The word – "dangerous" – had been underlined.

TEN

THIRTY MINUTES had passed since the two men had left the bedroom, taking with them the importance that had to be discussed, followed by the growl of angry voices from a room below. Cub was still taut with the memory of it, his mind swirling like the cloudy water on the chest of drawers. The girl was back at the bedside, humming a simple tune. She dunked the cloth and laid it warm and damp across his forehead. Slightly plump and slightly dowdy in a pale brown dress, she moved in a happy trance like a child playing a game with dolls, but she looked older than her years, the skin above her cheekbones cushioned by fatigue. He studied her pink-lidded eyes, and when she turned to him with all her honesty and innocence he saw Lucy Ryker standing behind her. He remembered the intensity with which the doctor's wife had cared for him, as if she had a greater understanding than her husband regardless of all his medical knowledge.

The girl held the cloth in midair and stared at the flame burning in the boy's dark gaze, the amber flare that was like honey held up to the light. Water seeped over her hand and dripped to the bed, leaving marks like shadow spots on the cover. 'You have nothing to worry about now,' she said. 'You are safe in my home.'

Cub heard the sounds again, replayed like a memory from the depths of the house: the thrust and parry of voices and the grind of furious feet on a wooden floor. He peered at the girl but she was unaware, floating in the bubble of the bedroom. He pulled himself up against the head rails and grabbed her arm. The cloth shuddered; water sprayed across his chest and her skin was hot between his fingers. 'I need to leave now,' he said. 'I need my horse.'

She stared at the grip of his hand, as severe as a tight cuff, and her face bloomed with horror until he opened his fingers and freed her; shaking a little, aching a little. His mind began to buzz. She shook her head and her ill-fastened hair bounced from side to side; a tendril escaped and trickled down her face. 'But you are not ready to leave yet. You must wait until you are whole again and strong.'

He sank, turned his head towards the window. He could see the snaggle-toothed buildings and the clouds scudding above. He could hear intermittent footsteps in the street, as though the walker dragged a leg; he could hear voices raised in greeting, a child skipping along the sidewalk as light as a gambolling lamb, the schlop schlop of a trotting mare.

'Where is my horse?' he said, sending his mind out into the dancing air, over mismatched roofs, away from packed earth and down to the gullies and crests of the plains. He hunted the hidden places, but they were vast and empty. He listened, but there were no echoes of wild hooves. And then heavy feet climbed the stairs and shattered his search like a stone thrown into still water.

The man came back into the room; the one from the street who had made the palomino rear. Cub remembered hitting the ground and the crunch of hooves inches from his head. He remembered smelling the bounce of earth as Wolf Wind galloped out of the town, the drub of sound that slowly eased and quietened, and the oblivion that came for him as his captor crouched beside his body.

Still only half-dressed, the fox-haired man fixed himself in the doorway. Reyna looked up at his bared chest, and looked away again quickly as though unnerved by the sight of curled hair. 'Uncle Thackeray, you need clothes,' she said with the pretence of a laugh, and fiddled with the high neck of her dress as if to insist on the message.

'On my way, Nugget,' he said. 'Though I had to step a while with your father in the office downstairs.' He spread a palm across his heart, as if to apologise for his semi-nakedness. 'But first I wanted to see your patient. See what else might have transpired.'

Reyna sent him half a glance. 'He is clear of fever, Uncle Thackeray, and all is well. When convenient I shall go and prepare for him some sustenance.'

'Why not take this opportunity, Nugget. I'll wait here. Have no fear for he will receive all attention.' The smile lifted his face and disappeared behind his moustache.

The girl slipped the wet cloth into the bowl, sweeping her skirt as though preparing wings for flight. 'I shall be as fleet as possible, for you must be as hungry as a bear in spring.' She stared at Cub, and he read something helpless, almost frantic in her eyes. But she was calm as she left the room, stepping around the man with the delicacy of a held breath.

Reyna's uncle watched the door as if through it he could see her quick, light step on the stairs, and then he turned towards the boy on the bed. 'You are a bit of a mystery.' He walked closer. 'Nobody around here has even a wisp of information about you.' He stopped in front of the window, and the early day outside threw him into instant and utter dusk. 'Why, you could be anybody.'

Cub struggled to see his eyes. 'I am grateful for your help.'

'Anyone else would have done the same.' The man stood completely still in his darkness, obstructing the window so that even the street sounds were muted. He seemed to grow, like a sponge taking in water.

'I have stayed too long,' Cub said. 'I must leave.'

'Not yet. First you should recover your strength.'

Cub looked up at the man. He could see the paler features of his face taking on residual light from the room. He could see the silver glint of his stare, as if he was trying to read what was in the boy's head.

'I have always been strong.'

Thackeray Dart's eyes widened a little. 'You see,' he said. 'This is something we know nothing about. You are something we know nothing about. Why, we do not yet know what to call you.'

For a while all sound hesitated outside in the street and there was a hush in the room, until a stumble of footsteps climbed the stairs beyond the half-open door and a young man stood on the threshold. The one that Cub knew from his sluggish mind, when he had been out of his body and sinking beneath the surface of the snakebite. The young man who had bent the boy's finger back with the crush of his hand, adding pain to the fire in his head; keeping his back to the door, so that the girl should not see what was burning in his face. But Cub had seen the loathing that had wrinkled the eyes to gashes and the spit glistening on his teeth, and now the young man was here again, half-empty with sleep and untidily dressed.

The red-haired man looked up, and a wave of irritation swept his face. 'Finally awake then, Clement?'

'Yes, Father; sorry, Father. But the day is yet new.'

'Even though the good news that the day has brought is now tired and tardy.' He leaned forward suddenly and gripped Cub's shoulder, and it was as shocking as an iron vice. 'See here; our young guest has finally recovered from fever.'

Clement ventured further into the room as though he did not know what else he should do, and pinned the boy to the bed with his glare. Thackeray Dart's grip tightened and Cub squeezed his hands into fists. This the older man noticed, and he smiled before he released his hold.

The round-faced girl came back into the bedroom,

balancing a tray that stretched her arms like a ballerina. 'Take care, Clem,' she said. 'Make a little space for me.'

She stepped around the young man and he watched her waddling beneath her awkward burden but made no move to take it from her, shamed by his father who strode forward and lifted it from her hands as though it weighed very little. Freed from the obstruction of his bulk, the sunlight warmed the window and relished the room, and Cub stared through the glass for something wild and open, but the unsure roof line opposite had not changed and the sky remained benign. Tame. No jagged plains like frozen waves, no echoes of falling rock; no sign of a stallion muzzled by rope.

But it felt safer to stare out of the window now that the small room had shrunk cruelly to the size of a cell, peopled by the curious. Cub was fettered by tight sheets and crazy things climbing the wallpaper, and when he sat high against the bedhead his skull swam in the wake of fever and his back tingled from healing stripes and fear. The industrious girl had set out her tray before him with plates and bowls and an excess of temptations that perhaps a child might appreciate. Cub saw it all in congealed colours from the edge of his sight, for the man with the silver star had appeared at the corner of his mind as if half-hidden behind the backs of the crowd, and he stood with power and knowledge, and watched the boy from beyond a padlocked door.

ELEVEN

SLEEP FELL unbidden and Cub's dreams fretted as one more day passed and the sheriff bided his time in the room downstairs. When the boy woke it was evening, and Reyna was still watching and waiting on the chair beside his bed. She wore a different dress on this different day, a gloss of pale pink, and her smile was the first thing he saw as sleep smoked away.

'Reyna,' he said, his voice breaking on her name. She lowered her eyes to her hands, clasped palm to palm as if in prayer, and the colour of her dress heightened the blush in her cheeks.

'And there I believe you have me at a disadvantage,' she said, 'while I am still in ignorance of your own name.'

'My name?' I have no name, he thought. 'My name, is Buck.'

'Buck.' She looked up with something like excitement, and he wanted to halt the questions before she could ask them.

'And you are Nugget when you are not Reyna.'

'Why, yes.' She smiled, and he noticed her dimples for the first time, as though fever had hung gauze over his sight. They transformed her into a pretty girl. 'I have been Nugget since childhood, when that was the only way I could pronounce my family name. My mother turned it into a pet name.'

But in this house of men, the stamp of boots and the heavy scent of animal hide, he had seen no sign of a mother. Even so, he felt strangely and immediately glad that the girl was not so isolated.

'My mother passed away a year ago,' she said as though she knew his thoughts. 'Not long after we'd moved here, to Liberation. And since then my pet name has become my inheritance.' She smiled again, and the dimples were pale, like ghosts.

'I am sorry,' he said, wondering about sadness and the death of a mother, and why it was that such a memory had seeped away from his own life.

'But I have much to be grateful for,' she said. 'How can I not be happy when so many of my family are with me still? My uncle, my cousin. My father.'

And yet your father is far from happy, he thought, and he wondered whether it had something to do with her uncle, and her cousin.

She gathered the full skirt of the pink dress between her hands and stood abruptly, as if she had said too much. 'You must be hungry, Buck. I will bring you some supper,' she muttered, bustling to the door. And then she stood there, uncertain, and lowered her eyes as she turned towards him. 'My father is a very busy man,' she said. 'Much of this busyness takes him away from home, you see. For many days at a time. And I wish…' She stopped and looked up, and her eyes were shining in the half-light from the passageway as though she had started to cry. 'I so wish that it would not.'

Her steps faded even as she clattered to the foot of the stairs, and at once the air was tentative with silence. Two men passed beneath the window on slovenly feet; one of them hawked, and spat. 'Bull's eye,' he spluttered when the gobbet hit the sidewalk with the sound of heavy rain. Both men snorted and stumbled away into their evening, and then silence oozed back into all the empty spaces of the house.

Cub pushed himself up against the bedhead, dislodging

the cover; without its protection his skin cooled quickly, exposed to sharp air lying in wait. He shivered, but it was from the cold and not the grip of fever, for he was stronger now. His feet met the coils of a rag rug when he stood from the bed. He took a step towards the window, towards the street outside where freedom slumbered and Wolf Wind was waiting to carry him through long grass and into the star-pricked night. He took another step and the room shifted, as though something had come loose inside his brain.

The window withdrew to the end of a long tunnel, too far to reach and too long to walk, and Cub fell back against the bed, shuddering like a newborn foal, listening to the remnants of drunken hilarity rip-roaring from the fringes of the town. The laughter tumbled along the sidewalk and smacked into the back of his head like a rifle butt; or a gun held by the man with a silver star on his chest.

Another day passed, and two more followed as slowly as a week. Cub endured the long hours, haunted by his weakness, waiting for the nights to come so that he could practise those steps again. And again; until his head was clear and he was certain that his legs would be strong enough to grip a stallion's flanks, to carry him away from the town of Liberation, from the round-faced girl and the lawman. Out there below the window the street was open and free; but the house wall was sheer and it was too far to fall. He could not climb down, and so he did the only other thing left for him to do. He waited.

And at the bottom of the stairs the sheriff waited also. Sunlight drifted through the door to the office where Ralf Norgate sat, smoothing the worn wooden arms of his chair. He thought of the boy, recovering his strength in the room above. He listened to his daughter's light tread and the jaunty rattle of the trays she carried; he listened to the impudence of his wife's sister's husband climbing the stairs two at a time like the wholehearted man he was, jigging to the crystal ting of the spurs on his boots. The sheriff waited, and after a few more days he heard Dart's knock, and felt the air suck away as the door opened.

'Busy, brother-in-law?' Thackeray walked into the room and looked around at the empty space, and then he answered his own question. 'No. I see there is a decided lack of crime in our fair town. Probably having a sheriff in his rightful place in this office for longer than a week has proved a potent deterrent, do you not think?'

Ralf turned to face him. 'But despite that, Thackeray, yes I am busy. So, is there something you wish to discuss?'

'Not as such.' The sharp eyes opened wide, and a smile slunk out from beneath the fulsome moustache. 'But I have some news regarding our virtually resident stranger upstairs…'

Ralf scratched the irritation at the back of his neck and felt bristles there. 'What about him, Thackeray?'

'It seems to me that the boy is anxious to travel again,' he said. 'Seems to me he will relinquish my son's bed when we are all in our slumbers, and hide his trail under the dust from a stallion's hooves.'

He turned to leave, but looked back again when he reached the door. Ralf had gone into his desk drawer and brought out the sheet of paper from the telegraph office, smoothing its creases with the edge of his thumb. Thackeray Dart saw all this, and he smiled with his eyes and walked away.

Cub came awake in the night, jumping from deep and still to vigilant. He read all the familiar outlines in the dark room, and listened to the rising and falling of the wind beyond the swaying drapes. The night was chill on his body when he drew his legs over the side of the bed, and his bare feet were first coddled by the rag rug and then tender on the floorboards. He went to the armchair and pulled on his clothes, borrowed and belonging, and the stiff boots where Daniel Ryker's money lay in secret; and under the sag of the chair he found the soft leather pouch and the hunting knife, lying in the dust as if they had been hiding.

Quiet as caution, the boy opened the door. He closed it behind him and stood outside in the passageway; the space where he had never ventured for all the days he had been an invalid. The house was holding its breath in a sweeping silence that retreated sporadically as the wind rose and fell outside. The stairs beckoned. They were steep and narrow and felt lethal with hidden alarms, but they flowed silently to the ground floor. Before him was the house door, topped by a panel of moonstone glass. It was the door that would lead him to wind-dusted streets, and his back straightened as he moved towards the promise that lay on the other side of the planed wood.

'That's far enough, Cub. Stay where I can see you.'

The sound was so sudden it stopped his ears, and for a moment he was deafened. But the fear had travelled with him from the bedroom; he had been afraid before he heard the man jumping from the shadows across the floor, and now he had no time to think. He lunged for the street door, little caring at the noise he made as his feet skidded over the boards. He turned the handle but the bolt was across. He ripped it away and tore the door open, and the town widened in front of him, fresh with the night and open to the sky. Cub reached into it as if in a dream, his back prickling as the man's footsteps rang closer and hands crashed down on his shoulders. He fought with the savagery that was the only emotion to rely upon after all those years in the defeated farmyard, twisting away from the man's grasp and kicking out to run through the doorway, and then to run and run towards the wildness beyond the brand-new town where perhaps the feral golden horse might still remember him.

But other hands were gripping him now, grinding his wrists up to his shoulder blades and jagging his screaming muscles. He tumbled over the threshold and jerked to his knees on the gritty hollowness of the sidewalk, and still he struggled; although by now it was useless.

Inside the house a soft sibilant light was dancing across the walls, washing the bleak and hopeless with gentle colour. The boy's eyes were drawn to it, and to the figure of Reyna standing halfway down the stairs in a long white robe, her round face rosy from the lamp she carried, her eyes flashing in the hissing light as she blinked, as she looked away, as she looked back, as she looked down.

Cub twisted his head round until his shoulders were screaming, and he saw the man who was forcing him to his knees; the fox-haired man who had probably saved his life on the day he had stepped in front of Wolf Wind and made him rear. Thackeray Dart looked down, and the flicker of a smile passed his eyes as he lifted the boy to his feet. There was a sigh that could have animated any of them, but it came from Ralf Norgate, committed and dutiful and correct as he stood beside his brother-in-law.

'I'm putting you under arrest, Cub,' the sheriff said. He reached out to shut the door, and the boy closed his eyes so that he didn't have to see. The ridiculous freedom disappeared, and the splutter of the lamp was the only sound left in the house.

TWELVE

THE FOOD had subsided as it cooled and now it was just a flat mess on the metal plate, and unrecognisable. Ralf Norgate stood with his hands by his sides and peered down to where the simple meal still lay in the spot where he had left it two hours earlier. Beside the plate a bed platform jutted out, suspended from the wall by sturdy chains. Cub sat cross-legged on the thin covering, his back squared up against the brickwork and his eyes pinpointing the bars opposite; pinpointing the gaps between them where there was life beyond the cell. He was completely motionless. He was barely breathing.

'Thirty hours and you've hardly eaten a thing,' Norgate said, but his prisoner ignored him. When the man spoke again his voice was lower and quieter; it hardly disturbed the prolonged sense of a breath being held. 'We shall be moving out early in the morning. It would be wise to eat something before then.'

That got the boy's attention, but only for a moment. Energy had flared through his body and dissipated into the emptiness that was all that was left in the cell. And as it disappeared the sheriff felt angry enough to grab him and shake, just to see whether some enforced movement, some violence, might bring him back to life. The man shook himself instead, picking up the sorry plate before he retreated from the jail and back into his office.

The hollow slam of the door doused him like a shower and left him ashamed, and he slouched in the creak of his desk chair, staring out of the window at the everyday that he and all the other inhabitants of this house took for granted. Cub was just a boy of sixteen, or maybe even younger, his body crisscrossed by newly-healed scars. Son or servant, his life must have been wretched, and when the sheriff took him back it would become wretched again. But the lawman had a duty to all honest people, and from the account telegraphed to him by Sheriff Clay Russett of Oasis the boy had violently assaulted one of the honest people of that town, and so he was guilty and Norgate had his job to do.

He stood, too abruptly; the chair bounced in surprise and grumbled across the floor to escape his vehemence, and he pushed it out of the way to get to the door that led from the office to the heart of the house.

'Where are you, Reyna?' Norgate's voice echoed back from the walls, and a casement rattled on the floor above. Sunshine beamed through the moonstone window and his back was cherished by its warmth, but darkness was churning inside him, and it felt almost indecent to be so cherished.

The kitchen door opened at the end of the passageway and Reyna stepped quickly from the room, as though she was hiding something that she did not wish him to see. Norgate pushed away from the stair handrail, and it shook with the force as he walked towards her. 'Daughter, I need you to do something for me.'

The girl watched him approach, shrinking from the gleam of silver on his chest. The closer he came to her the more the sun's shade collected in the corners, until it had grown to a swirling mist that obliterated everything.

'Reyna, the boy is refusing to eat. I want you to go and talk some sense into him.' He stood before her and spoke to the wall, as though the words might bounce back with an answer to it all, because it felt wrong to have locked up a guest who had been brought to life in his house. And after a while, when he became aware that Reyna had not replied, he peered down; and recoiled from the look on her face.

'I cannot do that, Father,' she said, and secreted herself behind the shadows. She looked at the floor, dismissing him. He felt as if he did not really know her, this beloved daughter who was all that remained of his beloved wife. Over the past year he had spent time away from his home, time increasing in length, when instead he should have been here watching her grow. He could see that she was a young woman now, not a girl, and it was a shock. It was a pain, spreading up through his feet and tugging at his scalp.

'What is the matter, Reyna? Dear girl, will you not tell me?'

She looked up at him so slowly that he was hardly aware, until he saw her eyes widen, delving deeply into his own as though there was something inside him that she needed to discover. 'The boy; he was incoherent when he arrived,' she said. 'When Uncle Thackeray brought him to this house he was incomplete. And I did everything that I could to put him back together.'

'You were remarkable…'

'I nursed him, day and night. I dealt with all his needs.'

'You nursed him with such ability…'

'He would have died if not for me.'

'He could not have had better…'

He stepped back, his cheek stinging. She had slapped him. She raised her hand again and came closer. 'Stop it, Father. Just stop it!'

Norgate grabbed his daughter's wrist. Her skin was hot and she was shaking, but she did not pull away. She folded herself against his chest and he held her as she sobbed. After a while her tears soaked through his shirt to slick his skin, and after a while more she was quiet again. He was in awe at how small she was, and why on earth he had kept himself away from her for so long.

'I nursed him,' she said slowly, 'until he had regained all his strength. He survived because of me. He is in your prison cell because of me.'

'Don't think like that, Reyna.'

'He is in your prison, and tomorrow you will return him to the indescribable life he thought he had escaped.'

'You cannot know…'

'But I do know.' She was staring at him. Her round face was pink from crying and his heart tumbled. 'I know because when he was delirious he was in a raving about it, about everything that has happened to him. It is abysmal, Father, and now he must be sent back to it. And I have betrayed him.'

She seemed to grow taller, smoothing her hair and stroking creases from her skirt. And when she looked up again she had poise and peace and determination. 'And it is because of these things that I will not see him, I will not speak to him, and I will no longer lead him down fruitless paths towards dead ends. I may have been naive, Father, but I have never been cruel.'

She opened the door, sucking the air and the circling shadows with her into the kitchen as she withdrew. Her father stood alone and thought of the boy who was sitting cross-legged on the hard bed shelf, staring into his future from behind grey metal bars, and for the first time in all the years since he had clipped the shiny new star to his chest, Ralf Norgate hated his job.

Cub dreamed of Wolf Wind that night. Two hours before dawn he awoke to the hoofbeats that had fallen out of his subconscious mind, beats as loud as the dream's echo in his brain, and he stood up by the small window expecting to see the stallion waiting for him under the moon's pallid shadow. But it was another horse that appeared, rocking along beneath a late traveller. A tired skewbald that turned crazy with bark-brown checks as it passed the bars of Cub's window, and stepped away into the sweep of the moon.

Night dragged slowly towards morning, and the sky was peppered with the dregs of dawn as Cub mounted a sturdy dun outside the sheriff's office. He sat with his eyes lowered and breathed wild air into cell-locked lungs. He knew only a blur of movement and the saddle creak beside him as Norgate climbed on to the back of a dapple-grey mare, but there was something else, and it raised his head from the dusty road to the building on the sidewalk. He saw the window beneath the roof where the drapes quivered like a veil. He saw Reyna as she stood watching the two riders on the street below, her face half-hidden behind draggled hair. He could see even from the street that she had been crying.

'Ready?' the sheriff said, flexing his body easily in the well-travelled leather as though he was glad to be leaving again, and Cub looked down at the cuffs that married his hands to the horn of his saddle; the rope that drifted in the morning breeze between his horse and the dapple-grey like an uncomfortable umbilical. And if he had a choice, then no, he would not be ready.

The mare started to walk into the street, and as the rope tightened the dun obediently followed. Cub looked up again at the window but the drapes were limp now, moving slightly in the breeze, and the room behind was dark with loss.

THIRTEEN

CUB'S ATTENTION was nudged by the stillness of a hawk. He glanced up at the sky before dropping his head with a tight blinking, seeing only the echo of the sun at the back of his eyes but remembering the beauty of the bird and the shimmer of its wings.

The residue of light leaked away slowly from his sight until he found himself looking at the rope that swung between the trotting horses, and he followed its guiding line to the man on the grey. Ralf Norgate leaned to his mount's easy pace and did not look behind him, but the boy's eyes were uncomfortable on his back. After a while Cub stopped waiting for the man to turn, and to still his mind he dropped his gaze to the dust that coughed up from the mare's hooves.

Their trail had led them to soft plains, uncurling like a flower seeking the sun, and the two horses steadily loped away from the town that had once meant something and was now a memory. Cub lifted his eyes again, catching the hawk before it dropped from its weaving, straight down and lost from sight; but he did not wish to see the ground when the sky above was empty and vast and free. He threw back his head until the world was obliterated, and his body soared closer to the clouds and felt wilder with each jerk of the horse beneath him. But nothing is level in the centre of space, and his ears began to buzz as his balance tipped. The land ebbed and flowed, but after a while the sick tide settled and he was aware that Ralf

Norgate was watching him.

'It seems to me we have quite a distance to travel,' the man said, 'and our journey may feel even longer if there is no speech between us. What do you say?'

He had wanted to talk after seeing the wild bird free in the sky, as motionless and golden as the sun, but his captor had been oblivious and now the spell was broken by the tug of his leash. The boy ignored him, and the sheriff made a grunt in his throat that could have been laughter. Cub thought back to the lawman's jail, the bars at the window, the hard bed where he had lain awake at night while the hours stretched into something eternal – and Norgate's laughter was iniquitous.

He kicked the dun until it squealed and reared into a gallop, and there again was the open door and the pull of early morning; the hollow wood sound from the sidewalk as Thackeray Dart brought him to his knees. Reyna stood once more on the stairs with her hands gripping her night robe and eyes as round as shock in her white face; and Cub heard the rope singing as it wrapped around the sheriff's body, half-dragging him from the saddle.

'Get back!' Fear cut into Ralf Norgate's voice as the mare was pulled sideways and he felt his balance failing. 'Get back, now!' he yelled. And the impulse of years drew his gun deftly from its holster.

The boy stared into the mouth of the weapon, and then he looked up at the man who was holding it. He relaxed his body until the gelding had slithered to a halt and stood quivering, churning the bit, and for a while that was the only sound before the sheriff holstered his gun and kicked the sweating mare back onto the trail. They walked and then they trotted, Cub following the grey horse with his eyes to the horizon, and Norgate strangled the strips of rein between his fingers and knew that there could be no speech between them now.

That first night they camped beneath the shelter of an

ancient tree, stripped of its leaves in starkly beautiful death out on the loneliness of the plain. They camped in silence and they ate their meagre rations in silence, and after swallowing bitter coffee Cub sat with his legs crossed and his eyes wide to the flames. Ralf Norgate leaned back in the shadows and stared at the firelight dancing across the boy's closed face, and wondered how much longer such a silence might last.

Before he settled for the night the sheriff built up the fire to a star burst, and cuffed his prisoner to one of the tree roots that grew like the raised veins on the back of an old man's hand. Cub seemed to be oblivious as Norgate fumbled the restraint beneath broken foliage, and he was grateful for that, but when the boy moved the chain sang its own reprimand, and something fell into the heart of the fire and sighed in response. And all through the night wild creatures kept the silence at bay.

Dawn arrived dressed in tatters. The sky groaned and a slow wind brewed from the north, slapping them with cold spittle as if reluctant to let them pass. By noon the country had turned as rugged as a furious sea; the two horses rode wild waves and the riders sought shelter beneath their cresting manes. The wind was exhausting; it fell away as slowly as it had struck, leaving disarray in its wake. When it finally appeared, the sun was a blessing hanging low in the west, casting a long gallop of shadows and gleaming in shards from scattered rocks. Birds flew again, their cries so distorted by the rubble that they drew near and they veered away, and nothing was in its right place. So that when it came, the crash of the rifle seemed dangerously close.

Distressed by the explosion, small animals scuffled for shelter under the rocks, and Ralf Norgate ducked beneath the reverberation and hauled on the grey's reins until her neck arched. Gunfire seared the air, two shots repeated by wayward echoes that multiplied the sound from behind them, and the sheriff's mare danced sideways as though on broken glass, tightening the rope between the horses and forcing the dun backwards.

The sheriff fought to pull the grey together and she stood shivering in distress, but Cub leaned over from his saddle and spoke the soft language that had cooled a fiery stallion as cowboys watched, and the mare whickered trust from the back of her throat and grew calm. Norgate had heard the words breaking the boy's silence, but they were unintelligible. He scanned the horizon until his eyes rested on a distortion of air, a lazy spiral like the aftermath from the hot barrel of a revolver. He saw secrecy and magic and gibberish, and he was too angry to be wise.

'There's something going on over there,' the sheriff said, 'and I want to know what it is.'

He collected his reins, leaning across the mare's neck and shocking her with his heels. She leaped into the air, tightening the rope and dragging the dun behind her. The animals strained upwards on a skid of loose chippings, slapped by shrubbery and a rain of dust. When another shot rang out it was shrill and sharp and menacing, but its echo died under the chaos of hoofbeats as the horses reached the rise.

Struggling for breath, the dapple-grey clattered to a halt, and as the rope slackened the dun rasped air and stood depleted, sweat-streaked and shaking; but the boy and the man sat in silence on the edge of the panorama that had opened below them to reveal a scoop of empty plain, crusted at the edge of the sky by the bite of hills. The same hills that Cub had stood beneath early one night, feeling the claw-scratch of his torn back as he reached up to shake the hand of Daniel Ryker before seeking the way ahead. And beyond them was the valley where desultory chickens were still churning the farmyard mud; where Haine Madison would be building up his rage with raw liquor while his wife and his brave daughter bent their heads to hide.

Down there, at the start of the great gouge of plain, was a turf road, cut to the bone by an age of wheels and hooves, and a stagecoach lay on its side in the centre, looking like a great dead animal in the late afternoon light. A slight figure in a dark suit lay crumpled on the ground close by, the neck of his pale shirt made obscenely vibrant by blood, his hands stretched out to the vehicle as if even in death he sought refuge. Further on a little way a larger man had fallen; swathed in a jacket as loose as a shroud, he lay on his back with one arm across his eyes as though to deny what had happened to him. Beside him stood two black horses, twinned inside heavy trappings and protected behind blinkers. They ignored the dead men, and the two who had caused their deaths: one standing on stunted legs by the horses' heads, his thick fists full of bridles; the other fumbling through the belly of the fallen coach as if ripping out entrails.

The man scrambled backwards through the broken door with a rifle in one hand and the handle of a rust-red cash box in the other, and he raised his gun to the sky and shook it twice. The late sun trickled down the barrel and dripped from the end as he stared along the road, his mouth a grin of pointed teeth nuzzled by crisp grey whiskers like a winter wolf. He waggled the rifle again and howled, 'Give praise, Joey, my friend; we have been blessed with a good haul.'

Spooked by the noise, one of the horses stamped forward, and the younger man by its head cursed and hauled on the bridle. 'A good haul and two good beasts,' he yelled back, and up on the ridge Ralf Norgate turned to the boy beside him.

'Can you see that money box? Can you see what's going on? I need to get down there.'

'Why?'

The sheriff gave him his full attention, but the boy was staring ahead, and it was as if he had not spoken at all. 'Because it is my duty,' the man said, and then Cub turned and looked straight into his eyes.

Norgate could feel a probing in his head; it was almost a violation. He leaned back to break the connection, but the boy blinked slowly as if he had learned enough. 'It is my duty,' the man repeated, sharply, like someone who knows he is wasting time. He tapped the star that glinted like a small shield on his vest and Cub looked away towards the distant hills, thinking of the smell of dark alleyways on the edge of Oasis where as a young boy he had taken risks and made plans to escape. Thinking of the doctor's wife, the scent of lavender in her hair. Closing his eyes so that he didn't have to think any more.

Stealthily, Norgate drew the horses away from the rise until they were out of sight and sound. He dismounted, leaving the reins hanging, and the grey mare dropped her head to search the rocks for grass and comfort. The sheriff stood by the dun's flank and weighed the key to the cuffs in his hand; weighed up risk with duty as though the decision had not already been made.

'I think you know that I will shoot you if you try to run.' Norgate looked up and Cub stared at the ground by his feet. He was so young, the strange boy who had been an unconscious guest in his house, and already it had come to this. 'And if I am taken by those below us, then they will be the ones who will find you and shoot you. And you know this also, don't you?'

Cub knew it also, and held his hands out for the cuffs to be unlocked and the rope removed. He dismounted and stood by the dun with one hand ready on its withers as though he might still have a chance.

Sliding his rifle from beneath the mare's saddle flap, the sheriff steered the boy to the side of the hill with the point of its long barrel. They began to descend, the boy followed by the man, stepping over broken boulders and scuffing the dried earth into turmoil; accompanied from the roadway below by arguments, the squeal of frightened animals, the sound of the fallen stagecoach having its sides kicked in just for the hell of it.

Ralf Norgate came to a halt halfway and drew Cub down with him, pushing the boy to the ground where the grass grew long, and warning for silence with one finger to his lips. He lengthened the rifle against his shoulder and crouched on his haunches like a wildcat preparing to leap. The pair below had collected themselves, finding the time at last to unharness the black horses, and the sheriff's voice cut across the rattle of chains like a siren.

'Stay right where you are! We have guns trained on you.'

That was the moment when the wind died and the men beneath the hill froze, as if both those things were connected. The horses, half-unharnessed, stamped in discomfort too close to the dead bodies and the blood, and Norgate rose fully to his feet, his head on one side as he sighted the rifle. 'No need to turn around; no need to move. Just the need to throw down your weapons…'

'You first, stranger!'

Without looking behind, Cub rolled sideways on the ground, but the sheriff had straightened and grown taller, whirling around with his grip on the rifle. His knuckles were as white as bone as he found the trigger, but for a second he hesitated – and it was a second too long.

A sharp noise galvanised the black horses and they scattered down the road, dragging the remnant of harness behind them to bounce over the rutted ground like a plaything. The noise they made covered the sheriff's cry of pain. He dropped the weapon in the grass and bent his head, and Cub rose swiftly to his feet in a thrust of energy and prepared to run – to the side of the hill, to the top of the rise, anywhere that was a way out. But a figure stepped from the bushes and stood in his path; a tall, thin man, camouflaged behind the colour of dust, his face in hiding under the broad brim of his hat. The barrel of his gun was hot with smoke and sharp with the scent of firing, and it was pointing at Cub's chest.

'Leaving so soon? I don't think I can allow that.' The man flicked the gun up and down. 'Are you bearing arms, boy?'

Cub raised his hands; he tried to see the man's mind but the eyes were buried, and the face was just a narrow white mask gouged by stubble.

'It looks like we understand each other.' The man waved the gun towards the sheriff. 'Give your friend some assistance, will you?'

Ralf Norgate was on his knees, gripping his right arm, his eyes smudged by red veins and a curling mist. Cub helped him to his feet, and the gunman's mouth twisted as he looked down at the glint of silver on the sheriff's chest. He turned his head and spat in the dust, and then he walked towards them, leaning sideways to scoop up the dropped rifle as he passed it. He walked fast, forcing the man and the boy backwards down what was left of the slope to the level of the vast plain. Norgate's feet tangled in the long grass and he stumbled; he would have fallen if Cub had not grabbed his shoulder. The boy felt the rigid muscles and the tremor beneath the skin; he recognised the primal fear. He recognised the human being behind the star.

The level ground was almost comforting, but there was a smell of death down here and the sharp tang of terrified horses; there was the buzz of danger as the two men came back from the tumbled stagecoach with the red box and a clutch of harness in their arms. They stood beside their companion, and for a few seconds there was no sound as they stared at the man in pain and the boy by his side, then they turned away with a squint of eyes, chewing over decisions like so much tough meat.

'I say we kill them, Fletcher.'

'No.' The tall, thin man shook his gun as if it had been the weapon doing the choosing.

'Why the hell not?' The man with the cash box spoke through his crisp grey beard, but his mouth didn't seem to be moving, and the words came to Cub from a very long way inside his head. 'For sure the coyotes will dispose of their bodies.'

'No, is what I said, Mitch, and I am noted for the best ideas.' The gun barrel nodded, the metal silvered by late light, and the man called Fletcher smiled; but his eyes were still hidden under the hat brim. 'Collect the horses. Come on, boys; time to go.'

Long shadows stepped high as the dun and the dapple-grey were brought down from the top of the hill, the sheriff's mare protesting as she clattered through loose stones. Cub mounted the dun at gun point, knocking stirrups with Ralf Norgate when his horse sidled away from the acrid smell of the man's blood.

They all started to move along the dust road, Fletcher in front and the other two men bringing up the rear with the stolen horses, herding the boy and the sheriff past the dead stagecoach where the silent bodies had already softened to unrecognisable humps in the half-light. Night clouds rolled over like a warning, and they rode straight into billows as black as the side of a mountain. The wind pricked icy needles through the boy's clothes, but after a mile his body was too numb to notice. After a few more he was fused to the saddle.

Cub and the lawman rode frozen and night-blind over scrub, the occasional flounce of hills, and sudden dips where trees flourished from underground water courses. At first the cabin appeared to them as a blacker shape in the blackness, illuminated by a firefly gleam through its small, mean window. The trees grew thicker around it as though they had been planted for protection, and the horses stumbled over their invisible roots towards the scent of wood smoke that bestowed welcome warmth as they came closer.

They were forced to dismount under a prod of weapons, but the sheriff staggered as he climbed from the saddle and fell against Cub, pinning him to the wall of the cabin and smearing blood across the front of his jacket. The door opened to lamplight; for a moment or two it was a painful spike in the boy's eyes. He hesitated on the threshold; he saw the outline of a spluttering stove and the shape of a man sitting beside it, and by that time any chance of escape back into the night had been closed off behind him.

FOURTEEN

UNREAL IN the dazzle, the single room was sparsely furnished and as welcoming as a void. Cub blinked the light from his eyes and a meagre table with a disparate trio of chairs came into focus. A camp bed webbed with shadows drooped beside the far wall and an armchair with one arm missing was cosying up to a black-bellied stove. The stove gave a belch of filthy smoke that writhed through the air like a lost soul, and the fat man in the armchair raised a small, neat foot and kicked it. It rocked with indignation and scuttled on stubby legs, and the man leaned forward and ground out the end of his cigar on the hot plate before peering through the shrouds of smoke at the crowd that filled the tight space.

'You are all killing the light.' His voice was high, almost shrill, and unaccountable for a man of his bulk. As the smoke settled his face came into view, loose jowls and sallow skin corralled by a nest of silver-grey hair. He wore round spectacles with thick lenses that exaggerated the sharpness of his pale eyes, and he adjusted them with a pudgy hand as though he could not believe what he was seeing.

'Oh my, we have guests. Tell me who these people are, Leo? Better still, tell me why the hell you've brought them here?' His petulance became more pronounced with each question.

Fletcher took off his hat and stood exposed, but the light from the lamp spluttering under the ceiling could not quite reach his eyes. 'Beg pardon for the imposition, Mr Cochrane, but the sheriff here interrupted us at our work.'

The fat man slithered to his feet and stood before Cub by the window; without his weight, the one-armed chair sagged like something exhausted. 'And how did you come across this fine young man, Leo?'

'He and the sheriff were together, Mr Cochrane.'

Cobwebs over the window transformed the darkness outside to a ghostly grey, and the fat man's reflection seemed incomplete as he reached out to touch the boy's hair, too gently, and smiled with glistening lips. 'Were they now?' His voice had a girlish playfulness. 'And I believe I can understand why.'

Cub looked through the razor-sharp eyes, and kept looking until the man faltered, his jowls shaking a little as if he had just woken from sleep. Ralf Norgate stumbled against the boy's body, but Cub did not react; it was as though he was merely a buttress holding back the man's weight. Cochrane squeezed his lips together and turned away, rubbing his palms over the shiny jacket as if to dry them.

'Whatever possessed you, Leo, to bring an upholder of the law to our establishment, and still with breath in him?'

Mitch bared his pointed wolf's teeth and slung the cash box on the table. He sprawled in a chair, its legs scraping uncomfortably across the earthen floor. 'I said we should kill them, Mr Cochrane,' he said. 'But Fletcher's come up with a better idea; or so he reckons.'

The fat man's magnified eyes disdained the wolf man, but feasted on the rust-red coffer. He went to the table, picked up the box with both hands and shook it under his ear, shuddering at the thick sounds from inside, his whole body energised by movement. 'Now what could have been better than to get rid of them both at the outset?' He swung around to face the tall man who was still standing in the shadows by the door as though deciding whether to stay or go. 'Is your idea grander than that, Leo?'

Fletcher smiled down at the floor as if he had seen something amusing on the hard-packed earth. 'We have with us a pair of hostages.'

Cochrane hooked his thumbs into the armholes of his grey vest and bounced on his feet from heel to toe, like a jerky rocking chair. He looked up at the ceiling, squinting in the lamplight. 'Hostages, eh?' His voice was quiet now, soft as velvet wrapped around a dagger. 'And how do you think that might work, Leo?'

Fletcher hesitated, and for a moment the silence in the cabin was stunning.

'Are you saying that we should take a note to the grieving relatives, imploring them for money or they will not see papa sheriff again in this lifetime?'

'I think that should be the course of action, Mr Cochrane.'

'Well, do you now?'

Cub glanced to where Fletcher stood straight-backed by the side of the room, and for the first time he could see the man's eyes, small and naked without the protection of his broad-brimmed hat.

'I'm thinking that…'

'You don't know how to think, you fool!' Cochrane screamed, slamming his hand on the table, and the uproar crashed around the small hut looking for a way out. Mitch's chair fell to the floor as he stood, and he stumbled over it like a clown.

Cub tested his weight on one leg and then on the other. The door was so flimsy that a simple push would be enough to set him free. They were unprepared, they were slow, they would only know he had run when they could no longer see him standing near the window. Unattended and still saddled, with their reins slung over tree branches, the horses were ready to carry him away. The boy tensed his muscles and turned towards the door, but Mitch was there now with slack-faced Joey, who looked like a guard that had forgotten what he should be guarding, until his eyes swivelled towards Cub.

Ralf Norgate was leaning against the wall near the two men. His useless arm hanging, he stared up at the boy through the glaze of fear. Cub knew he was thinking of Reyna who was born to care, whose mother was already dead, and whose fate was uncertain under the guidance of Thackeray Dart and his one, unmarried son. Reyna, the daughter who needed her father. The boy saw into the sheriff's future, and then he dropped his gaze to the floor and waited for the ripples of Cochrane's anger to settle. He was not prepared for the fat man's speed as he turned, his jacket flapping open to show the loaded gun belt that sagged beneath his belly.

'Let us finish what you should have finished back there where you found them, Leo,' Cochrane grunted, pulling the Colt from its holster with the swiftness of practise. In one smooth move, he had cocked the hammer and pointed the weapon at Norgate. Joey's feet agitated the ill-fitting door as he lurched away from danger, removing his under-endowed shadow from the wall and exposing the sheriff like a stag to the hunter.

Cub acted quickly, raising his eyes to the hungry mouth of the gun barrel as he stepped in front of the wounded man. Cochrane jerked his head back as if he could not believe it. 'Turn away, boy.' He flicked the gun sideways, and lamplight scraped the metal and sparked in Cub's eyes. But the boy did not turn away. The fat man took two steps towards him, his upholstered legs rubbing together with a grunt of frustration.

Ralf Norgate staggered a feeble dance and gripped Cub's shoulder with his whole hand. 'Too foolish,' he said. 'He will kill you.'

Cochrane settled before them on his rocking chair feet, toe to heel and heel to toe. 'Listen to the sheriff,' he said.

The gun nodded in his hand, and then it levelled on the boy's heart. 'You should listen to him, for I could kill you both with just the one bullet.'

'I do not think so.' Cub looked up and caught the jerk of hesitation in the man's eyes, outrageously huge behind the lenses.

Cochrane blinked. 'You are a pretty young boy and it would be a shame to destroy you.' He leaned forward and stroked the cold metal across Cub's cheek and under his chin, tilting his jaw. 'But maybe a necessity,' he said with a sugar-sweet smile.

Cub clenched his hands into fists until it hurt. 'The sheriff needs a doctor,' he said. 'Cochrane.'

The fat man breathed hard and gaped through his accommodating spectacles. 'Mr Cochrane. To you, boy, I can only be Mr Cochrane.'

'He has lost too much blood.'

'I advise you not to burden yourself with the sheriff's troubles, son, when it seems you are accumulating plenty of your own.' Cochrane chuckled then, an uncomfortably jolly sound from a man with a gun in his hand. 'Besides, he is going to lose a lot more blood before the day is out.'

'You will not kill him.'

'Will I not?' The fat man looked from right to left: to Fletcher standing motionless by the wall, to the winter wolf and the stunted man who were crouching beneath the meagre light as though seeking the protection of shadows. 'Our young friend claims that I will not kill this man,' he said. 'But how does he know this, boys? What makes him so sure of my magnanimity?'

The black-bellied stove in the corner coughed up a devil's horn of smoke from the hot plate. Cub watched the gun barrel scattering the vapour with a languid figure of eight, and he knew that the weapon was no longer hungry.

'I feel it is my duty to learn more about you,' Cochrane

said. 'For I declare, my son, that I find you intriguing.'

'I am not your son.'

'That is true.' Cochrane lifted the Colt and holstered it in one elegant swoop. He tugged straight the sides of his jacket, hiding the gun, and the air became benign. 'Then tell me whose son you might be.'

Cub jerked his head back to where Ralf Norgate was standing, unsteady but upright with duty. 'My father is here.' Norgate made a small sound in his throat but did not speak, and Cochrane stared at the sheriff as though surprised to see him still there, sagging against the wall and speckling the earth floor with his blood.

'You mean the lawman is your papa? Well, well.' Cochrane beckoned Fletcher's attention with his pudgy fingers. 'Leo, our guest is indisposed and requires a chair. See how white his face is? We must provide for him, and his brave and loving son, as best we can.' He turned back to Cub and smiled. Darkness leaped as the lamp guttered and for a second Cochrane's eyes were magnified moons, sharp and silver. 'And then we must decide what to do with our…hostages.'

Mitch and Joey slunk out into the dark to settle the horses for the night, opening the door to a gust of wind that wrought havoc in the small hut, plaguing the little stove and sheathing the crazed lamp in smoke. Fletcher left with them and returned with two coils of rope. He forced Norgate down in one of the chairs at the table and tied his arms behind him. The sheriff grunted in pain and slumped forward, his breath dulling the points of silver on his chest. Something shifted uneasily inside the stove as Fletcher roped Cub to the second chair. The fat man lifted the hot plate with a metal rod and fed the black belly from a pile of dried wood. He breathed vastly as he stood over the stove, as if the burning was giving off a wholesome scent, and tugged a voluminous handkerchief from his pocket to wipe his eyes clean of smuts.

'Exactly how should I deal with you, sheriff's son?' he said, sitting heavily in the remaining chair.

Cub watched him winding the spectacles back in place. 'How far can you see without those, Cochrane?'

There was a shivering silence after he had spoken, and then the fat man stood up and loomed over the boy, projecting his chair across the floor with a thrust of calf muscles. He pressed hands to the table with all his weight behind them, and the wings of his black jacket flared open so swiftly that one of its metal buttons bit into Cub's cheek and drew a sliver of blood. 'Mister! Mr Cochrane! You son of a bitch, I'm warning you…'

'Son of a sheriff. And if you look you might notice that my father is no longer conscious.'

Cub lifted his head and stared, piercing the sharp pale eyes, and the fat man shuddered as if something had knocked into the back of his skull. He pulled away slowly, his arms falling from the edge of the table as though they had been dragged. 'You need to keep him alive,' the boy said, each word singing in the stillness.

'So, what if your goddam father dies? Do you think that means anything to me?' Cochrane lowered his head, his well-fed jowls quivering with the effort to break the connection.

'If you kill a lawman, then many more lawmen will come for you.' Cub spat the words out on the ground before the grey-haired man, and dust puffed back from the dirt floor. 'They will destroy all your hiding places until they have hunted you down and then they will also destroy you.'

'Oh my, such concern for my wellbeing.' Cochrane's face twitched. 'And if you are seeking a little concern in return, try convincing me why I should keep you alive as well as your papa.'

'Because I am useful to you. I will deliver the ransom demand in return for my father's life.'

The boy's eyes seemed to change; Cochrane could see amber like the start of a fire behind the darkness of them, and his thoughts began to congeal until it became difficult to think. 'You will be of more use to me by revealing the whereabouts of your kinsfolk.' His spectacles bounced on his brow as he twisted the bridge of his nose for a sharp pain to clear his head, and the lamplight flashed crazily in the lenses as though it had been set free. 'And if you do not then I shall have to unleash Fletcher on you. Believe me, his ministration will be a mind-changing experience, and after it you will fall to your knees and plead for your soul.'

Cub shook his head and spoke quietly, in the voice that had once tamed a wild stallion to bear a rider. 'Do what you have to do.'

The fat man straightened and stared down at the boy secured with rope in a small cabin. And then he glanced up at the thin man standing by the wall, cracking knuckles like pistol shots, his face a narrow white mask shabby with stubble.

'Leo; deal with it,' Cochrane said, turning away so that he should not be obliged to see what was taking place behind him. He pulled the handkerchief from his pocket again and wound its blue and red checks around one lens and then the other of his spectacles, until he was satisfied with the way they sparkled in the light. His naked eyes seemed weak and reduced without their armour, and all actions were a blur before he fitted the glasses into the grooves at his temples and could distinguish the boy, leaning half out of his chair now with bloodied hair, and the imprint of Fletcher's fist blackening the side of his face.

Cub shook the thunder from his head, and opened eyes stained red from broken blood vessels. His mouth was numb and it was tricky to speak. 'No hostage if my father bleeds to death. No ransom.'

Cochrane pushed Fletcher aside and stood in his place. His blackness cut away the light, spreading like a slick over the table and the boy sitting beneath the cliff face of his bulk. 'You are forgetting that I also have you, and as of this moment, you are still alive.'

Cub lifted his head and saw the gun belt, a gasp of buttons on the grey vest, sweat stains on the collar where chins rested, the glare from thick lenses. He saw the man's head jerk as their eyes met, and after a while the sharpness behind the spectacles softened when Cochrane chuckled. The man took himself away from the table and the lamplight oozed back. 'Leo, come over here.'

Fletcher hesitated. 'You wanted me to deal with it, Mr Cochrane, and I haven't finished yet.'

'That is what I asked you to do, Leo.' The fat man waited, and all fell silent. 'And now I want you over here.'

But Fletcher did not move. He leered down at the boy trussed to the wooden chair like an offering, and squeezed his fists until the tendons were sharp as wire beneath his skin. 'I am ready to break him for you, Mr Cochrane; so that he falls to his knees and pleads for his soul.'

'No.' Cochrane took a step back, and his whole body juddered. He drew in a breath of the sour air; he didn't seem to notice the stink of battle. 'I don't think that will be necessary this time, Leo. I applaud your sense of duty, but maybe it is a trifle overwrought.'

The tall man came so close that Cub could hear the drag of his breathing; he pressed one fist against the side of the boy's head. 'We have unfinished business, you and me.' he said. 'Keep looking over your shoulder, boy, for that is the only way you will know that I am behind you.'

Fletcher's fist slid away, breaking the skin, and he went to join Cochrane in a corner of the cabin where the flicker of stove-shine spotted the darkest shadows. The fat man pulled out his handkerchief and wiped worried lines across his brow.

Cub stored the image away in a place where he would find it again with ease, and then there was nothing else to do but wait.

FIFTEEN

'THIS IS what I have decided.'

As if he had heard noises, Cochrane took three steps to the small window and cleared away some of the detritus hiding the view. Nothing was moving outside, but the darkness had been reduced; a tree was defined, and one of the tethered horses had woken and was searching the ground for fodder. The fat man rubbed a clearer hole in the dross and Cub saw stars through the glass, fading as he watched as though the light in them was dying.

'This is what I have decided,' Cochrane repeated as he turned to face the boy at the table, and the bound man slumping sideways from the other chair. The sheriff's face was pearly pale and slick with sweat; he was shaking, and making small sounds in his throat. Blood still dripped from the wound in his swollen arm, but the flow was weak now, as though too much of it had already been lost.

Cub stiffened as his captor drew near, a glimmer of shine staring from the worn fabric where his plump hands tugged the sides of his jacket. 'I believe the sheriff would benefit from some attention,' Cochrane said. 'Come and untie the gentleman's bonds, boys, and give him a tidy seat in the armchair; he is going nowhere in a hurry and we shall need to keep his hide glossy.' He paused, and his eyes flickered over the boy's face. 'And while you are at it, you can untie his son as well.'

Mitch sniggered, lips drawn back from his wolfish teeth. He pulled a knife from his belt and pointed it at

Cub's face, before sawing the knotted rope around his wrists until it parted with a sigh. He slashed Norgate's restraint and the sheriff took a fall towards the table; the two robbers lifted his weight and dragged him to the one-armed chair where he lay with his head lolling like a man asleep. Cub eased the blood back into his hands while Cochrane lowered himself into the vacated wooden chair beside him, folding his arms in a cumbersome way across the swell of his belly.

'The dawn is coming up. You and the unfortunate sheriff have been our guests for the better part of the night, and I don't even know your name.'

'I am known as Cub.' There was little point in hiding the fact.

'Is that right? As in bear cub, maybe?'

'As in wolf.'

'Truly an odd name to bestow on a child. Not the sort you'd expect a man of the law to give his son.'

Cub hesitated; rubbed the stiffness from his arms. 'The sheriff has no son.'

'No. Well.' Cochrane sat back with a smirk that gave his face a rosy glow. 'I kind of figured that, boy, seeing as how you share no redeeming features. So, what are you then – some sort of prisoner?'

Cub turned away and stared at the table.

'Too shy to tell me?' Cochrane cradled his belly with his arms. 'Well, it seems that you and me and the boys here ought to share some solidarity, and yet you stood in the way of the sheriff's bullet. It is a strange thing for a prisoner to do. There is a back story here, and I am a sucker for stories.'

Cub blinked, taking in the view before him: the sheriff a silent form by the stove and the two men who had moved away to the far wall. Although he could not see him, he knew from the griping of the scars left by Madison's whip that Fletcher was standing behind his back. 'I have a debt to pay,' Cub said. 'The sheriff's family saved my life, and now I owe him his.' He owed it to Reyna.

Cochrane nodded. 'Tell me where his folks reside.'

'I cannot do that.'

'Your loyalty is impressive, boy, but it is also growing tedious.'

'I told you, I owe him his life.'

'You tell me what I want to know and I will allow the sheriff to keep his life. I can do that, you see, because in here I am like a god.' Cochrane smiled, but there was no humour behind it. 'However, if you do not tell me then I shall take his life away, for if thwarted I can become a vengeful god. My wrath is all-powerful and all-seeing; my men will vouch for that. If they value their hides then they carry out my wishes to the letter, for they have no other choice. And neither do you.'

Cub hesitated. 'Why should I trust you?'

'Because I am about to trust you.' Cochrane raised his head, and his eyes were large behind the expansive lenses. 'For I believe that there is honour among thieves, and murderers, and all such wrongdoers who break the Lord's commandments. I just wonder what form your guilt might take, boy.'

Cub looked at the fat man sitting beside him at the table and Cochrane drew back from the boy's scrutiny, wincing as though something had scratched his soul. 'Well, all right then, I shall allow you to keep your guilt to yourself. But understand this, boy known as Wolf Cub, if you do not tell me what I wish to know then I shall have to kill you as well as the sheriff, and that would be a cruel, cruel waste.' He stared down at Cub's mouth and licked his own lips, and away from the bluster there was sadness.

'And if I do tell you, what then?'

'Then I shall let you go free.'

Fletcher moved forwards so fast his boots tangled with

a table leg. He swore loudly, and Cub stood to face him, the wooden chair rocking between them both like a peace-keeper. From his place by the gasping stove Ralf Norgate came awake, swimming up to the light through the fog in his brain.

'Leo. That is enough.' Cochrane pushed his bulk out of his seat.

'You're not going to let him go free?'

'That is what I said. He appears to be one of us.'

'He's nothing like us!'

Cub rubbed his face where the skin had been broken by the man's fist, and estimated how quickly he could move, how easily he might grab the gun from Fletcher's belt, how effortlessly he would fire it. And then he judged how long it might take Cochrane to pull out his own weapon and fire in return; and knew the senselessness of it all.

Fletcher took a step closer, cupping ready the curved handle of his gun as though he had picked up the boy's thoughts. The wolf cub was the prey and Fletcher the tall, thin hunter, eyes ringed with fatigue, face white behind the roughness of his beard. He did not need an excuse to kill.

'You'll find the sheriff's kin in the town of Liberation,' the boy said, without taking his eyes from Fletcher's face. 'Head south and east, a hard day's ride.'

Cochrane turned quickly for a man of his size. 'Get your horse ready, Mitch. You are familiar with the area, so you will be taking our request.'

Fletcher stood rigid. 'No. Let me go, Mr Cochrane. I am close with the area.'

'I need you here, Leo…'

'I am faster. You need faster, Mr Cochrane.'

The fat man frowned. 'I need swift and true as an arrow, Leo. And I need someone to leave right now.'

Fletcher pushed the chair aside; he knocked Mitch out

of the way and opened the door until it gaped. 'Then let me leave right now, Mr Cochrane,' he said, dragging the sides of his jacket together and fitting the hat over his eyes until his face folded into its shade.

Dawn chill gushed into the cabin; smoke scattered from the stove like a puppy at play and Cochrane flapped it away with a peevish hand. 'Okay, Leo, for I am truly too tired and too weary to argue with you. You know what to ask for. You know how much.' He sighed. It was a gentle sound, but only as soft as the glove around a fist. 'But I warn you, as I have warned others who have helped themselves to what I believe is mine, if you should even think about dealing me short then I will know about it, and my retribution shall be vigorous and painful.'

Fletcher nodded, his eyes unwavering. 'You're the boss, Mr Cochrane,' he said, and closed the door behind him. Cub could still see him through the small window, seeking the remaining darkness of the night as he went to his horse. Cochrane stood watching him as well, and when he turned around his podgy hands lifted the battered cash box from the edge of the table and played with the music it contained, the rustle of bills and tinkling of coins. His lips were greasy with pleasure. Sheriff Norgate stared at him, groggy from the pain that pulsed like an illness through his arm, and the sickness was heavy in his gut.

'You've paid your debt to the sheriff's kin, boy known as Wolf Cub. You are free to go.' Cochrane spoke without turning away from the rust-red coffer. 'I am as good as my word, you can count on it. But if you must go, you had best be quick about it,' he straightened and looked the boy over; his eyes were too hungry and too swollen, and Cub felt the sheriff's sickness in his own stomach. 'Because if I decide I need you with me after all then I will never allow you to leave.'

Outside, the tall, thin man was already on his way. The dark shapes of horse and rider moved past the window before it glimmered again with growing light, and Cub stretched the confines of the wooden chair from his body as he stepped towards the door. Mitch the winter wolf moved aside for him; pock-marked Joey with his pale frog's eyes backed away. The boy stood in their space and felt exonerated. He met the look on Cochrane's face as he turned around; it was as sharp and dangerous as a blade, even behind spectacles blinded by lamplight. Beyond him was the wounded man with the torn, bloody arm, whose stare was beseeching the boy for a sign that all the duty he had undertaken, without question, should one day be rewarded.

'Freedom is a nugget,' Cub told him across the bleak space, 'and I promise you that such a nugget will be yours again.'

Ralf Norgate closed his eyes to capture the image the boy's words had conjured, and Cub walked through the door into the gasp of cold dawn air. He did not look back.

The new morning was wide and empty and the dun's gallop cut through the air until it whistled. Cub rode south and east; the fresh sun spread around corners and through overhanging branches in intermittent flashes, and the outline of the tired moon faded in the growing light. Ghost trails of mist smeared the horse's coat so that the animal emerged glistening from their wake, coughing out vapour like puffs of cloud. Cub could hear its breath rasping as it galloped, and over the faltering of its hooves he began to hear the unreliable echo of another horse away to the side, where the ground was harder and higher and rattling with loose stones. The sounds had started softly but they grew clearer as the distance between the riders decreased, and it wasn't long before they were coming from somewhere much too close.

To confuse the man who pursued him, Cub steered the

dun towards places where trees were dense, but the animal stumbled on roots and skewed from the track. Bred to a stable it was not accustomed to wild riding, or ambush from hidden branches and snares in the underwood, and it would have been cruelty to push any further. Cub reined the horse to a standstill and turned around to face the way they had come. He sat high in the saddle to await the confrontation, and the dun stood on splayed legs with its head to the ground and the panting harsh in its throat. The air was as sharp as wine, and Cub opened his mouth and sucked his fill. He studied the land around him and the sky above him and the ground beneath him, and by the time the storm-cloud grey appeared, trotting forwards between the stunted bushes and misting the early morning with its breath, the boy had learned all he needed to learn.

Fletcher's face was half hidden by the broad brim of his hat but his eyes burned like separate spots of fire. 'Did I not warn you to keep looking over your shoulder, boy?' he said.

The grey horse was tall and strong, and the sound of its breathing made hardly a dent in the quiet of the fresh day; but the short night's rest and the fierceness of a hard gallop had already weakened the dun's little body, and Fletcher knew this as he pushed his horse closer between the rats' tail bushes. 'It's time to complete our unfinished business, you son of a bitch,' he said. His hands clenched like rocks around the strips of rein, and Cub felt the sting on his cheek where the man's fists had drawn blood.

'Get down.' Fletcher tugged the gun from his belt and aimed it at the boy's head. 'And give me one excuse to pull this trigger and put an end to your miserable life.'

Cub slipped to the ground. He noted the slant of the rifle holstered before the saddle on Fletcher's mount, and the collection of small stones lying like an offering close to where he stood. He raised his hands, palms forwards, and Fletcher smiled.

'Oh, I know you have no weapon, boy,' he said. 'But killing you unarmed will not sentence me to sleepless nights.'

Cub squeezed his hands together. 'Please don't shoot me, Leo. I'm begging you.'

Fletcher lifted his head until his hat was high. 'You surely are a spineless piece of filth,' he said, looking down at the boy from a squint of eyes before spitting a glob of phlegm that smacked into the ground by Cub's foot. 'There'll be nobody to mourn you,' he said, and held the gun out at arm's length with misjudged aggression.

Cub ducked aside, and the heat of the bullet sizzled the air by his ear. He stretched out a hand to the offering of stones and grabbed three, sending them up in a swift arc. They sang as they flew towards the dark grey horse, and one of them caught its muzzle. The animal screamed with pain and reared away, and Fletcher lost his scrabble for security in the tipping saddle and fell hard to the earth. He landed on his back, all the breath knocked from his lungs so that he lay stupidly amazed; and the gun fell away, coiling in the air before burying itself deep inside a tuft of undergrowth, where vicious thorns opened their greedy throats and swallowed.

The boy leaped to the squealing grey and grabbed the dangle of reins, touching the soft place under the horse's ear and speaking words that sank as gently as a swaddle of fleece into the animal's mind. The grey bent its head to hear the voice, and Cub swung to the saddle and kicked his feet into the stirrups. And then he looked down at the thin man on the ground.

Fletcher's hat had become dislodged in the tumble and now it rested on his chest like the hat of a corpse. But he was merely stunned, not dead. He opened his eyes; testing the air with confusion, finding the gentled grey and the boy sitting high on its back. Cub recalled how defenceless he had been, shackled to a wooden chair in the filthy cabin as the weight of the man's fist blackened his cheekbone; and he reached down to pull the rifle from its hold beneath the saddle. Fletcher's eyes followed him, showing the whites, and he dragged himself up until he was resting on the points of his elbows. He tried to stand, but his feet slid away hopelessly through morning-wet scrub.

'Don't shoot me,' he said, his voice struggling. 'Please, don't shoot.'

Cub stared down at the man grovelling on the ground; he opened his mouth, but there was nothing to say. There was nothing to do but replace the rifle in the holster and turn his back.

He gathered the reins and kicked Fletcher's horse towards the hard day's ride; and he tried not to think of what might be waiting for him at the end of it.

SIXTEEN

IT HAD been a stretch of days since Cub had first ridden into Reyna's town, awash with fever on the back of the unruly stallion, the buildings of Liberation swimming behind his hot eyes like a sick river. As he approached the wide main street once again he could remember very little of that other time, apart from the heightened fear of the imminent – that was still familiar; coursing through his blood as every step brought him closer to danger.

The storm-cloud grey could only walk now but it had carried him well, proving its worth in the passage over the land that he had already crossed, fastened to the dun's saddle by Ralf Norgate; fastened to the destiny of the thin man's fists, Cochrane's ultimatum and the sheriff's fundamental sense of duty. He had gained time over Leo Fletcher – an hour, maybe more – and now he sought some relief from the journey, swaying to the horse's movement as it plodded through the road dust. His mind was rolling as though he had been drugged by the long day of the hard ride, and the night waiting in the cabin for his time to die by the gun in Cochrane's hand. The desire to sleep was extreme, but before he could succumb he needed to do this foolish thing, this honourable thing; this duty for the dutiful sheriff, and for his daughter.

Cub drew level with the sheriff's office just as the day was finishing, and there were few people traversing the echoing sidewalk. The building seemed empty and silent as though nobody was home, but still he eased out of the saddle, which since the breaking of dawn had moulded itself to his body. The grey horse's hide was as cloudy as rain, but under the day's sweat it had turned to the colour of gloom. It was like an omen; and for a few seconds after sliding the reins over the hitching post, Cub was loath to leave the animal resting there, when already it could have carried him many miles towards certain freedom. Because his freedom would not be as certain now, after the thing he was about to do.

He stood listening and looking down to where the main street dust coarsened as it joined the open plain, and when he was sure he was not being observed he stared up at the bedroom window, where blue drapes that had once been the bars to a prison were now hanging powerless in the evening quiet. He stepped up to the sidewalk as if he was going into the sheriff's office, but turned instead down the alleyway towards the small yard at the rear of the house, where Reyna Norgate was busy taking down the day's washing.

Half hidden by the wall, Cub watched as she folded crisp garments into a wicker basket. She did not see him. She leaned down to pick up the bag of clothespins, and when she straightened it was with one wrist to the small of her back and the grimace of a middle-aged woman on her young girl's face.

Cub moved out of the shadows. 'I must speak with you, Reyna,' he said quietly, but still she jumped at the sound of his voice.

'You've come back,' she said, her face blooming with pleasure, and then it fell with alarm and she wrapped her arms around the little bag as though seeking some comfort. 'But I don't understand why you're here. And my father – is he with you?'

'No.' Cub went towards her, aware that he could now be seen from the house; that he might be about to lose everything he had gained after Cochrane had set him free.

The girl shook her head as if warding him off and he could do nothing but stand there, in view of the windows. The late sun glinted out of a cloud and gilded the yard and everything in it, and then Reyna came closer and lifted her hand to his cheek.

'What has happened to your face? Has there been trouble, Cub? Is my father in trouble?' She stroked his broken skin and he clasped her hand and took it back down to her side, squeezing until her fingers were pink.

'Reyna, there is no time and much to tell you.'

Her round face flushed and she started to weep, quietly and wearily, and just as wearily her knees folded. She would have crumpled if he had not stepped forward, and she fell into his arms as if only he could help her. Above the sound of her crying he heard the squeak of the door as it opened behind him, and the ring of spurs two seconds before Thackeray Dart grabbed him. Reyna stumbled away when the man wrenched him backwards and raised his fist, but Cub sidestepped the blow as it fell. The girl hauled on Dart's arm but she was too puny to combat his rage.

She shouted in his face. 'Uncle Thackeray; leave him be!' The cotton bag went spinning, scattering a hail of clothespins to the ground, and Dart's spurs rang with his fury as he crushed one of them underfoot.

'Let me deal with this, Reyna!'

'We need to listen to what Cub has to say. Uncle, please; it's important.'

'The boy is taken away from here with his hands tied across a saddle, and when he comes back he is freed and alone. What's important is how this has come about.'

'Then give him space to tell us.'

'You go and wait inside the house, Reyna. Leave me to settle this…'

'No!' She drew back her arm and hit him, but there was very little weight behind the blow and it made no impression. She hitched up her skirt to free her sharp-toed boot and kicked him hard on the shin. Thackeray Dart bit his tongue and swore mightily.

'This is my house, Uncle Thackeray.' Reyna stood in front of him and her voice was strong. Dart grew still and his eyes narrowed as he watched her. 'I am in charge here when my father is away,' she said. 'And I should not have to point out that you are merely a guest in my home.'

'Not merely a guest.' He frowned. 'I am family. Don't forget that.'

'Forgive me for saying, but that is only due to the sisterhood between my mother and my aunt. You are, in effect, no true relation of mine,' Reyna said, and then she was quiet as though such a truth had never occurred to her before.

Thackeray Dart jerked a glance behind him; a reminder that there was something he ought to be keeping an eye on. But Cub hadn't moved. He stood in the yard with his head raised, listening for hooves in the street outside. He needed to leave before Fletcher arrived on the winded dun, but the quarrel between the girl and her uncle was not yet exhausted.

'Why has the boy not run?' Dart said, as though he was asking himself.

'Cub is here with news of my father's whereabouts, Uncle Thackeray, and that is why he has not run.' Reyna pulled hard on the man's arm. 'He will tell us what he knows, and then we shall allow him to leave.'

Dart shook his head and turned towards the boy. 'We will have this discussion inside the house,' he said.

'We shall go inside my house to speak about Father, but before that we will stay out here until you agree that Cub shall go free.'

Dart scowled at the girl. 'The boy is a criminal; he must be detained.'

'What sort of criminal would put his future in jeopardy

by helping someone else?' Reyna stamped her aggravation and Dart stared at the ground, as if astounded that such a small foot could make so loud a noise. 'In the name of charity, Uncle, we must allow him his freedom!'

The man closed his eyes against the yelling. 'Very well, Reyna; very well,' he said, spitting the words through a clench of teeth. 'It is agreed.' He grabbed the back of his neck as though it was giving him pain, and then he held the door open for her to follow Cub into the kitchen.

'There is a lot of your mother in you,' Dart said as Reyna passed him, and she pinked, and didn't notice how firmly he closed the door, making the interior of the room even darker than the evening outside.

'I do not have much time,' Cub said, his eyes widening in the enclosed space. 'I will speak of what has happened and then I must go.' Reyna nodded; she laced her fingers together and pressed them against her waist to curb the emotions he could read from her face.

Thackeray Dart took himself over to the other door as though he was standing guard to the belly of the house, while Cub painted the picture of all that had taken place since that evening on the dirt track, where the stagecoach had been lying tipped and helpless, and Ralf Norgate had been unable to ignore the pull of duty. And he watched as the encroaching night dulled the kitchen window even further, and knew that Leo Fletcher was coming for him with one thorn-gored hand resting on the butt of his gun.

'Cochrane's man is dangerous,' Cub said, 'and he is near.'

Reyna swallowed. 'But if he wants money then I shall find it. I'll give him whatever he requires to ensure that Father will live.'

'Reyna, he cannot be trusted,' Cub said, and hesitated for only a moment before turning to Thackeray Dart. 'Trick him; lock him in the cell. You should reach the cabin by morning if you ride at speed. There are three men there guarding the sheriff; they are armed, but they will not expect your surprise. It is the only way.'

For a while Dart was statue-still, but his mind was busy – Cub could see it in his face. And then the man slapped the wall as if he had come to a momentous decision. 'I shall fight for him, Nugget. I shall liberate Ralf Norgate and bring him back here, and in one piece.'

Reyna's eyes narrowed. She went over and stared up at him. Penetrating. He had to look away. 'But why should you want to do that, Uncle,' she said quietly, 'when I know that you have always hated my father?'

Dart looked like somebody who had stepped in a trap. He shook his head, too fiercely. 'I have always admired Ralf for a fine man.'

'But that is not true, is it, Uncle Thackeray?'

'Your uncle makes plans, Reyna, for your marriage,' said Cub quietly. 'And he needs your father's approval.'

'What are you saying?' She turned towards him, the words tumbling to the back of her throat.

'He wants you to marry his son…'

'That is no business of yours.' Dart made a lunge towards the boy, his eyes as fierce as hate in the dusky light, but Reyna swung round too fast, her incredulity forcing him back against the wall.

'What does Cub mean, Uncle Thackeray?'

'He's just making trouble, Nugget, that's all it is. The boy is trouble. I should have left him to rot in the street that day, but instead I brought his poison into the house.'

'You want me to marry Clem? But why?'

'Your uncle has made his home here, Reyna, and he'll do whatever it takes to be allowed to stay,' Cub said, glancing up at the window to where the day was dying. The back of his neck prickled like a hundred insect bites and he had to end this conversation, he had to get out of this house. He had to get out of the town before it was too late.

Dart stared at the bedraggled boy, the hunger-thin boy with sharpness in his eyes, who had the gift to hear what there was to hear; and Reyna learned all she needed to know from her uncle's silence.

'So, it is true,' she said, but Dart was not listening, his head too full of questions. And he wondered just what else Cub had discovered.

'Yes. It is all true.'

Reyna turned towards the voice that was hiding behind the door, and the gap spread wider for her cousin to enter. He shambled into the room as though his shoulders were not strong enough to bear his body.

'Clement,' Thackeray Dart growled, like a dog. 'Hold your tongue.'

The younger man stood upright then; he became more substantial when he stepped out of the gloom. 'You used my mother as an excuse to secure a home for yourself, and you've been using me to make it permanent.'

Dart raised a hand as though he was about to strike his son, but then he relaxed, and laughed. 'One thing you have inherited from your mother's side of the family, Clement, is a flare for the fantastical.'

'You only brought that boy into this house to soften the way Reyna felt towards me.' Clement's voice rose, and his father stiffened as though the words had caused him pain. 'You used him to awaken her compassion.'

'Well, well.' Dart turned towards the window as though fascinated by what he could see outside. 'What a curiously detached memory you have.'

'I have a vivid memory, Father, for I also recall telling you that everything started to change when you found a place for him in my bedroom. And I was right about that, wasn't I?'

Thackeray Dart spun around and stared hard at his son. 'Stand straight, boy, for no husband-hunting woman is going to look twice at such an apology on legs.'

Clement smiled at that, but there was little mirth in his face. 'If you had ever stopped trying to make me into something after your own heart I could have learned to stand straight all by myself. But I'm standing very straight now, Father, and telling you that we'll both be riding to that cabin tonight, and we shall bring Uncle Ralf home together.'

The young man's declaration hung in the air for a while before dissolving, although Cub had barely heard it. He was looking out to the yard but seeing only the empty street at the front of the house. After a while he was aware of voices raised behind him, battling each other like stones in a can. The floor danced as footsteps scattered, and then there was a long silence which felt like forever to the boy who was listening for the horse that was carrying Leo Fletcher closer. When he turned around again the two men had disappeared, and there was only Reyna left in the kitchen, her face galvanised by outrage and excitement.

'Uncle Thackeray and Clement have gone to make preparation for my father's rescue,' she said. 'There will be no more freedom for the message bringer, Cub; you may be assured of that.'

'But even so he is nearby. It is his horse that I have left in the street, and you will be in danger if he learns from it that I have been here.'

'And what about you?' Reyna frowned. 'You risked everything to come back, just to save my father's life.'

'I came back because he is your father,' Cub said; and then he gave her the directions that would take Thackeray Dart and Clement to the miserable cabin, where Cochrane was sitting beside the stove like a myopic grub playing rattle the money in a rust-red box. She used the back of a store receipt to sketch out a map from his instruction, and after that there was nothing more they could do or say.

Reyna stared at Cub as if she was suddenly aware that she was never likely to see him again. There were words behind her eyes but she left them unsaid, although there was no need to voice what she was thinking because he already knew.

'Watch out for your uncle, Reyna; he is not a worthy man and has too much power over your cousin,' he said. 'Clement may prove himself, but only if they can be kept apart.' And then for a while he was quiet under her gaze. 'Your father is very brave, Nugget. He will survive.'

'And I'll make sure he never forgets what he owes you for his life.'

'You gave me back my own life,' Cub said. 'The debt is paid, and your father owes me nothing.'

Reyna followed the boy to the house door, and as they stepped out to the sidewalk together she handed over the battered pouch and the tinderbox, and the blade that had been taken from him on the morning that Thackeray Dart had twisted his arm at the open door. He had lost his freedom that day, but he had not lost the hunting knife. When he eased the sheath on to his belt it was as if a broken part of him had been made whole again, and suddenly he felt weightless.

The grey shook its head when he approached and Reyna held the bridle as he swung into the evening-cool saddle. She took his hand as he gathered the reins, and Cub touched her face with the tips of his fingers before kicking the horse to a canter that echoed the length of the street. When he reached the place where the town ended and the plains began he turned again. She was standing where he had left her, diminutive but strong, her head high and her skirt dancing in the breeze.

SEVENTEEN

NIGHTFALL BROUGHT the oblivion of darkness, and Cub sought the higher plains where rocks tumbled. Peace covered him as he slept. And he slept deeply, protected by cloud cover where owls flew like ghosts and little animals shrieked in fear of them. He slept as though he might never wake again; but wake he did, with crumpled limbs and the need, always the need, to keep his eyes open to fading tracks on the earth as he moved towards rugged ground in the distance. To keep wondering whether there was a chance that the palomino was still out there.

Noon was high by the time he gained the slopes. Flints breached the soil like pieces of shattered bone and the grass was scant and brown, and now it was easier to see fresher signs that another horse had passed that way. And Cub stopped wondering and began to hope.

Fletcher's grey stumbled through the heat haze on unsure legs and shook its head too listlessly to deter the flies. The saddle slipped sideways as Cub rode, as if the horse was wasting, and the boy's muscles were weak in the heat and stagnant air. The sun was burning oxygen and there did not seem to be enough left to breathe, so that when the grey's knees buckled it felt like something coming to an end.

Cub gripped the saddle to keep from falling and pulled the horse's head high, but the animal was going nowhere. He slid from its back and crawled like a dying thing to a rock that jutted from the land, sheltering a lizard under its lip. It was a good place to drop. He didn't see the earth rising to collect him, he didn't know the passing of time, but when he opened his eyes again the noon heat was a memory and his body a twist on the ground. The strap of Lucy's pouch was tight around his neck and it hurt to get to his feet. He stood as slowly as an old man, and knew without even looking that the grey horse had vanished as he'd slept, taking all hope with it and leaving him with nothing but the need to keep going.

Cub stretched the pains from his body and started out on foot. Shades pulled away from scrub and crumbling rocks, long and narrow and unearthly, and he walked until his stiff bones melted. He felt light and grew swift, and when the going was kind he dived through the turf and swam across pools of cloud-shadow that raced beneath the sun. The terrain ahead rose like a frozen wave, and as he came closer it surged higher. The sky began to darken as though a thin curtain was blocking the light, and he grabbed the swell of land and climbed until the foot slopes had fallen away and he was standing on the summit, fighting the air for every breath.

It was good to feel his muscles scream, good to hear the crashing of his heart. The breeze was as cool as mint, breathing through his shirt until sweat began to chill. He pulled his jacket tight as he gazed out from the top of the hill over a range that spread before him like a pedlar's wares. In this land of contrasts, the way ahead was a yawning mouth stretching towards dark and distant hills. It was a wilderness that afforded no hiding places; only a fool or a desperate boy who had lost his horse would walk across it, and Cub stood on the edge of it as naked as a hunter's prey.

He folded to the earth, resting his arms on his knees. The wind trickled through his hair and dried the sweat to a salty crust as the minutes passed, and the boy sat cross-legged under a sky like an upturned sea awash with clouds;

a lonely traveller caught in a split in his own time that had no beginning and the unlikelihood of any end.

After a while the colour of the sky changed from blue to a turquoise more beautiful than any jewel, and Cub caught sight of something stirring like a ghost-glimmer under the falling sun. It was drifting towards him, kicking up a maelstrom of grey dust across the plain, but all that Cub could hear was the air flow boxing his ears, as though the thing floating above the land was nothing but a mirage. Then as it came closer the dying light struck pale flashes that were like flags caught in the wind, and they became the flare of mane from a galloping horse, heat rising from the tawny hide as if its soul was escaping.

Cub was running down the slope before he realised he had moved. He missed the ground at the bottom and rolled in a clutch of small stones, and as he got to his feet they snatched at his eyes and fell useless behind him. He raced as though the descent from the hillside had given him power, sucking in air as if there could never be enough. The ground was thudding louder, and louder still from the echo of hooves as the wild space between them dissolved, and the days of fever in the sheriff's house, the capture, Cochrane and the hard ride back to Liberation became nothing but visions from a dream as he reached the stallion's side.

Lashed by the white tail, the boy gathered his last strength and leaped, shouting into the air as he hit the horse's flanks, wrapping his fists in mane and heaving himself onto Wolf Wind's back. The stallion raised his head to scream and the sound echoed away from the fold of hill, bruising Cub's ears as he grabbed for the halter. Wolf Wind reared, punishing the sky with his hooves, and Cub lay on the horse's neck with the magic in his voice until all was calm again. And it was like coming home.

*

The boy and the palomino rode through the empty days, and each night after each day Cub spoke his gentle words to the stallion until it grew still again and accepted the memory of him. The Rykers and the cowboys, Reyna with her trusting face and the sheriff with his shattered arm – Cub thought of them as he swayed to the horse's gait and left the past behind. Haine Madison on the broken-down farm and his daughter Sage, who had taken such risks for the boy's sake – these stayed in his memory longer, and their images became an imprint like a spirit's impression so that they would not fade. He couldn't leave them behind; they rode the stallion with him across the empty land, but as they fell into the background he grew stronger in the day's sun, fed and watered by squalls of wind and rain and hardened by Wolf Wind's steady pace.

Three days they rode, and then the time came that Cub looked down the beckoning country and learned, as if he scented it on the light wind, that the unknown land held perils and wildness sheltered within its dubious sanctuary. To pass through it safely he needed protection, and for that he had to find the company of people. This he knew, as the night wind blew the embers of his fire into the air and down again, and he sat before the star-prick glimmer of red that remained, worrying at the thought. He slept with it in the back of his mind and woke with it weighing heavily; he read it in the jerk of shadows that leaned before him as he rode, and he steered the palomino in a direction neither of them wished to follow.

Still distant and hiding below a slope of land, the town rang with loose stones and the thud of rock under thin earth. As they approached, Cub caught the tang of stifled air that spoke of people too thickly clothed for a summer's day, and the stallion sidestepped the ripe odours that reached out as though to draw them closer. They crossed the primeval rocks that calloused the ground, the terrain gradually gentling in tiers towards an area of squat buildings and devastation that had been cultivated out of wild earth. A few minutes later he found himself guiding the palomino towards the main street, soothing the horse with the touch of his hand and the back of his throat.

An ugly place, clumsily constructed and architecturally deprived, it lay at the bottom of a natural crater in the untamed country, and there was nothing to discover from the back of a skittish horse apart from the eyes of the curious. Cub took Wolf Wind away to where habitation was concealed behind a witch's thicket of trees, and there they passed a watchful night. The next day he twisted the halter rope around a withered branch and walked alone through the dusty streets as if he knew what he was looking for. He lingered in the shade as the sun began to bite, and for the first time he wondered what to do next. For the first time, he felt truly unsure.

The old man came out of his house, flexing his walking stick as if that might soften its rigidity. He stared up at the sky to greet the sun; he stared out at the rising land beyond the mean buildings, slapdash and haphazard and erected in the darkest hours of the night, so he thought, for he had been a carpenter in his youth and knew that the ways of the past were better. And then, when he could delay it no longer, he looked around at the place where he had come to spend the last of his life. And the knowledge of it lay uneasy in his stomach, as it did most days now. And like most days now, he took his constitutional in the mornings when the smell of the town was at its sweetest and the people were fresher. And that suited him best and gentled his displeasure, but he had become such an aged man that when he had strolled the length and breadth he was ready to take his ease on the bench beside the horse trough at the widest part of the main street, which the town planners who knew nothing had jokingly named the square. Here he would stay for the remainder of the morning and well after noon, watching the passing of life, the passing of the old ways; falling asleep and dreaming of being in his own young man's body, with the rest of his life ahead of him.

He sat in the spot where the bench's wooden seat was most comfortable and watched the boy walking through the town in his ill-fitting jacket, with trail dust making a patchwork of his pants. And when the boy came closer and ducked into the shade of one of the monstrous buildings, the old man was struck by the sun-whiteness of his hair and the agitation that shone clearly from his dark eyes.

'It seems to me that you might be lost, son.' The man called from the shadows that spread from the horse trough, camouflaging the bench and turning him into something invisible. But the boy had already seen him, and the man knew this from the depth of knowledge in those eyes, although he was knocked back by the barriers that sliced across them with the speed of a single blink. Was the boy hiding something? Or was it that he himself was hiding? The man was more than intrigued now; he was impatient. He tried again. 'If you're lost, as I believe you might be, then you need only ask for directions.'

The boy shook his head. He glanced up the main street and down again, and then he shielded his sight from the suddenness of the sun until the shadow was a black mask across his face. It surely was as though he was in hiding.

The old man stretched out one hand and let his fingers dangle over the horse trough. The water was like a cool breath on his skin. 'A stranger is a fascinating creature in a town like this,' he said. 'Particularly one such as yourself who is so remiss in the ways of speech.' The boy looked at him then, and smiled; it was an untried expression that stretched the planes of his face. It was uncomfortable to see, and the old man glanced down so that he did not have to. 'A town like this does not attract many visitors,' he said. 'Too close to the wild country for travellers.'

'The wild country?'

The boy's voice was young-old and as dusty as his clothing. The man looked up and met the gold in his eyes that was like sun shining through syrup. 'That's what I say. The unforgiving land; the wild country. Maybe stretching all the way to the ocean.'

'To the end,' the boy said. At least that was what the old man heard, but his ears had been playing him up for years now.

'You travelling that way on your own, son? Are you heading straight for trouble?'

It might be that the boy had heard enough for he seemed about to walk away; but still he stayed, square-shouldered and lean, muscles hardened by years of work carving the shape of his arms. He raised his head to scent the air, and licked his lips as though he could taste the danger that was ahead of him. The old man tried to read what was hidden in his face.

'Alone, you won't last a day,' he said. 'But I guess you know that already. Which is why you're walking around the town like a lost and uncertain soul, trying to decide the best course of action.'

The boy peered at him with what the man took to be disquiet. 'It is not easy to learn what might be inside a person from their skin,' he said.

'And yet I think I've learned more about you than you would wish anyone to know.'

'I think you have.'

'I was a city carpenter in my youth, and then I came out here where I could be free, and I became a scout and a ranger. They were lonely occupations,' the old man said, his memory shooting him back through the years. 'Maybe I recognise myself in you.'

'I am easy in my own company.'

The man remembered the freedom to ride and to run; to be dependent on sunshine and rain, and the protection of a kindly tree in the chill of the night time. He dug his stick in the ground and it bowed under the strain, and then he raised his head and stared until the street had disappeared, and he was alone again in the desert of his young manhood. He breathed deeply before speaking.

'Solitude has its benefits, son, but out there in the wilderness it would be nothing but rightly foolish.'

The layers of memory closed like a book, and slowly he returned to the body of an elderly man, resting his bones beside a horse trough in a slipshod town. 'Best thing would be to join with other folks who are intending to cross over,' he said. 'Best thing would be safety in numbers.'

The boy stood upright then, as though a burden had been taken from his shoulders. He seemed suddenly taller, but even younger with that spark in his eyes. 'Can you tell me where I will find such a company?'

'They travel in wagons from here, heading straight for the promised land. Not every day, not every week, but whenever there is a collection of fools who are blind to the delights that this town might offer them,' the old man bent his head to his chest and chuckled. 'And whenever there is a wagon master willing to guide them.'

'And do you know of a willing wagon master?'

Those dark eyes seemed almost black under their mask of shade, and the man wondered if there might be Indian blood in the boy's history. 'A wagon master is a thirsty man, so my advice would be to seek him in the saloon,' he said. 'If he's still sober I reckon he'll be pleased to meet you, for a train is only as strong as the people who travel with it. And I feel sure that you will prove to be of benefit.'

There was that smile again, and this time the light met the boy's face as if the sun was rising. The man saw his own freedom there and his heart felt eased with the memory of it. He raised his crooked hand and the boy shook it as though he was unsure, but his grip was strong, and the old man could still feel its warmth as he walked away, as if he had left his mark. And he had left an image too, of a furious horse bending to a greater power and the wisdom of soft words.

I wish I could go with you, the man thought, leaning back on the bench. Journey through the wild land with you on a horse that suffers no saddle and can run where it wishes. And he dipped his fingers into the water once again, deep enough to feel the sheen of ice beneath the surface.

Finding space between a pair of grander buildings, the saloon slouched like an apology halfway down the main street, and Cub pushed open its chest-high doors and left them flouncing behind him. Despite their limited size the shrunken doors effectively cut away the sun, and the light inside the room was subdued. The air was musty and coarse with the scent of beer and cheap tobacco. There were few customers this early in the day, although those few had already made inroads into the shelves of liquor and were well on the way to oblivion.

The bartender wiped his hands on a beer-brown towel as the boy approached, and stood straight and tall with narrowing eyes. 'You need to be of a certain age to drink in this establishment.' His voice was practised and loud enough to float above the noise of inebriation. 'And you have a few more years to grow, boy.'

A customer wearing a round hat like a chopped ball leaned into the counter and chortled, as if the barman had cracked a joke. He pushed the hat so far to the back of his head that it was in danger of falling, and grabbed his glass like the raft of a drowning man. The spirit it contained fell in drops to the shiny wood and sizzled dull spots in the varnish, and the movement attracted the attention of the beribboned woman at the nearby table.

She stopped filing her nails and raised pencilled brows

to the bartender. 'Cut it out with the lecture, Henry. He might only be a boy, but he surely is a pretty one,' she said, flexing the pointed toes of lilac-leather shoes where they rested on a neighbouring chair. 'And that makes a welcome change from the sight of your miserable face.'

Enhanced by paint, the beauty spot by the side of her mouth danced with mischief when she grinned, and the barman scowled, his eyes disappearing between pockets of flesh. He turned his back on her and attacked the counter top with the dirty towel, but she ignored him, beckoning to Cub with glossy red fingertips. 'Come over to me, my sugar.' She slipped her feet from the chair with a bounce of merriment and tidied straggled hair behind her ear as though the tired, dusty boy was her new acquaintance. 'You are just what I need to shatter the tedium that has been my day so far.'

Cub made his way towards her, and as he came closer he could see the lines of a hard life peeking from beneath heavy face powder and lips falsely plumped by strong colour. The velvet of her dress was rubbed and crudely mended and her hair was brassy and tickled with grey, but her eyes were kind and thoughtful and perceptive. She reached forward and took his hand, reading years of rough farm work from his skin, and she knew she wanted to help him, this boy who was young enough to be her son. But she knew also that it was not her help he was seeking. 'Where are you headed, honey?' she said. 'Tell Mary-Jo what it is you need.'

'Ma'am,' he said. 'I'm looking for a wagon master.'

'But where are you headed?' she repeated, thinking of wheels racketing through the wild country, and of sleeping beneath a canvas cover.

'For a place where it is good to be free,' Cub said. The words floated through the fug of stale beer, and his spirits floated with them. Suddenly everything seemed possible.

'If it's a wagon master you need then you won't go far

wrong with me.' The voice was as dry as smoke, and seemed to appear from nowhere much, that is if the table by the wall where the lights were shaded and darkness was a cloak could be nowhere. A brown-haired man in a brown-checked shirt sat there drinking, his eyes gleaming like two points of pewter over the top of the glass.

Mary-Jo dropped Cub's hand with reluctance and picked up her nail file from the tabletop as he moved away, and he stopped at the corner where the man was feeding himself from a squat cigar, and scratching the rough-weave at his chest as though that might help to draw the smoke into his lungs. 'Take yourself a seat, young sir.' The man clumped the glass on the table, agitating its contents, and raised his right arm to the boy. 'And if I offer you the hand of friendship, will you give me your name?'

Cub scraped out a wooden chair and shook the man's hand across whisky stains on the table. For a while he pondered the question and he pondered his answer, and he thought of the place where he was going to be free. 'I am known as Cub,' he said, but he was looking down at the floor as he said it, and the words were almost an apology.

'And I am known as Faulkner,' the man said, squinting at him through the clinging smoke. 'Christian Faulkner; that is my name.' He raised his chin out of the shadows to finish his drink, and the sudden flash of light from the empty glass was blinding. 'Tell me what I might do for you, Mr Cub, and I will tell you if I am able to do it.'

'I need your help to cross the wild country,' the boy said.

Faulkner grinned and cocked an eyebrow. 'Then I'd be glad to give it, for I shall shortly be guiding a train in that direction. Just how many people and how many wagons might there be in your party?'

Cub paused. 'I have no wagon. There is no one else. I

have nothing else.' Nothing of any use, he thought, but then he felt it beneath his foot, the bulk of notes that lined his boot, and he remembered the generosity of the dark-haired doctor. 'Although I have the means to pay for your guidance.'

'Then it sounds to me like you have all that is required.' He might be young, the boy, less than organised, but he was resolute. Christian Faulkner read determination in the strange brown stare, and he liked that. 'And if you can be ready to start out at dawn on the day after tomorrow, Cub, then I look forward to travelling with you.'

EIGHTEEN

THERE WAS little strength in the sun that early in the morning; it rose behind them, lemon-cool in an amethyst sky, painting the eternal plain with long lean shadows.

Christian Faulkner's train seemed under-subscribed, but he was not dissatisfied. He mounted his piebald and led it away from the ugly town, the horse's mane tossing like a black and white flag as it trotted in front of the four lumbering wagons. Cub and the palomino slipped into place at the rear like an afterthought, stepping through the bounce of wheel dust that turned the ground invisible. Between them, the boy and the wagon master herded the train forward into blunter shadows as the sun progressed through the hours: flying high like an angel above the canvas roofs; burning to oblivion as the evening of that first day arrived, and the wagons were pulled nose to tail in a circle on the floor of the plain, like a dog preparing its bed for the night.

As the wheels stopped turning everything that was weary gasped and groaned, and after that there was a period of silence as though nobody could quite believe that they had finally come to a halt. Dust sighed as it settled, and then hands were clapped and animals released from their trappings to graze the unforgiving ground. Each covered wagon was full of strangers and Cub kept away. The dusk fell in swathes and he watched as the light from cooking fires bloomed across the canvas roofs. The wagons shifted to the dance of tired people coming back to life, and Cub wandered off to where his horse was waiting in a separate world, ears pricked towards the way they had come as if he could still sense the mares he had left far behind.

It was as he passed one of the wagons that Cub heard the growl, and the rumble growing from its belly like a rock fall at the back of a cave. Disturbance stretched long and dark down the canvas side, and a sleek shape leaped from the puckered opening and rounded the wheels. Shackled by the fury, Cub stared into the wolf's savage jaws and the teeth bared to bite. His fingers found the handle of Ryker's knife and the evening grew darker.

He caught a rush of movement as someone dropped from the end of the wagon and squeezed the scruff of the animal's neck with an unprotected hand. It was a small boy, thin enough to be insubstantial in the evening's ethereal light, brown hair flopping like a web of sugared silk. The wolf snuffled and turned with its muzzle flaring, and Cub unsheathed the knife and started forward into the danger of jaws that were no more than an arm's length from the child's throat.

'It's all right.' The boy's voice was slight, too quiet for the open air. 'Rust is protective, and he can be scaresome when he is too much so, but he won't attack you.'

Cub's senses were as sharp now as the wolf's bite; he heard what the boy said and he listened to the fear inside him as he looked down at the chestnut coat, the plumed tail; the dog. And then he trembled.

'Really sorry to fright you, sir.' Concern had added strength to the boy's frail voice, but Cub was staring at the animal's teeth and remembering the sharpness of snake fangs in his ankle, and the fever that had dragged him down towards death. And still he trembled.

'Don't just stand out there, Randy. Ask the young fella in!'

The voice that came from inside the vehicle was brittle

with age, and it rumbled like the dog's growl – like falling rock in a cave. The young boy jumped at the sound of it, gripped the dog's neck with one hand and herded Cub towards the canvas opening with the other. And when he followed it was in a crooked way, as if his right shoe was filled with broken glass.

Cub bedded the knife in its sheath and felt the ground grow solid beneath his feet. The puckered entrance to the wagon was a-dazzle as an oil lamp flared into light inside and for a blind moment all shapes were smothered, but his sight cleared quickly enough for him to recognise a padded bench beneath the wagon's wall and a man sitting there, his back following the contours of the shadow-streaked canvas. His similarity to the boy with the limp was evident in the narrow skull and the pointed jaw, the birdlike and fragile bones; although the dusty hair was sparse and patchy on the man's head, and his face was a wrinkled mask of weathered skin surrounding eyes that were dull with age. But his cheeks lifted when he smiled, and the film over his sight cleared to a sparkle in the oil flame.

He beckoned so greatly that his slight body bounced. 'Come on up, young fella, come in and find yourself a seat. And a great welcome to you.'

Cub could see no harm in him, and climbed wooden steps into the canvas tunnel where a taller man might have had trouble standing upright. Chests and rolled bags heaped all around him, folded cloths and unidentifiable objects swathed in bright material. There was a box on its side, and he sat on it. The old man stared at him with fascination, and bounced a little more as the young boy climbed into the small space; and the dog slumped to the cluttered floor to add its musty heat to the end of the day.

'We have all of us voyaged many hours,' the man was saying, 'and our expedition has only just commenced. It seems to me that you might be an experienced traveller, so would you say we are in for a long trek?'

Cub thought of dust settling behind the doctor's buggy and the scratch of his back as he climbed the foothills. He saw Ryde St John hiding under the brim of his hat, the town where he had fallen prey to the lawman's star, the stagecoach lying beside dead men in the road. Already he had travelled far, but the end of his journey was still unbelievably distant.

He slumped forwards, and the box seat tilted as though to expel him to the riotous mess on the floor. He had to get away. The stallion was out there on the open plain; a glimmer of gold under the darkening sky. The horse was dancing through loose stones on wicked black hooves, its head raised to point the way to the end of it, and he had to leave. Now.

The old man was still speaking, but his voice had faded to something slight and unattended, like the voice of the young boy with the broken-glass limp. He seemed to be asking a question. He leaned forward and grabbed Cub's arm; his face was a crumple of lines, but it meant nothing. It meant nothing until he gripped with his age-bent fingers and a scorch of pain seared the boy's skin, bringing him back to life and the sound of the man's voice. 'There seems to be something amiss with our guest, Randy,' he was saying. 'There is something at odds with you, young man, and I suspect its name might be hunger.'

Cub stared at the filmy eyes and knew the strength and ferocity hiding there. The hand squeezing his wrist felt firm and secure. Dependable. He had never depended on anyone but himself before this day, and he was bone-deep with weariness. The old man scanned Cub's face and leaned back. His voice was soothing, like falling onto a bed of moss. 'It is not easy to travel on your own with people you have never met before and do not yet know if you can trust. Am I right?'

'I am alone. It is natural.'

'There is nothing natural about loneliness, my boy. It is not natural to be lost inside yourself.'

But the man knew nothing about him, or of the childhood he had spent in his own silence because it was safer that way. Memories dulled by years had once been vivid with the skill of acrobats and jugglers, falls from painted horses, pain from broken bones. The stink of sweat and greasepaint, and the prickle of straw laid over mud to protect the feet of those who had come to watch. The man knew nothing about the small boy who had walked on his own beside the wagon, his mouth soft with whispers for the skittish mule, while she who had been his mother lay abed beneath the canvas roof with the bottle cradled to her breast, its comfort as swift and devastating as the demands of yet another lover.

The child had learned quickly that the only consolation to be found was inside himself; he had learned well, but the old man with fogged eyes could know nothing of this. Neither could the boy seated on the floor of the wagon, gently stretching out the dog's ears so that they shone pink under the flickering lamplight. Nevertheless, the man seemed subdued, as if he had delved too deeply into his guest's mind and now knew more than was comfortable.

'I have often been accused of allowing my tongue to gallop away from me,' he said. 'It seems I've lived too long on my own to know how to keep it harnessed, and I apologise.' He smiled, and his face rearranged itself into well-used lines. 'But there is one thing you can offer me, son, and that is your name.'

'I am called Cub.' Although his mother had regularly cursed him with other words.

'Well, I am sometimes known as Red, but my complete name is Benjamin Redmayne,' the old man said. 'And along with my grandson, Randal, I am hoping to start a fine new life on the west coast of our great country.'

The small boy had looked up at the sound of his name.

In the sweep of lamplight his eyes seemed too large for his face, accentuated by dark circles. 'It is always summer on the west coast,' he said. His voice faded as soon as he spoke, as if swallowed by the bundles of belongings that surrounded them like well-loved friends. His grandfather leaned down and stroked the boy's silky hair.

'That's what they say, Randy. That's what they say.'

The child smiled and lay down with the dog, nestling his cheek in feathers of fur and pulling the animal's ears with gentle hands. The skin of his face seemed unnaturally pale, but the network of veins beneath the surface had turned it an ethereal blue. The old man dropped his voice and spoke as if for the moment he had forgotten the boy sitting on the box by his side. 'The healthy healing sun; that is all we can hope for, Randy. And plentiful food.'

He slapped his knees. 'Will you join us for supper, young fella? For it looks to me that you are accustomed to going too long between meals.'

And you are friendless and have lost your family, he surmised, struck suddenly by the starkness of Cub's collar bones, carved by light and shadow. I would like us to become your second family for as long as this adventure lasts, the old man thought. I would like that, for sure.

NINETEEN

'WE CAN stop here for a short respite, folks.'

Christian Faulkner's piebald cantered to the end of the train and the man's voice floated behind him as he passed the straining animals. Wagons slowed to a standstill as if the wheels were seizing solid, and hot wood started to sag in the heat of the noon sun. The passengers climbed from their elevated seats like people that might never walk normally again, rubbing their backs and stretching for handfuls of sky, branching off to the fuzz of bushes to obey nature's call. Their voices were lost to the vastness of the country as they talked.

Cub allowed the stallion to make its way towards the open land, where the wagons' dirty grey roofs seemed washed clean by distance, and when the horse was comfortable in its own skin he slid from its back to the hard ground. There was a gentle peace here, where the stillness went as deep as an arrow to the heart of the earth, and Cub sat for a while in the horse's shade with his eyes closed. But he knew, even before the stallion moved, that someone was watching him.

Wolf Wind kicked dirt from the ground by Cub's face; the sound was raw and violent, and Cub squinted in the flailing grit. There was a boy standing a few feet away, short and dark and curly-haired, too thickly dressed for the heat of the day in clumsily fastened clothing, as if he was wearing as much as he owned to save on storage. The palomino bellowed at the intruder and shook its head to toss him away, and the lash of its tail felt like rain on Cub's face.

'That stallion looks half wild,' the boy said, fear battling with awe in his voice. 'Will he attack me?'

Cub got to his feet and pressed the bunched muscles in the horse's neck with a calming hand until all was still again. 'He will not attack you.'

The boy shrugged his shoulders, but they barely moved under the stiff clothing. 'Well, as long as you can hear what is going on in his head.'

Wolf Wind stamped the hard earth; the sound was muted and hollow and made the sturdy stranger think of secret caves under his feet. But for Cub the throb beneath the land surged like the pulse of hidden water, and he certainly could hear what was going on in the stallion's head. He could also hear insistence in the yell of the man who stood before one of the wagons that had come to rest on uneven ground. Tilting awkwardly, it was a chaotic shape under the bright sky, and ragged bushes beneath its wheels shivered in the heat. The pair of oxen caught between the shafts lowed with mourning as the man shouted, and he slapped a dusty rump and waved instead. The movement shook his short body from side to side, and the overdressed boy raised his hand in reply and turned back to Cub with the sun full in his eyes.

'My folks want to learn everything about you, so they told me to come over and collect you.' Two dimples pressed his cheeks when he grinned, like sudden thumbprints. 'So, would you be up to meeting them?' he said, beckoning eagerly as he turned back the way he had come, and rolling slightly in his cumbersome clothes as he walked towards the wagons. Cub waited a few seconds before following him, leaving the stallion by itself on the edge of the plain.

A hum of voices rose to greet the two boys as they approached the idling wagon train, finally splitting into separate conversations that coalesced with the smell of animal droppings, the clatter of life and the rattle of harness, as though the assembly represented small homesteads in an embryonic town. The bawling oxen bawled again and rolled frightened eyes that stared white, and the dark-haired boy touched each one with a flat palm, as if he had learned from Cub how to hear what was going on inside the creatures' heads. He grinned up at the woman who was sitting with her baby on the wooden seat of the wagon; glossy brown braids embracing her head, she was as elevated as a queen above the man who had yelled at them. He was still there beside the unhappy oxen, his stocky legs planted square, and the similarity between him and the bedecked boy was easy to see in the disobedient hair, the tipped noses, and the same dimples hiding in their cheeks.

Shrill sounds sang from beneath the wagon canvas, and it roiled like a pregnant belly and gave birth to a girl and a boy, eyes shining like violet jewels in the sun as they stared through the opening at Cub. Their mother shifted her infant from hip to lap as though the slight weight was nearly more than she could manage, and the tiny girl peered out from beneath the exaggerated brim of her yellow bonnet. She blinked in the noise her siblings were making as they slid from the side of the wagon, and clutched the air because she wanted to go with them. But the woman leaned forward, the sun glinting like rain on the chain around her neck, and whispered something in the baby's ear that delighted her with a clap of her starfish hands.

The man stood before Cub, pressing fists above his hips as though his elbows were wings. He was not tall; he could look the boy in the face, and when he grinned his eyes almost disappeared until they were a mere glint of violet beneath dark brows. But they were clear eyes, and they appraised him from behind the smile. 'Well met, young fellow,' he said, dropping his arms to his sides as if he had come to a decision, and holding out a hand for Cub to shake that was incongruously large and square for someone of his stature.

His skin was dry and calloused, and the boy knew the years of hardship behind the man's greeting. The man shook firmly and let go, but the memory of roughness that had been the boy's life lingered for a while longer, and he was struck by the sun-brown eyes, and the barriers that slid across them like a wall until there was nothing to see.

'The name is Rory Callahan, and I bid you welcome.' The man's voice was as soft and smoky as moss in a fire, and there was a singing lilt at the end of his words. As well as a wink to his eye when he turned towards the wagon and the woman sitting above him, the baby girl in her arms chuggling to herself in the vast openness of plain and air and sky. 'This is my wife, Kathleen, and our darling girl, little Maeve.'

The woman smiled at her husband with indulgent eyes, and the green of them turned pale blue for an instant in the depths of the sun. And as she nodded to Cub the same sun sparked red glints from her hair until it seemed to be ablaze. 'Good afternoon to you,' she said, as if they were just passing in the street. 'And you have already met Finn. So, that also is good.'

Gleaming in the light, the chain at her neck scooped free for a moment as she leaned over the side of the wagon. The little girl in her lap made a grab for it, but the mother teased it away from her grasp and tucked an escape of ringlets back beneath the primrose bonnet.

The curly-haired boy looked up at her. 'For sure, he has met me already, Ma, but who would know whether for good or not?' He grinned at Cub with his father's dimples, and the sweat of the journey beading his top lip like a budding moustache. 'So, I am Finn; my brother is Killian and my other sister is Aoife. And now you know us and we know you not at all.'

The silence then was sudden, an implosion inside the muddle of talk that seeped over from the other wagons containing the private lives of people yet undiscovered. And Cub wished to remain undiscovered as well, but his new acquaintances were watching him with their square, open faces, wisps of dark hair curling, astonishing eyes the colour of the early morning sky. They were waiting for him to become known. 'I am Cub,' he said, reluctantly, as if he was giving away something of himself that could not be retracted.

Finn laughed, bent double with his hands on his knees. 'What sort of a name is that?' he snorted.

'It is all that I have,' said the fair-haired boy, and the woman sitting above them was the only one to see his young face grow old as he spoke.

She made to rise, clutching her heavy skirt with one hand and clasping the little girl around the middle with the other, so that as her mother stood the child soared into the air and fixed Cub with clear eyes the colour of sun-touched lavender. Knowing infant eyes that penetrated the wall he had built around himself until, with an exhaustion that struck from nowhere, he let the barriers fall. He felt a sudden lightness that allowed him to float high enough to see how sharp the land was where it crested the horizon; almost high enough to know what was in store for them on the other side. The baby smiled with the joy of being in her mother's arms and lifted her small hands as if bestowing blessings.

Rory Callahan helped his wife down from the wagon seat. She seemed reduced on the ground, suddenly shorter beside him, and the sly glint of silver in her hair stole away with her youth. 'I apologise, Cub, for the rudeness of my family,' she said, 'but I shall try to make amends by offering you some refreshment.'

She passed the baby to her daughter and went around to the rear of the wagon, unburdened but still with a bend to her back. The little girl gurgled and buried her hands in her sister's long hair, until it seemed that she was reaching into a glossy black waterfall; and when Aoife turned to see Cub watching this, colour flushed her cheeks before she could look away again. Her mother called to him, and he moved into the shade at the rear of the wagon and took the glass of watered beer from her. The young girl wandered away then with her sister in her arms, but she looked back to where the dark-eyed boy was standing by the tailboard, and where her mother bustled and her father talked, and her big brother bristled with importance as he listened.

'We hail from the west of Ireland. I was born poor and raised that way as well. It was the same for everybody where the families were big and there were small pickings available to fill all the bellies.' Rory Callahan breathed the words, and each one lifted like a murmur from his throat, grit-encrusted. 'A more beautiful country on this earth I have yet to see, but I tell you a hard living is akin to a wasted life. I saw too much of it as I was a-growing, so when I had a family of my own I wanted more for them than my ma and da could ever bestow on me or my brothers.' He looked away then, weaving his fingers together so that the muscles of his arms knotted, and there was fog in his voice. 'Though they never gave up on the trying.'

His wife reached out a hand, and her touch seemed to release the tautness of his shoulders, as though all his tension flowed along her fingers and was dispersed into the sultry air. He looked at her as if only he knew she was there. 'We are heading for the golden land, my darling Kate and all our darling children. We are going forward to find wealth and happiness and to live a better life.'

'There will be no going back,' Kathleen said softly; the

brave words hovered without protection in the air, and Cub caught the tail of them, falling like a frightened bird. She was smiling at Rory's glorying face, but the smile was a rigid white line around her lips and did not quite find her eyes.

'Oh, but why should we want to go back, Ma?' Finn urged, standing beside his father, square-faced and sturdy and very young. 'When Da is taking us all the way to the rainbow's end?'

Rory chuckled and pushed at the boy's hair but his wife said nothing more; she just cupped her hands around the drink and seemed to fade into herself. Although when Christian Faulkner climbed back on the piebald and called for the wheels to begin their rolling, Kathleen became the mother again; searching for young Killian, and for Aoife with Maeve playing in her arms.

Cub thanked them and turned to wade back through the slam of heat to where the stallion was resting, a solitary dark outline on the edge of the wild. Canvas bustled and harness clattered as the wagoners readied themselves for the journey to Rory's promised land, and one by one they followed the piebald's lead. All but for the last wagon, for although the yoked oxen stood primed, the man sitting above them was merely gripping the reins. He was staring ahead but seeing nothing, as though awaiting the woman's permission to move.

Tall and thin and totally enclosed, the woman was standing as still as a rock beside the low-slung wagon, buttoned to the neck in a dress the colour of old leaves with a bonnet severe around her head and fastened as tight as strangulation. And it was only when Cub drew level that she looked up. Her eyes were fiercely masked by the bonnet's shadow, but he could read contempt in her distorted mouth and the squeeze of white skin at her nostrils. Her lips moved painfully around a word that he could barely hear, and then she coughed and drew back her head.

The spittle landed on the ground near him, a liquid shine that was soon swallowed by the thirsty earth, and the sour memory of hatred in Martha Madison's eyes slammed into the back of his mind. Everything he thought he was leaving behind was right there in the inflexible body of the woman, who had now twisted away from him as though she found it difficult to stand upright. She climbed up to the bench and took her place beside the black-coated man, and they sat together like two statues hewn from dried earth and dead leaves.

She must have given her permission, for the man flicked reins over the oxen's backs and the wagon moved away. Cub moved away too, more slowly this time, until only the dark dregs of saliva were left on the ground to show where he had been standing.

TWENTY

LAMP-SHINE BATHED the underside of the canvas roof like warmed honey, and brought in a fidget of insects to play with the light as evening fell. Benjamin Redmayne yawned mightily in the soporific hush and leaned back on his rug-covered bench as though it was an easy chair, and well padded. Sitting with his damaged foot splayed as if it did not belong to his body, Randal spread out on the wooden floor and stroked the soft hair behind the dog's ears. Between them was spun a peaceful web; Cub could feel the touch of its silk from the low crate where he sat at the end of the wagon, resting his arms on bent knees.

What remained of the evening meal lay scattered on the jutting ledges of parcels and boxes, and the hill slopes of bags where Redmayne's china plates were balancing, only an accidental knock away from breakage. Benjamin had already taken down the bottle that was stored in his makeshift kitchen. Dusty with age, it had been awaiting its deflowering at the journey's end. Perhaps it had been a foolish extravagance, purchased to celebrate a new home, a new life, a fresh start; but in this uncertain wilderness it seemed more appropriate to fete the present instead.

Two glasses flashed fire from the edges of light as he poured the brandy. He offered one to his guest and Cub took it with care, as if he had never received before.

'I believe,' the old man said, 'that the weather will turn tomorrow and we shall have rain. We shall have the relief of a thirsty earth and the hindrance of muddy wheels.'

'I will get out the cans tomorrow, Grandfather.' Randal spoke from behind the dog's head, and it was as if his words had breathed over the animal's own tongue, lolling pink and wet between lethal teeth. 'If I put them out in time we should collect a goodly supply of fresh water and we will not go thirsty.'

Benjamin looked down at the boy. 'A wise decision, Randy. You have an old head on young shoulders.' He pushed at the dog with his foot and it coughed a lazy growl. 'And Rust is none so fragrant these days. Perhaps the rain will be cleansing, too.'

Cub brought the glass to his lips and the spirit opened the back of his nose before he tasted it. It ignited fire in his throat as he swallowed, and that felt good. 'It will rain in the morning,' he said. 'It will rain hard but it may not last long enough for you to collect much water.'

Benjamin Redmayne eyed him over the rim of his glass. 'Interested to know your opinion, Cub. I would be interested also to know how you know.'

'I learn what the weather teaches me.'

The old man sipped brandy and sighed with pleasure. 'What else, pray, has the weather taught you?'

'When it is angry I seek shelter; when it is content I count it as a friend.'

'That may be so, but does it teach you how to survive solitude? Is it whispering in your ear to be mindful of savagery in the palomino's heart; to beware the whites of its eyes? Does it help you to live in wildness yourself?'

The boy filled his mouth and swallowed, and the fire of the spirit was fierce to his stomach. He held the glass between both hands, he looked up but said nothing and Benjamin studied his face, carved into stillness by the unearthly light and pinpricked by a flicker of insects.

'Please forgive my blatant curiosity, Cub, but I find you intriguing. I want to know why you are here with us on this pilgrims' wagon train, where you are going and what you will do when you arrive. I want to know the story of where you come from, who you have left behind. What you have left behind.'

Cub stared at the floor where Randal sat, crooked and silent; the only sound was the dog's laboured panting and the only movement the shivering of its wolf's pelt. 'I have no story,' he said.

'Everybody has a story, but perhaps you choose not to share yours.'

'I have no story.'

The old man lifted his glass and pulled at the drink as though giving himself time. 'How old are you, Cub?'

The boy seemed to wince, and a moment later the shutters came down over his face. But Benjamin had seen perplexity in the dark gaze, and with it he had sensed panic. 'Forgive me,' he said. 'I am a foolish old man who has not yet learned to think before speaking. You ask Randy and he will tell you. I am a liability and a challenge, and I apologise…'

'I do not know.'

'What do you not know?'

Cub sat with the empty glass forgotten in his hand, and his eyes were asking for help. 'How old I am.'

'Oh.' Redmayne straightened his spine until it twinged. 'Were you never told?'

'No.'

'But didn't your parents…?'

'I had a mother. I was with her as a child. Then she was gone.'

The man placed his feet flat on the floor and leaned forward. 'Where did she go, Cub?'

'She died.'

'I am sorry.'

'Are you?'

'Well, of course. To lose your mother so young? Why, that's tragic.'

Questions were building up, too many for his head to hold, but even so it was a while before Benjamin could speak again. 'Who took over the care of you, Cub?'

'I did.'

'You were a child, and yet you had nobody to look out for you?' He was sickly hot in his heavy shirt. He was his grandson's only relative on earth. He was a stupid old man with a limited lifespan, in charge of a vulnerable young boy.

'My mother died and after that I was in the way. They threw food at me; I survived.'

'Who were these people?'

'The travellers.' The players and performers; the jesters and the jugglers tumbling beneath sky blue canvas. His mother had died and he became a parasite, and then a commodity.

'How long ago was this?'

'Some years.' Seven years. 'I do not know.' I do not want to know.

Redmayne opened his mouth, but this time the words could not get past the obstruction in his throat where the questions were threatening to choke him. He stared at the sprawl of dog on the floor and his grandson stared back at him, large frightened eyes in a pale face webbed by defenceless blue veins. Benjamin smiled; as hard as he could. 'There is nothing to worry about, Randy,' he lied. 'All is well.'

When he turned back he knew from one look at Cub's face that the boy had locked everything else he might have said inside where it was safe, and the old man cursed himself for his foolishness and tried again.

'Each person has a story, Cub. You just need to look at the others who travel with us on this epic journey. The Callahans, for instance: an Irish family with aspirations. I have seen the hope in Rory's eyes when he bids me a good day,' and the desperate look the man was hiding until he thought himself unremarked, of a wrong-footed idiot who had everything to lose. 'The Thatcher family have a story indeed, as do the Dyeston couple and their child. Our guide, Mr Faulkner; now that would be the one to hear: the story of a silent loner.' Much like yourself, Benjamin thought as Cub placed the glass on the rough plank floor, his mystery blanketed by the bending of his head and the control in his voice.

'Who are they, the Thatchers?'

'Septimus and Elfrida Thatcher and their two identical daughters. Have you not yet met them?' Benjamin smiled, but there was no mirth in it. 'Quakers, quite possibly. Good people; without doubt they are good people.'

But he did not believe what he was saying. Cub knew this as though he had looked inside the old man's mind. He saw again the severe bonnet over the pinched nostrils, the breathless word that had twisted the woman's lips so painfully. Abomination, the word had been. He saw the stolid man on the wagon seat staring straight ahead as his wife cursed the boy and spat at his abominable feet.

Benjamin Redmayne's good people.

The next day the sky opened. Randal Redmayne hung his cans from hooks along the wagon sides and, mindful of Cub's words the evening before, he touched each one with hope before leaving them to swing in the plod of the harnessed horse. Heavy drops of rain sent up small explosions from the earth and pattered its loud applause over the canvas roofs until they were saturated. It soaked Cub's clothes and gilded the palomino's hide, and everything felt cool and good after the fierce sun. But by midday the angry clouds were placated and the rain had stopped; and Randal's cans were only half-full.

Christian Faulkner flung back his tarred cape with the clatter of bat wings, tipping a spill from the brim of his hat before it could extinguish the stump of cigar between his lips. He heard the rush of water as soon as the rainfall had been silenced, and he led the four wagons, and the boy riding, towards the place where a stream had grown to a torrent that was sinuous and sly, gulping down a jeopardy of small plants from its banks.

Abandoning their vehicles, and the harnessed animals that edged forward clumsily to drink, the wagoners collected by the swamp; a small congregation in rejoicing where the overflow had beaten the earth into submission. Finn Callahan picked flat stones from the ground and bounced them across the water and Rust clambered after them, paddling wildly through the ripples with his head proud. Benjamin Redmayne rested one protective hand on his grandson's shoulder to prevent him from following the dog into the flow, and little Maeve clapped and crowed in her mother's arms.

But the Thatcher daughters stood together, two girls lapping adulthood, bonneted and buttoned to the neck in shadow-grey, silently watching the other children play. Cub could see their father, sombre as a preacher in his black coat, stepping down from where the wagon had been hauled up to higher ground, but the mother remained upright and indifferent on the uncomfortable seat, strait-lacing intact.

The boy turned the stallion away as though he had witnessed as much as he could stomach and rode the horse downstream, stamping wings of spray into the air where a flood had climbed across the path. The sounds of the wagon train fell into the background and disappeared, and after a while the land passed a clump of trees and dipped to where the rain had widened the watercourse and filled a pool.

Sunshine played through the clouds and lifted curls of steam from Wolf Wind's flanks as he drank from the shallows, his bent neck a burnished scimitar. Cub pulled off clothes that were reluctant with wet and took them with him into the pool, rubbing out sweat and dirt and all the days that had gone before, and leaving everything eagle-spread over a grab of thorn bushes that were growing up through replenished water. He swam out to the centre and sank to the bottom through waving shafts of light, where weeds looped like tresses and grabbed his heels as though praying for him to stay. For as long as he could he kneeled on the mud beneath the water's shifting skin, hearing nothing but liquid kisses.

It was time to leave when the air began to lose its heat; he breathed it deep into his lungs as he waded to the side, blinking the drizzle from his eyes. The flood was already withdrawing, and its evaporation was a mirage above the ground. Cub tramped through the slime and stood on relinquished grass, pushing the swim from his body with his hands. The pool had almost receded from beneath the thorn bushes, and he reached high for the clothes he had spread in surrender to the sun; when he pulled them on they were still damp, but the warmth of his skin eased them into place. He felt lighter, as though he had floated away from the wagon trail, away from the falling and the failing and the long road that led back to the farm, the stink of cheap whisky from Madison's mouth and the coils of leather pushed into his belt. He was as buoyant now as he had been in the water, and there was a voice in his head telling him he was nearly there; he was going to make it.

Head down and snatching grass, the stallion flicked a tail and held it high as though he, too, had stepped into the place where the air was lifting. He stamped further downstream when Cub came towards him and reared away as if the man-fear had returned; but the boy made the calming language and waited, and when it was time to mount he steered Wolf Wind back towards the wagon train, where the sounds of excitement had subsided.

As they passed the clump of trees the stallion shied, troubled by what might be concealed there, but the boy kneed him forward into a canter on the open ground. He was riding high on his horse, he felt weightless, shining in the sun; he did not see who was hiding in the centre of the thicket and watching him leave, one arm squeezing a slender bole and a claw of fingers digging into the bark.

TWENTY-ONE

AFTER THE cloudburst, the terrain altered. Perhaps the onslaught had washed away the familiar and replaced it with an alien world, one that led them to a soft sway of land that was unexpectedly transformed into a sea of swoops and hollows, raging over loose rocks that seemed to have lost their moorings. The wagon train clung to the path as it climbed and then plunged; the animals strained, heads lowered, plagued by stones and a frenzy of insects. But Christian Faulkner was unconcerned; he sat his stoical piebald with the wagoners in his trust as he led them through the switchback towards a gentle gully with slopes to either side, and if his horse was bothered by the clash of utensils hanging from the bed roll on its rump it gave no indication.

Redmayne's wagon was the first in line to enter the gorge, and Benjamin took heart from the man who rode in front. 'Our guide is not flustered,' he told his grandson, seated beside him at the fore. 'Do you not agree, Randy, that we should put our trust in a leader who seems to know where he is taking us?'

The child nodded, but after trying so hard not to be jolted to the ground he wasn't that bothered about who it was he should trust. He grabbed the edge of the seat and peered around to where Septimus Thatcher was driving his team like a man made of stone under a flat-brimmed hat. Randal stared hard, willing the statue to move, but he stared too long and Thatcher's eyes shrivelled, his glower slicing through the boy's scalp like a blade before he could escape. His wife sat beside him in a tight dress and slid her face back inside the bonnet where everything was dark. The bench was narrow for two people, but even so their bodies did not touch.

It was silent on the driver's seat of the Thatcher wagon, and although the conveyance rattled in pain all else around it and all that was inside it dwelt in the same hush; even the two sisters jolting between the wheels. They stared out the back through the drawn edges of canvas to where Finn was driving the Callahan oxen with his elbows on his knees; eight-year-old Killian bouncing beside him and adding to the precariousness. Finn grinned at the big eyes in the pale faces that peered like timid ghosts from the wagon in front, and lifted his round hat by its curled brim in greeting. The girls withdrew swiftly beneath the canvas, and under its protection they reached out to each other and gripped hands in dismay; in excitement.

Bringing up the rear, the Dyeston wagon pulled free from the ones that went before until the distance between them was stretched thin to the point of breakage; and as it laboured the back-left wheel kicked aside a large rock and rolled awkwardly into its gap, bending like a fractured limb. The horse dragged it forward a few feet before the sturdy driver could rein it to a standstill, and the screech of the wounded wheel pumped the damage even further into the axle until the wagon slumped in submission and the grinding stopped. A wailing started up beneath the canvas shroud like the bellow of a trapped animal, and the palomino heard it as the yelling of men who were coming with ropes. He slashed at the sky with angry hooves until Cub turned him towards the wilderness and gave him his head. And when they reached a place where the wailing was cloaked by the cries of birds, he left the stallion to his liberty and headed back on foot to the disabled wagon.

Dyeston was leaning his weight into the wheel as though he expected his own stocky strength would be enough to lift the vehicle and set its broken bone. There was a creaking of wood and the sound of splintering, but nothing was moving. He took off his hat and wiped his forehead with the back of a hand, turning as Cub came closer. 'Morning,' he said with a smile that made his wide face ruddy, 'but not a good one as far as I can see.' As abruptly as a change of mood he turned and kicked the offending wheel, and the splintering sound whinged again from its place beneath the wagon.

Cub held out a hand. 'You will break something.'

'That has already happened, it seems to me.'

'Let me have a look.'

He crouched beside the tired wheel of the old wagon and the sway-backed horse. The trapped animal bellow that had spooked the stallion was quieter now, and then it snuffled away to nothing behind a young woman's voice, and her soothing words made him think of Reyna as he crawled underneath. He could see the damage directly above him; he could feel the torn wood, but when the horse stepped sideways in its traces the structure teetered like a warning above the boy's head. A hand grabbed his left calf and shook.

'Reckless. Come away from there. You will get yourself killed if this contraption should collapse.'

Cub slithered out from under the wagon with the hand guiding him. 'What do you think you're doing, boy?' Christian Faulkner helped him to his feet, and then he peered beneath the wounded vehicle. 'What have you found under there?'

'The wheel is not broken, it is only the jointing that has come apart.' Cub brushed wood dust from his eyes. 'It can be mended.'

Stocky and firm as a tree trunk, the wagon's driver nodded and rubbed the pale hat forwards and backwards over his tousled head. 'It is not as bad as we thought, Bethy,' he said, 'and we are therefore saved.'

The young woman who had climbed from the wagon was too slight to have been in much danger from its collapse, but she clutched the baby, wrapped in a lemon-yellow shawl, as though she was protecting the most precious prize. The child had stopped its snuffling and was gazing up at the sky in silent wonder. Dyeston drew his wife to him with a deceptively strong grip and the baby was engulfed like the filling in a sandwich, her tiny body almost swallowed by his burliness.

'Any assistance required here?' Rory was stepping without care over loose rocks to reach them, but young Finn followed more cautiously, rubbing his hands on the seat of his pants as though preparing to help.

Christian Faulkner squatted like a long-legged hound at rest and peered under the disabled wagon. 'I believe,' he said, straightening up with a wince and a click of his knee, 'that what is required is all the assistance we can get, so that the dislocated part of this wheel can be relocated and perhaps a peg applied for strength.' He turned to the wagoner. 'What say you to that, Jeremiah?'

Dyeston took a step back from the wagon master's proximity and the rattle of his smoky voice; he seemed to hold his wife's shoulder ever tighter as he drew her away. 'My grateful thanks to all concerned, that is what I say. What do you think, Bethy?'

There were too many curious eyes and the young woman crumpled a little under the scrutiny, her cheeks flushing with more than the sun's heat. 'I am certain that you will find a solution to the problem, Jeremiah,' she said, scuttling away to a large boulder halfway up the side of the slope where she sat playing with her child like a little girl with a toy, for she hardly seemed more than a child herself. Kathleen Callahan came across with Maeve in her arms, and went to join them both. Bethy was civil to the older woman, but it was clear that she wished to be left alone so that she could watch her husband as he found a solution to the problem.

Albeit mismatched in height as well as age, Jeremiah Dyeston and Rory and Christian took the weight of the wagon against their backs and heaved it into the air, so that Finn could crawl underneath to assist Cub with replacing the joint that had come away. Loose implements travelled across the floor inside as everything shifted, and the wheel dangled like a broken wing, groaning as it moved.

Christian Faulkner's arms bunched with strain as he gripped the side of the cart. 'Lord above, but we would surely benefit from extra assistance.' He spat the words as if each one was painful. 'I have asked the good man Thatcher, but it seems we ought to have known already of the feeble state of his back.'

'It is likely that at the end of this business,' Rory grunted, 'his feebleness will have infected us all.'

There was no sign of interest from Septimus Thatcher or his wife, but the two daughters had come near to the Callahans' wagon to watch, heads safely hidden inside their bonnets.

Their hats were like helmets, Killian thought, as he stood on the bump of track halfway between the silent girls and the fascination of what the men were doing. Or bellows, maybe, fanning the flame. He watched the girls more closely then, and when Elfrida Thatcher yelled he was the only one to see how utterly her voice extinguished the spark of life in their eyes.

'Mercy,' the woman shouted, and it took Killian a while to realise that the word was a name and not a cry for help. 'Charity. Return here this instant! The devil is all around you.'

The girls made no sound as they obeyed their mother, as silent as wraiths in long grey dresses, and when one of them turned her head for a moment and stared at the young boy, all Killian could see were empty eye sockets in the deep shadow cast by the bonnet. He shivered because it meant that the devil already had her in its grip, and he crossed himself to keep the demons away. And then he peered over at his brother and his brother's friend, and wondered if something evil might have reached out for them too, so evening-dark was the space underneath the crippled wagon, so obliterated by the devil's dust.

It was after the job was done that the clouds formed thick curtains to hide the heat of the sun, and the men sitting around with the rocks at their backs were glad of it as they stretched the strain from their arms.

Fully restored, the wagon was stable again, and Bethy Dyeston dispensed beer from the tailboard as if it was so much largesse; but it was gratefully drunk, and after a brief time of drinking and a longer time without eating, the men grew merrier, and flexed the proud muscles that had held up a wagon until what was broken had been repaired, and what was once a small group of strangers had become comrades. Rory offered Finn some of his beer and slung an arm around his shoulders; Benjamin Redmayne came over with his grandson, some dry biscuits and a wedge of cheese, and Randal and Killian went away together to throw sticks for the dog. It had turned into a party, loud with loosened voices and plenty of back-slapping.

Cub sat on the slope above them, taking peace from the scene, picking rough wood splinters from his hands and thinking of the cool water that had washed away severity the day before. Thinking that in just a little while he would collect Wolf Wind and ride back to the remnants of the pond, and if the darkness came down as he was away then he might sleep by the waterside that night, and if he did not follow in the dusty wake of the wagon train again then he might do better to find his own way forward and at his own speed. And he was thinking of how much further he had to travel to get to the end of it, when he heard the shout.

'She's gone!'

From his greater height Cub was the first to see Mrs Callahan running towards her husband with Maeve in her arms; the first to see the look on her face before the merrymakers staggered to their feet, knocking into each other on the uneven ground.

Rory Callahan thrust his beer bottle at Jeremiah and stepped forward to meet his wife as she rounded the Dyestons' wagon. 'What is it, Kate?' He grabbed her elbows and leaned down to hear. 'Who has gone?'

'Aoife. Rory, I cannot find her.' She seemed to shrink, holding on to his arm as if it was the only thing keeping her upright. Her braids held more evidence of grey than mahogany now, as though she had suddenly grown older, and the little girl on her hip began to wail with fear because she did not recognise her own mother. Kathleen woke to the sound as if to a trigger, and shifted the child higher so that their breasts were touching.

'I have called for her. I have looked everywhere. I climbed to the top of the slope here and I could see just so far, but I could not see Aoife.' She gazed up at her husband, her face a pit of hopelessness surrounded by Maeve's soft curls. 'My little girl. My baby. Oh, dear God.'

Rory staggered like a man who had lost his place, and Benjamin Redmayne gripped his shoulder. 'She cannot yet have gone far, Mr Callahan, or your wife would have seen her. This land may be a roll of hills but it is a clear and empty space.'

Rory considered the kind old eyes, saw the intelligence there and knew the man wanted to be right. 'Aoife hides,' he said. 'Empty or not, she finds concealment in unlikely spaces.'

'Then if she is hiding she cannot be lost. Do you see?'

'But Mr Redmayne, why should Aoife be hiding?' Fear was scratching Kathleen's face with cruel lines. Her eyes were murky green, like an illness. 'What has happened to make her hide from us?'

Christian Faulkner slapped his hat against his thigh, dust rising and settling on dust as he dragged it over his head. 'We are losing time,' he said. 'Two horses are ready to ride. We shall go out to find your daughter, Mrs Callahan, and we will bring her back. You must not worry.' He looked around and caught the boy, still standing on the slope. 'I'll go to the left of this gorge, Cub, and you head out to the right. Swiftly now.'

The palomino had wandered to the top of the rise and stood in outline against the swirl of cloud, his head high as though troubled by the confusion below. His ears were flat-tempered against his skull as Cub ran to him, a steady lope over the tricky ground and slowing as he approached. The stallion reared, attacking the sky and the man-threat, and as his front legs reached the ground again Cub leaped for the halter rope and fought the horse until he was on its back. His grip was tight on the arch of Wolf Wind's head and his mouth met the flick of the horse's ear. The animal turned in circles as it tried to follow the disjointed, mesmerising words.

Maeve was clambering at her mother's neck. Kathleen looked up and tried to smile encouragement through the wisps of baby hair as Cub took Wolf Wind to the edge of the hill above her, steering the stallion down one side and up the other of the small canyon, and disturbing a rain of earth and stones that trickled behind them as they disappeared. Christian Faulkner's piebald climbed away to the left, and the wagon master leaned forward over its mottled neck and let the animal have its head.

Nothing remained of the earlier camaraderie as the wagons were left behind in the rocky cavern, and Rory and his wife stood alone, listening to the staccato rhythm of hooves that faded as soon as the two riders were lost from sight.

TWENTY-TWO

THERE WERE so many places to hide in the dips and bows of land, under the plunge of rocks and beneath the ledges, crouching in shallow caves that stank with the memory of the animals that had sheltered there before. The wind up here had a mournful voice that haunted the space above the boulders and whimpered near the ground. But Aoife's voice was louder when she screamed.

She had lifted the skirts above her knees to free her legs. She had run up the slopes where the trail was clear and high-stepped the cumbersome stones where it was not, until she was melting in the heat that had turned her bodice into something repulsive. But that did not matter, because the higher she climbed the greater the feeling of exhilaration to have escaped the slow plod of wagons, the constant reek of animals and the drudge of wheels; the monotonous grind that her life had become. Her family were irrelevant; she had no time for the people who had decided her future without asking what she thought about it; without even giving a desperate damn. Up here they no longer existed and she was free and she was invincible.

And that was why she made the mistake.

Cub threw his head back, opened his ears, scented the air like an animal. He slowed Wolf Wind, pulling on the halter rope until the stallion stiffened and became still. It was ill fortune that this land was unforgiving. There would have been nowhere to hide in the very heart of the plains country apart from the stumble of rocks, trees rough-barked for survival, fertile places like splashes of green paint. But where the land was steeper he could hear little above the harsh breathing of his horse and the unearthly wind-moan, and he could detect no living movement – no Aoife – from the edge of his mind. He had sensed nothing unusual about the girl that could have rendered her invisible to his search, or prepared her for a strenuous climb such as this from the stony track where the wagons waited, far behind and deep below. There had been nothing to tell him that she had lifted her skirts for the freedom to run.

Time had passed since the girl had disappeared, and he had ridden the palomino hard. The echoes of Christian Faulkner's hunt over on the other side of the canyon had fallen to hush, and there was still no sign of her. Cub slid from the stallion's back and left the horse nosing around for grass as he climbed the hill. The slope was sharper here, precarious with stones, with clattering rock shards and resilient stalks exploring crevices for life. He used both hands to pull himself up, topping the rise where the land levelled for a long breath before it began to slope upwards again. And he heard the flap of material before he saw the biscuit-brown of her skirt at the place where she was half-concealed behind the rock stack.

He knew before he reached her that something was amiss, because it was only her skirt that was moving in the fidget of wind. Aoife was leaning back with her arm over her eyes, but beneath its protection he could see that she had been crying. He knelt beside her in the grit, disturbing a long-legged insect that ran away and left them to it. 'Aoife,' he said. 'Where are you hurting?'

Her chin quivered as if the sound of his voice had snapped something inside her. 'I've twisted my ankle.' She dropped her arm and stared up at him, big eyes made even bigger by thick lashes, glistening as she started to cry again. She rubbed her nose with a fist. 'Oh, God help me, I think it's broken.'

She was wearing boots of patched leather, lovingly mended but scuffed now by the difficult ground. She offered him her damaged foot and Cub unlaced the boot and carefully drew it away. Her stocking was darned and thin, and her ankle was rubbed raw and swelling, but under his touch he knew that the bones were whole.

'It is not broken; you have only weakened it.' He sat back on his heels and smiled. 'If that was all that stopped you then you have done well to get this far.'

Aoife blushed, a brighter pink topping the sun's burn. She cupped her ankle and squeezed gently, as though with healing hands. 'Climbing is easy; I have always done it. This country, the rocks, the hills, it is the same where I live. Where I used to live.' She shook her head to chase away confusion. 'I miss it so much.'

Her thin shoulders panicked when she started to sob, as pitiful as a terrified animal. She reached out her hands like a child asking for help and he held her because for those few moments she was vulnerable. Her chin shook against his neck and the tears were warm spots on his back. His skin felt fresh where they fell, and the wind touched him there and mourned with the girl. 'I hate it here,' Aoife said with her head on his shoulder, and her breath was hot where the wind was chill. 'This is not my home.' She pulled away to look at him. 'I want to go back to Ireland.' Cub dropped his hands but hers were still a harness around his neck. 'I want to be untamed, like you. You have such a good life.'

'You do not know that.' He shook his head and made to move away, but those arms were strong and she was not setting him free. He reached up, tried to unlace her fingers. 'Your family need you, Aoife. Your life is with them, and it will also be good.'

He did not want to hurt her but he needed to open her fingers. There was too much of a grip around his neck. 'Your parents are afraid for you. We have to get you back.' One of her nails was scratching his skin. The harder she pressed the deeper it scratched. 'Let go of me, Aoife.'

His shoulders started to ache. The girl was staring up at him but he could not look at her; she dropped her head, her arms softened and he began to calm down. Too much. He was not prepared for the kiss.

She gripped his mouth with her lips, biting with small sharp teeth. He felt her licking his blood and recoiled, no longer caring whether he might hurt her. Hoping he might hurt her. He shouted, 'Don't do that!' He tried to stand but she pounced like an animal, and he had to clutch her waist to stop her falling on stones. She embraced him, arms tight around his neck; he felt her body, catlike inside the roughspun dress.

'I love you, Cub. I love you so much.'

'Aoife. No.'

'I trailed you yesterday, when you took that horse downstream. I saw you at the pool. I watched you in the water.'

He had stripped off his clothes and swum naked. He had felt completely liberated, free from everything and everyone, and all the time she had been watching him. 'You have to let me go, Aoife.'

She leaned forward to kiss him again and he pushed her away. He stumbled backwards on the uneven ground, but Aoife didn't follow him. She was quiet now, perching against a stone platform with one small hand gripping the side. The strange hunger seemed to have been sated, taking the woman from her and leaving a child. Long hair black in the shade, wild with red lights in the sun; large lilac eyes wide open on his face. A child. He had felt her feline body inside the brown dress. He was hot with shame. He was cold with fear.

'Don't you want me, Cub?' she spoke very softly, but even so he heard.

'Put your boot on.' He could not look at her. 'We have to go back.'

'I love you, Cub.'

'You know nothing about me.'

'I know plenty.'

Sulky. The child was certainly back again, drawing on her boot, her bottom lip glowering with discomfort. She tied the lace with her child's fingers. Her stockinged leg was slender, and she stretched it forward and wriggled her weak ankle. She took a while to cover it with her skirt. 'There,' she said. 'Just as you wish, Cub.'

All was normal again. 'Can you stand?'

'If you will help me.' She held up her hand.

She was shorter than him, but he had not noticed that before. All those days had passed and he had not really seen her. She had never stood this close to him, never wrapped her arms around his body the way she was doing now. He tried not to touch her.

'Aoife, I cannot. You are a child.'

'I am a woman and I have been in love with you since that first day.'

'You are a little girl, and you are playing me for a fool. Let me go.'

It was sudden, the way her hands fumbled at his belt. The heat slammed into his head. He wrenched her away and she cried out, gripping her wrist until her fingers turned first white and then red. Her eyes glittered. 'You hurt me!'

She had managed to unlatch the buckle, he tried to fasten it, he tried to keep his eye on her. She came towards him with her mouth open, pink tongue, small pointed teeth. He grabbed her arm and tugged, and the wind screamed too close to his ear. But no, it was not the wind making that appalling noise; it was the girl.

Aoife fought him as he dragged her down the hill, screeching, resisting, stumbling on her injured foot. The slope seemed steeper now, precarious; they skidded and fell in the dust, and she threw back her head and squealed. He held her arm until she was hobbled but still she fought, flailing against him with her free hand, her nails clawing the side of his face. The wounds stung in the wind-blown grit but Cub barely felt the pain. He pulled her towards the restless stallion until his muscles began to cramp with the force, and he knew it was going to be impossible.

'Why are you doing this?' He grabbed her shoulders and shook her, not caring how hard. Aoife's hair tangled around her face, and something tore.

And then she screamed.

'Stop!'

The heavy word fell on them from nowhere, flattening the dust cloud like thrown water. Cub stood still. His arms were aching; Aoife was a small thing in front of him, shaking under his hands. The word's echo withdrew but the man who had yelled it was silent now, sitting on the sweating piebald with his face in shadow. The animal was breathing hard, its painted hide messy with foam. The horse sidestepped and kicked the hill, and further away the palomino shied at the stone-clatter sound.

Aoife pulled away and stumbled over the rocks to the wagon master's horse. 'Mr Faulkner, help me.' She stood young and defenceless by his stirrup and raised her hands as she had raised them to Cub. Her hair was an unruly tumble down her back; one of her sleeves had torn away from the seam, and the skin was very pure underneath. Without a word, the man reached down and lifted her up as if she weighed nothing at all. She settled behind his saddle with her small hands around his waist, and turned her head away as he looked down at the boy.

'Do your belt up,' he said.

There had been desperation in Cub's face the day he had walked into the saloon to seek a wagon master, but there had also been fortitude. Christian Faulkner had liked what he had seen then; he saw it now as the boy stood below him, hiding nothing behind his eyes.

'It is not how it looks,' Cub said, and his voice seemed to come from some hopeless place.

'Get on your horse and follow me,' Faulkner told him, too aware that the girl was sitting with her small breasts pressed hard against his back, and that her hands felt hot around his waist. When he dipped his head, he could still see the echo of the cat-claw scratches she had left on the boy's skin.

TWENTY-THREE

THEY WERE all waiting, spread like a tableau around the idle wagons as if they had not moved at all since the two horses had been ridden away. As if they needed to see dust smoking in the distance before they could discern the drub of hooves, the scuffle of stones and the rattle of the bit; before they saw the piebald picking its way over broken ground with the double load on its back, and the stallion stepping high as the boy rode from somewhere behind.

Kathleen Callahan was shaking; she held Maeve's little body so tightly that the baby grew fearful and whimpered her distress. Finn reached up to take her from his mother, teasing the child with whispers until she had settled into a happier place beneath his chin; and Kathleen tucked a length of skirt between her fingers and stepped out to greet her daughter. But Rory leaned forwards and stopped her, his grip tight around her wrist. He had seen Aoife's tumbled hair and the way she was clinging to the wagon master, her stone-white face and the look in her eyes. He had seen all these things and he held his wife so fiercely he could almost hear her pulse.

'Damn you, Rory Callahan. Let me go to our girl.' Kathleen pulled at her husband's hand until he realised what he was doing and released her, but he did not like to see her running towards the piebald as it came to a halt before them and the wagon master helped Aoife down. He did not like the sounds his daughter was making as she tripped on the clumsy ground and stumbled into her mother's arms. He did not like the piercing sounds from her throat because they were turning him inside out.

Christian Faulkner dismounted slowly and arranged the reins to hang to his satisfaction. He smoothed a side of the saddle blanket and eased the piebald's forelock where it had been snagged by the bridle. And then he turned to make sure that from somewhere behind him Cub was slipping from the palomino's back. 'Come, boy,' he said, and his words were light; but his face was as dark as a warning.

Rory stared at his wife and his daughter; stunned by the enormity of wanting to know what had happened, and the muteness of wanting not to know. Faulkner walked towards them, vigilant over the hazardous ground, too aware that Rory's eyes were asking him to say something that might make sense of it all and knowing that there was nothing he could say. He was relieved when the Irishman turned towards the boy who followed in silence, shielding his face behind blankness, and as they came closer the wagon master raised his hand as though to ward off immediate questions. 'She is in one piece,' was all he said.

Kathleen Callahan turned on him with the girl in her arms. 'Oh no, Mr Faulkner, for sure my Aoife is not. She is here with us, but she is not whole. Can you not see? Rory, will you not see?'

'Hush, wife.'

'Damn you then! This is our daughter.' Kathleen clutched Aoife by the shoulders and pushed her forward. 'Look at her!'

Standing in the shadow of the wagon, almost invisible in the gloom of her clothing, Elfrida Thatcher sucked in her breath. It was a shocking sound, almost painful; she made the sign of the cross over her buttoned-up chest as though she was gazing into the pit of evil. Rory did not want to think of evil as he surveyed his daughter standing before him, her hair wild with misuse, her clothes ripped and dirty, her face distorted by distress. 'Aoife,' he said. 'Darling. What has happened to you?'

She pointed beyond Christian Faulkner to where the boy was standing, quiet and still. 'He tried to touch me, Daddy. He tried so hard, but I wouldn't let him.' And she teetered, unsupported on her injured ankle, because her mother had taken her hands away.

Kathleen's skirt swept the stones into life as she ran past her husband, past the wagon master, past Benjamin Redmayne who had stepped into her path to stop her; and when she reached Cub she raised her fists and forced him back against the rocks, hitting him with murderous force but little accuracy until they fell together in the bitty dust and the gash of stones. And when Christian Faulkner lifted her away she fought him instead.

Cub got to his feet and stood before her. He didn't move as she screamed into his face, straining forwards from Faulkner's prevention. 'Do you know how much I want to kill you?'

Her voice broke and echoed down the rock gully and the babies took fear from it and started to cry. The people were all staring at him, those whose lives he had been sharing. The people who had accepted him were peeling away his skin. 'I have done nothing,' he said, but the words were inconsequential, corroded by biting eyes and dipped in guilt by the crying of the innocent.

And from somewhere at the edge of the gathering came the shriek, like a saw when it finds a nail inside the wood. 'Satan's work; that is what you have done!' Elfrida Thatcher stood by her wagon where she knew herself to be safe, and she stabbed at the distance between them with her finger. 'You are the devil in human form!'

Benjamin Redmayne turned sharply. 'Mrs Thatcher; that is enough!' He stumbled like an old man but his frail voice had grown powerful. 'There is no need for words like those.'

'What there is no need for is one such as him in the company of honest and God-fearing folk.'

'You have no right…'

'Old man, I have the right of all that is good. Unlike you, I do not seek to hide behind a vicious dog when the Saviour is my protector.'

'Oh, for heaven's sake!'

'For the sake of heaven and all the angels, and of our wondrous Lord, Himself!'

Kathleen Callahan was limp now in the wagon master's arms. He set her down on a boulder, scoured smooth by the wind's teeth, and she slumped as though she might never be able to stand straight again. Bethy Dyeston shushed her frightened child and shook off her reticence. She climbed the stony path to sit beside the woman, gathering her close; and the baby reached out her arms to them both.

Christian Faulkner looked over at the boy standing so alone on the rock slope, and then down at the soured woman by the wagons, her face aflame with righteousness under the scold's bridle of her bonnet. 'I believe we have heard enough, Mrs Thatcher.'

'You are all fools. Do you not recognise the heathen in your midst? He rides a great wild beast, he comes from nowhere, he owns nothing, not even a good Christian name. For all that we know he has absconded from a madhouse; from a prison. He is dangerous!' She turned abruptly and spat into the dust beside the wagon. 'No one is safe while you are alive, creature of sin.'

'Woman, you have the foulest mind.' Benjamin Redmayne coughed over the words, but when he saw his grandson's frightened eyes he felt ashamed.

Faulkner shook his head, scattering a frustration of dust. 'Mr Thatcher, would you kindly control your wife?' But the man was sitting as upright as a preacher on the wagon's unforgiving seat, and even though he turned his head as if to acknowledge the question there was nothing to see beneath the brim of his wide, round hat.

The wagon master gazed up at the late afternoon sky that glowered above them as if in disapproval. He slapped his own hat against his leg and watched as the dirt filtered away towards where Cub stood motionless on the slope. He was streaked grey like something carved from the earth, and Christian Faulkner could see that he was already completely alone. 'Rightly or wrongly, boy,' the man said, 'you need to leave.'

Cub lifted his head, and a piece of that solitude escaped from his eyes, so that the wagon master felt the scratch of something dismal; a flash of hopelessness, swiftly smothered as he turned away from them all. He climbed the slope, the noise of the wind covering the sound of the people he was leaving behind, and when he reached the palomino he could hardly move for weariness; for the fear that this might always be the path his life would take. And then from behind him came a rushing and a rustling, and Wolf Wind reared away and left Cub alone to meet the person who had climbed the slope after him.

Finn Callahan stood firmly on the precipitous ground, square and sturdy like his father, with the same dimples hidden now on his sullen face. He was holding the leather pouch that Cub had left in his mother's protection. 'I took you for a friend,' he said. 'My family welcomed you in and you turned on us all.' Cub shook his head, but the younger boy could not see it through the anger in his eyes. 'You have damaged my sister and that means that we are all damaged. I am glad you are leaving. I only want to see the end of you.'

Finn threw the pouch on the ground before slithering back down the slope, half running in his desire to get away from the one who was standing above him and making a funnel from his hands. 'Your sister is damaging me with her lies,' Cub shouted. 'I have done nothing to her, and that is the truth.' But the wind whisked up and broke the words to pieces on the rocks before they could reach the other boy.

He led Wolf Wind away from the late sun as if it would have hurt his eyes to stare into its fire. He walked to the soporific rhythm of the stallion's hooves and the escort of small insects that were waking to the cooling air. He did not think of anything much, he did not see much of anything; he only knew how far he had walked when he looked up to the night that was gathering before him like a pregnant sail, and when he turned around the dying sun stopped his breath with its beauty, flaring the sky as red as a dancer's skirt. The four wagons had gone, swallowed inside the wound in the earth where voices echoed from the rocks and perished on the ground as if they had never been.

Cub looped the bag containing everything he owned over his head. He pulled himself up to the strong, pale back and swung the horse around to face the end of the day. He thought of the gentleness he had learned from Lucy Ryker's smile and Reyna's ministry; he thought of Kathleen Callahan's anger as she beat him to the rocks with her fists. All were as if they had never been, and he was on his own again. Blue-black clouds soared behind him into growing darkness, and he knew that this was the way it would always be.

TWENTY-FOUR

THE LUMBERING wagons had held him back like a leash and Cub travelled faster without them, eating the ground under the lope of the stallion's hooves. He sat high and sucked sky into his lungs until his heart swelled, and the land rose and fell before him. Time had passed and his hair had grown; sun-whitened, it soared like a horse's mane over his ears as he rode the palomino towards the end of it. It was all he had wanted since Daniel Ryker had left him alone beneath the hill, and now he knew it was close.

They made good speed and slept unhindered beneath regal stars, but the day dawned when the stallion woke uneasy, testing the air with flattened ears and white-rimmed eyes. There was something different out on the landscape, and when the boy woke and saw Wolf Wind outlined against the early light, he knew it too. It was later in the day that Cub rode the stallion towards a chaos of rock that was heaped like an upturned bowl in the shallows of the plain. Late sunshine splashed the cairn with points of colour, and they spread to become many colours as a pony emerged from behind the crumble of boulders.

Silver-grey, with darker spots like a scattering of paint across its rump, the animal stood completely still. The half-naked man on its back stared at the boy and the boy stared at the man, so that for a while it was as though their souls were mingling. But then the breeze kicked up, rippling the rider's hair and plaiting the coloured feathers in the pony's mane, and the man twisted round and stabbed the sky with his fist. His siren-call scorched Cub's ears and ricocheted from the unquiet mess of rock, and a small band of Indians came up from the heart of it on a jostle of horses. They emerged from beneath the earth and rode for the plain, converging in a stream that flowed towards the boy.

Cub wrenched the halter and Wolf Wind pivoted, churning the dust and screaming; the sound rose to the air to become one with the cries of the Indians as the stallion began to run. They galloped blind through the mud cloud; they galloped faster until the wind filled the boy's shirt and spilled hair into his eyes when he looked back over his shoulder, so that he could barely see the distant line of horses behind him. After a while they grew more distant; after a while again they had fallen away to nothing.

The stallion juddered to a halt and Cub stretched until his muscles locked, and he could hear again above the throbbing of his blood. A mesh of clouds covered the sun and his skin cooled to a shiver that swept across his body as he slipped to the ground, leaning against the horse's flank until the animal had stopped trembling. He knew what he had to do next. He fought the knowledge with resentment, wrapping pale ropes of mane around his fists until his fingers were sore with anger. Wolf Wind dipped his neck and licked salt from the boy's skin, and the roughness of his tongue at least was comforting.

Killian Callahan was the first to notice the low wake of dust heading their way. The small boy was trudging at the rear of his family's wagon, and when he stopped suddenly the oxen hauling the following wagon shied and bellowed and knocked him sideways. Killian cursed with his father's voice and pushed the animals away, then pointed with an arrow-straight finger. 'Look there yonder!'

It had taken longer to return because reluctance was as awkward as a hobbling rope. Cub had seen the shambling wagons from way beyond when they were mere insects dotting the distance, far-off but so exposed in this vast wilderness of scrub and tree and corrugated ground, and the sound of complaining wheels was a low chant of effort and toil crossing the plain. Since the evening of the Indians the stallion had settled to a lope that had carried them over the miles and through the hours, but they were tired now in the rising warmth of the new day, and Cub slowed to a walk as he neared the bulbous wagons. When he saw the other horse riding out from the train to meet him he stayed Wolf Wind with a word, and an emptiness in his stomach that was not hunger, and sat the broad golden back to wait for Christian Faulkner to approach. It did not take long for the piebald to reach him.

The wagon master eased himself forward in the saddle. 'I did not expect to see you again, Cub,' he said, pushing up his hat and scratching his scalp as far as he could reach. 'No indeed, I was not expecting this.'

'It was never in my mind to return.'

'Well, to tell you the truth, that surprises me.' Faulkner rearranged his hat until he was satisfied. 'It surprises me that you have remained unaware of the strength of feeling here, a mystic such as yourself.'

'I know that I am hated.'

'No.' As though he was being recalled, the man glanced back at the group of wagons and the people who had climbed from their seats and the ends of puckered canvas. 'No, Cub, since that was only when we believed what we had been given to believe and foolishly did not allow time to investigate.'

'And what have you been given to believe now?' The boy followed Faulkner's glance to where the wagoners were standing. Everything might have looked normal, had it not been for the unearthly silence, or the fact that there was nothing to see of the dark-haired girl.

'I like to think we now know the truth, blazing as it does from a mire of lies.' Christian's smile dragged lines across his face. 'And it is fitting that you have returned.' He kicked the piebald half a circle around, and looked back at the boy sitting the stallion, loose-limbed and white-knuckled. 'Will you come with me?'

He had to; he was here to follow Christian Faulkner towards the group of people who had expelled him. His hold on the halter rope tightened but Wolf Wind froze, stiff-legged and shuddering. Cub dropped to the ground and stood beside the horse, gripping the white mane as though for safety. The wagon people had formed a close group now; they were watching him like a small band of trappers, and his scalp prickled in the sting of their eyes. The stallion smelled his fear; he bit Cub's arm with a viciousness that tore his shirt and drew blood, and the boy swore and slapped the horse's flank, driving him away towards the tangle of grass through which they had just ridden.

He followed the piebald alone, walking in its hoof tracks with the wind's teeth sharp inside his torn sleeve. Christian Faulkner had already reached the wagons and he sat waiting, low in the saddle, but when Cub had covered the short distance between them the wagon master turned his head away, as though he had led the boy into a trap and had no wish to view the consequences.

There was still no sign of Aoife at the Callahan wagon; perhaps she had turned away as well in order not to see the vengeance her father was about to inflict. But instead of his fist her father was holding out an open palm to the boy, his face childlike with embarrassment. 'Before you think to blame us, Cub, know that we were only seeing what had been put before us to see. Our crime was to believe in our own child.'

Kathleen came to stand by her husband's side; she bent her head to hide her eyes, but the boy could smell her natural perfume and it was like a leaf-rich wood on a summer evening. 'It was wrong of me to attack you,' she said. 'Did I hurt you, Cub? I do not want to think that I did.'

'We know the truth of what happened, you see.' Rory placed a reassuringly heavy hand on the boy's shoulder. 'Aoife confessed to everything, just after you had ridden away on your fast horse; too fast for us to prevent you from leaving. She made trouble for you and that was difficult to forgive, but at heart she is an honest girl. Kate and me, we could not bear to think that we have raised a deceitful child.'

His wife brushed hair from her face, and when she looked up at the boy her eyes were as green as spring grass in the sun. 'We hope that you can learn to forgive her too, Cub. Forgive Aoife and forgive us.'

There was something warm pushing between his fingers; Rust's tongue tasting the sweat on his skin. He cupped the dog's muzzle with his hand, and behind him Benjamin Redmayne stroked down the wolf hair on its neck. 'You should know, Cub, that we are all delighted to have you back,' the old man said, but disjointedly because his gaze was fixed on Elfrida Thatcher. The buttoned-up woman was a dull figure in the wagon's shade, although her frown had been too sharp to hide. She shot Redmayne a jagged glance down the barrel of her bonnet, but that only made him smile.

Christian Faulkner came up beside the boy, the piebald's reins wrapped around his wrist as though he was a hitching post. 'I have led many trains through lands like these, and each one brings with it a mix of the well-meaning and the ill-informed. This train,' he jerked his hand and pulled the reins, and the horse nodded as if in agreement, 'is no exception, but even so you have not been deterred from riding with us again.'

'Wagon master.' Cub stepped closer. 'I was chased by Indians. You needed to know, and that is why I have come back.'

Christian Faulkner leaned forward; the piebald shook its head and the reins snaked from his arm. 'How far away was this?'

'A distance to the west. I have ridden hard to get here and the riding was swift. You have a herd of four wagons and the travelling is slow. If you pass through their territory you will be at their mercy.'

'Then we must prepare ourselves to fight.' Benjamin Redmayne was standing too close not to overhear what had been said, and his retort had been shrill. But then he straightened and spoke with a younger man's voice. 'We all knew what might transpire before we joined this wagon train, Christian. We know what to expect and we are not afraid.'

The children were playing their seeking game, weaving in and out of hideaways in the scrub. Babies gurgled and women laughed, but the wagon master stood back from the gentle sounds and his words were quiet. 'We are not journeying through Indian lands, Mr Redmayne. I would never choose to take the vulnerable in that direction. If Cub was challenged by renegades, then this could be very bad for us.'

Benjamin's eyes hardened as he twisted towards the boy. No longer an elderly man, he had turned into a fighter. 'How many Indians were in the party?' He reached out as though to grab Cub's collar, to shake him.

'I could not be sure.'

'But how many do you think?'

'Maybe the fingers of two hands.'

Redmayne faced the wagon master. 'Not so many then, Christian. And we will be ready for them. We have five full-grown men. We have two who are nearly men.'

'We have three women.'

They had not noticed that the children had abandoned their games and the mothers had ceased their laughter, and now Kathleen was there in front of them; her hair scattering as she beat her chest with a fist. 'Three women who can use a rifle, Christian.'

'Well, about that I cannot be sure…'

'But I am. A mother will fight when her children are threatened.'

And Bethy Dyeston was there too, her baby in her arms. 'Mr Faulkner, if you need me to use a firearm, then know that I have done so since a young girl. My pa taught me; there were no boys in my family.'

'Do you see?' Kathleen Callahan rose on the soles of her feet and spoke over the heads of the men before her. 'Mrs Thatcher, are you one with us?'

The laden wagon was still and silent. There was no reply from within. It was as though the two quiet girls and their mother had vanished, but if everyone listened carefully they might be able to hear them breathing as they hid their faces behind canvas walls, while the thin, reedy man stood by the side of the wagon and stared away as though he did not wish to see what was in front of him. 'We are opposed to all violence,' he called out to them, 'and we will not fight.'

Christian smiled, but the rest of his face was hidden beneath the brim of his hat. 'With respect to you, brother, are there not times when principles might be overlooked, particularly if innocent lives are put in danger?'

Septimus Thatcher bristled, and turned a fanatical stare towards them. 'Nevertheless, Mr Faulkner, our views and our faith remain sacrosanct.' Then he dropped his head, as though the wagon master had been dismissed. 'My family shall pray for you all.'

'Then we are obliged to you for that small favour, Mr Thatcher.' Faulkner looked away as if he had seen enough and faced the small group before him. 'It appears that we are on our own,' he said.

Benjamin Redmayne swore and shook his head, as if ridding it of something unpleasant. 'We shall be better off on our own,' he said. 'We have no use for the disobliging, Mr Faulkner, but what we do need is for you to tell us what we must do. And, if you please, as fast as you have a mind to it.'

Christian Faulkner indeed had a mind to it.

He led them deeper into the open country where nothing would be hidden from them; a place that was wild with winds and blown dust, where they unharnessed the animals and pulled the wagons around in a small, tight ring that they linked together with boxes, chests, chairs and rolls of mattresses. The wagons were gutted; every movable object was brought out to choke up gaps in the fortress walls until privacy had been exorcised, and neighbour breathed on neighbour in the constricted space where all was safely gathered in. The people waited and the day passed, and by evening stretched nerves were loose with fatigue, and the animals that had joined them inside the refuge were sharp-haired and rank with distress.

When he was a child Cub had lain beneath the wagon that contained his mother and the only way of life he knew at the time; now these other children lay beneath their own wagons, knowing the same trepidation he had known but for a different reason. They were children with families to protect them and he remembered none of that for himself, although everyone that mattered right now was here with him: Benjamin and young Randal, gripping the red hide of the dog as if he wanted it to carry him away; Kathleen and Rory, his shoulders bent from the weight of wagon-shifting. Aoife had come out of hiding to help her brother with the animals; she turned her face from Cub as if pretending she couldn't see him, but Finn sought his forgiveness with just one glance, and then hid his eyes also as he grappled with the great bellowing heads of oxen. Bethy Dyeston moulded a baby's cradle from blankets pulled from her bed, and her husband eased her panic in a cradle made from his own arms. Septimus Thatcher opened his pale, empty stare and refused to see as he knelt on the ground beside his daughters and his wife. Their earnest prayers echoed like a hollow wind in a cavern and died away to nothing.

Cub stood at the edge of the vortex and held Wolf Wind's head rigid until the horse had stopped shuddering; he stood like that for so long that his arms grew useless with aching. Christian Faulkner came over; he was far too close in this confinement but the stallion was exhausted by anxiety and Faulkner remained undisturbed, tall above the barricades, turning his head from north, and all around again to north. 'There is nothing to see,' he said. 'Perhaps this day they will leave us be?'

Cub surveyed the empty plain. 'This day and this night. And maybe even longer, until we are thinking that they will not come at all.'

The wagon master gazed about him at the squeeze of people, the mess of animals, the whole paraphernalia of wagon life. 'We are captives of our own fear, but we will not be able to live this way for too long,' he said. 'If the Indians are hunting our scent we are surely making it easy for them.'

'Then they will be here soon,' Cub said, and Faulkner shivered because with six words the boy had brought the danger home.

TWENTY-FIVE

IT WAS shortly after noon the following day that the Indians came, so stealthily that lookout Jeremiah Dyeston would never have noticed had it not been for the dust clouds. He called out the warning that was too loud for the cramped space, and above his shout a gentle breeze arose like a sigh of relief and swept the garrison with energy.

Cub leaned against a packing case and scanned the line of approaching horsemen. There were many Indians now taking the place of the few that had chased him from the path he had been trying to follow, it seemed so long ago. Two days and two nights had been taken from his life, enough time for the Indians to have regrouped and replenished, and now twenty or so half-naked, fully armed warriors were racing towards a handful of people. Frightened people, with a limited armoury of firearms, blades and hammers; pebbles and catapults; forks and knives from Redmayne's canteen of cutlery.

Cub gripped the handle of Daniel Ryker's hunting knife, and his elbow knocked the wagon master who was standing by his shoulder; the man was too silent and too still, his left eyelid in spasm beneath his dusty hat. The boy's hand began to ache, but when he relinquished the knife handle he felt powerless. 'Mr Faulkner, can we hold them off?'

Faulkner shook a little as if the words had loosened something inside him, and swallowed before he could speak. 'With a damned good try, we shall.'

The Indians were close now, the air thick with their screams. The shudder of galloping ponies crept into the blood of the wagon people, and it was as if their bodies were solid and they could no longer move. Christian Faulkner stood frozen like the others, but he glimpsed a shift in the air around him; his bones creaked when he turned to look. One of the Thatcher girls had thrown herself against a wall of mattresses as if she needed to be engulfed. She could have been Charity, she might have been Mercy – it was difficult to differentiate when the whole family seemed moulded from the same severe cloth – but when she looked up at him she was only a child, and he knew he had to protect her.

'All you men, now is the time,' he called out. 'You have your weapons and you know how to use them. Women and children, get yourselves beneath the wagons. And have courage, people, for we shall endure this.'

'Courage we need courage we shall endure!' Aoife Callahan, shrilling on the edge of hysteria as her mother herded her beneath a gutted wagon. She looked up at Cub before she disappeared and the boy was impaled by the terror in her eyes, for she was very young and very afraid and she needed him to kill for her.

Horse hooves pounded from the heart of the earth until it seemed there was nothing else but the passion – no screaming babies lying beneath the wagons, no bellowing animals tethered tightly behind flimsy walls; and if any of the men were yelling out their feelings as they clutched their rifles in petrified hands it was impossible to judge which of them was the most frightened. The Indians were getting near on wild-eyed ponies that would break through the barricade, break their legs on the wagon wheels, break their necks; coming so close to the wagons that the air simmered with body heat and splintered as the riders twisted away like one living creature to orbit the walls, charging taut bows, swinging tomahawks into grip, grinding rifles into shoulders.

Guiding the horses with their knees, bodies supple to the gallop and long hair rippling like fire from strips of buckskin around their heads, the Indians bombarded the makeshift fort. The dust they had summoned rained down on the group inside until everything was obliterated under the sting of grit, and beneath it the wagoners panicked, firing hopeless shots that flew wide of their mark. Rifles were emptied and new ones grabbed from the stockpile while wives relinquished their hoarse babies to the ground and reloaded the smoking weapons. And all that time, beneath the quiet wagon, the Thatcher family huddled together with their hands over their ears and their mouths and their eyes.

Benjamin Redmayne was the first to kill, his arms so tense that the rifle stock knocked back into his shoulder and left the bruise that would haunt him for days afterwards. The Indian rode into the way of the bullet and it seemed to be the retort that heaved him from his horse and laid him out on the ground. The old man dropped the weapon as if it had caught fire and stared at the casualty, lying forever still; chest bright with blood, and arms spread as though he was asking why. His face was too smooth; he couldn't have been much more than a boy. Benjamin saw someone's grandson, and he put his hands over his face because he did not want to see any more. He only knew that the Indians had gone because of the sudden drop in sound that left his ears ringing.

They had wheeled their mounts around on hind legs and galloped away in a single stream of speed, but before they left one of them had jumped to the ground and lifted the dead boy to lie across his horse's withers; and when he remounted to follow his people the sound of lamentation broke in his throat, a cry of grief that faded as the Indians disappeared. The silence that descended was oppressive, but one by one the prisoners of the barricade moved, a short dance to life, and the noise they made grew stronger as they dared to hope. And Rust gave a single bark, a triumphant sound that set oxen groaning and horses stamping as if easing cramped muscles.

The dog's bark pierced Christian Faulkner's skull like an arrow; he stretched until his bones clicked, and looked over the walls. The battlefield was a churn of dust, grey stuff smoking above the ground like something ghostly. The place where the Indian had fallen was marked with his blood. Faulkner reached out to Benjamin Redmayne and clutched his shoulder, and the man took his hands from his face but did not look up. He tried to speak but his throat was too dry; he whispered the words like a penitent in a confessional. 'I have never killed anyone before.'

'Self-defence, Mr Redmayne.'

'Did you see his face, Christian? He was just a boy.'

'He was a warrior with a rifle, and he was trying to kill you.'

That was when Benjamin looked up. 'He was still too young to die, Mr Faulkner.'

He had disintegrated. Old and bewildered, he raised his hands and turned around, and Kathleen Callahan stood before him, her children staring up at her from between their wagon's wheels. 'Mrs Callahan,' he said, as she took his arm and moved him away. 'I don't think I can do this; I don't want to kill anyone else,' he mumbled, his head bent against hers.

Rory stood by Christian Faulkner, his face grimed with sweat and dust and the rifle hanging in his hand, and watched his wife walk with the old man through the clutter to a quieter place. 'Are we safe, wagon master? What happens now?' His eyes were as pale as silver in the dirt on his face, and they tracked Jeremiah Dyeston's stocky body as he came towards them.

'Tell us when we can leave, Christian.' Dyeston rested his rifle against his reliable shoulder. 'I need to get Bethy and the baby to safety, so why are you hesitating?'

Wolf Wind was growing restless at his tether, tension sharpening every muscle. 'The safest place right now is here,' Cub said, and pushed the borrowed gun he had been using into his belt before reaching up for the stallion's halter.

'Now what can that boy know about it?' Dyeston's voice was rising, battering at the ache in Faulkner's head. The wagon master watched as Cub spread his hand down the palomino's hide, and felt himself dissolving into the gentle language that was easing the animal's distress.

'At times, Mr Dyeston,' he said, 'I believe that boy knows more than me about many things.'

'But they have gone, Christian. Can you not see? The Indians have gone.' Dyeston's voice rose higher. He dragged the rifle from his shoulder and shook it to make his point, and the sun fell from the barrel and into Christian Faulkner's eye so that he was blinded for a while, and only the others could see the dust that had begun to rise in the distance. And then he saw Kathleen Callahan tying waves of loosened hair back with a rip of material and picking up Benjamin Redmayne's rifle from the ground.

'When her children are threatened a mother will fight,' she said, and positioned herself against the barricade with the rifle at her shoulder. No one tried to stop her.

Warriors stampeded towards them, firing arrows into the sky and yelling like wolves, and the clutch of animals trapped inside the flimsy fortress howled in reply. It was as if the noise itself manifested the stink of fear and spent ammunition. The ground sizzled, the air shimmered above scorched rifles, and the belongings of desperate people began to disintegrate. Boxes jumped with bullets, wooden crates splintered; mattresses imploded under the stab of arrows, liberating small white feathers that drifted calmly over the enclosure and lay as soft as blessings across the mane of the exhausted stallion. Then above the uproar that was turning the day to nonsense, Cub heard a girl scream.

Aoife was leaning from the cave beneath the wagon, stretching her arms until her fingers were grasping air. Her mother dropped the rifle and threw herself down beside her daughter, and Cub saw the girl gripping the woman's shoulders until her knuckles were bone-white. Kathleen shook, stumbled when she tried to stand, fell to her knees again as though she was in fever. She stared up from the ground and caught the boy watching her. She opened her mouth but there were no words.

Cub slid the revolver into his belt; the metal was hot against his skin, it cramped his ribs when he crouched down by the Callahan wagon to hear what Kathleen was trying to say. The children lay looking up at him, white faces in deep shadow framed by the wagon's wheels. Aoife's fingers clutched at her mother's skirt and convulsed on a grab of earth. Her nails had gouged her own palms; he could see half-moons of blood when she raised her hand to point beneath the wagon where it should have been blind-black and safe under cover. But the cover was split now and the light and colour and movement beyond were shocking. Out in the dazzle, like a small bright flower blooming in the dust, he could see Maeve crawling.

Kathleen's lips moved and still she could not speak, but her eyes were eloquent, and the palest green as if her colour was seeping away. Cub twisted round to see Jeremiah Dyeston leaning over the barricade, staring at what was beyond, the rifle forgotten in his hands. Christian Faulkner looked away from the turmoil and down at the boy as his lips formed the baby's name, and then Cub slid beneath the wagon.

He knocked the children aside with the force of him, finding the small gap in the defensive wall that Maeve had found, and when the heat hit his face he hesitated, for just a moment, before he pushed through into chaos. He rose to his haunches, and ahead of him the little girl grew brighter in the sun, her blue dress like a splash of sky, vivid against the dust. She was far too easy to see. He came up to a crouch and ran across the ground, thunder breaking beneath his feet. Only seven steps, but it felt as though he was emptying his body into a ravine with no bottom as the safety of the makeshift fortress disappeared behind him and he reached out for the child.

Her arm was plump and warm and infinitely fragile. She turned around to look at him, and her laughter made an obscenity of the death fight, the thrashing legs of the paint ponies, the burn of rifles. She sat with her heels together, stretching her arms to be lifted; he wrapped her body to his belly so that her baby heart beat against his own, and turned to face the pitifully inadequate wagons. Flimsy wheels and billowing canvas were before him, the pockmarked mattresses, the splintered boxes, but out here he was lost, his back exposed to frenzy and the vulnerable child with her head tucked beneath his chin.

He began to run the seven endless steps back, but danger was as dark as death behind him and a shadow crossed his heart. A shadow crossed his path as the horse galloped towards him and he dipped his head to protect the child's as a rifle coughed, too close. Heat zipped under his hair and down the side of his face, and dust puffed up by his feet. His mouth was wet, a curtain had dropped over his eyes and he could no longer see the ground, or the wagons that were close enough now to swallow sound. He was running blind when he reached them, the sturdy wood knocked him back and he stumbled to his knees, pushing blood from his eyes so that he could make out which way he was facing.

There was a horse standing stiff-legged behind him, a silver-grey with coloured feathers in its mane and a scattering of dark spots across its rump. The man on its back was staring at Cub, his eyes alight as he remembered the chase across the shallow plains, and the boy on the stallion that had outrun even the fleetest of his mustangs. He raised his rifle as though offering it to the sky and yelled his siren scream, and the ring of horses slowed dramatically, pulled back squealing on their haunches. The warriors clustered around the silver-grey, looking more like a social gathering than a small party of killers, and then, as one, they galloped away.

Cub heard the hoofbeats fade to nothing as he began to crumple, as though someone was turning off the sound. He tried hard to fall on his back so that the child in his arms would not be crushed. He did not feel the ground.

Everything had changed when he opened his eyes. He could hear the chirrup of nocturnal insects but no thunder, he could taste the nutshell tang of wood but no dust. He looked up for the sky but that too had vanished, and there was a canvas roof curving over his head in its stead, dented with light and shade as the wind played. He was lying on a wounded mattress with a cluster of bullet holes under his ear, as if the wadding had been chewed by giant moths. Something across his head was restricting his movement and somebody stayed his hand when he reached up to push it away.

'You must not do that.'

Cub tried to look round to see whose warm, soft hand it was, and Aoife was sitting beside him. She was smiling, but the smile began to falter as the light from the oil lamp flared and guttered. 'Please don't stare at me,' she said behind the shadows dancing over her face.

All memory was returning, and now he knew it was a bandage that someone had bound tight enough around his skull to deaden the pain, although it was still pulsing across his forehead. 'How long have I been out, Aoife?'

'A couple of hours. Since the Indians left.'

'Left for good.'

'Yes, they did.' She was answering the question he had not asked. 'And Christian has assured us that they will not attack again.'

He remembered a silver-grey pony with marks like rain on its rump. He remembered trying to turn so that he should fall on his back with the little girl clutched to his chest. 'The baby; is she okay?'

'Ah, sure Maeve is fine. She has no fear, that one; the bravest of us all.' Aoife watched him from the shelter of her long, black lashes. 'I brought you trouble and for that you saved my little sister's life.'

She coloured slightly, looking down at her fingers as she wove them together on the edge of the mattress. 'Christian told us that you would be conscious again in a few hours; and he was right.'

She had her brothers' eyes; she had her mother's fire in her blood. In a few short years, she would keep her father awake with worry.

'Christian is such a wonderful man,' she said, 'and I love him, Cub. I love him so much.'

TWENTY-SIX

EVENING HAD come and the sun was low, a quivering fireball about to sink below the horizon where even the land was burning. The sky sighed relief in the breeze that had riffled up from the lees of the day, and Cub reached out for night and the coolness of the moon. Even from this distance he thought he could still discern the knife blade of ridge where he had waited with the palomino, watching as Christian Faulkner and the families from the wagon train slowly disappeared into boiling dust clouds out on the plains.

But the farewell was two days behind him now, and growing as pale as the memory of those people in whose company he had once touched death. They were out of his life and he was alone. But he was better off alone. After the long, hard ride he and the stallion were near to exhaustion, but the land rolled before him and at the end of it was the promise, and as he shielded his eyes from the sun's last rays he could finally see the toil of weeks converging into this supreme moment, when the horizon was close enough to touch.

Half a mile away a stateline patrol straggled the ground, their uniforms grey with dust but worshipped to bronze by the late sun. It had been a tough day and a long one for the handful of worn-out men who were following their sergeant back to base. They did not ask for much, just their food and their sleep and a few free hours to numb the dregs of evening. They never expected much either, for that would be the dream of a fool. But they all knew that Trooper Claythorne was a fool, for he was the man whose eye had been caught by the moving speck in the panorama of empty country, flecked with gold by the sun; he was the fool who had brought it to the sergeant's attention.

'Seems to be a lone rider down there aways, Sarge,' the trooper said, peering along his raised arm as though it was the sight of a rifle.

The sergeant thought the same way as the others; he wanted food, he wanted rest. He wanted to kill Trooper Claythorne. He followed the pointing finger with gritty eyes and gritted teeth. 'Well, soldier, and so there is.'

Claythorne waited, like a puppy panting to play. 'Don't you reckon he's worth investigating, Sarge?'

'No. I think not. He is of no consequence.'

The puppy wagged its tail and bounced a little. 'Might be he's a cowboy or a saddle tramp, but no one is safe all alone on these plains. I reckon we should take ourselves a look at him, Sarge,' Claythorne said, smiling a little smile. 'Don't you?'

A length of time had stretched since a boy had climbed a hill and found a horse; but time meant nothing when it took just seconds for the gods to cast their die. Cub knew there had always been too much at stake, even before he twisted round and saw men in tarnished uniforms coming for him like something from a nightmare.

He ground his heels into Wolf Wind's flanks. The horse reared to unseat him, but the boy had no time for gentle words. He wrenched the stallion's head and kicked him towards the sun, clashing cries with the animal's scream. A volley of small stones exploded from the hooves like a gun shot, but Cub could still hear stunned disbelief in the voice that had called out for him to stop. He lay flat across the stallion's mane with horse sweat in his eyes and poured Wolf Wind towards the sun's fire and its treacherous mirage; and for a while the ride could have been perpetual.

But nothing is perpetual; he knew that when the big horse began to falter. It was gradual, it was inescapable, and then everything was still. The distant land felt so close he could reach it within two heartbeats; it stretched so far away that it shrank and sank, and his mind grew black and the air was dead, and Cub was an apparition hanging in dust. He opened his throat for the sorcery that had compelled the stallion to bear a rider, but his heart was hollow and the words would not come. Although that did not matter, for the spirit of a long-haired man was with him now; the quiet man who had once carried a lonely child on his shoulders and taught him the language of horses. A breath of wind smoothed Cub's hair like the touch of a hand and left gentleness behind. And nothing mattered any longer.

The sergeant levelled his gelding with the palomino and made a grab for the tattered rope as if it might run again, but the spent stallion was heaving chunks of air and could barely stand. The boy sat motionless on its back. The soldier eased down in his saddle until his horse staggered sideways beneath the weight. 'What the hell were you thinking?' he said. 'Why did you run from us?'

It was the evening of a long, long day; the sergeant sat in uniformed authority on an army horse, and was being made to look stupid by a silent boy on a crazy stallion. Petulant with spite he gripped the runaway's shoulder and twisted him round, and when Cub turned towards him the man's arm fell useless to his side, halted by the trail of tears on the boy's face; and everything that spoke of the end of it.

...TO THE VERY END

TWENTY-SEVEN

OASIS CONFRONTED him like a firing squad before a condemned man. Nothing fundamental about the place had changed, although the summer had widened cracks in window frames and wooden walls, and its storms had dug holes in the road and torn shingles from roofs. And things had aged since the night when a bitten moon had ruled the sky and Cub had climbed the foothills beyond: weeds flourished through gaps in the sidewalk, and the listless town flag was faded and strangled by wind snarls – but the people leaning from half-open doorways still damned him; their eyes still prickled in the way of before. They were also prickling the lieutenant who was walking with him, and the man rubbed them from the back of his neck as he led the boy from the stagecoach to the dull brown building that was squatting like a mongrel dog halfway down the street.

There were three people standing outside the sheriff's office – a couple and a man on his own. As Lieutenant Clyne came nearer their intensity gripped his interest and lifted it away from the rest of the shabby town. The couple stood close together: a neatly dressed man in his late thirties, who lowered his eyes to the ground and turned away as if he would have preferred to be in some other place; and a pretty, and much younger, woman, who was clasping her partner's arm as though she needed his help to stay upright. She held him so tightly that all her emotion was centred on her hands; she must have been hurting him but, like hers, his face was safe and impassive.

And then there was this other man: gaunt to the point of emaciation, and tall, as if he had been stretched. He was dressed in a slouch of clothes, his arms folded like a cage across his bony chest and his hat pulled down so low that his nose and eyes had all but disappeared beneath its shelter. Only his mouth was exposed, open in a rictus grin. Clyne could hear him breathing; it was too hard and too fast, and it caused the soldier to falter because there was something incorrect about it. He sensed that the one who walked beside him had faltered also and his steps had become leaden. He put his hand on the boy's shoulder and it felt as though he was guiding him into danger.

That was how it had felt on the evening that the small patrol had returned to the border fort with the boy cleaving to the back of the sergeant's saddle; ragged and dirty, his body shaped by malnutrition but strung out on a residual energy that kept him on his feet in the lieutenant's poorly-lit office. The dregs of fight still boiled inside the black pits of his eyes, but he was hiding behind a barrier that was impossible to breach. The officer's exhaustive questioning had revealed no answers, and in exasperation he had flung out a comment about the stallion, the fine palomino that was already heading into mythical status inside the isolated fort, and for just a moment the boy had stood taller and a light had sparked in his eyes; after that he had simply hung his head and stared at the floor, until the lieutenant had finally bowed in defeat and called for a guard to take him to the lockup.

Clyne was remembering this as he and his companion reached the mongrel-dog building. The door opened as though summoned by their approach and the sheriff of Oasis stepped out, grey hair curling like a nimbus. He greeted the silent couple standing before his office with a nod and a touch of his hat brim, but stepped in front of the other man as though he thought to protect the soldier who had appeared before him on the gritty street, and the boy he had brought with him.

'Sheriff Russett?' The officer tapped a salute to his forehead. 'I am Lieutenant Lewis Clyne, sir.'

'Come right in, Lieutenant Clyne,' Russett said, and Clyne took the boy's arm as they approached. But they had to step around the skeletal man for he did not move to accommodate them.

People were watching from the buildings or clustering in small groups on the sidewalk, fanning away the sultry heat with inadequate hands. It did not feel normal. The entire population of Oasis seemed voracious, almost inhuman in their curiosity; feeding on the reaction of the gaunt man who was staring at the boy so intently that even dimmed his eyes were pale and as hard as stone. Chilling eyes they were, turning the boy's arm to ice under the lieutenant's hand.

The air inside the office was sluggish; two flies were weaving around in a desultory way, knocking into the windowpane in a drunken rhythm, and Clyne empathised with their craving to be set free. The sheriff raised the sash and followed the flies out into the street with his eyes, but when he tugged the window into place again the room seemed too quiet, as if something was holding its breath. The lieutenant gathered sheets of paper from the pouch at his belt, and they bunched in his fist as the skeletal man came to stand in the doorway, sucking out the air. The soldier took a deep breath before smoothing the paperwork out on the desk, but his hand was shaking and nothing felt right.

'Sheriff Russett, I believe you will find everything here to be in order,' he said. The handing over of a human being, like the severing of all hope – how could that be the correct order of anything? He pointed at the line of dots on the last sheet. 'I just require your signature, if you please.'

There was too much of a hush in the stifled room. The skin on Russett's face seemed slack with weariness and reluctance, and Clyne knew without a doubt that he too was uncomfortable with what was going on in his office.

'Are you feeling unwell, Lieutenant?' The sheriff was peering at him with some consternation, and the soldier wondered if indeed there might be something wrong with him. He knew what it felt like to be a fly battering a windowpane for escape; escape from the wraith-like boy at his side, the man at the door blocking all life from the room, the strange uneasy couple out in the street – nothing here was in its proper place.

The sweat was cold on his back, and he adjusted his uniform. 'I am quite well, thank you, Sheriff Russett. It has been a long journey, that is all.'

What lies we tell to hide what we really feel – a wrong journey is what it had been. He knew that now when it was too late.

They had left the fort and ridden twenty miles to reach the first stagecoach post, and it had been a strange and silent ride with the boy, followed by a relay of coaches through barely-glimpsed towns. A constant drudge of days, and nights passed in badly-aired boarding houses as his prisoner slept at the local jail. He had been unsettling company, the boy, and at times unnaturally still even when the going grew strenuous. Now and then the lieutenant had lost him; that was the only way he could describe the ease with which the boy distanced himself, as if there were moments in that tedious journey when his mind stretched away and his body went to find it. The soldier had to squint to make sure he was still there on the seat beside him. The boy became ethereal, although that might have been the effect of his hair; such cornfield lightness not being a familiar partner for sun-weathered skin and dark eyes. Striking looks: he was half angel, half damned; too otherworldly somehow to have been spawned in a town like this, that some blinkered fool had named Oasis. It was as distant from any fertile haven in the middle of a desert as it could get. In fact, this dry and crumbling place was a desert itself, the lieutenant had thought as he climbed from the final stagecoach and eased the twist in his back. No matter what the boy had done to merit the label of dangerous criminal, it seemed a crime on its own that the mettle of this unusual young man should be quenched in such a town; and yet he suspected that the boy's heart had already withered at his interception on the evening plain where the borders joined, and he had been dead inside ever since.

But the soldier's reply had seemed to satisfy the sheriff, or perhaps he was just as eager as Clyne to complete these soulless proceedings, for he signed swiftly on the line of dots and straightened up. The lieutenant gathered the documents and restored them to his pouch, duty fulfilled, nothing to keep him in this place any longer. But then he thought he heard a sigh; it hovered in the room for a moment and fell to the floor on an echo of hopelessness as Russett turned towards the door.

'Since for some reason Martha has decided to drop the assault charge,' he said, 'I guess I'll have to hand him over to you, Haine.'

The bony man stepped inside the office and the light he had been blocking flashed through the room with something like joy, but Lieutenant Clyne found himself looking at the boy with the sun-white hair. He saw a tremor running down his body faster than eyes could follow as Haine Madison grabbed him, and he faced the man with his head raised. They stared at each other for what seemed like the measure of three heartbeats, and then Madison slowly squeezed the boy's shoulder until the muscles in his scrawny arm were rigid. 'Don't you worry, Sheriff,' he said. 'He won't be the cause of any more trouble; I'll make sure of that.'

Crowding into the soldier's ears, the words echoed in his mind as the thin man and the boy walked together into the burning street, and he and the lawman were left standing by the desk. He had to clear his throat before he could speak.

'I was informed that the man there was the boy's father.'

Sheriff Russett made a sour mouth. 'In a way, he is the only father Cub ever had.'

'But no kin by blood?' Clyne's chest felt hollow.

Russett picked up the sheet of paper lying on his desk and held it in both hands, the better to absorb its official importance. The document was as dry as the look on his face. 'Haine Madison's wife never bore him a son to help run the farm, but he took himself off somewhere for a while about seven years ago, and when he returned he had Cub with him. He told anyone who was interested that the boy was his son, but he told them nothing more.'

'You said he did not have a son…'

'No. I said his wife never bore him a son.'

'I see.'

'I guess we all have our secrets, but whether Haine was lying to Martha or embarrassing her with the truth, that rundown farm is an uneasy place to live.'

'Blood kin or no, it seems that the boy was brought in to take on the work there.'

'He was, and he will again now that he is back; and if he does not wish to, then Madison will beat him. Blood kin or no.'

The sheriff opened a drawer in his desk and slid the piece of paper inside, and then the office was as clear as the lieutenant's conscience, until Russett glanced up at the young officer in his sweat-stained uniform. 'And I am truly sorry that the kid didn't make it.'

'He was described as dangerous, and the job to bring him back here fell to me.' Clyne stood tall by the window, dragging his military tunic smooth of creases. 'I am just doing my duty, Sheriff Russett.'

'The way I just do mine, soldier. But even so that can't turn it into a good thing.'

The lieutenant had had enough. The office behind his back sulked in the day's heat; it felt oppressive, and he searched the street outside for release. The desire to get as far away as he could from this cheerless town was compelling, but the half-open door did not seem wide enough to set him free. Through its gap he could see the neatly bearded man and the pretty young woman standing on the road where the sun was showing no mercy. The man was perfectly still but the woman had become animated, stretching up to speak to him, leaning around to peer down the street with one hand protecting her eyes. Clyne wondered why she had ventured out with her head bare when all the other women of the town were bonneted against the fierceness of the sun. The light was oiling off her coiled braid of hair like something alive and her body was thrumming with it, but the man who was shaking his head beside her seemed untouched by the iron heat. She stood as if frozen by his response, and then she saw the soldier in the doorway of the sheriff's office and reached out her hand to him as if he was her last resort; but as Clyne stepped out into glaring light it was the lean, dark man who spoke first, almost over her head.

'Lieutenant, my wife would like to know whether you accompanied the boy all the way back to Oasis.'

As though suddenly enervated by the heat the young woman dropped her hand and her shoulders sagged. She said nothing but her eyes were huge and swept the soldier's face; it made him uncomfortable to think that maybe she was trying to read his mind. He bent his head to break the connection, tapping the brim of his hat to her. 'Yes, ma'am, that is so.'

'Then did Cub manage to reach his destination?' Her

mouth tumbled over the words, and her husband folded his arm around her waist as if to anchor her to the ground.

Clyne saw the empty country and the frontier line that he did not think could be anyone's destination. He saw the clouds of that day and how in the cool breath of evening they had stretched thin towards darkness, the way the woman had stretched her arm to him. 'He was at the border, ma'am.'

The dark man looked up at the sky; his brows were drawn together, shadowing his face. 'Would you please tell us what happened?' he said, and the soldier read the question's echo from the woman's eyes; remarkable eyes, the darkest blue he had ever seen.

'The boy…'

'His name is Cub.' She spoke abruptly, and too loudly for the lazy afternoon. Her husband's hand tightened around her waist and she frowned as if in pain.

'Pardon me, ma'am. Cub was a matter of miles from the frontier when he drew the attention of one of my patrols. The men would have left him alone but he chose to run from them and they were obliged to give chase.'

'It seems that an ill-advised fate brought about his capture, Lucy.' The dark man tucked his wife closer and spoke with his mouth against her hair. She was crumpling as if all her energy had deserted her, and he seemed to be holding her up with that protective arm.

'But I believe in right, Daniel,' she said, 'and fate has nothing to do with it.'

'I suspect that he would have got clean away,' Lewis Clyne said, 'if his horse had not tired.'

And he knew that it was true, that it was right for the boy not to return to this town, that fate had only intervened because of the palomino. The couple looked at each other and something passed between them that excluded the soldier and everything else around them.

'So, it was that he found the horse.' The dark man said; the words were breathed and the soldier knew it was not a question. 'He told me that would happen, Lieutenant, but I did not believe him. There is some power about him and I mistook its strength for foolishness. But I was the fool; I know that now.' And he and his wife walked away together through the flying dust and past the weathered buildings, leaving the soldier standing on the sidewalk and wanting more; for the man's words had highlighted a need inside his soul and it was something to do with the horse.

The horse had quickly become legend among soldiers who were hungry for spirits and fire after so many months of bleak semi-existence inside the border fort. The rich tale had begun rolling on the evening that the patrol had staggered in with the boy shackled behind the leader's saddle. The story of the palomino, dusty to the colour of sand, wearied to a standstill with drool pooling from its mouth; the stallion that had fought them with the devil in its eye. Not one of them had got near enough to rope the animal, and it had grown in its frenzy as they all tried, until the boy on its back had deliberately thrown himself to the ground so that the horse should be free to run; whipped by the tattered halter rope and near to collapse.

And there was this other thing, this something else to tack on to the end of the tale, so that when he returned to the stockade after the days of his coming journey, the lieutenant might enlist its help to keep the legend alive a while longer. For towards the end of the slow and weary trek in the relay of stagecoaches, his mind dulled to the scream of tedium by the relentless panorama, the soldier's eye had been imprinted by a sudden glint of gold from the window, a splash of joy that transformed the barren land into something lush. Hungry for more he had shifted on the unforgiving seat, and it was then that he saw the stallion, galloping with the coach. It was too far away to be clear, and there was no sound as though even the wind was silent, but the horse was flying, mane and tail curved like wings and hooves skimming the low-lying dust. The lieutenant had lifted his hand and spread it against the light as if he might be able to clasp the gold and hold it for a while, but then the leather bench had creaked with astonishment as his companion leaned past him, and when the soldier turned he saw the dark eyes flaring; he saw the spark of gold in them like sudden life as the boy stared out to the palomino.

Lieutenant Clyne had opened his mouth to speak, but no words came for his throat was empty. It was the boy who spoke; for the first time since his detention under the setting sun, his confinement in the lockup at the fort, the interminable journey in one stagecoach after another with the soldier who was only doing his duty. And he said just the two words.

'Wolf Wind.'

TWENTY-EIGHT

HE HAD believed that he would never see the farm again; he had pushed it so far to the back of his mind that it was a stranger of a place, and he had to sit for a while on the old piebald mare in the heart of the yard until the familiar began its trick of reforming.

The dusk-hour had arrived; its soft shadow was touching the rough edges of the steading and easing its desolation, and the light was as sleepy as half-closed eyes. Leather protested as Madison dismounted the chestnut gelding. He threw reins at the boy. 'Deal with the animals,' he said. 'I don't need their work – not now that you are returned to us.'

Cub started to climb down from the mare, but the man reached out as if he could not wait and pulled him off-balance. He knew the pain of the ground before he struck it and the threat of the farmer standing above him, black in the evening shadow. 'You appear to have taken a tumble, boy,' the man said. 'I think you should be more careful from now on. Careful what you say and careful what you do.' Bent elbows and fists knuckled on his hips, he had the look of a loaded crossbow. 'Careful in your skin, boy. Do you hear what I'm saying?'

Cub got to his knees and he got to his feet, but he went flying to the rattle of stones when the man struck him. Madison crossed the yard and rested his foot on the boy's head, pushing his face into the mud and the animal dirt until he was choking, and Cub wondered if this was where it was going to end; pinned under Haine Madison's boot with the stink of muck in his nostrils. He wondered if he was glad that it was going to end, and when he felt himself passing out he closed his eyes and sank into the peace of it, until the man lifted his boot away and let the air back in. Cub gasped and coughed and scattered grit as he stood, and this time he was careful in his skin.

'Do you understand me now?' Madison said, and Cub nodded; but that was not good enough. The man shouted in his face, his breath heavy with the whisky stink he'd picked up in the town that day, waiting for the stagecoach to arrive. 'Do you hear me, you shit-swallowing bastard?'

'I hear you,' Cub said, but it was not easy to speak when sharp stones were cutting his throat. 'I understand.'

Madison flicked a thumb at the horses. 'Deal with the animals; set them loose in the corral then come straight back here. The chores have been building up since you left, and you're starting on them right now.'

That night the sky was black and the stars too embedded to shine. Darkness shimmered behind his eyes. He could only imagine outlines, but the familiar map was stronger in his mind now. It had solidified through the hours he had worked, unable to rest in the knowledge that Madison was standing there with the coil of whip tucked in his belt, just waiting for an excuse to flex it. The man was swaying behind him, lifting the bottle to his mouth and stumbling as he swallowed. He became easier to identify as the boy's eyes grew accustomed to the blackout, and he became easier to avoid as the alcohol made mischief with his brain. And further into the darkness, mending fences to the music of night insects but unable to see the nails or even the hammer, Cub left the farmer where he had rolled over on the ground and walked away into a deeper land, the place where the smallholding reached its own border and the hill began to curve in a gentle canter towards Oasis. The grind of Madison's snores faded behind him as Cub walked, until he was finally alone; staring blindly towards the foothills where it had all begun; reaching back in time to the moment when Daniel Ryker had reined in his buggy horse and set him free.

But the foothills seemed a lifetime away, and Cub was mortally tired. Weariness had slithered into his bones and formed an old man from the body of a boy. Behind him lay the cowboys hunting the palomino's mares and the lawman who had tried to do his duty; the cabin in the wood where Cochrane waited, and wagons full of people with secrets to keep. They were all used, all useless, and the farm was pulling him back like a hound's leash around his neck.

The barn was almost invisible in the dark but the smell of horse was comforting, and the straw was feather-soft for someone who had grown accustomed to sleeping on the earth. That was where he found rest; and that was where Sage found him too, early in the morning. Still so early that the yard was slumbering under her feet, and the sweet scent of new day had not yet been swamped by the stink of the farm.

She pushed through the gaping door and stared into haunting gloom, and everything was hanging in sorrow like a heavy curtain and flickering as if it could not quite reach the floor. She knew the boy had to be there; he would have been nowhere else now that he was back, unless her pa had already killed him and hidden his body under a clutch of scrub out on the lonely land. Unless he had escaped again into the night, or Sheriff Russett had told them wrong and it was a stranger that the soldier man had brought back to them on overland stagecoaches. Maybe some other forlorn soul had been dumped in the darkness, and it was not the boy huddling up to the wooden wall like he needed its straightness to bring him some ease – and she knew how that felt late at night, when her pa was a monster drowning in his drink outside the place where she slept.

She stood on the threshold of the barn and called, but his name barely emerged over her tongue for fear of it being picked up by others across the dawn-peaceful yard. She said it again, just a little louder. Cub. It echoed like thunder in her ears; it tasted like an awkward word that she had not used for a while, but she was sure that it belonged to the one lying on that scatter of straw, for he had lifted his head and turned towards the sound of it. And he said her name back to her. His voice croaked like he had gravel in his throat, but the way he said it was wonderful. Sage. The girl dipped her head to glory in it, and her hair rippled like a horse's mane. She took four short steps to cross the floor and kneeled by his side. Bed-rosy and shawled, she was robed for sleep, comforted by shadows that were concealing her state of undress from the boy who, weeks back, had held her to him as tightly as a lover as they rode the chestnut gelding into town.

Cub pushed himself away from the wall, his shoulders high as though his neck was hurting. His hands and his clothes were still caked with field mud, and a finger of dawn light was stroking his face, showing all the scratches and crusts of blood. The girl knew who had inflicted these hurts, and it was all her fault. But she had only meant to help when she took Cub to the doctor on the night of the beating, and she had willingly borne her pa's fury the next morning, even though her heart was leaking at the thought that she might never see the boy again.

'All the ills you have suffered are due to me and what I did,' she mourned, but even in the half-light she could see his frown.

'No, Sage.' He tried to smile, with his poor damaged face that had never been able to smile much before. 'It is because of what you did that good things happened.'

His voice was husk-dry but the words were mighty; they unshackled such a burden that she could feel her soul lift. And then everything she wanted to say to the boy who had been returned to her vanished like mist in the morning, because of the way he was looking at her. The hair tightened on the back of her neck; she could feel it crackling against her skin. His eyes were black, as though they had absorbed as much of her as they would hold. They gripped her so completely that for a while she could not move.

Cub's hand was resting on the spread of filthy straw between them, ingrained with dirt as it had always been. She reached out for it. His fingers crabbed as if to hold on to something only he could see, but they uncoiled one by one when her skin touched his. All his strength flowed into her body; all her warmth flowed into his. It was as though they had become one spirit.

And then he jerked up his head to hear the commotion coming from the yard, and a second after that the whole farm would have heard the wooden door of the barn slamming open, quaking like a jerk of sobs as it bounced off the wall. Sage knew without turning around that her pa was standing on the threshold, for she could see his unearthly reflection in the boy's eyes before that strange veil came down over them and kept the lustre away. And everything grew cold when their hands slid apart.

'There's something wrong happening here?' Madison pressed further into the barn and stumbled as he skidded on the loose straw. 'For sure this does not look right to me,' he said, and he came close enough for his daughter to catch the draggled stench of him, the grab of the liquor stink that always brought the vomit to the back of her throat.

She forced herself to face him, slowly though, for he was not welcome to her. His clothes were wrinkled and stained with mud and grass and his hair was wild with disarray, as though he had been dug up from a grave. When he pushed her backwards his hand left a sleek of cold wet ground on her nightgown. 'What are you doing here, girl, and undressed like that?' he said. 'What in hell?'

He shoved her again and she fell, sprawling with her face to the barn wall. She heard Cub stand up, she felt his hands helping her to her feet, she saw him collecting her shawl from the straw before the man grabbed his arm and tore him away. The boy skated across the ground but did not fall, straightening with discomfort until he was upright again, and there was a silence when he turned around. The air was stunned, crackling with flying straw and chips of husk, but everything else was still as Madison and the boy she had always been advised to call "brother" faced each other. And in the peculiarity of that hush she had time to see what was different about him, and it was that Cub had grown.

Yes, he was lean, his bones stark at the open top of his shirt and his cheeks hollow, but during the invisible weeks when he had been someplace else he had got taller. He stood over her, his yellow hair falling around his ears, and she had to look upwards to see his eyes. Sage grew slowly, she was never far from the ground, but even though he was not as lofty as her pa, Cub's shoulders were reaching higher. There was a slick of fear over Madison's face, for the boy was becoming a man; he had fierce young antlers and agility and he could dance out of danger. The girl felt a fizz of excitement because things had already changed and there was more change on the way.

Her pa's expression distorted as he stared at the boy, as if scoured with cunning, and from behind his back he unhooked that great leather serpent of a whip. Sage could swear he slept with it; that he made a pillow from its spiral at night and warmed his wasted body in its coils, all but the frozen heart of him. That devil's tail had tasted blood but was always hungry for more, and the girl knew from the way he stood, clawed like tree roots, that Cub feared the thing. Hell, she feared it too, but still she opened her mouth for her pa's attention to fall on her and not on the boy.

'I came here to afford my brother some welcome, Pa, now that he has been brought back to us.'

'You would welcome an animal? For that's what he is; a rat in a rat hole.'

The man spat on the bitty ground behind him, and then he started laughing. His teeth were yellow and his daughter could almost see the green stink of his breath choking out between them. 'You keep your distance from him, girl,' he said. 'Because for sure this animal will turn on you the way he's turned on the rest of us.'

She said nothing back to him. There was little point when he could not hear much above his own mumblings, like he was conversing with the whisky-slathered part of his brain.

Madison pushed Cub out into the yard where the day was fledging and it was time to work again, and the girl followed from the barn. Over beyond the house and Martha's meagre garden, that with its gasp of greenery and wizened produce was a lot of effort for not much effect, Sage could hear her trees singing; the ones she looked for out on the hill slopes in that pinch of time when there was no one else around and she was in her solitude. Her trees were speckled with little birds and they were singing about freedom as Cub walked out to the fields; as the girl stood shivering under the thin shawl that he had lifted away from the muck on the barn floor, and offered to her as though it was a gift.

TWENTY-NINE

CUB WELCOMED the protection of night. He slept when he could but nothing was easy, for even when he had been felled by exhaustion sleep was still elusive, like something mischievous laughing from the blackened corners of the barn. He might sink for an hour or so, more if he was lucky, and that brought oblivion for a while; but he was awake long before dawn, listening to yard sounds through the wooden walls, smelling the pungent straw that prickled ridges in his skin, tasting the bile of hunger as it rose to the back of his throat.

He did not move. If he moved, the rope would grip his wrists and crunch his bones; if he moved, he would remember how tightly the farmer had knotted him to the restraining ring. And time stopped until Madison stood in the doorway of the barn, curdling the dawn's light; the early breeze dragging in the feral smell of him as he kicked his way across the straw, clumsy with the knots, hawking balls of spittle to the walls like shots of slime that narrowly missed the shackled boy with rope burns at his wrists.

Those first days had jerked like the persistent tug of a leash, and then they had pulled into a smooth passing of hours that jumped each other's backs, without end. Nothing that he had lived through before had felt so hopeless. It was as though the place had despaired in his absence: the fields had become a tangle of crops allowed to die, the repairs had been neglected and the animals left unfed. He avoided their hungry eyes in case he should glimpse his own wretchedness from their reflection.

The weather deviated from good to poor and back again. Rainfall was sporadic and sudden; water assaulted him like so many knife thrusts, but it was soothing after the heat. The showers were swift and the sun followed, just as the nights followed the days, rising like cool ghosts from the shelter of the hills.

But the evenings were the best, for only after the long day's work did Madison give him leave to drink from the yard pump and rinse the dross from his body in its sparse water. In the evenings Martha Madison scattered a tin plate with food, that was only ever enough to make him feel that all might be well again, before captivity sucked him back into the barn.

And then one night there were no more ropes to hold him. One night, when the boy had grown thinner than the day he had returned, his body strung tighter with muscle and his hair longer against his neck, Madison had drawn the beam over the stable door but left the trussing ring bare.

Cub woke suddenly as if he had fallen, sweat oiling his skin. The night was as thick as tar, but he was still inside the dream of angry people. They slithered towards him in the way that dreams shift, as though nothing happened but everything was happening; they lifted high their sticks and hammers and branches from trees until the sky was black with the menace that had woken him to the barn. He lay on the ground and wondered why his breathing was soft and why his heart was rested, because he could still see the horror of the dream when everything else was so hidden, like creatures of nightmare under the cloak of complete darkness. Although it was not quite so complete, the darkness, because there was somebody waiting by the open door, a silhouette etched against the sky, a long stick raised to strike.

They could not move, either of them: the boy by the wall and the girl at the threshold, her nightgown pleating in the breeze. She forced a sound from the back of her throat to show Cub that she was no apparition sliding into his sleep. He spoke her name as if it was a question. He was asking so much just by saying her name. She found that she still had it in her hand, the heavy piece of wood she had taken from its supports before releasing the door, and when she dropped it the clatter was like a rebuke, as though the bar was chiding her for its disturbance. The breeze tugged her nightgown again and she shivered as if from cold. But it wasn't that at all; it was because she was not sure.

'What is it?' Cub said, and the sharp words seemed to attack her from all corners of the barn. The girl could hear the straw snapping as he pulled himself to his feet, and in the gloom his dark shape stood like something fearful by the wall. She muffled the night sounds as she dragged the door back into its hole, but the quiet was claustrophobic and there was nothing right about it.

'What are you doing here, Sage?' He was asking the question that she was asking herself, even though she had no answer. But his voice had chased away the brooding silence, and it made the girl feel she was not on her own in this enclosed place; that perhaps she even had a right to be there. She moved nearer until she could hear him breathing. She drew comfort from it, but Cub took a step away. 'What has happened?'

There were thorns in his voice, and suspicion; Sage stood still and raised her hands as if to pacify, but it was too dark for him to notice the gesture. 'Nothing has happened; I can't sleep, is all. I had to see you, Cub,' she said, leaning towards his outline, and her skin crawled as if there was some unearthly creature enclosed with them;

slinking in the corner shadows, or hiding on the platform above that sometimes creaked with the gusts if there was a wind out in the yard. But the barn this night was ghostly quiet; it started up a shivering that tricked a mew of fear from her throat, and the floor rustled as he came towards her.

He took her arms. Sage felt as if he was holding her upright, and that she would never fall again because of it. He was staring into her face as though he knew what she was thinking despite the obliterating darkness.

'It's not easy to see anything at night,' he said quietly, but there was still that sharpness at the back of his voice, and it made the girl crazy for a while.

'I am angry with the soldier who brought you back. I want to find a way to help you; I want to put things right. But I don't know…I can't think…'

Her pulse raced; she was shaking. Her cheeks were wet and she was not sure how that had happened. Perhaps someone had been crying. It couldn't have been her; after all those years as the daughter of Haine Madison she believed that she had lost the wherewithal to cry. Even so, she was glad that Cub couldn't see the tears.

'You have already helped me, Sage,' he said. 'You took me to the doctor's house.' His voice had changed, as if it was easing over a blockage in his throat, but if his face had changed also he was hiding it behind the dark. 'You took me there that night so that I might find freedom on the other side of a hill.'

His words were strong, but behind them there was desolation. It made her think of a broken wall that nobody could be bothered to rebuild, a crumble of weed-kissed stones to be stepped on or kicked aside. But then she thought of how freedom might feel. Maybe it was like riding through the rain on a summer's day, or jumping into a void so deep that the ground below simply disappeared. It was the sound of birds flying with nothing beneath them but air and nothing above but the sun. Surely no image of freedom could be more beautiful than that.

'Will you tell me about it?' she said, but he was so quiet that she wondered if he was going to answer, or even if he could.

Then Cub reached for her hand and pulled her down to sit with him, their backs to the wall. He rubbed the ring on her little finger, as though he needed the touch of silver to help him speak of everything that had happened since the night of the solemn moon, when they had followed the track from the valley to the town. When it had still been dark enough for lamps to be lighted, and for the tending of wounds that her pa had made, with that brutality he always found in the whisky bottle. That was the night she had left the boy huddled on Dr Ryker's couch, returning alone to the farm to wait for the dawn to change their lives; and although it had been too early for the cock to crow or for her pa to wake to a new fury, Cub's future had already begun.

And here he was now, pulling pictures of that future from his mind like a conjuror and lighting a fire behind them, so that even in the pitch-dark of the barn Sage could see everything that had arisen from that night; everything she had made possible.

When the minutes had passed and he had finished his tale, she began to float back from the air to the pressure of grit beneath the straw and the warmth of his body beside hers. It felt good and it felt right, even though in her guilt and her greed she sometimes wished that the night ride into Oasis had never happened. She had missed his dark eyes and his wild hair, the width of his shoulders and the strength in his hands. She had missed watching him from a hidden place beside the house as he stripped to the edge of decency at the day's end, and the sinuous pleasure he took in rinsing his body under the pump.

A stronger wind had brewed up outside the barn as if the air itself had been excited by Cub's story; it urged away the silence that might have fallen as they sat with their hands clasped together. The girl could find nothing to say; the pictures that Cub had drawn were in her head now, whipped up to adventure, almost dreamlike, and each picture was touched with the gold of the palomino that he had guided with a rough rope halter. It seemed to her that they had both flown through the sky like birds, and that for sure and certain this was what it meant to be free.

'The ranch man wanted me to give the horse a name,' the boy said, his voice clearing holes in the darkness and bringing in the shine. 'I saw fire and rain and the sound of thunder. I saw everything wild; and that was Wolf Wind,' he said, and then he was quiet again, listening to the memory of a stallion's scream as he and the girl settled one with the other, putting the night aside. And Sage gathered Cub's words to a safe place at the back of her mind until it seemed they were united in that way also; as if by sharing his tale he had spread out the story of his life, filling her with more of himself than she had ever known.

The weeks away had altered him, he was a different Cub; the one from before would never have been with her like this, sitting so close that she could almost feel the pulsing of his blood. And she was a different Sage, for she knew the question even before he asked it.

There was a rustle of straw as Cub got to his feet; another as he pulled her up to stand before him. He was very still, and then he put his arms around her, just as he had on the night they had ridden the chestnut to Oasis. She had felt his heat and the need in him then; she felt it again now as she held him; their bodies melding in the dark as though they were already joined. But she could not speak. She wanted his question again; to hear that need in his voice as he asked it. The need for her to lie down with him, for as long as possible; for at least until the dawn.

The second asking was gentle; the question hung in the air like a soft echo. And when she raised her head to give him her answer, he lifted it away with his kiss.

THIRTY

THE DAYS passed slowly, heavy with work and the presence of Haine Madison. Cub was never alone when the man stood waiting for him to falter, pulling coils of leather through his fingers until the boy was conscious of nothing but the movement as he toiled and his back protested, as his arms crabbed and his head filled with the ache of the sun. But he persevered, and Madison swished leather on the ground behind him and had no cause to come any closer. And eventually, as Cub expected, his diligence began to stumble and he appeared later at the periphery of the boy's sight, and departed earlier to take his ease, along with what might be left in the bottle. But still Cub worked as though the man was standing over him, as though the smell of the man was forcing him through the day to get just those few steps ahead to where the air was fresher, and he could see the distant hills shimmering with freedom in the heat. But they did not seem so far away now that he had discovered this new life.

Each night when the wind was kind and the morning still so far away that it might never happen, Sage came to pass the dark hours with him in the barn, their one shadow as rich and deep as a stormy sky. Their bodies grew sleek with the pleasures of love, and after the love she left him sleeping naked in the place he had chosen for their bed, as though the hard ground was the softest mattress. The nightmares had gone, for it was their time together that Cub dreamed of now, until dawn woke him to the empty space where Sage had been lying. Everything else: the backbreaking work, the burn of the sun and the flailing rain, the hatred of the whip that Madison wrapped in his hand like a test of his own strength; all of that was worth enduring when the day finished on such a note.

But nothing is static and everything can change, even over the course of one night. One empty night when Sage did not come to the barn to join with him on a bed of straw, and the hours dragged past so slowly that time seemed to hang suspended from the dusty rafters, just as he imagined death might feel. The next day ached as though it was full of complaint, and the sun creaked across the sky like an old man and fell behind devil clouds that had boiled into a solid mass. The rain started, and that was a relief, because each drop took its own time and the drops that followed meant that the day was passing, although all it did was lead into another cold and endless night, pool-deep with memories. Cub dived there and swam until he was exhausted; until it was gruelling to ride the hills again on the back of the stallion towards futile dreams, and the return to captivity in a decaying farmyard was brutal.

He counted seven nights before sleep became easier again. The place where he had lain with Sage grew cold and the threads of hair that she had left behind, like a promise to return, disappeared into the scrambled dust of the floor. When the eighth night came the darkness was as hollow as before, and the other life had vanished as if it had been mere fabrication.

The external sounds of that night were a nocturnal language, like the cough of a corralled horse or the bark of a fox – but when the turbulence ruptured his sleep he recognised the voices that were hitting the barn wall as though trying to beat their way inside.

Cub was on his feet before he was fully awake. He could hear the three of them in the yard, the rowdiness knocked from one to the other like physical pain – Madison and Martha battling, Sage fighting the onslaught of words. He found himself by the door with his hands flat on the boards, as if all it needed was one push to get out there to protect the girl. He kicked the restriction in front of him; it bent away moaning and sprang back puffing wood dust in his face, and all sound beyond the barn fell away with an abruptness that dulled his ears. Cub waited, his arms still raised to the door, floating in the lull as though he had been lifted from the ground. There was a scuffling; two quick beats came from the packed earth, and when the wood rattled against his hands he stepped back from the warning into the belly of the barn.

The door swung open to blackness and everything was invisible in the sudden depth of it, but then his sight was swayed by the girl's pale nightgown, her hair pulled tight in the mother's grip. Madison stood before him, as black as the devil; he drove inside the pitiful building, scattering the space until it seemed to shrink back in fear, grabbing Cub's arm and throwing him out into the yard. The boy tripped and fell, and when he tried to stand the man was already there with a boot raised to kick him across the dirt, as though he was animal feed trussed up in a sack.

Cub let himself go limp; rolling easily from Madison's attack until he found a space to get to his feet. The man lunged but the boy retreated; Madison lost his footing and fell in the dust and the yard rocked with impact, but when he stood again the leather was coiled in his fist, looking like a collection of bracelets in the half light. Cub lowered his head at the sight of it; he saw Sage struggling; he heard her scream. She wrenched away from her mother and leaped forward, her gown crowding her body and taking on its own life; and her father was unprepared. She grabbed the whip with both hands and threw it across the yard, and it hissed like a snake and collapsed in the scum of the shallow pond.

Madison held Sage's arms to her sides as if her bones might bend, but she raised her head and shouted in his face, her breath escaping as though from punctured lungs; and when Madison hurled his daughter away she skidded across the ground and lay still. Cub jumped for the man's face, but he had not heard Martha closing in on her quiet feet. She wrenched him to his knees with her fists in his scalp and her screams shocking his ears. When she let go he tried to crawl towards the fallen girl, but Madison was crouching like an animal before him, the smell of his anger as sharp as his outline.

Spittle sprayed the yard as the man turned towards his wife. 'Woman, what stinking habits have you been teaching your daughter?'

Martha stepped away from the blackness in his face. 'Not me; that devil is yours! Your son, in my home. You have never allowed me to forget.'

'Crazy mare, the fault is yours alone. If you had borne me a son I would not have had to go elsewhere to make one.'

The woman covered her ears; her eyes glittered as she stared at him. 'And the one that you sired is just as filthy as you.'

Madison gave a roar; he jerked upright with a speed that swallowed all other sound. And then there was silence, so sudden that reality seemed to take a step back from the cowering woman, the fleshless man, the boy who was coming to his feet. The girl who was already standing, pale nightgown flapping behind her as she ran towards Madison, punching his chest with puny fists that he grabbed as though they were just drifts of air.

'That you can lie with your own brother? You shame me, girl. You shame her,' he nodded at Martha but his eyes still blazed into Sage's face as he shook her, almost lifting her from the ground.

Her long hair soared and plummeted; it sang in Cub's

ears like the wind skimming through a stallion's mane. It moved with its own soul, in the same way as his mother's hair, that when he was a child he believed to be spun from sunlight for the colour of it. His mother had long golden hair and silver in her eyes; and she had borne a dark-eyed boy.

Unbidden, a memory slipped through the blockage in his mind. A horse had thrown him; it was too big and he was too young, and the fall had opened a cut on his forehead that had wept into his eyes, like the tears that he never cried. And from somewhere his mother had found pity for him, and as she staunched the flow she spoke to him of the Indian who had lingered one summer long enough to plant the boy's seed in her belly. The Indian who had remained as the child began to grow, but for whom there was to be no forever. And here was Madison, with his skull's head and his eyes like a cloudy sky, spouting into his daughter's face all the lies that she and the boy had been told to believe were the truth.

Cub stood steady; the stony ground rose and fell under his feet, but the memory was holding him upright. 'I am not your son,' he said, and the man turned at his voice and rumbled in his throat with something that might have been a laugh.

'That is right. You are no longer my son.'

'I am another man's son, Haine Madison,' Cub said, savaging the name. 'And my mother never knew you.'

Madison looked down at him, knocked back by the power in his dark eyes. It gave the man pause; but only for a moment. He released his daughter too swiftly for her to balance on the earth; too swiftly he reached out and gripped the boy's arm, twisting it behind his back. He dragged Cub towards the barn, where the door was still knocking senselessly to and fro in the raw throat of wind, and with strength in anger he pushed him inside. 'What I have in store for you,' he said, 'can wait until day.'

Cub rattled across the shreds of straw and knocked into the wall where the darkness was complete, but he turned too late to retaliate, hearing only the board being thrust into place in its supports and tasting the dust that had arisen like grit on his tongue.

The scuffling continued outside, but no words were spoken to paint its image, and then the sounds reduced as they retreated towards the house and doors were slammed against the night. But still Cub stood by the darkness of the barn wall and listened, until all there was to hear came whistling in through slits in the wood, telling him of the empty yard and the gradual stretch of night as the minutes passed.

He was surrounded by stillness, as vibrant as a held breath, as though there was someone else in the barn with him, turning him towards the door so that he could see the feeble light that surrounded it like something drawn with a grey pencil. The boy thought about the bar that was locking him in and he stared until his eyes burned, watching the blackness of the door and its frame of tarnished light. He sent his mind out until he was standing in the yard, facing the roughness of the wooden wall, pinpointing the door and the heavy beam that crossed it, resting on the metal supports like an arm in a sling. A bar suspended by hooks. A bar that rattled when the wind was strong, as if eager to lift and be gone.

Cub tried to slide his fingers into the slit of subdued light, but the gap was too narrow. He sank to the invisible floor and searched around with his hands flat, but all his mind could read from the feel of it were fragments of earth and the scratch of straw. He explored the walls, rubbing his hands through coarseness until the sounds that echoed back to him roared like rain falling in the yard, but when he paused to listen there was nothing but silence out there, holding its breath and waiting, just like the someone else that was trapped inside with him. He went from wall to wall, high and low, and his hand caught on sharpness in the wood. He felt the stab of splinters and the sting of blood starting; little wounds from the broken shard that he gripped and ripped from the wall until it was a dagger in his hand.

The night was waning; encroaching dawn shone a paler light around the ill-fitting door, and it meant that time was leaking away. Cub wedged the splinter under the shadow of the bar and levered it up with both his hands and all his strength. The heavy constraint fought the flimsy slice of wood but it lifted an inch. It lifted two inches and Cub's muscles locked, but he could not hold it. The splinter snapped and he skidded backwards across the ground; threshing the straw with his hands, fishing for the piece of wood in the blindness of the barn. It had not fallen far. Stunted from the break the segment was thicker now and stronger. He rammed it underneath the bar, pushing it up until his back was taut with pain. The wood disintegrated from the pressure, turning to chips in his hand, but he could hear the bar toppling from the hooks on the other side of the wall. It hit the yard with a defeated ring, and there was nothing left to hold him prisoner.

The door swung outwards with an elderly creak and the dregs of night rushed into his face, as cold as hatred. He crouched to halve his height and ran across the yard, reaching the wooden wall too soon, grabbing the porch post to check his speed. He waited for discovery, but there were no sounds prickling the air. There was no one to stop him slithering into the shadows at the back of the house, where Sage's casement was partly lifted and the age-faded flowers on the drapes shook their heads as if warning him of what he might find inside. He heaved the window higher and peered through slants of darkness into a room that was as silent as a held breath.

It was small and severe, like a cage, with an armless wooden chair against one wall and a simple chest against another. Sage lay with her back to him, slumped in a foetus curl on top of her narrow mattress, and she did not respond when Cub murmured her name. He climbed over the sill and stood with his muscles tensed, and Sage dreamed that somebody had come into her room. She woke to the shock of it. He saw her mouth open before she turned towards him and he knew that she was afraid; he covered the cry with his hand so that it was as muted as a whisper. She recognised him in the half-light. She sighed; there was something limitless in the sound she made, as though now that he was here the next step could not be far away. Cub breathed her name again – Sage. It tasted like fresh air on his tongue.

'I am leaving,' he said, 'and you are coming with me.' But she shook her head with a slight movement that was as dismissive as a slap.

'I cannot come with you,' she said, 'because my pa will not allow it.' And when Cub saw the rope that trussed her arms to her legs he felt a rage as fierce as fire.

He attacked the knots like a starving animal tearing at meat and Sage whimpered because she did not recognise the boy she had taken as her gentle lover. He heard it as a sound of pain and was ashamed. He grabbed her hands, his thumb rubbing the little silver ring, and soon his warmth had stopped her shaking.

'I don't know what to do.' His words fell to nothing as though a sink hole had opened in front of him.

'You have to get away from here,' Sage said, her voice cracking with the need for quiet.

'I will not go without you.' His fingers gnawed again at the knots around her wrists until she pulled away.

'You must, Cub; but when the sun comes up I shall follow you. For I am a sinner in the eyes of my kin. I am unclean, and no longer welcome here.'

'And I am to blame.' He reared up and spat the words; it was as though a trap had opened and set a demon free.

Sage tried to calm him with her hobbled hands. Her fingers stretched out to the darkness, but he was too far away and she couldn't reach.

'When he brought you to our farm all those years ago, Pa told me I should know you as my brother.' She saw the boy flinch, as though he had been stung. 'But we share no kinship, and you are blameless. We are both blameless for loving each other.'

She knew her tears were coming before his face blurred; they pushed up from the place that still longed for good things to happen, much as it had when she was a child and believed in magic. Her hair fell across her mouth as if to smother her; Cub moved it aside and touched her lips. 'It was the Indian who sired me, Sage,' he said, seeing only the long-haired man, his brows painted with strange designs. 'There is no alikeness between your pa and me, and there is no shame in what you and I have done.'

'No shame,' she whispered; a soft echo of his words that felt like something pure had crept into the mean little room with them. Outside the rain had started to fall; it sounded like a hundred running feet and the air from the open window was wholesome, but Cub's skin had been rubbed raw by the passing of time.

'Sage, I have to leave,' he said.

'But first you must listen to me.' She couldn't read his eyes, black in the pre-dawn haze. 'My pa talks when he drinks, and what he says he would know better to keep to himself sober. Last night he was sucking the bottle like he needed to reach its soul.' Last night her pa had been outside her window, ready to catch her as she climbed over the sill on her way to the barn after a week of abstinence. He had thrown her against the side of the house so hard that even the animals in the corral were jumping, and she had learned that good cannot last and bad will go on forever if no one stands up to it. 'Last night he was talking about Wolf Wind.'

Cub started backwards as if he had been struck. 'Tell me what he said.' His voice seemed to come from a stranger's throat, as though he had split into two people. The girl searched, but his eyes were impenetrable and she did not know where he had gone.

'A golden horse was seen in the hills on the day the soldier brought you in,' she said. 'The people were excited, they spread stories around the town and Pa listened to them.' She fell silent, and for a while the rainfall was loud, and urgent. Water sprayed in through the window and fell on the boy's back like a warning.

'Sage, tell me what he said.'

Her lover was standing by her bed, and she hesitated before she spoke. She knew that as soon as she told him what her pa had said, something would be unleashed that could not be controlled. 'He's already been out once to search for the stallion, Cub, and the next time he is going with a rifle.'

Rain bombarded the farmyard and invaded the small room. It was so cold that it burned the girl's skin, and she was afraid. It was so sharp that it pricked the back of the boy's head and he felt anger, fiercer than any he had felt before.

He glanced at the nudge of light that was coming in through the window and saw the danger it was bringing. 'You must get yourself to the Rykers' house as soon as Madison frees these ropes.'

'Are you heading there now?' she said. 'Will you wait for me there?'

Cub hesitated. 'The doctor's wife will want to take care of you.'

'Pa is throwing me out of my home and Ma is not standing in his path to stop it, but the doctor's wife will take care of me.' Something spiky had crawled into her voice. 'My heart is closed to my true kin, Cub.'

He cupped her face in his hands and bent down to kiss

her, straightening up too quickly to hear the words she whispered. She turned her head to watch him leave but the boy had already gone, and the flowered drapes were settling back into place behind him.

THIRTY-ONE

OASIS WAS deserted that early in the morning, and desolate in the rain. The small trees in the Rykers' garden bent in sorrow and puddles rejected Cub's feet, for his thin-soled boots spread puddles of their own. The bell-pull was still in hiding behind bushes to the side of the door although his fingers were too numb to feel it. He thought of the first time he had heard the bell chiming on the night that Sage had brought him here, sitting tight behind her on the gelding's back. He thought of the Sage he had had to abandon, rope-trussed on her bed, and in the fire of anger he forgot the chill of his own wet skin.

The darkened window above the door rolled up at his summons and the woman looked down on him, just as she had before.

'Mrs Ryker…'

'Cub!' She almost shouted his name, holding a hand over her mouth a second too late to stop the shrillness. She deserted the window abruptly and he was alone under the weeping sky, then the door opened to the flickering light in Daniel Ryker's hand.

The man was tousle-haired from the break in his sleep, but his eyes were quick. 'Get yourself inside,' he said, and stepped back to where the lamplight was as pale as butter and as soft as slumber. Cub wanted to sink beneath its gentle stutter. He stood blinking as the water dripped in cold splashes from his hair; he barely felt Lucy Ryker's hand cuffing his wrist.

'You must be chilled to the bone. Come with me, I will fetch you a towel,' she said, and he followed her into the wood-panelled room where the piquant scents of leather and bitter ointment had become familiar. The doctor busied himself with setting the lamp on a small round table as the young woman brought the towel; and then she stepped away, clutching the neck of her gown as though seeking its protection.

'Has there been some trouble?' Daniel said, and the word was mountainous. Cub staggered beneath its weight, and when Ryker took his arm he gave himself up to the man's strength and the edge of the leather couch.

Lucy lifted the towel from his hands and pressed it over his head and his body until the stiffness had receded and the shivering had stopped. But still she pressed, as though she didn't want to set him free.

Her husband turned the desk chair to face the room, and sat with his fists on his knees as if he was about to force himself forwards. Lamplight wavered beside him like a strange shadow. 'You have come here for a reason,' he said. 'And if it is our assistance you need then we shall gladly give it, but first tell us why.'

The flame flickered, settled, chased away the darkness. It was difficult to speak in this place where he had once tasted independence, but staring into the light seemed to help. 'It is as it was before,' Cub said, unaware that Lucy was peering through the open door with tension lifting her shoulders, as though she was looking for an excuse to escape; as though it hurt her to be in the same room as the boy.

'Has anything happened?' Daniel's question was startling. Just three words, but they encompassed the mass of dark days that had squeezed the rundown farm in the valley back into Cub's hard, dry existence, and everything he had achieved on the plains, across the hills and through the lowlands had been for nothing.

'I was in debt to Madison for the time that I was away,' the boy said, 'and he has been working me to pay it off.'

Lucy's head jerked as if she was trying to avoid the words.

'And now there is Sage.' Cub thought of the girl lying hobbled like a calf, and he shivered inside his damp clothes.

Daniel Ryker straightened a little. 'Now there is Sage?'

'They are throwing her out of her home.' Cub saw Madison knotting ropes around his daughter's arms, and Martha watching as he did so.

'But she is barely more than a child. Why on earth would her parents do such a thing?' Lucy had stepped towards her husband's chair, so suddenly that her heavy braid swung away as if to escape her anger.

Cub could not meet her eyes. 'Because Sage is with me now.'

'With you? I do not understand…'

'We are lovers, Mrs Ryker.'

The whole room was silent, apart from the sigh of the lamp and the welter of rain hitting the window, and then a volley of creaks attacked the ceiling as though ghosts were dancing in the upstairs room. Lucy held the towel to her face as she crossed to the door, nearly falling in her desperation to get away. Her footsteps clipped up the staircase before Cub could speak again.

'Things are changing,' he said. 'And they cannot be changed back.'

Daniel Ryker rose from his chair and lifted the lamp, glancing upwards as if searching for his wife. 'Come this way, Cub,' he said, stepping from the room without waiting so that the darkness swallowed the echo of light, and the boy followed him quickly, because there was not much time left.

Encroaching dawn was pearly-grey through the glass in the house door, and when the dark man turned his head its shine played along the edges of his profile and bared the age lines crossing his forehead. 'Lucy is right, for Sage is too young to be cast out on her own.' He stood still then, and faced the boy. 'And we have been led to believe that she is your sister.'

Cub shook his head. 'Sage would only be my sister if Haine Madison had sired me.'

'But hadn't he?'

'I have no sister, Dr Ryker. And Sage has no brother.'

Daniel was quiet for a moment, and then he dropped his stare and sighed to a guttering of flame. 'When lies are conjured for the sake of appearance, that's when problems arise.'

As if she had been waiting for a signal, Lucy appeared at the top of the stairs. She hovered there for a while, as though deciding whether to descend. Maybe she would have preferred to stay with the ghosts, for her eyes were downcast, and Cub could not read her thoughts. Although he noticed the tear-glisten on her cheek before she could slap it away.

'Mrs Ryker, I have upset you and I am sorry,' he said, because she looked wretched, and he thought he knew the reason why. 'But I swear that Sage is not my sister.'

Lucy came to the bottom tread with a finger to her lips. 'Hush now, Cub,' she said, and then she tilted her head away, as if she was still too agitated to look at him. 'If that is what you tell us, then that is what we must believe.'

'After she has gone from that place I told her to come to you.' He studied the woman's face. 'She has nowhere else to go, Mrs Ryker.'

She nodded, standing beside her husband but still so far away. 'Then this is the right home for her. Have no fear, Cub; we shall take care of your girl.' There was regret in her voice, and something deeper in the look she gave the boy, but he was intent on the brightening daylight, and missed it.

'I found a horse, the time before,' he said. 'I broke a stallion to bear a rider. He followed the stagecoach when the soldier brought me back, and now I must find him again, before Madison does.'

Ryker put his arm around his wife's shoulders, and after a moment she turned her head and smiled up at him with her mouth. 'I have heard the tale of a palomino that has been seen on the hills,' the man said. 'I had thought to dismiss it as mere rumour, but you tell me he belongs to you, Cub?'

'He belongs to nobody, but he allows me to ride him.'

'I feel you have a wealth of stories that would be rich in the telling,' the doctor said. 'But now is not the time.'

Not with the sky lightening more for every passing minute, and Haine Madison heaving his bones from the wormhole of his bed to find the barn empty of all but worn straw and dust motes.

'Dr Ryker, will you help me to track the stallion?'

'Just wait a minute.' Lucy came towards him, and he braced himself. Shapes shifted through the mist of fatigue, and for a moment he saw Madison bearing down on him with one hand on his whip instead of the slight figure of the doctor's wife with her braided hair. 'Wait a while, Cub. Surely you are not talking of going away again?'

'He cannot find me here.'

'I am aware of that. But remember the consequences before you take a step you might end up regretting.'

Cub stared at the flame in the doctor's lamp as if that might help to incinerate his memory of the consequences. 'Mrs Ryker,' he said. 'It is the only step I can take.'

Lucy held up her hands and let them drop to her sides. 'Daniel and I were by the sheriff's office on the day that the lieutenant brought you back.'

'I know.' He'd seen them there, watching as he was herded through the town like an animal.

'Should we also be present at your recapture?'

'There will be no recapture.'

She leaned forward with her hands raised and pushed him with such force that he slid across the floorboards in his wet boots and almost fell. 'How dare you, Cub. You cannot say that. You cannot…'

His back was against the wall; its firmness felt like the only thing holding him up until the doctor clutched his arm and added his own strength. And then Daniel turned to his wife and spoke softly, but with grit in his voice. 'Tell the boy what you would do if you were in his skin, Lucy. But choose wisely, as if your own life depended on it.'

She stared at her husband's eyes, white-rimmed in the dark corridor, and then she turned her head and her chin quivered. She bit down on her lip to still it. 'Oh, just go and find the horse. Send the boy on his way, Daniel, and put an end to it.' The insecure lamplight caught wetness in the corner of her eye before she walked away to the kitchen and slammed the door.

Time had passed; the night was disappearing like dregs of smoke from the outlines of buildings across the street. The moon was an apparition hanging lower in the sky and as it grew weaker the threat of discovery strengthened. The doctor left to change his clothes, and as soon as he was dressed he went into the yard to harness the pony to the buggy. Cub held aside a clutch of drapes at the front room window and watched the danger grow into a new day. He hadn't heard the door opening, but saw Lucy's reflection in the glass before her footsteps crossed the floor. She bowed her head when he turned towards her, so that her braid followed a spiral of its own momentum. It took her a while to speak.

'There is something inside telling me that nothing good will come of this,' she said, and then she looked up. 'And I am so afraid for you.'

He did not reply; he had nothing to say.

'I should like to believe that there is another way,' she said, and her eyes were as wide as a child's in the dull room. 'But that is not so, is it, Cub?'

'There is no other way, Mrs Ryker.'

She came closer, too quickly; her perfume filled his head. She wrapped her arms around him and her hands gripped his back, each fingertip burning through his shirt. Her hair spread like silk over his skin. 'Promise me you'll take care of yourself,' she whispered, so quietly that he had to bend his ear to her lips. 'You have no idea how much I…'

'Are you ready to go?' The dark doctor stood in the doorway with the buggy whip in his hand. He flailed it in the air and Lucy heard its hiss of impatience. Her hands dropped to her sides, but Cub's skin was still hot where she had held him.

'He is ready, Daniel,' she said. 'He has always been ready.'

She followed them to the back of the house where the bay mare was waiting in the buggy's harness, and pulled her robe tight in the dawn chill as they climbed to the seat. The doctor guided the horse towards the quiet street and when they had gone his wife was still standing in the empty yard, swaddled in her night clothes. She searched the sky for answers, and returned to the house without them.

They set out for the high ground, and the day rose swiftly at their backs as if to force them onwards. Everything in the distance was coated with purple gauze that was as soft as plush, and nothing seemed real. There were no signs to follow, but still they travelled forwards until the foot slopes were climbing before them like a jumping-off point for the swell of hills. Daniel trained the bay in a swerve and the buggy creaked its resistance when he urged the pony faster, and as they ascended they searched, and listened, and tested the air.

Distances became vaster the higher they climbed, and the valley floor pulled away. The day bloomed and its light ignited fresh colour, making the ground easier to read. They passed areas of recent dung on the damp earth, and the evidence of unshod hooves that grew fainter as the grass began to thin. As they scaled the hill only a trace remained, until the layer of soil had worn away and dust grew as thick as a false turf cloaking the rocks. Cub gripped the edge of the hard seat and leaned from the side of the buggy; he looked but there was nothing to see, he listened but there was nothing to hear, and unease travelled with him like a silent, unwanted companion.

From afar, the canyon was practically invisible, lying in wait like a secret slash in the unpredictable ground. It widened as the buggy drew closer, wheels humming through the residue of rainwater as the dark driver guided the bay towards the hidden gorge. He cornered the little horse around the edge and followed the track as it descended, furred with moss and angry with sharp stones, and the rock teeth above chewed away the sun until only the stretch of canyon was visible beneath them. The boy and the man slid into a fog of shadows that turned day back into night, and the buggy sank further into a nibble of stones until the going became hazardous. The bay's hooves seemed to exhume a raw chill from the ground, pricked and seething with a wash of sound, until the place was pervaded by an extraordinary hush that even the echoes avoided.

And then they saw it ahead of them, the splash of colour caught in stillness between the rocks and the desperate scrub.

Dr Ryker pulled on the reins, jerking the mare to a stop before he was aware of what he had done, and he and the boy sat motionless on the bench, drowning in silence. The sky above the canyon lips came alive as the new sun rose, cut about by the two large birds that followed each other on circles of early warmth as though keeping a watch over the stallion lying on his side in the grass, the sparse yellow blades pushing away from his hide as if they had tried to escape from the spot where he had fallen. The palomino's mane and tail spread like banners over the ground, pale as clouds in the dull shade, and he could have been merely asleep at the bottom of the gorge – but for the small round hole just visible under the hang of his forelock, matted by a protestation of flies, and the thread of blood spoiling the white hairs on his muzzle.

Cub stared at the death on the ground, and there was nothing in his heart as he climbed down from the buggy on numbed feet that could not feel the spring in the earth, or the crush of the rocks beneath. Disbelief fought him for every step he took towards the palomino in the grass, so that he sank to the ground as though his strength had gone. The colour of the stallion's hide was now as bleak as something that had been used up and discarded, and it made an old man of the boy who stroked drying blood from the bullet hole between the horse's eyes, his fingers driving flies into the air for a while. Only a while, for they were persistent and they were hungry, and they were impatient for him to leave.

Daniel looked down at the boy and the horse and felt empty. The bay whinnied, a shrill sound, fear in her throat. She stepped high and rattled the harness, and he looked instead at the reins lying dormant in his hands, and called the pony away with a tug to the left. She went willingly, twisting the buggy sideways so that one wheel complained, clattering on loose rocks before it settled again to follow the mare's pace out of the canyon and towards the day's warmth.

Cub was unaware that the doctor had gone; he did not

hear the low mutter of the wheels or the whisper of an echo. A slight breeze winged down from the canyon side and shivered his hair, but he did not feel the coolness on his skin. He had closed his eyes so that he would not see his own grief washing Wolf Wind's blood into the earth.

And when Daniel Ryker had eased the bay mare's disquiet and guided her back through the mouth of the gorge, the two large birds were still waiting and watching in spirals of air above the ground. The flies had clustered again, black around the bullet hole – but the palomino was lying alone; and the boy had vanished.

THIRTY-TWO

CUB KNEW the direction to follow by the blaze of the sun behind him, growing bright already despite the day's infancy, and he let his feet take him there, scuffing through brown-grey mud as though it was just another obstacle. He could feel hard ground through the soles of his boots, worn thin following the weight of weeks that had pulled him across the wild country towards the end of it, when he had been so close to the company of strangers that solitude thereafter had fashioned a natural distance. Since parting with the wagon train the stallion had been his only companion; at least that had been the way of it once, although it could never be the way again.

He walked blind as the sun rose and dried the wet earth, but beneath its blaze his body shivered with an internal chill. All that was pitiless brought back memories of how far he and Wolf Wind had travelled. He saw Christian Faulkner's painted horse and the sway of canvas roofs, the half-smile lifting Uncle Thackeray's moustache, the rub of shine on Cochrane's jacket. He saw the cowboy who had offered him a golden prize, and the stallion lived again – his mane as alive as a writhe of snakes as he raced early evening shadows; as the wind shattered the fury of his screams; as the dust flared like flags around his pale hide…

Cub lost the path; his feet fell away and he stumbled back to balance, his spine jarring from tail to skull. He knew how far he had come by the height of the sun and the new clouds that had grown from nothing, and he could almost hear the crash of gloom in their swathe. He stood still, moving his shoulders to ease his back, and there it was, stretched below him – a fall of dirt and rock and struggling scrub, scattering as the land levelled, as though reluctant to reach any further into the abyss where the farm sat hunched and grey. Everything waited for his next step, and as he took that step downwards, following the hill curve towards the valley, the sun surrendered to a swell of cloud and the colours died. There was a sudden silence as the wind-fidget fell; a hush like the hesitation on a cliff edge where the pull of gravity is inescapable. Cub walked into the hush with grit beneath his feet, and the silence followed until he was touching the weathered boards of the farmhouse.

The yard was deserted, but for Martha Madison's scrawny chickens that pecked with aimless desolation at the embittered ground. The air was thick. For a while the boy could not move in the viscous light; his hand dropped from the rough wood as if his muscles had turned to lead. There was a weight on the back of his neck that was like a fist pushing him down, and Cub closed his eyes and wondered if it meant that he could spread himself across the ground and sleep, and whether that might be a final sleep with nothing following, and whether he might dream as he slept and if the dream might flare into brilliant light before he came to an end. But when he looked again everything had changed; the stupor cleared away as though fog had lifted from the valley bottom and left brightness behind. There were no more obstructions, and Cub knew what he had to do; he knew that it had to be done before he could sleep, and long before he would ever want to dream again.

He moved with the farmhouse by his shoulder and stopped at the corner. To the one side the new day was fresh, but the wooden boards to the other pulled away into uncertainty, and the light was as dull as a poor man's lamp. Still caught under a veil of cloud, the rising sun had lost its strength and the air smelled slimy, like something growing in a cave. The window halfway along the wall was low to the ground, it drew back from its frame in a sulk but gaped like an invitation beside the tightly closed door, and Cub stepped towards it, as quiet as caution. The atmosphere was electric, as though a storm was boiling up from the wash of pale sky, and when he reached the window the short hairs between his shoulder blades were standing erect.

The room fell away from the casement like something uneasy in the shadows, just as he had seen it the first time, when he was a frightened little boy in a world of strangers. The sparsely furnished place shuffled with apology; it was like a homestead where nobody lived and nobody cared, apart from the occasional glare of incongruity where Martha Madison had once brought in an ornament, a decoration, a tapestry bird in a carved frame – bright blue, fire red, sun yellow. The colours had fought the colourless room until their hearts gave out, but in defiance she had left the bird hanging there ready to catch a lonely child's eye; to make him believe that he had been brought to a place he could know of as home. Those were the days when he had still been able to hope, but then the years had taken the rest of his life and Cub had found it easier to sink into their heaviness, for riding the weight of them with his head up would have earned a fool's destruction. This much had he learned, and from the first taste of Madison's whip he had learned also that to keep silent bought invisibility.

It had been seven years since he had sought the fading colours that Martha had fastened to the walls, but in the depths of days he began to see himself in the dying of their light, and the walls had fallen blank. He looked in through the window now and they caught his eye like something new, a hesitation from the reality that had grown him from a young boy to a young man. And the second's pause was enough for Haine Madison. In the gloom of the room, on the edge of his chair, the man waited; he leaned forward, his elbows seeking the dip in the centre of the raw-wood table. He caught sight of the boy at the window, and the shadows of his face deepened around his smile.

Cub knew him with a shock, even though he was already prepared to see him there inside the room. Strength flowed from the earth and he used it to kick in the door from the porch. It thundered against the wall and quivered back like a thing stunned, but the farmer was oblivious to the violence. He reached for a moss-green bottle on the table and his hand shook as he emptied it into his glass. The trickle of liquid was a soporific sound after the thunder; gentle, like rain reaching a gasping land. Cub heard the battered door closing behind him, sealing him inside the house with the heavy light and the silence. His back prickled as though something else had crept in after him, but the room was empty – apart from the man, and the smell of him.

'The woman is out in the fields, which means that we won't be disturbed.' Madison's voice was too close in the intimate space. He leaned back until his chair screeched and lifted the whisky to his mouth. 'Your ma was real upset that you'd run away again, but I know your true colours, boy, and they're all shades of yellow.' No light hit the glass when he drank. Cub saw the dead thing in the hand of the man who sucked the life from all he touched, but for the fierce spirit in the whip that lay sleeping at the end of the table; snake-curved, snake-vicious.

'So now it's just you and me, all alone where no one can see us, I reckon.' Madison took another pull from the glass, and the level of the liquid it contained fell like defeat.

Cub strained his senses as he felt for her. 'Where is Sage?'

'Sage? Well, she's gone. Left first thing; surprised you didn't meet each other on the road. But then you wouldn't be here stinking up this room, would you? You would be too busy rutting in the bushes, you and your sister.' The man looked over the rim of the glass at him; his eyes were sour in the half-light.

'You make me sick, Madison.'

The farmer straightened in his seat, his black outline climbing the wall like something from a nightmare. 'That is a curious thing to hear from trash like you.' His voice was quieter, as if it had retreated inside the heavy light.

A thunder cloud was gathering in the room, just below the sway of the ceiling; Cub felt it like a weight pushing him into the floor. He looked at the man sitting in front of him, and it was as if he had never seen him before. This encounter began to feel unstable, as though everything that was once natural had been turned on its head; and he was the child again, maybe nine years old, relinquishing the company of a travelling band for a life of internment with his new pa and his new ma. A child with a man's head, already hardened and scared to show his feelings but still a child, piloted by hope.

Cub stared at the farmer until his eyes ached, and then he looked down at the rough planks under his feet, and the faded rug that Martha Madison had once believed might bring new life into the old house. The floorboards had slowly pulled apart over the years and now there were gaps between them; a perspective of crevices, some as deep and as wide as his thumb, filled with the detritus of decades.

A streak of sunshine passed through the window. It swept a straight line across the grainy wood and bounced a glint of light off the curve of metal; and the skin on Cub's back prickled when he recognised the silver ring lying in the dip between the boards. The ring that the girl had worn forever, like a lucky charm around her little finger.

'What have you done to Sage?' he said to the man sitting at the table. 'Where is she?'

'Well, are you deaf as well as stupid?' The farmer lifted the glass and shook it a little to see how much he had left to drink. 'Your sister has gone, like I told you. Don't query me, you piece of shit.'

Cub stepped across the floorboards, over the gap where the ring was sleeping in its bed of dust. 'Have you hurt her?'

'Any hurt done to my girl is yours alone, boy.' The farmer put down the glass and sat in stillness, watching as he came closer. 'Your sister was just fine until you fouled her innocence. Now she has taken her filthy sins to another's door, for she is no longer welcome at mine.'

'Sage is not my sister.'

Madison widened his jaundiced eyes and the light around his head grew sickly. 'Now how can that be, when you are both my spawn? The woman out there is her dam, but she bore me no son, so I had to make you in another's belly.'

'I am not your son.'

'And believe this,' the man said, and began to rise from the chair as the boy drew nearer. 'If I had known it was you growing from the seed I spat inside her I would have stuck my knife in the same hole that I used to make you and torn you both to bloody rips.'

'My ma never knew you.' Cub felt the edge of the table against his thighs and pressed into the sharpness of it. 'I am not your son. I am the son of Dark Wolf.' Horse man, whisperer, bareback rider. 'And you are nothing.'

The room was humming. The boy and the man stood in silence on either side of the bow-backed table, but the air was strident, and something tore when Madison spoke.

'For certain she knew me. Your ma was a whore in a coloured wagon, and as long as I threw money at her she would oblige me any way I wanted.'

Cub shook his head. Memory ignited to a vicious flame and nothing could stop the years as they parted and disappeared, dropping him behind the coloured wagon where it was anchored to the greensward at the edge of some town.

What town? The child could not know that as he sat dwarfed by wheels that slashed his skin with spoke-shadow, watching the three riggers as they sniffed the air for rain that was going to fall, before raising the poles and the canopy for the makeshift ring. The canopy that was like a pocket of sky brought down from the clouds; canvas mottled with holes that let in the light. The men rigged a pale blue heaven, freckled with sun spots, and they called things out to the child they knew was in hiding behind the painted wagon. They walked past him with their poles and coils of rope, and sometimes the things they called were friendly and sometimes not; and when they were not he learned that it was the fault of the alcohol that floated like clouds around their heads.

Jugglers, tumblers, jesters and horse handlers, they all danced under the upturned sky of the canvas canopy, and sometimes they too were friendly; but when they were not the little boy hid from them in the place where the horses lived. Long-legged stallions wetting him with their moist breath and warming him with their warmth; speaking to him in a tongue that was often easier to understand than the language of the people around him. That was the place where the horse-talker lived as well; the dark-eyed man with skin the colour of earth who had given Cub his hair and his eyes, and his face and his name. Who had taught him how to speak to the twitch-eared stallions; how to lift away to another plane; how to fade to invisible. The man who tied his long hair back with a strip of buckskin so that he could sit above the nameless towns and sing the prayers of ancient people to the sky and the wind and the trees.

Dark Wolf the horse man, who had held the little boy's golden-haired mother in his arms as though she was the sweetest gift.

'Your ma was a raddled woman. She was diseased and disgusting, but she sure had her uses.'

Cub jerked as though the words had slapped his ears, and Haine Madison was there, leaning towards him across the table. The gentle horse man vanished into a past life as the farmer licked his lips and smiled through the shine on them. 'She was so raddled that she couldn't do much more than lie down,' he said, and his voice shivered the hairs at the base of the boy's scalp. 'But she had her best uses when she was flat on her back.'

'Shut up.'

'Oh yeah. And do you remember that wagon of hers? You remember that bed she had in that wagon? I can remember the stink of her in that bed in that wagon. I can remember the place underneath that wagon where she made you sleep when she had company. Did the wagon rock above your head when she had company? Were you afraid that it might break and crush you where you lay beneath it when that filthy whore had company?'

'Shut up!'

'That red man was killed; the native who sired you. Do you remember that time, boy, when your pa was shot? That was when your ma turned back into the slut. She said it was for the need of money, but the real fact is that she enjoyed the feel of a man's...'

Cub lunged. Madison knew it the moment before and stepped sideways too nimbly for a drunkard who had sunk a full glass so early in the morning. He pushed the boy backwards with an elbow to his throat and stretched towards the sleeping snake of plaited leather, and it woke in his hand and unrolled to the floor like a wave of hair. The farmer cracked the whip, it buzzed through the air and bit into Cub's cheek, but the boy was faster. He grabbed the leather tail and twisted it around his fist and tugged. The man lost his grip on the handle and the weapon sang across the room, hitting the wall like a dead thing. Martha Madison's faded tapestry in its carved frame shuddered, slithered sideways, hung helplessly as the whip fell to the floor.

'She had you young and took no care of you.' Madison held the edges of the table; it was shaking from his hands. A foam of spit collected at the sides of his mouth and sprayed the air. 'She couldn't even care for the child I put in her belly. My child. My real son. They died together and that was the end of them and riddance to the filth. I took you in because nobody else wanted you. I paid that circus good money for you, and I gave you a home. I am the closest to family you ever had.'

Cub stared at the grey face of the drunkard who had held his life in a vice for so many years, but all he could see was the horse man, his skin carved with tattoos that crinkled when he smiled; and all he could see were the stallions he rode across sawdust rings, under the sky canopy, outside the walls of unknown towns.

'I saved your miserable hide, and for why? So that you could spit in my eye?' Madison stood away from the table and wiped his mouth with the back of his hand. 'So that you can shoot your feral seed into gutless females, just like that mongrel stallion you brought back with you?'

The dark-eyed man with magic in his tongue stood shoulder to shoulder with the boy, and the blood that flowed through them was the evening breeze above the land and the animals that fought in the forests. It was the quiet light of a molten moon that had rippled through the stream where a palomino stood haltered by the cowboys' ropes, and was tamed to bear the Indian's son.

'Decent folk will not allow vicious beasts to live. Do you not know that, boy?' The farmer slipped a hand behind his back and took a step forward. 'We do not consent to the notion of freedom when it comes to killers.'

The Indian's son felt the heartbeat of a brave stallion. He felt the dust under his hands, and the cooling hide of a dead horse.

'The only thing to do when it comes to killers,' Haine Madison said, 'is to kill them first. Do you not know that either?' And when he turned the corner of the table he was holding the knife he had taken from his belt. 'That golden horse died well,' he said, raising the blade so swiftly that its steel tip whispered through the air like scissors through silk, and he pointed the knife at the boy's heart. 'He fought my aim but he could not outrun the rifle.'

He studied Cub's face through the pall of alcohol. The barriers had come down over the dark eyes and there was nothing different to see there, but the boy's shoulders were straight and his head was high and pulling him back into shadows, and Haine Madison learned everything he needed to know about him from the places where he could not hide. 'The stallion had to die, and it was a shame,' he said. 'But that is just nature teaching us to destroy vermin before we ourselves are destroyed.'

Cub blinked slowly until his thoughts scattered and his mind was clear, and when he opened his eyes again his sight was boundless, and Haine Madison was caught like a fish on the end of a spear. 'I said it was a shame the stallion had to die,' the man said loudly, as though the boy had to be hollered out of stupidity, and he rubbed his forehead with a fist as if to clear what was twisting his head out of shape. 'Because I could have gone far with that horse. I could have been someone with a ride like that.'

Deep holes began to open under the farmer's feet as he stood in the unwholesome room, holding a knife to the heart of a still, silent boy, and Cub tightened his shoulders until his muscles bunched. He moved his head away from the light that was digging through the window and his eyes disappeared behind darkness. Madison squinted, trying to bring the boy's face back into focus; he took a step closer until he could see better, and then he brought the blade up, its tip seeking the skin beneath Cub's jaw. His hand tightened around the handle as if all he needed was one excuse.

'Do you understand what I'm telling you, half-breed? Am I making myself clear?' he said. 'I shot the horse that you stole from some outlandish mountain. You cast your ungodly native spells and the beast followed you back here. You ravished my girl so I rode out early just to kill your animal, and you were too late to stop it happening. I took an eye for the one you took from me. As I see it, I have been blessed by the holy word of gospel.'

A hush had fallen, as though the sun's power that was encroaching on the growing day had spun a gentle cloak. Light softened the hard edges in all the corners of the room; it sucked the sharpness from the air and Haine Madison's arm began to ache. The point of the blade became rounded and fell away from the boy's throat, wavering in spirals as though dancing to some music in the man's head. But it wasn't music he had chosen. He scowled and held the knife tighter.

'I have no more use for you,' he said. 'You turned into a big problem, but now you've handed me the solution. You ambushed me; threatened me with my own knife. I had to kill you to save myself, and I shall be blameless for what else could I have done?' Madison grinned, bubbles of saliva on his teeth. 'Well, the folk in Oasis know all about your wickedness by now. They remember the day that you attacked your ma and ran off like a coward…'

There was a sudden flash from the blade and Cub jerked back. But the knife had not been meant for him; the farmer lifted it from his own forearm where the slash was already welling with red tears. He grinned through spittle and showed the boy his bloody arm. 'You were trying to kill me and I defended myself. Who wouldn't understand that?' he said. And then he lunged.

Cub twisted away. The blade tore his shirt but missed his body, and he knocked it out of the man's hand. The farmer staggered on uneven feet and fell heavily, groping for the weapon as it tumbled to the floor like a wounded bird, but the boy was there first. He kicked the knife to the far side of the room and stood over the fallen man, fists clenched until everything hurt, and Madison felt his power like an enraged beast in the enclosed space. The farmer hid behind his slashed arm, smearing his face with his own blood. He peered up through his hands and saw fire.

It was only for seconds that Cub stood above the man who had been his captor for so many years and who now unwound helplessly at his feet, but it felt like the passing of his life. And when it was over he slipped back into his body and became still and silent once again; until he felt it growing inside him, the gasping pain that twisted his gut and his belly and his scalp as if it was tearing him in half. The grief was unbearable but then it was gone, leaving in its place a calmness that he had never experienced before.

He rose into the air above the pathetic heap on the floorboards, the sprawl of the whip by one wall and the bloodied blade against the other. As he opened the door he turned his back on darkness and the sun shone in his face. The purity of the morning was heartbreaking, and Cub stepped into it over the threshold. Light gushed inside the room as though nothing could hold it back, but it did not reach the floor where things lay cold among the dust balls; where Haine Madison dipped his head in shadows and was unaware of the glory that was just out of reach.

The farmyard was blooming with the new day, and the squawk and clatter of the fowl by the frayed edges of the pond sounded as brave as the start of a life. The boy filled his lungs with clean air and began to run. He ran from the house and the tumbling barn, across the cracked earth and the fright of the chickens, away from the caustic past towards the distant purple hills. He ran fast to break free, and when the crumbling ground became the rut-scored track that climbed to Oasis, the bonds disintegrated and scattered under his feet.

He did not see Martha Madison standing by the barn door, field dirt dropping from the rake she held in her hand, but when he had pulled himself out of the valley and the farm was behind him he could still feel the strange scratching, as if eyes had been watching him leave, and for a while his back prickled beneath pale scars, and then even that dissolved into what had gone before.

THIRTY-THREE

DANIEL RYKER closed the door and the house sank under shadow. His home was as silent as a hesitation in time, until he caught the rustle of a skirt as his wife crossed the parlour. She stood in the doorway, swathed by subterranean light from the window and reaching for the tail of her braid as though she needed something to hold on to. 'You have been gone a goodly while, husband. Has anything happened?'

She spoke so quietly that her voice barely left her throat, and he came back to himself, surprised to find that he was standing there. He touched her arm as he walked past and she gripped her hair like a friend, turning to watch him falling heavily into the first chair he reached, hands loose by his knees. Silence stretched between them, and Lucy pulled the braid until her scalp wrenched. Her skirt muttered as she went towards him. 'Please tell me what has happened?' she said, shrill now where before she had been quiet.

'Something is wrong.' Ryker stared down at the floor. 'We found the horse.'

'But that cannot be what is wrong.' She was unearthly in the half-light.

'The horse had been shot, Lucy. The horse is dead.' She swayed on her feet and he was suddenly afraid for her. 'You must be exhausted. Come and sit down.'

He stood back from his chair as if to usher his wife into it, but she flapped away his hand. 'I have too much to do.' She moved quickly to the door, but stopped there, facing him again. 'Do you have anything else to tell me, Daniel? Where is Cub?'

'I left him with the stallion.'

'On his own?'

'For a little while. I drove around; when I returned the boy had gone.'

'You left him alone?'

She spoke as though she was holding something back, and he felt a flare of irritation. 'Yes, Lucy, I left him alone with his horse and then he disappeared. I searched for as long as I could, but it was as if he'd gone into hiding. The boy can make himself invisible, you know this. He was hiding from me, and I am baffled.'

A strange thing seemed to happen to the woman standing at the room's threshold; her outline shimmered and became double. To his tired eyes it was as if her soul had been ejected from her body, until he saw Sage Madison standing there behind her, half hidden by the door frame. Her long hair flowed from her face as though caught in a sudden draught, and the weary man felt her eyes burning through his skull. She said, 'I know where he might have gone,' and then the house door rattled.

All three of them turned towards the sound but only Lucy moved, sweeping forwards to welcome, reprimand, defend the boy she wanted to find standing outside on the path. She was not ready to see the sheriff with his face still creased from lack of sleep, and two mounted men behind him with bullets belted around their waists and rifles holstered at their saddles.

'Forgive my disturbance, ma'am, but is the doctor here?' Russett lifted the wide hat from his head and held it down by his leg, and when Daniel stepped to the parlour door the sheriff could barely make him out in the slouch of shadows. 'Haine Madison's son again, Dr Ryker,' he said to the murky space where he thought the man was standing.

Ryker drew himself upright, but with difficulty, for the air around him was sticky. 'Then there has been some trouble,' he said, loudly enough for the armed horsemen waiting in the street to lift their heads and stare.

'For sure there has been some trouble, and we need to find the boy before there is more.' Russett touched the pointed badge on his chest as though to remind himself of his duties.

Lucy pushed past her husband. She glared up at the sheriff, trying to read what was in his head. 'Will you tell me what you are doing here? You and these men.'

'We need to find him, Mrs Ryker.' Russett stepped back a little from the fury in her face. 'And I'm asking if the doctor will join us in the search.'

'Why?' Her voice hit the quiet morning like heavy rain. 'Is Cub hurt?'

'I have no knowledge of that. What I do know is that Haine Madison is dead. His wife drove into town a while ago; she told us he had been stabbed, but she was unable to tell us anything more.'

And then Lucy seemed to crumple, as if the fire in her had been quenched, and over her head the lawman caught sight of the girl listening from the darkness. He slammed his hat against his leg. 'Is that Sage Madison over there?' he said. 'I'm sorry for your loss, Miss Madison. Damn me, if I had known you were here I would have stayed your ma before she took herself back to the farm.'

Daniel Ryker looked at his wife; he looked behind him to where the girl was standing so still. He inspected his heart and found anger and unease, and the desire to be exempt from all responsibility. He said, 'Lucy, please will you take Sage into the parlour?' and she threw him a look he did not care to read before she ushered the girl away.

'I would not have wanted her to hear that about her pa,' the sheriff said. 'It was unfortunate.'

The doctor faced him and wondered if anything was real. He felt enormously tired. 'Are you telling us that Cub stabbed Haine Madison to death?'

'Well now, Daniel, I am unlikely to know for sure, but from what Martha had to tell me it seems that he did.' Russett turned to the men behind him and the restlessness of their horses. 'Whichever way the truth unfolds, we need to find him.' He turned back, quiet for a moment, raising his eyebrows. 'Do you have any information you would like to share with me, Dr Ryker?'

Just an early morning buggy ride towards the hills, the dark man thought; just the desperately still form of the horse in the grass. He shook his head.

'And will you join us in our search?'

'You know well that my first obligation is to Mrs Madison. And I guess there is no one else you can ask to pronounce the man dead?'

'At least you can offer that assistance, Dr Ryker.' The sheriff shrugged and tucked his hat back on his head. 'I expect the boy to have made for the hills again, like he did that last time.' He twisted on the path to leave, and threw the next words over his shoulder. 'Would I be right in this assumption, Doctor?'

Daniel closed the door, listening until the hoof-clatter was swallowed by the wood. He shook a little, balancing on his tightrope over the abyss, and then he went to face the women.

A bit of space, that was all he wanted; just some time on his own. It was the reason he'd headed straight for the foothills instead of following the track towards Oasis and the Rykers; and Sage. Quiet space in which to collect his thoughts before he took up the reins of the rest of his life; and he found it in the small cave that might almost have been lying in wait for him, halfway up the slope of rocks and scrubby vegetation.

Cub bent down, pushing through twisted grass and the whip of foliage until the hollow cupped him close and drew him in, and when his sight cleared he could see the earth walls, whiskered with roots, and the scattering of twigs on the floor. He tested the air; it was fetid with the scent of animals, but the stink was weak and he knew that what had been sheltering there had left during the night, herding its young before it. The cave was sheltering him now; the human cub crouching in the mess on a floor that was still shaking from his heartbeat.

Damp with sweat, the shirt collar gripped his throat like a noose. Cub pulled it away, exacerbating the ache in his skull; he took a mouthful of air, and then another until his breathing boomed like dull thunder from crumbling walls. Sunshine spotted the fronds that bearded the mouth of the cave and the boy leaned back against bristled earth, watching light dancing in the heat until exhaustion crept from his feet, and there was nothing he could do to fight it. He slept, and dreamed of mud and fire, and when he woke the pain behind his eyes had turned to hammering, as though it had taken on its own existence. It was coming out of the walls, it was all around. He rose on his haunches to the throb of hoofbeats, climbing the slopes towards the burrow where he had hoped to find solitude.

Cub made himself small and hugged the ground, edging forward into the sun's glare. He saw dried earth puffing like smoke, he heard a struggle of winded horses. He backed off to where the ceiling met the floor and coiled like a creature in the darkness, chin to chest, the weight of the soil above dulling everything but the pain in his head.

Still persistent but turning ghostly, the drumming told him that the horses were slowing, and when they stopped the silence was a void. Cub searched it with all his senses. He caught the muffle of men speaking; he smelled hot leather and swallowed the taste of horse hide. He leaned forward to ease the strain on his legs, and he waited for them to leave him alone.

There was a clattering as the horses began to move again; unsteady hooves skidding across the thin soil and sparking the rocks beneath. Gradually the sounds receded, but still Cub waited, and after a while silence settled like windblown ash and it was as though the hill had never been disturbed. He crept to where light was dappling the mouth of the cave. The sun was hot there, even though a breeze had whisked up since he had been cupped by shelter. It slapped the sides of the hill and chuckled across his face, urging him out into the open.

Cub pushed through the vegetation at the lip of the cave and slid into the shadow of a rock hollow, and wide to either side rode three men, scything the ground with their eyes. The tang of the horses rose rich and full to the back of his throat, and something turned black inside him as he watched them. He recognised the two men who rode behind the sheriff. They had been among those who had passed sentence from half-open doors on the day that the soldier had brought him back to Oasis, like a gift to a drunken farmer; and they were out there now with their condemnation and their guns, hunting for prey.

Above him, high on the ridge of the hill, crusts of rock and scrub bled into waves of muted green as though the ground had been smoothed to patches of velvet. Like the sun on his face he saw it with hope and he knew he could reach the summit and disappear, so quietly that the men with their searching eyes would go unrewarded. And that made him smile, and it made him reckless, and he slithered away from the lair and began to climb, until the little cave was indistinguishable from the rest of the hill and the riders had shrunk beneath him, as harmless as toys.

The higher he climbed the closer he came to the brow,

and the terrain changed with each step so that the smoothness became a crumple of stones, loose and easy, and the green was fighting bare rock for survival. The wind was wild where the sky was near, it wrapped around the boy and tugged, and he bent to the ground and anchored himself with his hands. Broken stalks stabbed under his nails and raked his arms, and hair blew into his eyes so that he was blind to the boulder until he grabbed it and felt it roll from his fingers.

It joined the slide of stones; he heard them tumbling, knocking from the rocks and skidding down the hill with little hammer blows; musical notes like a clatter of conversation. There was nothing that Cub could do to stop them falling except to watch as they betrayed him.

Sheriff Russett and the two men had spread wide in a triangle and if the stones had fallen into the empty spaces between them he would have been okay; he could have climbed again until the summit had scooped him towards a different future. But the hill rang with disharmony as they scattered. One of the horses stepped high in the air with a squeal of pain that was like anger in the howl of the wind, and the man on its back eased it calm again before he looked around. He looked up and pointed and yelled, so that everyone could see the boy clinging to the side of a hill where there was no place left to hide.

He tried to run, his body battered and his muscles screaming. The ground was unforgiving; the horse came closer on tremulous hooves, slipped back on a slither of stones and choked on the bit. Cub could feel its fear, but its rider was tenacious. When the animal baulked at the treacherous slope the man dismounted; he left the horse stiff-legged and shuddering, and began to pull himself up over broken rocks and powdered earth that swirled like gritty mist, choking the air grey. And then Cub knew that there was nothing more he could do.

He turned around, and the wind hit him in the face.

Sheriff Russett was only feet away, coughing out dust against his fist. The other horses were climbing carefully, their riders tilting hats against the bluster to shade the judgement in their eyes, but Russett stood bow-legged in the onslaught of wind and the cutting slope, breathing like a man in pain. Cub could tell that the sheriff was unable to go much further, which was tough for the lawman, but maybe not for him.

He took one step backwards with his heel digging into the slope. He took another and his thigh muscles clenched as he prepared to face the hill again, and after that the wind-blitzed summit that had looked so neat and smooth from the mouth of the cave. His feet were sure and light, and it was not far to climb; and ahead of him was the rest of his life.

But he heard the scuff of leather and a serrated click, and the sheriff's voice rasping like a man with cigar smoke in his lungs. 'Time to come quietly, Cub. If you should try to escape I shall have to shoot you, and I really do not want to do such a thing,' Russett said, and then he sighed, as if it was such a thing he would do in a moment, despite the regret.

The man's weapon was pointing at his chest. It was like the end of everything. 'You do not need the gun,' the boy said. 'I have done nothing wrong.'

'Just hand over the knife, Cub. Easy now.'

'Sheriff Russett, I have done nothing wrong.'

Russett snapped into action, holstering his gun as he stepped forward and squeezed the boy's shoulders until it hurt. 'Where is the goddam knife?'

Cub looked at the man in front of him; he looked down at the two men below. The sheriff's fingers were angry, but he did not pull away from the pain. 'There is no knife.'

Russett stared hard at him. Cub was assaulted by the man's mind and he did nothing to protect himself. After a while the sheriff released his grip and shook his head as though searching for sense. 'Come on now, Cub,' he said, holding out his left hand as if it was a friendly greeting instead of a shackle-maker.

He clicked the cuffs around the boy's wrists. The wind spun webs through the metal and along the sheriff's arm as he dragged Cub down to where the grey mare was nosing the ground for greenery. The man mounted and helped the boy up behind him, easing forward as though to make space. Cub gripped the saddle and swayed with the horse as they began to move, stepping slowly and carefully through wicked stones until the hilltop was a mere mound of sharp rocks and no longer the gateway to a vast new land.

Wind-tussled, the first of the two riders slumped silently in wait, his muddy eyes exploring the boy as the double-loaded horse came near. He pushed out wet lips and nodded, as if in agreement with himself, and the sheriff gathered the grey mare's reins and rode in front, leading the men from path to path as they followed the slope downwards.

They arrived in Oasis limp from the power of the sun, animals and riders uniform to the colour of mud. Diminished by its burden the sheriff's grey laboured behind, but the other horses were lighter, lifting their heads to the scent of warm, still water in the half-empty trough and moving down the street towards it before reins yanked them back. The riders dismounted on creaking stirrups; bashing dusty hats against their thighs they left the horses shivering at the hitching post below the sheriff's office. As Russett's grey came near one of the men reached up behind the saddle and hauled Cub down by his arm.

He nearly unseated the sheriff as he fell, hitting the road so hard that his cuffed hands were numbed and useless, and the blackness was roiling inside him. The man leaned over him with the promise of danger, eyes shining like earth-coloured pebbles. He was familiar to the boy now, and still unsteady from his association with the saloon, where once he could have been found sinking the drink at a table half covered by Haine Madison and an emptying bottle. But the long relationship with cheap whisky had made a bungle of the man, and Cub rolled to his feet and easily avoided one shapeless righthand blow, stepping back from another to pain in his heels as they cracked against the rise of the sidewalk.

And then Russett was there in front of the boy, forcing the attacker away with a hand raised for calm. 'Enough, Pete,' he said. 'Craddock, that is enough.'

The man shuffled as though the ground was moving. 'Murdering little shit; murdering bastard,' he said through the saliva gathering at the corners of his mouth. 'Haine Madison was just a fine…a fine man.'

'Okay.' The sheriff raised his other hand and stepped forwards, gripping the man's shoulder as though he had some sympathy. Craddock stood still, he drew an arm across the mess on his face and stared downwards. 'I want to thank you for your help, Pete,' Russett said, and looked around at the other one who had positioned himself between the two horses in a perfect symmetry of animal and man. 'I want to thank both of you for your time,' he said, and set Craddock loose. 'Go on now, back to your businesses.'

He stood by the sidewalk, waiting, and when the two men had gone he turned to Cub, touching the firearm at his belt. 'I wouldn't want to use this on you, boy, so don't make it necessary. Okay?' he said, speaking quietly to hide the words from people passing by, slowly curious, sharply listening.

They stepped up to the sheriff's office together with dirt shimmering from their clothes like a disturbance of the light. Almost politely, the man stood aside so that his guest might precede him into the building, but something crawled on the back of Cub's neck before the door closed.

He looked around to see Sage watching him from the other side of the street. She was standing so still that the trickle of sunlight following the slope of her face could have been rain falling on a statue, until she lifted her fingers to brush the wetness away.

THIRTY-FOUR

TWO SMALL cells were tucked like an embarrassment off a narrow corridor at the back of the sheriff's office, but only one was in use. It was quiet in there where the roll of wheels, the knock of hooves and the rise and fall of town noise had become separated by walls. Any sound that seeped through had to travel second-hand from the outer office, and that made it feel like being inside a box within a box; a box with steel bars and no privacy, a bucket by the brick wall and a biscuit-hard mattress on a wooden shelf. It smelled of emptiness, as though haunted by the ghosts of melancholia, and it was as dusky as evening when the sun is hidden.

Cub saw Sage again, standing at the side of the road as other lives rolled around her. Imprisoned in isolation he saw her over and over, as though his mind was so busy with that last sight of her that nothing would clear it. Apart from the infrequent interruption when food was brought in covered dishes on a small tray by a squat, chunk of a woman, who stood waiting for Russett to unlock the cell door with her eyes cast down as though she had no wish to be tainted by the sins of the prisoner. Apart from the sheriff on that first day, sitting at his desk in the outer office with his back to the street, so that Cub who was sitting opposite him could see that the world outside the window was as unreal as a magic lantern show.

'Tell me why you went to the farm.'

'I needed answers.'

'To what questions?'

'I needed to know why Madison had killed my horse.'

'Where was this? Where was the horse killed?'

'Where the slopes start climbing to the big hills.'

'How did you get there?'

'I…walked.'

'With nobody to assist you?'

'I was alone.'

'So how did you get back to the farm?'

'Walked.'

'You walk fast.'

'I walk fast.'

'And did you get your answers when you went to the farm?'

'Yes.'

'Did you get them from Haine Madison?'

'He told me what I wanted to know.'

'Displeased you with his answers, did he?'

'He told me what I wanted to know.'

'And then you stabbed him.'

'I did not touch him.'

'You went to the farm with a knife and stabbed Haine Madison to death.'

'I did not touch him, Sheriff Russett. Madison had the knife; he cut his arm with it.'

'Now why should he do such a thing?'

'So that when he killed me it would look like self-defence.'

'Is that right, Cub? Is that what happened?'

'That is what happened.'

'Tell me where the knife went?'

'He dropped it. I left Madison lying on the floor and the knife was there with him.'

'And even then, you did not hurt him?'

'There was no need. He was already broken when I left him.'

'What do you mean by that?'

'He was drunk; he could not stand.'

'Did you stab Haine Madison and then dispose of the knife?'

'I did not. I did not.'

'If that is the case,' the sheriff straightened from the desk as though an invisible rope had tugged him upright, 'tell me who did?'

Cub stared out to the sidewalk where a woman and a girl were clattering along on busy feet that needed to be someplace else as quickly as possible. As they passed the window the woman gazed downwards as though in silent conversation with the boards, but the girl turned her head towards the lure of the dark office. She looked straight at the boy in his unsettled seat and smiled until her face was afire and her eyes were slits. The heat from her greeting hit the back of Cub's head and ignited something that could have been hope.

'I don't know who killed Haine Madison, Sheriff,' he said, 'but I swear that it was not me.'

'Seems you have visitors.'

Russett's voice preceded him as he came through his office door into the thin corridor, exorcising the ghost of despondency that was hanging over the cell. Cub had gone away into himself, stretched out on the bed-shelf with his eyes shut, and he was unaware until the voice became a noise that dispelled the plains, the acres of land beneath the stallion's hooves, the swathes of sky above his head and the buffet of wind across his ears.

The ceiling fell as he was dragged back to the present; he swung his feet to the floor, stood slowly, and looked up. Daniel Ryker was there in the passageway with his pale-haired wife beside him. The boy's eyes flashed in the residue of office light as he waited for Russett to unlock the cell. He waited for the hinges to release the door, his muscles tensed for the open space that the bars had been guarding, and for the tantalising second when he might have the chance to make a run for it.

But that was just a fantasy, and nothing had changed. The door was locked and unforgiving, and the lawman stood before it with his hands empty of keys. When he spoke again the words were mere gibberish. Cub watched him walk back to his office, taking the light and leaving the dusk. Leaving the Rykers alone in the corridor.

Lucy opened her mouth, and then closed it as though her voice had been defeated. She gripped the lock and tugged with a strength that might bend iron, until her husband eased her hands away and held them safely in his.

'That he should be imprisoned like a pariah! Where is the justice?'

She blasted the words and the doctor said, 'I am sorry,' as if he was apologising for more than the boy's captivity. But Lucy was unappeased, as though she had heard it all before.

She wrenched her fingers free and grabbed the bars again, passion deep in her eyes. The door rattled like a mad thing. Cub stood erect, the backs of his legs pressed against the mattress, and when she caught the power of his gaze she fell beneath the ease of it and grew calm, dropping her hands from the bars as though astonished to find that she was holding them.

'Cub,' she said, and for a moment she might have said more, but lost the strength to say it. She faded into the twilight, taking with her the question she could not bring herself to ask.

And then the boy was afraid that they would walk away and he would be left alone with nothing but pointless memories. 'No,' he answered the question she had not asked. 'I did not kill Haine Madison.'

Lucy studied the low ceiling and the bare walls; she

studied her husband's face. 'Daniel, we have to get him out of this cage.' The doctor moored her with a hand and shook his head. She struggled out of his grasp. 'Damn you, husband. Why will you not help me to help him?'

Ryker's brow thundered. He hit the bars with the flat of his hand and glared through them to the motionless boy in the centre of the cell. 'Before I decide whether to help you,' he said, 'I need you to tell me what happened.'

Cub told him everything.

Once more he walked away from the stallion lying in a dead gallop beneath the two harbingers in the sky; and as he walked his mind was filled with the weeks that had gone before, so that those images were all he was seeing as he followed the folds of land down to where the farm still sat like something that should be forgotten. And when he reached the crusted yard and the slimy pond and the graceless farmhouse, he had already forfeited an hour of his life for the sake of the coiled whip and the moss-green bottle, for Sage's silver ring glinting from the floor and the knife in Haine Madison's hand.

An eye for an eye, the farmer had said. You ravished my girl, I killed your animal, he had said. You attacked me with my own knife so I killed you. And I shall be without blame.

Dr Ryker and his wife stood listening as Cub spoke of Madison lying de-fanged and de-clawed but still alive at his feet; of leaving the unfortunate history behind him as he departed. Feeling nothing beyond the sparseness of livestock and the scatter of crops and the pity of it all. And there was a moment of silence when he had finished speaking, until Lucy gasped as though she was learning to breathe.

She spread her fingers through the cage bars and wanted only to reach the boy inside. 'My belief in your innocence has never wavered,' she said. 'And I trust my husband has decided correctly, for he is a good man.'

The good man raised his head as though her words had lifted him, and there was the same determination in his eyes that Cub remembered seeing in the half light of early morning, carried whip-flayed on the chestnut's back to the Rykers' house. Carried in by the girl.

'Did Sage come to you,' he said, 'on that morning?'

Lucy's hands played dull music as they slid from the bars. 'Indeed; she sought succour with us, as you told us she would.'

'She is safe?'

The doctor nodded. 'Yes, Cub, she is safe,' he said, and for a moment something gentle smoothed the lines from his eyes.

But his wife saw none of this, and neither did she see the boy's shoulders relaxing under her husband's words. Instead she saw the girl withdrawing to the shelter of her hair, as day followed day; she saw the way Sage gripped her belly with folded arms as though she was holding secrets inside. In her mind Lucy saw this but said nothing, and all thoughts and plans remained unspoken in the quietness until the sheriff stepped into the passageway, followed by a scarf of yellow lamplight that stunted his shape in its shadow. He took away the doctor and his wife and the hope from their parting words. And when they left they took the yellow light with them as well.

THIRTY-FIVE

MARTHA MADISON stood at the open door of the house and looked out over the farmyard as if she had never seen it before. The ground had sunk, as though a relentless suction beneath the surface was tugging the hard-packed soil, and the area was as concave as a dish; compacted from the years of feet and hooves and wheels like a lowly creature beaten into submission. Like the boy. The boy who had walked across this desperate enclosed space each day of the seven years since he had been brought to the farm under cover of Haine's darkness. Haine's spawn; the unspeakable son of the ungodly. Martha wondered if her husband had found God now; whether there was such a spirit in the place where he had gone.

She leaned from the door and stared at the bedraggled farmyard and the crumple of fields, where stony soil and clods of unmanageable dirt would trip her feet, tipping her head towards the ground until she could see nothing but her rooted old boots. But there were no clods up towards the sky where the gloss of hills lay under a haze of distance. The ground up there was close-cropped, pale blue and dove grey, and the trees bore soft, dark branches. Martha stretched out her hands and felt gentleness on her skin; and she longed, as she had always longed, to walk on that velvet and float in that air.

But the boy had got there first. The bastard had sullied her sacred place. He had found freedom for a while and the while had lasted for weeks but felt like years, because of the vileness of her husband when he learned what it was to work one hand down. The hottest time of the year, the remorseless toil of urging food from the land for the humans and the animals; the need for those who were left behind to break their backs while the runaway had been basking in Martha Madison's dream of freedom.

The arrival of Haine's by-blow seven years before had been nothing but a bad omen under cover of secrecy and sin. And on the day that Madison had died the boy had escaped again. He had abandoned Martha's husband to the floor and flown across the yard as if there were no dips in the exhausted ground, no stones to trip, no responsibility to drag him backwards. Maybe it was down to the badness inside him in the first instance that those dips had come about, and the unforgiving ground and the tripping stones. Maybe it had always been down to him. And now it was all over and Martha had to face coping on her own, and that also was down to the boy.

Martha had driven to Oasis in the cart that day, and it had been empty. She was unfamiliar with such emptiness. When she went to town it was customary to carry produce: what she could glean from the fields, the animals and the chickens; what she had trapped on the open swathes, or shot as she moved softly through the scrubland. She took cakes of corn bread, dead bundles of rabbits, eggs she had prised from the scruffs of chickens, misshapen turnips, the occasional clutch of flowers from the garden she had stolen from land behind the house. She took everything she could sell to those who had no such things, and gave Tobias Kendall what was left to stock his shelves in return for a handful of coins and a supercilious smile. But on that day the cart was as unstable as intoxication without its expected weight; the chestnut skimmed the ground like a colt, and it was almost thrilling to drive that fast to report the death of her husband. The wind had fluttered her hair and she felt free; she felt her youth again, when she had been an excited bride who had yet to learn about the older man she had married.

When Martha wound the reins around the hitching post on that day, the chestnut had hung its head as though in mourning for its master's passing. The town itself had bowed in sympathy; even though Lionel Darkling's sorrow had been a professional mask to conceal his gleam of calculation, for Haine Madison had been a tall man and would require a costly coffin. Martha expected no less from an undertaker; but Sheriff Russett had gripped her shoulder for a moment after she gave him her news, and when he took his hand away he left his warmth on her skin. It unnerved her to feel the touch of compassion, the touch of a man, after so long; although she stayed strong, making sure she had her words ready for the sheriff to hear. Words that painted the picture of what had happened in the farmhouse as that day had awoken and stretched its arms; before the chickens started their clamouring, before the drag yanked her down as it did every blessed morning. And Russett had nodded, as though he had anticipated everything she had come to tell him; as though he had foreseen it on the day the soldier had brought the boy back to Oasis and it had begun, all over again.

If such a thing was possible, Martha had felt even lighter as she drove the chestnut back to the valley; the cart had bounced over the ground as though it was taking flight. Her husband was where she had left him before harnessing the horse and driving away, still lying across the floorboards with his arms awkward and the open-mouthed surprise on his face. The pool of blood under his body had spread further, as slick and cold as fish skin and blackened by exposure to the air. She thought his eyes had been shut but she returned to half-open slits. Fear stiffened the hair on the back of her neck and she was sealed to the floor, because even after what had happened he was still judging her and recording her failings, flinging them in her face with the back of his hand. Even in death nothing would change and she could never escape, and so she had bowed her head and waited for Haine Madison's retribution.

But there had been silence instead, for his eyes were not watching her through the whisky glaze, they were watching what had taken place the moment before he had died; and although it was already fading, like something sliding back into the past, Martha shuddered. Bravely she had approached the carnage of overturned chairs and broken glass, stepping towards where Haine Madison had been lying with his arms spread as though to welcome her. The blood on the floor was still bright red; it was the flies that had turned it black. They rose in a cloud as she intruded and the noise they made sickened the silence of death. When they came to rest again a few of them had landed on her husband's face like a crawl of spots.

On the day of his demise Haine Madison had studied his wife through dreaming eyes and flies had ventured into his gaping mouth like invited guests. Martha's empty stomach had heaved, and she had run outside to the splintered wall to vomit bile in his honour. But more days had passed since then, and here she was now, standing at the open door of the house and listening to the morning bird. It opened its heart and sang something sweet and powerful that pierced the clean sky, and at that moment Martha wondered what her daughter was doing.

At that moment Sage was leaning from the bedroom window of the doctor's house. From the branches by her head a bird was singing something sweet and powerful, and the drapes waved as though the creature's miniscule breath held the breeze. The girl took it with her as she stared across the street, to the narrow passageway that led from the back of the sheriff's office, where Cub was caged behind shadows. She brought him the song of the bird, and it tickled Sheriff Russett's ears as he stepped into the gloom of the corridor.

He had left the office door ajar, and the blade of light opened a second door in the darkness. The sheriff's dull brown shirt flashed a rich chestnut as he passed it and stood before the boy's cell.

'Another morning, Cub,' he said, and his voice was as strident as an alarm call in the cramp of space. The man felt his own pulse jerk, but his bellow had had no effect on the figure slumped on the bed-shelf across the cell. 'Another morning, and breakfast is on its way,' he eased his voice, but still expected no reaction. For the past few days the meagre meal trays had been discarded to the floor, the food barely touched.

The boy was sitting in dusk, his edges fuzzy as though he was starting to fade. He did not even look up at the slash of light knifing the corridor wall. 'Received a message from the telegraph office,' Russett said, adjusting the volume of his voice even further until he was practically whispering beneath the hush, and it was like meeting the inside of a church after a full-throated street. 'A few more days and the judge's circuit will bring him here. Just a few more days and we can sort out these particulars.'

He paused, but received nothing. 'Are you listening, boy?' he said, and his impatience lifted Cub's gaze from the dirty floor. The darkness inside the boy's eye sockets was a void; it cut into the back of Russett's mind, and for a moment the man knew how emptiness felt.

THIRTY-SIX

THE JUDGE was on his circuit. Haine Madison had been murdered and justice and retribution would shortly be arriving in a stagecoach. Cub sat in the cell as the day's shadows lengthened, and there was nothing to see beyond the heavy block walls. Inactivity made sluggish with his limbs until they became porous and dismantled. The mattress grew ridges like molten iron solidifying over compressed rock, and slowly, relentlessly, the boy began to break.

He didn't know that the doctor's wife was standing on the other side of the bars, or that as Russett had preceded her to the small passageway the woman had seen what appeared to be an empty cell. The atmosphere was powdery, as though every prisoner who had resided in this place had left a little of themselves behind – flakes of emotion hanging in layers – and Lucy pulled the collar of her dress high so that the slivers should not reach her heart. Words formed on her lips for the sheriff who walked without expression, as if he had noticed nothing unusual about the void where Cub should have been. She lifted her hand to grab his arm, to halt him, to shout in his face; but then she saw the boy. He was still there in the disillusion of the cell, forcing himself back against the wall as though he wished to push through its impediment to another plane, and she grabbed the cell door instead, squeezing until the bars flared hot.

Sheriff Russett patted her arm before he turned back

to his office, and she welcomed the gesture; sought after the memory of it as the corridor grew dark again and the sense of despondency was as unnerving as the presence of an eavesdropper.

'Cub.' Lucy whispered, as if anything louder may tip the balance, and she waited, and watched him lift his head until she could see his eyes. They were too dark, too dull; nothing was left of the spark which had once ignited the gold that shone like the edge of his soul. He looked at the woman standing behind the bars, but he did not seem to recognise her and he did not speak.

'I am going to help you,' she said, 'but you need to help me first.' When she stopped talking the quiet was almost crippling. 'You must speak about it, Cub. Do you hear me? How can anyone else believe you are blameless when you are condemning yourself with silence?'

The atmosphere imploded as her voice rose; crushed by the need to stir some life back into his dead eyes. 'Don't you understand what will happen to you when the judge reaches Oasis?' Lucy pressed her face against the cell door, and the bars imprinted her skin with ferocious lines. 'You are facing a murder charge, Cub. You have offered no proof of the innocence you claim and so the judge will have no other choice but to find you guilty. And I am so afraid for you.'

This boy had crossed the hills on foot, bandages easing the stripes on his back; he had tamed a wild stallion to bear a rider and travelled miles to fulfil his quest. This boy had been dragged back from the pinnacle and the consequences had been harsh; but nothing had crushed his mettle before. Now his body was a shell; it was as if he had gone away inside himself because nowhere else was safe. And Lucy felt a rage building that burned the blood in her veins.

'Do you want to suffer the penalty, Cub? Do you want to be hanged for another's crime?' Her voice slammed from the walls; it crept through the closed door at the end of the passageway into the sheriff's office where Russett sat against the back of his chair, breathing hard as the wrath of the doctor's wife slithered under his scalp. But it was quelled as suddenly as it had erupted, as if something had been slotted into place.

Cub stared through the bars into the woman's face; endless black eyes, but with the spark struggling to life behind them. The gold was a pinprick, like the embryonic fire in the centre of kindling; like a flame taking hold and growing stronger. The spirit was returning to his eyes, and his face took colour and came from the shadows. Lucy Ryker was gripping the cell door; he saw the fierce lines that were marking her cheeks; he saw them starting to fade when she stood back into the passageway, drawing him to his feet.

'Somebody else is responsible, Cub,' she said, her voice cracking as though rage had bruised her throat, but she spoke quietly and the warmth was there again. 'Who is it? Who was with you at the farm that morning? Think very carefully and tell me what you can remember.'

And then her voice fell into a whisper. 'I cannot – I will not – lose you,' she said, so softly that her words did not quite reach him.

She was a young woman, just a few years older than the boy, even though he had no age. She had given him warm clothes, food, the hunting knife in its sheath. She had shared her own fierceness so that he should come alive again, and now she was offering him hope. He thought back to the morning that he had sat with the dead stallion, fighting flies for the beauty of the horse for as long as he could. He saw the farmer sprawling on the floor, too drunk to focus and as crushed as a spider. He saw the knife lying harmless on the boards and the whip in its dead coils by the wall. And he searched his memory until he was standing at the threshold of the house once more, his nostrils clogged with farmyard stench, his ears picking up the chickens, the creak of wooden walls, the distant voices of animals that sounded like the scuffle of hidden feet.

His hair had prickled as though someone had breathed on the back of his neck; as though he was imagining eyes watching him as he ran towards the land where maybe, just maybe, he could finally and absolutely be free.

'The place was empty,' he said. 'There was no one else around.' And then he paused, because there might have been something.

Lucy unclenched her fingers and there was pain when she tried to straighten them. Tears waited at the back of her throat but she managed to smile at the boy standing in the middle of the cell. His head was raised as though hunting a scent from beyond the jail walls; a breeze that rolled across from the purple foothills bringing with it the sweet smell of possibility. He walked forwards until the barred door became an obstruction, and Lucy had to tip her head back to see his eyes. They had been fogged with dullness, but now the fog had lifted and they were shining. Darkness in the corridor receded as Cub looked down on the honey-haired woman, and she felt the swell of her pulse like the crash and retreat of waves.

'Mrs Ryker.' He slid his hand through the bars. Lucy gripped it with both of hers, pressed it until the blood surged between them, and when she let him go her skin tingled, as if she was taking part of his soul away with her. She sucked a breath and held it, and only then could she speak again.

'What about Sage's mother?' she said. 'Cub, where was Martha that day?'

'He said she was out in the field.'

'But she may have seen something; or someone.' Lucy frowned. 'Why has she not come forward to help you?'

She was already prepared, but the hairs still tightened

on the back of her neck when he answered.

'Because she wants me dead.'

And she always had. Ever since the day he arrived at the barren farm; a small boy needing to belong after the dismantling of the other life, with its jugglers and jesters and sky-blue canopy. After the dark-eyed man who sang with the spirits and conversed with horses; after the passing of the golden-haired mother. A small boy who could not understand why Haine Madison's wife disliked him so much. He knew he must have done something to displease her, but she had never given him a reason for the loathing that flared from her eyes. She had never spoken to him with anything but disgust, and that hadn't changed. Once despised, he had always been despised.

'Martha Madison is our only hope, Cub,' Lucy said. 'She is going to tell us everything. I shall make quite sure of it.'

But it was difficult to know how, when the boy's life was in balance, and the weights were in the hands of a woman who wanted nothing more than to see him hang.

THIRTY-SEVEN

MARTHA THOUGHT she could hear the rumble of buggy wheels, but it must have been early thunder falling from the blameless sky. She shrugged away the sound, and bent back to pull weeds – the only crop that managed to thrive in this forgotten land.

The land that dropped into the valley disappeared like well water pumped into gasping earth, and the farm disappeared with it, hidden from thought and interest; although the unwelcome had been no impediment for the doctor who had driven himself across from the town to certify the death. But that had been an ache of days ago. A wedge of time had passed since then and the wound had begun to heal, leaving a ridge of awareness in her heart like a scar, like a reminder, if she needed to be reminded, of the half-life that had gone before.

Even in death the thin man had demanded, dismissing her with contempt, holding her captive to his rule from the level of the floor; but the wooden boards, where his blood had spread like something set free, were now clean. On her knees Martha had scrubbed, raising paleness from the stain; taking joy from the empty house, the gentle way it creaked itself to sleep at night and stretched awake to days that had never felt so fresh. The stoop in her back eased and she stood as straight as the woman she used to be, free to stare at the trees spiking the horizon like sparse fur on the flanks of an old dog.

The man was in the ground now, buried in the field of

graves at the edge of the town. She had been the only one to watch his coffin disappearing into its hole, for there had been no Sage to stand beside her. Her husband was beneath the earth and she was safe, but still she woke throughout the night, fearing the stumbled footfall outside her window, the sozzled curse that Haine had learned from the whisky demon, his tongue oiled by uneasy slime from the bottom of the glass. She was cut by barbs of imagination that brought him to life, stalking the farmyard when the night was black, scratching the walls with his nails, tantalising her with fear. But she had barred the door to him. She had bolted and barricaded and he could not get through. Haine Madison's spirit was an impotent wisp of air, the simple wail of wind in the chimney, a vile memory; she would no longer suffer the back of his hand, the swift punch like the blow from a padded hammer, the spit of obscenities that had once left a putrid imprint on her skin, until it had become as hard and shiny as a shell.

This was the way she was thinking on the day she heard the wheels that sounded like a warning of thunder from a blameless sky. The sound grew in intensity, wafting towards and away from her as the wind played. But only when it became steadfast did she look up from the soil at the back of the house where she was urging life into puny flowers. The buggy was getting near by then, and she saw that there were two women sitting high behind the horse. She could not identify who was guiding the reins but she recognised the one who sat beside her, hands clasped in her lap, shoulders squared as if she was fearful of what might come. As if she had learned the art of modesty, maybe. Martha had not known her daughter to be dressed in such splendour before, with her hair tucked to the top of her head like a lady, and she hid a catch of breath behind her fingers as she watched the buggy arrive, bouncing an ungainly dance where the land ended and the farmyard began.

The driver of the bay mare was attired as if calling on friends. She took time to stack the reins tidily, as though rehearsing the words that she had come there to say, before sitting straight-backed on the bench and bending her head to the farmer's widow. Fresh and serene in her lilac dress, the woman saw the struggle of flowers in the hard earth and the dangle of weeds in a hand, skirts that were as dull as a dusty day and thin lips in a thin face; and Martha felt the heat from her eyes as though she was standing too close to the sun, and took a small step away to break the grip before she realised she had done so.

'Mrs Madison?' The woman's voice was clear though tentative, as if to make certain that she was addressing that very person. But Martha did not know her, and when she looked to her daughter for an explanation Sage was somewhere other, staring down at her demure hands as though waiting to be introduced. Martha felt like the stranger; she straightened her back with displeasure and focused on the woman with the glossy neat hair, who was sitting so close to the unnatural girl that they seemed well acquainted. It was a friendship that sliced away the mother standing below and sharpened the sting in her tongue.

'Who are you and what are you doing here?'

'Mrs Madison, my name is Lucy Ryker.'

This then was the doctor's wife. The woman with her carefully coiled braid, the owner of clean petticoats that rustled as she climbed down from the buggy to confront the mother at her own height. This was a woman who had no right to be standing in the crusty mire of a lost hope farmyard, compelling with eyes where the whites were too wide. A woman who brought unease into Martha's heart, because she knew things; because she had guessed.

'Sage has been staying in my house since she left her home,' the woman said, lifting her head towards the girl.

'Why does she not come down from there?' Martha folded her arms, clutching the thin sleeves of her dress.

The weeds slithered from her fingers. 'Get yourself down here, daughter,' she demanded.

Sage didn't look at her mother; she looked instead at Lucy as if needing her permission to step from the buggy and stand beside the bay. She held her skirt like wings as though preparing for flight, and sought protection behind her hair. In Martha's memory, it was something she had always done, but now the girl's hair was bunched tight to the top of her head and could no longer offer her a safeguard.

'Might we speak with you, Mrs Madison?' Lucy said.

Martha tightened her arms and felt the sharp points of her elbows. 'If you wish to speak, then go ahead.'

'I was thinking that it may be more comfortable to speak inside the house, if you would allow it.' A rogue breeze ruffled Lucy's dress and it cracked like a flag around her legs. A scent reached Martha's nostrils, and it was as if the garment had been woven from the very flowers that coloured it. The perfume unlocked childhood memories that circumstances had forced to the back of the widow's mind, and relaxed her like a hot bath. She turned to lead them towards the door, guiding her daughter as if she was a stranger in her mother's home.

The house was dark inside and stifling beneath its blanket of heat, and the obliteration of farmyard sounds left a hum in the air. Martha nodded at the table and Lucy drew out a chair to sit, but Sage hesitated for a moment by the doorway, as though she had not expected to enter the house ever again, and sought shadows by the wall where she could hide, her hands crossed over her belly.

Martha folded into the second chair. The humming dispersed in the sticky air, and the silence it left behind felt like the moment before falling.

'Mrs Madison,' Lucy leaned across the table, and her eyes lent further heat to the room. 'Although this might be painful for you, we need to talk about the morning that your husband died.'

'And why do you need to do that, Mrs Ryker?'

'Because whatever transpired that day could make the difference between life and death…'

'Already there has been one death.'

'Indeed. But we are hoping to prevent another…'

'And how can you expect my help in preventing any such thing?'

The doctor's wife clasped her hands together on the tabletop. 'What you can tell us may save a life, and I beg it of you, Mrs Madison,' she said, and then she bowed her head until it seemed that she was praying. All Martha saw was how the dingy room muted but could not quench entirely the shine of the woman's hair, and not for the first time she was discomfited by all that this house, this miserable farm, had meant to her: complete isolation, as though she had been suffering from a disease; the twenty-year disease of being Haine Madison's wife. But when Lucy parted her hands she brought back a little coolness like an answer to her prayer, dousing some of the room's heat.

Sage stepped across the floor towards the two women, passing over the spot where her father had fallen in his last inebriation, spitting vitriol at his spouse as he tried to get to his feet; the place haunted by the ghost of blood stains that Martha had attacked with the scrubbing brush until her hands were swollen. It was to have been her final chore to follow his death; but now the doctor's wife was pleading with her to perform this other chore, and the asking was too much.

She put her hands over her eyes until she felt alone in the room. 'I don't know what to do,' she said, her voice laden with the years she had spent never knowing what to do. But this time she was not alone, and her hands were gripped by gentle fingers that smothered the rough skin with softness like a kiss.

‘We will both help you, Martha.’ There was excitement in Lucy’s voice, and the rise of relief. ‘Sage and I will help you.’

‘Sage?’ Martha looked around and the girl was there, like someone else’s daughter in the gentlewoman’s dress and uplifted hair, her head raised by her own excitement. Martha stared at her with hope, with regret, with the loss of years and the gift of years to come, and Sage looked at her mother and smiled with a face so unused to smiles that she was transformed into something fresh and beautiful.

Lucy’s hands were rich with her untroubled pulse and smoothed by her tranquil life, and Martha’s hands lay between them, made ragged by relentless toil. She thought that she could stay there forever, sitting in idleness in the company of this indulged woman while the animals lowed for their feed and the broken fences disintegrated and the house sank further into the ground. Perhaps she could borrow some gossamer from Lucy Ryker and use it to weave a glorious future.

‘It will be fine,’ the woman was saying, exaggerating syllables with the squeeze of her fingers. ‘Just help us to help the boy, Martha.’

The boy. The words tumbled as though the ceiling was coming towards her. Martha pulled her hands away and raised them high, flailing at the pressure; trying to push at whatever was squashing her skull before the bones should break. The connection with the lilac woman shattered like the end of a beautiful dream, and reality was twice as painful. It was unendurable to be sitting there enveloped in a false and glittering mist while the sweat stains spread across the back of her dress and the farm would always and forever be her prison.

Martha shot to her feet and her chair skittered. Lucy jerked backwards and her eyes grew wide again, and Sage took a step behind her to hide from the mother.

'There is nothing I can do for you.' Martha's voice rose higher with the words. 'Nothing I will do to help that murderer!'

'Mrs Madison. Please.' Lucy stood like an angel in her own pool of light. Martha saw her uplifted arm, the brandishing of blame from her fingers; she felt the woman reaching into her soul. 'Please tell us what happened that morning. You are the only one who can.'

'Not me. The boy can. Ask him, and he will tell you that he took a knife and used it on my husband until his life flowed away with the blood, and he left him lying. Down there.' She pointed to the rough floor where she had scrubbed until her fingers were claws around the brush. 'You are standing on my husband's blood.' She shouted the words so that they would hear. And then there was silence, broken by Sage, sobbing as though her heart had burst. The mother saw that the doctor's wife was holding the girl in her arms, and after a while the fury inside her was subdued to an aching, that was as strong as the pain of her daughter's distress.

'No, Martha. Cub is innocent,' Lucy said, and her voice was firm now. 'And you may have been the last person to see Haine Madison alive.'

'Mrs Ryker, you are condemning me.'

'Mrs Madison, nobody has the right to condemn you. But if you hide the truth then you yourself will condemn the boy to death.'

'It is his word against mine…'

'This is not a competition, Mrs Madison. This is the redemption of an innocent life.'

Martha began to shake as though a whirlwind had taken control of her body, spreading from her feet to the roots of her hair. 'My husband abhorred me because I was unable to birth a son for him.' Her teeth juddered, cutting holes in the words. 'And because I'd failed him he found someone else to do the job. The boy is his spawn out of another woman's flanks.'

'But even if that were so, Martha, how can Cub be to blame?'

'And how can you blame me for the way I felt when he was brought to my house?'

'I only feel sympathy for you, Martha, not blame.'

The shaking had stilled, but she was too heavy for her swollen feet. She sought the chair again; it had pulled away from the table and she sat on its island with her eyes to the floor so that she wouldn't have to face the lilac woman, or the girl who was still her daughter, despite the ladylike disguise.

'That boy is my husband's bastard,' Martha said to the boards, the places that she had scoured clear of blood. 'And because of him I have had to endure the fruit of infidelity for seven long years.' There was a murmur of petticoats. Martha could almost taste the silky sound as Sage stepped forward and crouched at her feet.

'But none of that is true, Ma,' the girl said, and it was soothing where she touched her mother's hand. Martha remembered the perfume of her baby's skin, and when she looked up into Sage's eyes she noticed that they were beautiful. 'Cub is not my brother. Pa was lying to you. He never had a son; he only had me.'

Martha could not take her eyes off her astonishing child, the gloss of youth, the shine of hope. 'Why?' she said. 'Why should he lie when it hurt me so much?'

'Because he wanted it to,' Sage said, and colour flared in her face, the colour of anger and the years of hiding behind her hair for protection. 'He hurt everyone. But now he is dead, and when he has finally gone I will be grateful!'

'Hush, Sage. Do not speak like this of your pa; of the departed…'

'I need to speak like this, Ma, because he has not yet departed; he is still here in this room, on this land and in all our minds. He has perished but his vileness remains. He is still hurting us, and Cub is the one he wants to hurt most of all. But with your help we can be rid of him. You must tell us what happened that morning, to save Cub's life and put an end to this haunting.'

Lucy Ryker stood waiting with her hand to her mouth as the minutes died, while in her mind the boy was slumped over himself in the dark cell at the back of the sheriff's office, and the rest of his life was passing too fast. Martha heard weeping, and saw tears like sapphire glitter in her daughter's eyes. 'I am begging you,' the girl said. 'If you love me then help me. Help Cub and help me.'

Time leaked through the gloom in the farmhouse. The wooden walls ticked with the day's heat and Martha Madison stared at the two roads in front of her: one of them came to a sudden end, but the other was wide open, shimmering with guilt all the way to the horizon. She looked down at the floor again, because she no longer wished to see the little child her daughter had once been, trusting and loving and ignorant of all that the future held in store for her.

'I have told you what happened,' she said. 'Now leave me be. Both of you.'

She stood at the door and stared across the muddle as the buggy wheels clattered away. It was a hopeless sound; it left her feeling as though something had been pulled from her heart and thrown into the air, and the wind had ripped it to pieces so that it would never return. She could still feel Lucy Ryker's soft hands in her own, but the memory was going to fade into nothing. If she lived in the way of the doctor's wife she too might grow fine skin, lose the heavy knuckles of harsh winters, the black lines of toil embedded too deeply to wash away. Perhaps she too might wear crisp clean clothes that smelled of flowers and oil her hair to a gleam on the top of her head. She might already have received those glorious gifts if she had not met Haine Madison; if she had not believed the visions that wafted behind his lies. Twenty years ago, there had still been a chance to outrun the life she never expected. But she had been a headstrong young bride, gladly turning her back on her own kin for fear that her future would be ruined by their overblown concerns.

Ruin her future! Only one person had done that and he was dealt with and dispatched, and now she wanted to grow back into herself. It was all she wanted, and nothing would be allowed to turn those tables against her again.

THIRTY-EIGHT

THERE WAS a sudden and harsh fall of rain that night, almost like the release after a period of great tension. Like a release it should have cleared the air of fog and tasted of all things fresh and new, but although there had been a torrent it had been brisk, it had misbehaved like a tantrum and achieved nothing. If anything, the pulse of darkness hanging over the cell was palpable, whisked up by the storm into an unease that beat a patchy rhythm from wall to narrow wall. Beneath it Cub had grown transparent, and if he should open his eyes he would see nothing in front of him.

The tray of food was still on the floor by the door, where it had been placed the previous evening; it was providing a meal for the flies that were now accustomed to the waste, but they rose to greet Sheriff Russett as he came out from his office. He found himself wading into the murk, and when he stood by the cell it pulled at him as if to drag him down. He shuffled his feet to break the hold, but each day it lingered just that bit longer.

'The judge will be in town soon, Cub; two days' time now.'

The boy did not move; he may have been in the deepest sleep, or perhaps the strange fog was an incubus lying on his chest and slowly starving him of air. But the sheriff had grown as accustomed as the pampered flies to the trances that appeared to suck him so dry he might crumble through the wooden slats into some spellbound place. Russett knew that Cub was not asleep when the enchantment held him; that he had heard the man's words and understood what they meant, and the sheriff spoke no more until he was back in his office, along with the chill that had followed him from the corridor.

Gasping its last like a landed fish, the residue of rain slowly disappeared into the ground so that at first there was a gloss across the road that echoed the heavy clouds, and then the wheeled ruts were dry again and the sky had risen. But the weather had not finished with them yet, for a new darkness was swelling like an evil temper. The day was apprehensive, and tendrils of that disquiet found the girl who stood at the window of the doctor's house, the cleaning cloth forgotten in her hand. Sage held herself so still that it was as if she was no longer there. Cub was so motionless in the cell across the road that it was as if he was no longer there. They were unconscious of each other; their minds were whole with each other. They shared the same unease and could not move with it.

Lucy watched the girl from the doorway, wishing there was something she could do to alleviate her own misery. She collected herself together and entered the room at a bustle to hand out activity and stave off the day's relentless hold, dragging Sage back from wherever she had been. Her entrance was so abrupt that the girl was shocked awake, astonished to find that she was in the Rykers' house with a cloth in her hand, that her employer was jostling the room with sudden movement and a brightness to her mouth that didn't quite reach her eyes. Sage shouted when she had only meant to whisper.

'I don't know what else we can do to help him.'

Lucy put her hands on the girl's shoulders, fragile with bone beneath the borrowed dress, slid them down her arms and gripped fingers that were as cold as rain and as dry as sorrow, and after a while Sage lifted her head. Her eyes were saturated. Lucy recognised the need in them, and her own inability to promise that all would be well. 'We have already done as much as we can,' she said instead. 'His succour rests with higher hands now.'

Invisible hands; hands sitting in judgement.

'I went to the church to see the priest,' the girl said, as if the room was empty and she was merely voicing her thoughts. 'I told him things that I have told no one else. He pressed his hand on my head as if he was pushing his wisdom into my brain. He advised me to pray and the answers would open like petals in my heart; but my heart is already too full and there is no room for anything else to lodge there. The man in the church should have given me the answers, Mrs Ryker. A priest should know what to do.'

Lucy squeezed her fingers. 'My dear girl, the priest is limited. He endures the frailty of a human body and is not divine. But you are right for he does have wisdom.'

'What use is that to Cub, Mrs Ryker? Wisdom will not open the cell door and set him free. Wisdom should never have brought him to a place where he must barter for his life with a man he's never met. A man who can't know him the way I do.'

Lucy bit her tongue to kill the words she might have spoken. It all seemed so futile. The day before, Martha Madison had been resolute; dismissing them from the farm like a broom sweeping away detritus. The woman held in her hands the answers that the priest had predicted, but they were destined never to open like his promised petals unless there was a part of her heart that could cultivate forgiveness. Forgiveness of the boy in the cell, and of herself.

Sage's mother had been sucked nut-dry by life until her heart was a shrivelled kernel, but Lucy Ryker had seen how she lamented her daughter's tears, and it made her think of irrigation. She looked at the sorrow in Sage's eyes now and saw a thread of hope.

But two days later the thread had stretched to a strand of gossamer, and Judge Gerald Hopgood arrived in town.

The stagecoach had ploughed the last miles through liquid mud that spat from the wheels and coated the horses' flanks with slurry. It eased its way through the ill-fitting door along with the bitterest of draughts, violating the fine leather on the man's feet and the cuffs of his expensive pants. He could not recall ever having ridden in such an abysmal conveyance, which was in truth not much more than a sieve. The first thing he craved in private and demanded in authority as soon as he arrived in this godforsaken place was a hot bath. There was a scurry as suitable accommodation was found for him, and the only obstacle to his comfort seemed to be the bow-shouldered sheriff who had arrived at the door of the stagecoach to bid him welcome. As if the judge could ever feel an affinity with this grotesque settlement, when he himself dwelled in spacious rooms in a city where men were employed to sweep the paths in front of his home. But the sheriff wore the blinkers of long association and knew nothing about the despicability he could not see beyond his nose. Indeed, the lawman would do well to spend a few minutes pondering this truth as Hopgood sought peace and solitude in the saloon's private bath tub.

Sheriff Russett returned to his office, dashing water from his hat at the doorway. The rain was as relentless as a stampede of buffalo; it was as pitiless as bad luck, for he had seen how it had shaken the judge's power of balanced opinion. He thought of the boy waiting in the cell for his future to be decided, and he hoped that such a decision was to be fair and just in such irascible hands.

Lucy had heard the commotion arising from the centre of town, where the stagecoach had been disgorging its passenger: the disapproval, the volley of complaints, the prejudgement – as if the town itself was responsible for the weather. She saw Sheriff Russett return to his office with his shoulders beaten down by rain, but she could not see his face under the brim of his hat, just the straight line of his mouth inside the bristle of beard. The thread of hope was still there in her parlour where it had woven itself two days earlier, but it was only visible in sunlight now and vanished behind the storm that lay in the room. And Lucy was troubled.

Judge Hopgood inspected the ground before stepping from the swinging doors of the saloon, but the boards of the sidewalk were no longer as grey as an untended winter garden; they were regaining the colour of sand, which meant that while he had been taking his bath and making the most of the kitchen's meagre menu, the rain must have ceased. The boards looked warm, and the judge felt warm as well, for unlike the limited kitchen the measures of liquor from behind the counter had been plentiful; therefore, he began to feel friendlier towards the town as he made the short way to the sheriff's office and rapped on the door with the carnelian in his signet ring. As he entered the man was already rising from his chair, and he greeted Hopgood with the handshake that the disgruntled judge had spurned at the time of the downpour and its creeping mud. The sheriff was still bow-shouldered, but in whisky-inspired magnanimity the judge accepted it as the inevitable fight against lawlessness that was weighing him down, and he smiled at the doleful face before him, lifting the flaps of his coat before seeking a comfortable position on the hard chair he had been offered. And then Russett started to explain.

A man had been murdered. Judge Hopgood rubbed his hands together and placed them palms downwards on the desk. The well-manicured nails shone like pale tips to his freckled fingers and he studied them with approval as the sheriff talked, picturing the scene of the hard-working farmer killed in his own home by the boy he had welcomed into his family; the boy who had profited from kindness, bed, board and a solid future but had repaid his benefactor with undeniable viciousness. No outstanding points were raised to query guilt; why, there was even a potential witness to the deed – the dead man's widow, no less. It sounded perfectly clear to the judge that it was to be an investigation in name alone. Although, Hopgood surmised, the sheriff was not satisfied. The lines between the man's eyes clawed deeper as he spoke; his voice grated with dislike as he talked of the murder victim, Haine Madison; it grew tremulous with regret as he described the boy who had done the deed. It was as if Sheriff Russett himself was sitting as judge, condemning and vindicating with wild inconsistency; summoning a cloud to disturb the perfect clarity that should have allowed Hopgood an early return to the sparkling pavements of his home.

And then the woman came to the sheriff's door; as well dressed as a lady from the city, but bonnetless, as though she had left her house in too much of a hurry, or even considered her coiffure unimportant. Her hair was as dishevelled as if she had tended it in the morning in one frame of mind and yet another had taken hold of her as the day progressed. Oh yes, he had recognised a city lady, like his own dear Tilda, who was at that moment waiting in their spacious house for his return at the end of the circuit, taking delicate tea with the other groomed ladies of her acquaintance under the genteel tick of an ormolu clock. But this woman appearing at the sheriff's office was a firebrand with flaming eyes and forgotten hair, and she came straight over to the desk and spoke without waiting for an introduction.

'There has been an injustice,' she said, 'and I beg of you to allow me time to prove it.'

Judge Hopgood rose to his feet with automatic good manners, and a smile that only lifted the edges of his mouth. 'My dear lady…'

'The boy is innocent. I am convinced of it.' Her voice was rising with the fire in her eyes; she was losing control and the judge frowned his annoyance.

The sheriff came around the side of the desk with his hand raised. 'Mrs Ryker, I understand your anxiety but you may well be making things more difficult…'

'But I only wish to make them easier, Sheriff Russett, however pleading the truth from another could very well prove to be difficult.' She turned to the portly judge in his beautiful clothes. 'That is why I need you to allow me more time.'

Although more time might have been something that Hopgood was unwilling to offer when he could already visualise his wife growing peevish beneath the persistent clock, flicking the folds of her skirt with exasperation as his circuit came to an end and there was still no sign of him. But the young woman's eyes were truly compelling; they seemed to reach inside him and squeeze his heart: an atrophied organ where excitement had once dwelled, before being quashed by one godforsaken town after another, and humanity's unceasing desire for its own destruction. Mrs Ryker's frenzy stopped his breath until he began to feel faint, and when he started to breathe again he was unsteadied by the thud of his heart and the heat that rose to his throat.

He stared at the woman, whose cheeks were streaked as though she had earlier rubbed away tears and left the shadow of passion on her skin, so fierce and pure was her belief. Russett was trying to turn her towards the door where she would unravel in the street, and the judge wanted none of it. He reached out a hand and stepped forward, and they became a trio, pushing and pulling and pleading and appeasing, until the woman spun away from the sheriff and grabbed Hopgood's arm with both hands. A fever climbed up through his coat sleeve until he thought he would not be able to bear it.

'My dear lady, you must be seated. Please do not worry for I shall listen to everything you say, but first you must calm yourself.' For my sake, calm yourself, he thought. And when she released his arm and sank slowly into the vacant chair the judge wilted, and he tried to remember when he had last felt so fatigued. He dropped his weight to the edge of the desk where Russett was standing like a tired man resting himself on his fists, bowed down by his own battles against corruption. Hopgood felt the leak of sympathy through holes in his cynical soul.

'Judge Hopgood, this is Lucy Ryker,' the sheriff began. 'Her husband is the doctor of Oasis…'

'Daniel would be here with me now, but today people are lining up to see him.' Lucy shook her head and her hair flew. 'Far too many sick people for such a small town, so I am thinking that they have come merely to ogle Sage.'

The judge frowned. 'Who is this Sage?'

'Sage Madison,' Russett straightened up from the desk, but his shoulders were still bowed. 'The daughter of Haine Madison, the deceased.'

'The monster.' The woman's voice was rising again, like a tornado that she could not control. 'Haine Madison was a monstrous man…'

'Madam, you must understand that if you do not contain yourself I shall be unable to listen further.' It was a voice more suited for a courtroom than the tight walls around them and the strength of it knocked Lucy back in the chair, but she looked at the man sitting above her and knew that she had his attention.

'I understand,' she said, but what she understood was that finally she had found someone who might help. She closed her eyes and sighed, and it was as if the build up of weeks dissipated in one deep breath, and finally she had permission to be calm. It was a sigh that raised the office ceiling until the air felt fresh again and everything was ready to hear Lucy Ryker speak.

Judge Hopgood saw himself perching in discomfort on the edge of a wooden desk, and that it had become an unseemly place to be. He stood up, adjusted the flaps of his coat and the stiff tie at his throat with satisfaction, and paced to the window because his legs needed to move. The panes of glass were lively with the picture of the main street of Oasis: the slouch of riders rocking to the slide of hooves; the stately glide of older ladies along the sidewalk and the energy of the young ones heading home with laden baskets; the disparate kick of boots as clumps of men made for the saloon, and the singular purpose that led tradesmen from their businesses at the close of day. While Hopgood absorbed what he could see through the window, his mind absorbed everything he was hearing behind him, as the woman told the story of the offender who was waiting in a cell at the back of the office for his future to unfold. Even though he was still invisible, the eloquence of Lucy's words was painting him in flesh and blood, and the judge would not have been surprised if he had turned around to find the boy taking up his own space in the office.

But when he did turn around there were still just the two of them; the grey-faced sheriff sitting behind his desk, and the fervent young woman who had finished speaking and was watching Hopgood with the fire hovering at the back of her eyes. Such vehemence; the judge wondered whether the absent doctor was a worthy husband for so passionate a woman, and he wondered also about the merit of the invisible prisoner who had obviously won her over.

'Well,' he said, tucking hands behind his back and rocking on his heels; becoming a courtroom judge once more. 'Now that I have heard the plea for the defence, I believe it is time I spoke to the young man you wish me to exonerate. And then, Mrs Ryker, I need to ask if your husband will allow you to accompany me in the morning, when I propose to make a visit to the victim's widow.'

THIRTY-NINE

THE BROKEN axle had defeated her, together with the mutter of thunder behind the hills. Martha stood beside the twisted cart and heard the rumble as a yowling of giant beasts that wished only to tear her to pieces, dismembered and scattered and consumed by dust like everything else that struggled for life in this deathly place. And when that happened she would be glad; free from all concern for the failing crops and the hungry animals, as well as the flowers that had given up hope in the garden she tended at the back of the house.

She had never felt more alone. Even in drunkenness, when the husband was alive the fields had been cultivated, Sage had kept busy in the house, and the boy – well, he had worked as though he were three in number. But they were all gone now, taking their usefulness with them, and Martha leaned on the fractured wagon in the last gasp of the farmyard and knew she was finished. Gathering her frayed hem around her, she sat down where she was, heedless of the mud, the ordure, the protuberant eyes of skinny hens that pecked for sustenance in the miserly ground at her feet. They jabbed at her legs, leaving angry gashes that she hid beneath her skirt, and nipped her hands in retaliation when she shooed them away. Martha was hungry as well, sitting surrounded by chicken meat, although by now the hens were too wizened beneath their feathers to provide much nourishment, and she was too weary to care.

Thunder came again, muted this time. The giant beasts kept rolling towards her and Martha thought that perhaps it would be wiser to lie down on the earth to greet them, so that when the end came at least it would be quick. And it was fast approaching, for the rumbling grew louder and closer until the ground began to vibrate. But then it stopped, just as suddenly as the false thunder she had imagined on the day that the doctor's wife had arrived at the farm to denounce her.

All was quiet again, except for the rattle of harness, the halting hooves on the other side of the farmyard and the voices raised in query; and Martha sat in the dirt and stared at the buggy that had appeared again beside the house, the bay mare snorting for air and the people descending from the vehicle. They approached as though they had some fear of her and it was as before, when the woman had come to beg for clemency for the wild boy, bringing Sage in her fine clothes to add ballast to her plea. She had brought Sage with her again, recognisable this time in homespun and calico, as though the first visit had not been a lesson enough. And she'd brought a stranger along as well. She introduced him as a judge, and that made sense for he had a snout like a pig, snuffling for evidence. A rotund gentleman, too smartly dressed for the slovenly farm – he picked his dainty way over animal shit, rubbing smears of matter into sharply creased pants until his rosy cheeks were a scowl of disgust.

The young woman came swiftly across the yard and crouched down in the muck to wind her arms around the mother's shoulders. She helped her to stand as though she was an invalid. She said kind things in a soft voice that crept in under the armour of years to where Martha was weakest.

'There, there,' the young woman said, holding the mother's head against the heavenly perfume at her neck, and Martha wanted nothing more than to sink into the memory of her own mother's love; the memory of that far-off time before the man had crushed her future beneath his muddied boots.

'Shall we go in the house, Martha?' the woman said, and led her across the yard and into the wooden shack, where Martha knew the floor needed sweeping; and for a moment she was bothered that her guests would look unkindly on her sluggish housework. But they were not guests that she had invited. They were intruders who wanted something from her that she was unwilling to give.

She flung off the soft arms and glared about her. They were all inside the house now, the uninvited: the young woman, her dress smeared with crud from the yard; the stout man, his lips thinned by distaste; and Sage with her anguished face, too frail and too hungry and looking for somewhere to hide. Afraid to come any closer; desperate to come closer. Desperate for her mother to come closer.

Martha opened her arms and the girl stood as if in shock, but then she started to move into the room, slowly at first and then faster, until she met her mother in the centre. When Martha held her, it was as if they had been moulded together.

Dear God, Martha thought inside the collar of her daughter's thin arms, the comfort muffling sharp places in her mind. Dear God, as Sage glided across the floor with her towards the inadequate table, and they sat there with hands clasped and the warmth lifting the grey sky and feeding the birdsong. Sage's eyes were wide and level, no longer downcast. She had been growing; she had turned into a young woman and her mother had been too lost in her own misery to notice her transition. Martha held the youthful hand as if it could remind her of what she had lost in the days when she had risen at dawn and worked until dusk, keeping her head down and her mouth so tight that her tongue had become desiccated with disuse. Their heads were almost touching as she held Sage's hand, and the girl spoke close to her ear so that the words were for her alone. There were promises and dreams and wishes in the words, weaving a rosy future in the bleakness of the room. Dear God, thought Martha, that any kind of future might be possible when in the past all that had existed had been the present.

Sage said the boy's name; it was a sharp word that pierced the tenderness and brought Martha back into her skin, but the rosiness remained and so she was content to rest easy as her daughter spoke. Although Sage's words were digging for answers and Martha was afeared that the girl might discover what she had hidden. She was afeared of the well-nourished man with the intelligent face who was standing in her house, listening carefully for snippets. He had opened his mouth to predatory teeth and Martha shrank from the bite of judgement.

'I cannot help you,' she said, lowering her eyes to dismiss them, but the room was too full of people and she panicked. She tried to break the connection with Sage but the fingers were insistent and the will was fierce, and the mother could not escape the daughter's inquisition. Sage was the strong one now and Martha could not fight any longer; but still she tried.

'I cannot tell you anything,' she said. 'You will have to leave.'

'Please, Ma.' The girl squeezed the captive hands as though she was milking her mother for the truth. 'Only you know what happened here that morning, and Cub's life is at stake if you do not speak of it.'

Then two unwanted lives will be over, and when that is done she will be unencumbered; the ghosts will leave her be and it shall finally be her turn to live. How could her daughter not understand?

'That man's by-blow…' Martha swallowed, but the bitter taste was still there on her tongue, as if the past had adhered in layers that could never be eradicated. 'I have had to live with my husband's bastard for too many years, so why should I lift a finger to help him now?'

'Because not to do so would be unjust.' The doctor's wife had come closer, as though she had been slowly sliding across the floor towards them like a snake with a poisonous mouth. Like Madison's sharp fanged whip that had splintered the air under his hand. The last time Martha had seen the coil of plaited leather it had been impotent in a death spiral on the floor of this room, and the man's hand had been reaching for its viciousness to stop her mouth. But his mouth had been stopped instead and she had seen it finish. And the woman in her fine dress, with yard shit turning the lilac purple where it was drying in patches, why should she consider that unjust?

The mother tried to pull away but Sage would not let her go. Martha was frightened by the girl's eyes, their sharpness penetrating her mind and searching for the truth beneath wrappings of righteousness, and something deflated inside her until she could not bear it.

'Daughter, do you not remember? At first there were three of us, and then a fourth was brought to the farm and that other one was an invader; he was not welcome but there was nothing I could do to prevent him coming. The husband was always strong and I was too weak, but you were my only child and I knew that I had to stay alive so that he would vent his cruelty on me and you would be safe from it. I could cope with the beatings and the hurts, they were physical and they healed, but then he brought his bastard here, and that wound has never healed.'

'Cub is not his son, Ma, he is not my brother…'

'But for seven years I believed it to be true. And I hated. I hated the woman who birthed the child that the husband had fathered. I hated that the child would grow from a boy to a man, and when Madison was gone the baseborn would inherit what was left. And when that day came there would be no more need for you or me, so what would happen then, daughter? How much longer could I protect you when the farm had gone to the invader and we were cast out?'

'You protected me so well, and I'll always be grateful.' Isolated in her own misery Sage had been blind to her mother's. They had been separated by all-consuming toil and self-erected barriers. The bond between them had been fallow, but by the grace of God it was not yet too late. 'We are safe now, Ma. We are still together.'

'Sage, we have not been together since you were a little girl.'

Martha felt the depth of sorrow in what she was saying and there were tears in her eyes. There was something odd about the blurring of the room, as though she had been tightly folded away inside herself for so long that the ability to cry had faded. The memory flashed through her mind of the day the stray had arrived; the curious child who was content to sit before the husband on his saddle and had not yet learned to fear Madison's temper. The boy's eyes had been strange even then: dark until the sun set them alight, and so clear that maybe he could see what lay beyond the starkness of his new existence. And the day that the husband had flaunted the proof of his betrayal had been the last time she had cried, long and hard and silently through the night, with the knowledge that the mark of adultery was lying on straw in the barn across the yard, and nothing would ever be the same again.

Her daughter had been so young and so needy; a plump little girl with laughter in her eyes and curls in her hair. But the laughter had faded and Sage's hair had become a curtain to hide behind, and Martha knew that it was because of her and because of Madison. And even though he was now beyond the veil he could still direct the way she should feel, and maybe that was what the doctor's wife was referring to when she said it was unjust.

'Is it too late?' Martha looked around, pushing wetness

from her sight until the room came into focus again and the three who shared the space with her were clearer. Through the open door she could see into the yard where the sun fell in knife-edged rays, as though paradise had come down to the dirt where chickens grovelled, and turned the filthy pond into something miraculous that reflected the sky.

The sweet-scented woman knelt beside the table, and Martha winced for her knees. 'It can never be too late,' Lucy Ryker said, her eyes as far-seeing and vivid as the boy's eyes had been when he had first come to the farm. 'It is never too late to put things right, Martha.'

Sage stroked the back of her mother's hand, reading her story from the raised veins and cracked skin. 'Ma, only you know what happened the morning that Pa passed away, and you must speak of it for there is a life at the mercy of what you can tell us, and it is a life that deserves to be saved.'

Martha felt prickles like sudden surprises on her hand, and she saw that her daughter was weeping, gently at first and then with anguish. Lucy Ryker leaned forward, and the two women pressed hands to the girl's head as though to urge their own strength into her body. Fingers laced where the hands touched, and they stared at each other over Sage's hair, until the girl looked up and began to speak, her sight still blurred. Too blurred to notice Lucy recoiling from the words.

'I am in love with him.'

Dear God, Martha thought. 'With your brother? You cannot…'

'Listen to me!' Sage's voice was too shrill; it stung her mother's ears. It stung everyone in the room, and they all listened. 'Pa bought Cub. He paid money for an orphan from a travelling circus and told you he was his son,' she said, biting every word. 'Cub's father was an Indian horse whisperer. He has never been my brother. You have to believe me.'

'But all those years…'

'All those lies.'

'…All those wasted years.'

Martha looked back and saw him again; debauching wooden boards with his drunkenness. Spitting in her face and sliding on the blood from his self-inflicted wound as he tried to stand.

Lucy Ryker touched the woman's arm and brought her forward to the present, to floorboards that she had scrubbed clean of evidence. 'Even now in death he lies to you,' the doctor's wife said, 'and he has trained you so well that you still bear allegiance to him. But it has become a dangerous thing to honour the memory of a bully, for it overweighs the balance and puts innocence in jeopardy. And Cub is too young to die.'

She frowned as if in pain, swaying from the table as she battled with some inner turmoil, and Martha caught sight of the well-dressed man standing close to the door. It looked like he had just entered the house, even though he had been there the whole time. He was too upright and motionless for a body carrying such weight, and she could see that he was accustomed to being seated; but he had heard every word that had been spoken in the room, for they were playing behind his eyes in a calculation; as though he was a mathematician solving a problem.

This man was holding the scales of justice. The balance was inconsistent; but there was nothing else she could do.

The chair sighed in relief when she rose, brushing down her skirt and folding the material around her legs, as though giving herself time to make the decision to turn and face the stranger at the doorway. Even the boards on which she stood were guilty from the history of her husband's death, for this was where his blood had flowed until it began to disappear into the wood on the day that she had seen the boy leaving through the open door. She had hidden behind the house and watched as he ran into the morning, and then she had gone inside to find the husband on the floor. He had been lying shut-eyed and open-mouthed and silent, and her heart had leaped to a conclusion. But he was far from dead.

He snorted a breath like one coming awake, spat her disappointment back in her face, hated her once again for her barrenness, for her uselessness. He climbed to his feet, he gripped her by the throat, he raised his fist.

'I have something to tell you,' Martha said.

Judge Hopgood took one step towards her in his very fine shoes and nodded. 'Madam, I am only too ready to hear what it is.'

FORTY

RAIN FOLLOWED them back to Oasis, the corpulent man and the doctor's wife squeezing together on the buggy bench, the girl finding more space in the hollow behind them. Lucy's hair was wild with lack of tending; it unravelled down her back to join the wind, but she did not care. The judge's shoes were past ruin now; he cast a glance at the sodden leather, but he did not care. Sage felt each collision with the stones beneath the buggy wheels and every jolt echoed in her body, but she did not care. The horse strained towards the town, its head hanging over puddles and its back quaking from the chill; and nobody really cared.

Lucy halted the bay in front of the sheriff's office and the sound of rain filled the silence that remained after the wood-crack and leather-creak ceased. The judge's feet swam inside his shoes as he climbed down from the seat, and he realised that it felt as unpleasant as sweat on a chilly day. The rain trickled down Lucy's back from her mangle of hair and she recoiled from the touch of its fishy fingers. Sage struggled to her feet, and the muscles in her back cramped with a viciousness she could feel all the way round to her belly. She stroked the discomfort away with her hands.

Martha had refused to accompany them and so they left her behind on the squalid farm; it was as if she had become rooted to the dirt and direness and could accept no other way of life. She was still standing in the yard when Lucy drove the buggy away, animals gleaning by her feet as though her own body was providing for them, and as the clouds descended her figure took on the colour of the ground and her clothes the texture. Sage waved as they went; it was not a salute but an acknowledgement of kinship and a promise to return. She twisted around too fast to face the track into Oasis and did not see the look on Martha's face, or the way she was holding that promise to her heart with both hands.

Sheriff Russett rose from his desk as the three of them flooded through the door, trailing greedy rain that clung to their heels. He lifted his arms as if he was holding warm blankets, but they came no further into the office, needing to melt back into the street again to seek their own warmth, and the judge stopped him with a hand that was accustomed to being obeyed.

'In time, I shall report on what has occurred,' he said, 'but first I shall need…' He considered the two women by his side. 'We shall all need, to change from ramshackle to refreshed.'

'Well, I can see that.' Russett wondered if the weight of the judge's saturated suit might make the man's feet any more leaden. And he wondered if Lucy Ryker was feeling as ill as she looked, and whether what had occurred had been the cause of it. He stepped forward to take her arm as they all turned towards the door, hesitating on the threshold as though testing the water before they dived back into the shower. She peered around at his touch and smiled; the smile seemed normal and gave him heart as she gathered Sage about the shoulders, and they splashed out to the street to be swallowed by the downpour.

Judge Hopgood stood for a while under the shelter of the sidewalk canopy, exuding the back-of-the-throat smell of wet wool. 'Sheriff Russett, I shall require an audience with the prisoner again, and as soon as possible,' he said. 'But not as soon as I would like, thanks to this dratted climate of yours.' And then he sighed at the onslaught before him and did indeed walk on leaden feet towards the saloon.

Russett fed the stove with axe-whittled logs before he returned to his desk, and for a while the office was filled with the hissing of green wood and the gentle ricochet of rain hitting the metal chimney above the roof. But before the logs had been half consumed by fire the judge was back, standing outside the cells in a fresh suit and another pair of shoes.

Hopgood considered the light in the corridor to be unusually murky, as though the air was swirling with fog. It was a fog crowded with eccentric shapes, or beings that belonged to other times and other planes. The only human, warm with blood and breath, was the prisoner in the cage; but he was not easy to see through the dark matter.

The judge shook his head and rubbed his eyes until the fog lifted, and he could differentiate the boy standing in the middle of the cell, watching the two men who had brought with them a smear of office light like a candle flame. There was very little to read from his face until he blinked, and that hesitation made him nothing more than a young man who was awaiting a decision on his future with dread at the back of his throat.

'This time I believe it would be far easier to converse without bars between us,' Hopgood said, indicating the metal lock. 'Sheriff Russett, would you oblige?'

The sheriff worked with the rattle of keys and the cell door opened with its resistant sound, permitting the judge access. The limited gap squeezed him as he entered, although the lawman seemed unaware of his discomfort, raising three fingers as if in blessing as he vacated the passageway and left the air heavy behind him. Hopgood rested his bulk on the bed platform, indicating that he had allowed space for the boy, and when Cub took his seat there his weight barely made a hollow in the meagre mattress. Too thin, the judge decided; not eating. Quite understandable, in the circumstances.

The floor was washed by a pale reflection of rain through the small window, and the music of downpour in the road outside was as gentle as a lullaby, promising dreams. Hopgood relaxed back against the brickwork, which felt strangely comforting through his clothing. The day before the window's reflection had been of the warm street and the open sky, and the boy in the cell had been whole, but now it was difficult to see him when he was little more than a dark shape in an overall darkness, and the judge imagined him vanishing like a phantom through the wall. He knocked Cub's arm with an elbow as he slipped off his spectacles to rub the focus back to his eyes, and the boy flinched. The judge wondered how many times before had he flinched from blows that had left the echo of abrasions on his skin.

'Well now,' said the man. 'I have been down to the farmstead and spoken with Mrs Martha Madison, as I told you I would. How should I refer to the lady? As your employer? Your stepmother?' Cub's shoulders tightened and the judge waited, but there was still silence. 'No matter,' he said, 'for I have learned interesting things this day.' The three women teaching him what he needed to know; each in their own way. 'Did I mention that I was driven there by the doctor's wife, accompanied by Mrs Madison's daughter?'

Cub turned his head, and the judge caught a reflection of light at the edge of his eye. It was like stepping into a pool and finding warm water beneath the sun's rays.

'Mrs Ryker is a woman with fierce opinions, and she is convinced of your innocence, young man. Indeed, she is an unavoidable woman.' The boy was staring at him, reluctant to look away, as though blowing on a weak spark that might with luck inflame a beacon on the hill. 'Be assured that I sit up and take notice of people like Mrs Ryker, for they are the ones that will point me in the right direction,' Hopgood said. And then he leaned forward and looked straight into the stare. 'Shall we talk about Miss Madison?'

Cub opened and closed his mouth, as though chasing his mind for words, and when he spoke there was grit in his voice. 'I do not want Sage to see me in here.'

'And why is that? Because you killed her father?'

'I did not kill him. I told you this yesterday.'

'Yesterday, young man, you told me not very much,' the judge said. 'And you are going to deny murder, are you not, when its fruits are inescapable?'

'I did not kill him. That is the truth.'

'Ah.' Hopgood folded one knee over the other and sharpened the crease of his pants leg between finger and thumb. 'There is nothing as shy as truth. It hides beneath the dark where it feels safe and we must dig and dig to bring it up to the light. And only if we are lucky do we get to it in time.' He turned again to the boy at his side and sensed barriers around him, but they were there to protect and not to hide. 'Give me your attention, Cub, for I am prospecting as deeply and as ferociously as I can.'

The boy leaned back against the wall and closed his eyes. He was barely sixteen years old, seventeen at a stretch, but there was a long history in the squared shoulders and the white-skinned hands gripping the mattress. 'I had no wish to kill him. I learned young that life is sacred,' he said, looking back to where his gentle father had stood one day with a bird in his hands, wing mangled by some animal in the wood. The horse man, crooning magic as he stroked fear from feathers and healed with his rising falling whispers. 'Madison was too drunk to stand. He fell and he dropped the knife.'

'Which was when you picked it up and stabbed him with it.'

'I did not touch it; I kicked it away; it hit the wall.' The blade glinted and the whip coiled; they were only waiting for hands to bring them to life, and he remembered how fiercely his fingers had itched.

'There was a wound in Haine Madison's arm. Did you cut him, Cub?'

'He cut himself.'

'Now why should he do such a thing?'

'Because I would not.'

Everyone will believe that you came here to kill me, Madison had said. I was just defending myself. Nobody could blame me for that.

'He was drunk, he fell, and he dropped the knife.'

Madison dropped the knife and the final restraint was shattered. Cub had stood over the man sprawled on the floor, fighting to keep his balance while the whole of his life up to that point careered through the room, hitting one wall after another. And then he had run into the heartbreak of daylight that opened like the gateway to a life yet to come.

'You left Haine Madison lying on the floor.'

'He was watching me leave,' with that strange look on his face that was something like awe. 'He was alive. He could not have died from the cut. I don't know how it happened.'

The cell rattled with words, and the judge waited for them to fall away to silence. 'Indeed, Haine Madison did not die of the cut to his arm,' he said. 'Sheriff Russett has informed me that he was pierced through the heart; a wound that was probably inflicted with the same knife that you tell me you kicked across the room. The knife that has no existence because no trace of it can be found.'

Outside the rain had stopped; the street still sloshed to the sound of wheels through mud but brightness had grown from the small window, transforming the iron bars to arrows of silver. 'Truth may be timid, it may be shy, but it can never resist relentless digging,' Hopgood said. And then he turned, and stared. 'On that morning, Cub, were you alone with the man who was killed?'

The boy stiffened; he pushed himself away from the bed shelf, and the judge felt the breeze against the side of his face as Cub moved into the centre of the cell, standing straight in the yellow light that seemed to gild his pale hair and throw his shadow out to the passageway. Hopgood peered through the unreliable thickness of his spectacles at the shadow of another that had come to stand beside him, and he felt a strength emanating from the boy and the strange outline, so that the cell burned with a radiance that was more than daylight. But it lasted for a moment, and might never have happened at all.

'I saw no one,' Cub said, recalling the pull of freedom that had brought him out of the valley that morning and the scratch of eyes that might have been watching him leave. 'But that does not mean I was alone.'

'No.' The judge smacked both knees before rising from his austere seat, and one of them retaliated with a twinge that made him relish the prospect of a leisurely retirement. 'Indeed, it does not.'

Hopgood stepped towards the bars and raised a hand as though to ring some bell that might bring Russett through the door with keys at the ready, but turned around instead to face the boy. 'I am in no doubt that you will be glad to see the back of this accommodation,' he said. 'I presume you have some place else to go?'

Cub was still standing at the centre of the cell. His body seemed to become more defined as he listened to the man's words, as though suckled by hope. The strange shadow that had appeared by his side was no longer evident, so perhaps the light had changed. It had certainly reached the boy's eyes, and possibly as far as his soul.

FORTY-ONE

STORM CLOUDS sped from overhead all the way to the hills, and the day was drawing away. The harsh flood of rain had ceased, leaving its dregs swimming over soft mud, buildings still wet and dripping from the onslaught, and a gentle wind that carried the scent of autumn on its wings. The sun glanced through feathers of mist out to the west and shadows deepened as its power spread.

Gerald Hopgood tucked his nightshirt into the carpet bag and closed its mouth. The bag swung easily in his hand when he lifted it. His luggage was always lighter when he was about to leave than when he had yet to arrive and that never ceased to astonish him. He surmised that it was probably down to a law of physics, as the law of desire might well be too unscientific. He left the saloon with a flourish of the half-height doors and, relishing the fact that he was unlikely to come this way again within a decade of blue moons, beamed benignly the length of the short and stocky street.

Two men were standing outside Russett's office: the bowed build of the sheriff himself, and the taller man with the neat beard, whom the judge recognised as the husband of honey-haired Lucy, that magnificent young woman. Hopgood had seen something of his own wife in her; just a glimpse perhaps, and a quality of Tilda's that had been bullied into the background over time and the strains of a lengthening marriage, but he had enjoyed the nudge of memory.

'Dr Ryker,' Hopgood said, approaching the men and resting the carpet bag by his feet. A dapper gentleman, he thought, without doubt a goodly citizen. Kind, too; that was unmistakable. Just consider what he had done to help the wretched boy. 'I trust you are well? And your wife also?'

'Yes indeed; we are both of us in excellent health,' the dark man said, and he seemed to stand taller and more upright, as though their wellbeing was something that pleased him immensely.

'Might Mrs Ryker be waiting for you somewhere?' Hopgood said. 'I should like to applaud that lady's bare-knuckled fight for justice.' He smiled to himself, looking around as though Lucy should be within hearing. But she was not, and that left him feeling almost bereft.

Daniel Ryker shook his head. 'My wife dislikes having to wait for anything; not even the grinding wheels of your law,' he said. 'She cares deeply about what she believes to be right, Judge Hopgood, and cannot rest until hunger is satisfied. Lucy is a fine woman, and I am a lucky fellow.'

Hopgood smiled politely at the lucky fellow, whose wife was evidently closer to the age of the unusual young man she had been determined to save, than she was of her dull but reliable husband. And he wondered if the husband was aware of just how close. 'That is a pleasure to learn, Dr Ryker.'

'I am glad you think so,' Daniel said, 'for it appears that I also have you to thank for what has transpired.' He looked the stout man in the eye; it was a fierce look, and Hopgood slipped off his spectacles so that he could polish the gleaming lenses and avert his own eyes.

'Just doing my duty,' he said. 'That is all.'

'Then may I shake the hand of a man who does his duty so exceptionally well.'

Hopgood shook the offered hand; he shook the dusty sheriff's hand, and his duty was complete. But still he felt strangely disappointed, as though he had walked into a room full of unfamiliar faces when he had been expecting friends. 'I am on my way home, gentlemen,' he said, 'but I regret having missed Mrs Ryker.'

'She left in the buggy a short while ago with Sage Madison,' Russett said, sliding off his hat and pushing back his hair as he replaced it. 'Seems they had to follow him.'

'Follow him?'

'The boy. He started walking, straight after I set him free. Down the main street and out of the town. It looked like he was being pulled by a rope.'

'And do you know where he might have gone?'

'Why, back the way he had come. It is difficult to believe,' Russett said, 'but he was heading in the direction of the Madison farm, and that unfortunate woman who seems to have been the cause of so much trouble.'

'Indeed.' The judge looked down and adjusted the fit of his immaculate coat. 'The dread of recrimination arising from the need for self-defence is enough to make any person unfortunate.' He glanced sideways at the sheriff. 'In my professional opinion.'

The doctor was peering upwards, screwing his eyes from the day's light, unaware of the understanding that passed between the lawman and the man of law, and the silence that signified the end of the matter. 'He went by me in the street,' the dark man said. 'He barely noticed me, even though I was standing in his path. When I asked him where he was going he said just four words in reply.'

Hopgood lifted his carpet bag and weighed it in his hand. 'I should like to hear what they were, Dr Ryker.'

'She needs my help. That is what he said; and he was not looking at me as he said it. It was as if he was looking at something that was too distant for anyone else to see.'

Daniel turned back to the portly judge, and his eyes were clear. 'That boy has travelled far for some place he was desperate to reach. It seems strange to think that perhaps it was always just over the ridge at the end of town.'

Cub shivered slightly in the new wind and hunched his shoulders as he stepped down the main street and out of the town. Walking steadily in the direction of the shingle road, he hardly noticed the puddled water that seeped into his boots and spattered the legs of his pants. It was the route he had followed so many times in the past that only now did he realise how automatically his feet had turned towards it. He was staring straight ahead, oblivious of Oasis and all it represented, allowing his thoughts to take him further than his sight, whisking him away to the gentle rise that was the warning before the dip in the road, the sudden slope into the valley where the farm looked out to distant hills.

Martha Madison's farm. He still had a little way to go before he reached it, and this was not the time for walking. As though he could barely wait for the invisible boundary where the town met the beginning of the wild, Cub fell into the elongated run that he had once learned from the horse man. For this was the way that Dark Wolf had covered the ground; pacing swift and silent through trees, between the frozen waves of hills, beside the dance of wide rivers; carrying his son on his shoulders in the years before the child had grown strong enough to run by his side. Those few short years that had only lasted until the man was no more.

Deep in the memory of his father the young man loped. His head was high and the sky all around was vast, sweet with the play of breezes and the scent of leaf fall. He followed the clouds with his eyes and saw Wolf Wind in a gallop of vapour. Birds swooped, crying out, and he thought he could hear the stallion screaming above their voices. It made him feel whole for a moment, until the cloud mass imploded, scattering like the flare of a horse's mane.

Land rose like a caution under his feet, directing his eyes to where the slope fell away into afternoon shadows. He stood tall and spread his gaze from the broken crags of distant hills down towards the valley that he had known for nearly half his life. But when he felt the drub of hooves through his soles he ran again. Not to escape, for the speed of the wheels that were chasing him was thrilling as opposed to frightening, but just for the elation of being free to run. He didn't need to look round to identify who was driving the buggy and who was sitting beside her, leaning forwards from the bench as if that might encourage the mare to greater speed.

The farm appeared, crouching in its dip; as broken and forlorn as he had always remembered. But peacefulness was lying on it now, as though something soft and gentle had tumbled like snow to hide the spikes and the sores and dull the crazy ghosts of pain. And when he saw it Cub stopped running and stood waiting for the buggy to strain to a halt behind him. He heard the bay snorting as it chewed at the bit and stamped the ground with the need to move again, and the boy felt the little horse's exhilaration as if he was inside the animal's head. And when he turned around he could see the girl's white fingers gripping the bench as though she was afraid to let go.

The driver secured the reins and climbed down, lifting her yellow skirts high like a dancer preparing to waltz. The bay skipped to its own music and Sage jounced in her seat as she watched Lucy crossing over to greet the boy, her narrow boots flattening clods of earth and leaving pieces of broken ground to show where she had walked. The woman didn't speak, she held him very tightly, biting his neck with her lips as she breathed his name. Cub put his arms around her, but then he let her go, searching instead for the girl on the buggy seat. The warmth he had left on Lucy's skin cooled too quickly, but nobody noticed the desolation in her eyes, or the sudden bitterness that soured her beauty.

Cub went to stand by the wheel. The mare slithered sideways and he laid his hand on her neck until she was calm and snorting the ground for grass. The sun edged from behind a cloud as Sage looked down at the boy, and she saw that he was now a man, tall and straight. His eyes were dark in the shade but endless where the light struck them, and he was staring at her as if she was all he needed to see. He reached for her hand and their fingers locked, and then he lifted the girl down to the ground where everything was brand new and held her as tightly as the doctor's wife had held him.

They took little notice of the rising falling plain and the portentous clouds, or of Lucy Ryker, who had already climbed to the buggy seat and twisted the bay towards the town. She was gripping the reins so tightly that the pain must have been almost too much to bear, and the moan of the wheels when they started to roll might instead have been the voice of the woman in the yellow dress. But that also went unnoticed.

Politely, as if asking permission, the rain began again. The sky clenched as dark as a premature dusk, but so slowly that the burn of colours remained like an echo long after they had faded. Cub wiped away the drops that kissed the girl's cheeks; they were falling too fast and he could not tell the rain from the tears. He put his arm around her as they turned to face the valley, and the farm that was waiting in the centre of the dip.

The wind carried them, joined together, down the slope.

Printed in Great Britain
by Amazon